JOURNEY
of the HEART

DANICE ALLEN

DIVERSIONBOOKS

Also by Danice Allen

Arms of a Stranger
Beloved Rivals
Remember Me
The Perfect Gentleman
The Spring Begins

Diversion Books
A Division of Diversion Publishing Corp.
443 Park Avenue South, Suite 1008
New York, New York 10016
www.DiversionBooks.com

For more information, email info@diversionbooks.com

First Diversion Books edition August 2014.
Print ISBN: 978-1-62681-683-1
eBook ISBN: 978-1-62681-406-6

To Lorena Belle Phillips Ford
A sassy, smart, loving, understanding,
exasperating, and unique lady—my mother
Love you, Mom

PROLOGUE

Edinburgh
Christmas Eve, 1831

From the craggy, volcanic heights of majestic Castle Rock to the bustling, shop-lined thoroughfare of Princes Street below, from the smallest, darkest garret of smoke-begrimed Old Town to the bright candle-lit warmth of New Town's most elegant drawing room, Christmas Day trembled on the edge of a snowy night before.

No discriminator of persons, the holiday spirit had sprinkled its merrymaking dust on rich and poor, old and young alike. The city teemed with jovial, desperate humanity. One gentleman was desperate to find just the right silver salts bottle for his Aunt Lizzy before the shops closed, while another less prosperous fellow was desperate simply to haggle a good price from the poulterer for an adequately fleshed goose to satisfy the rumbling stomachs and gladden the hopeful hearts of his several offspring. Still others—the most wretched and ragged of Edinburgh's bursting population—had only the modest wish of finding themselves no more hungry and cold by morning light than they presently were.

Unaware that so much suffering existed in the shadowy wynds that were the narrow off-lanes of High Street in Old Town, Gabrielle Tavistock strolled along Princes Street in the snug safety of two other females as blissfully ignorant as herself. Exactly five paces behind them walked an abigail and a groom, both of them encumbered with packages and whiling away the time they had to spend toting for the Quality by flirting outrageously with each other.

Gabrielle felt herself in a world of enchantment. The persistent wind from the Firth of Forth had obligingly calmed, seemingly for the convenience of the last-minute shoppers who streamed up and down the street in their myriad colorful redingotes and cloaks like schools of tropical fish. A lacy, powder-soft snow fell and piled in delicate mounds everywhere and on everyone.

Like Gabrielle's heart, the air was filled with a delicious ambience of anticipation. That morning she'd received a reply to the letter she'd written to Zachary Wickham about her betrothal to Rory Cameron, Marquess of Lome, and in it he'd indicated that he would be paying her a congratulatory visit in a matter of days, cutting short his usual month-long holiday stay with Alex, her sister, Beth, and the children in Surrey.

Over ten years ago, Zachary and his older brother, Alex, had become reunited after a separation that was forced upon them by their father. They had been extremely close ever since, even though Alex had ended up married to Zach's betrothed. Beth, Gabrielle's sister, had been engaged to Zach before Alex made his dramatic appearance in Cornwall on the eve of their grandfather's funeral. The Tavistocks' estate in Cornwall marched with the Wickhams', and, as neighbors, friends, and lovers, their lives had become fatally intertwined.

As far as Gabrielle was concerned, however, all that was ancient history. The details of said ancient history served in the present only as corroboration that Zach had indeed made some personal sacrifices to hie himself up to Scotland so hastily to meet Gabrielle's husband-to-be. These facts gave Gabrielle a much-needed dose of renewed hope. Just the prospect of seeing Zach again after a three-month absence made her feel as though she were walking on air.

Beneath her parasol, which exactly matched her emerald green, ermine-lined mantle, and with her feet encased in velvet, leather-soled boots, Gabrielle was protected from the cold and dampness and was in "high gig," as Zach used to say. With her honey-blond curls framing her face beneath the wide brim of a fur-trimmed bonnet and with such a radiant smile on her face, it was no wonder that many gentlemen stared as they passed by. Aunt Clarissa, who as Gabrielle's paid companion and chaperon was supposed to repress the odious ogles of strange men by glaring them down, was raptly window-gazing and as inattentive as usual.

"Gabrielle! Oh, look at that precious doll!" exclaimed Regina Murray, Gabrielle's other companion. She grasped Gabrielle's arm and turned her to face a shop window filled with toys. Archery sets, sailboats, stuffed dogs and monkeys, miniature cribs, scarlet-coated soldiers, and several dolls cluttered the display table that had been pushed up to the window.

A sign above the door declared the shopkeeper to be the happy recipient of a very recent shipment of sheepskin-covered drums from Germany. There amongst the toy drums, as if given a special spot away from the other dolls in order to showcase her superior attributes, stood the doll Regina referred to. It had auburn hair similar to Regina's and a porcelain face of fragile beauty. Her sapphire blue evening gown was in the current mode, with gigot sleeves and a gathered fichu draped from one ivory shoulder to the other. The doll was beautiful.

Gabrielle sighed and brushed back with one white-mittened hand a damp curl that had loosened and fallen into her eyes. "Regina," she said in a playfully chiding tone, "I wish you wouldn't bring to my attention every doll that happens to strike your fancy! I've already bought two dolls apiece for both my nieces, and one for—" She lowered her voice. "Aunt Clarissa." Then, in a louder voice, she said, "You're supposed to be helping me choose a Christmas present for Rory. Isn't that right, Aunt Clarissa?"

By now Aunt Clarissa was several steps ahead of them, her nose, a mere bump of a feature that barely held up her spectacles, practically pressed against the glass in front of a millinery shop. In addition to Aunt Clarissa's constant distracted state, she was shortsighted. This happenstance made Gabrielle's mother's choice of Clarissa for chaperon even more incomprehensible. Gabrielle could only suppose that her mother was too harried and sick to be put to the trouble of finding a more qualified chaperon at short notice. Mrs. Tavistock, widowed and ailing from a recent bout of rheumatism, was only too happy to send her daughter to Scotland to spend the winter with Regina and her family, all of whom she'd met during Gabrielle's debut London Season last spring.

The fact was, Mrs. Tavistock was miffed with Gabrielle for neglecting to accept any of the several offers of marriage she'd received from very suitable, and sometimes titled, gentlemen. Though Gabrielle came from a good family in Cornwall and was well dowered—her mother told her woefully and often—at the age of nineteen she was no longer a young girl and had no business turning up her nose at such offers simply because she wasn't in love with the fellows who begged her to wed them. But all that was a moot point now, Gabrielle reflected happily. She was officially engaged and would no longer be plagued by her mother's fretful remonstrances.

"What, my love? Did you say something?" Aunt Clarissa's attention was caught at last. She turned in Gabrielle's direction, then shuffled carefully back along the walkway, which had been made rather slick by the street-sweeper's hasty scraping, to stand before her niece. With her gray hair topped by an unadorned gray bonnet, her thin shoulders snugly fit into a plain gray mantle, and her tiny, narrow feet shod in very functional, sturdy black boots, Aunt Clarissa's collective appearance gave the impression of a dormouse. She had a habit, too, of waggling her fingers nervously in front of her whenever she was trying to pay attention or frame a difficult sentence.

"I only wanted you to help me resist that beautiful doll in the window, Auntie," said Gabrielle teasingly, indicating the porcelain temptress with a tilt of her head. "It will not suit for Rory, and I don't need any more to send to Surrey for the little girls, therefore I had ought to pass it by with nary another glance."

Aunt Clarissa moved to the window and leaned close, supporting her light weight by placing the fingertips of both splayed hands against the glass. "And well you should, my dear, for what's to do with so many dolls? You've already purchased all you need! I can understand your wishing me to help you resist this one, since I haven't any use for the frippery things myself," she said, speaking in her odd way, forcing each syllable through pursed lips, "and since Regina is so addicted to collecting them and lends you little resolution against spending your money so freely—" She squinted hard, then exclaimed, "Good heavens, my dear! She's quite ravishing, isn't she? Are you sure Victoria or Cecily don't need another one? Perhaps they don't have one with precisely *that* color of hair!"

"There, you see!" Regina interrupted, poking Gabrielle's shoulder with the end of her muff. "Your aunt agrees with me! This doll shouldn't be passed up. If you don't want to give her to your nieces because of some silly notion that you might spoil them, keep it yourself! *I'd* buy it, but I've spent all my allowance and don't dare ask Papa for another farthing."

Gabrielle shook her head and smiled. She was in such a halcyon mood she could have given in to Regina's urging or flatly refused to indulge in a rather pointless expenditure and been happy with either decision. Then, as Regina joined Aunt Clarissa at the window in her close inspection of the doll, Gabrielle's attention was caught by the sound of children caroling. This was not an unusual sound, of course. They'd listened to and given pennies to several little knots of singers already that evening. But there was something different about this group of carolers, something rather poignant in their tinny, off-key rendition of "God Rest Ye Merry Gentlemen."

The carolers were about three shops ahead. While Regina and Aunt Clarissa sighed and cooed over the doll and discussed between themselves why Gabrielle ought to buy it, Gabrielle walked up the street unnoticed by the other two women to catch a glimpse of the urchins who were singing her favorite Christmas hymn. It was a small group of only four, and since they weren't exactly melodic, no one had stopped to listen to them.

They weren't very handsome, either, she realized when she finally stood close to them. By the light of the hissing gas lamp just above them, she could plainly see their sharp-featured little faces poking out of the ragged scarves that had been wound about their heads for warmth. The tattered ends of their oversized, hand-me-down coats dragged in the street. There were three boys, ranging in sizes that suggested the eldest to be no more than ten, and the two others each probably a year younger than the one before. Judging by their facial similarities, Gabrielle realized they must be a family.

The youngest was a girl. She was a tiny creature holding a low-burning, tallow work candle. Her mittens had long since worn down to the knuckles and served as poor protection for her wee hands against the cold. She was engulfed in a shapeless garment of heavy brown wool, the wet hem of her skirt hanging to the ground. Her wrap almost looked as though it had once been a man's redingote which had been somehow shortened and taken in to fit the little girl. With the proper clothes and enough food to plump up her sweet face, she might be quite pretty, Gabrielle thought, pity twisting painfully in her chest. She had never seen such ragged children on Princes Street before. None of the other carolers had looked half so pathetic. When the children realized she wasn't going to pass them by, their thin faces brightened and their song increased in volume if not, perhaps, in precision of tune.

"Och, miss, dinna mind these little beggars!" said a dark, bearded man in a bright apron, who appeared on the front stoop of the liquor shop they stood by. He thrust his head round the corner of the half-opened door. "They ought not t' be beggin' down here in New Town, but had ought to keep t' Ol' Town and t' others like 'em." He turned to the children, who bravely though faintly continued their carol despite his sudden intimidating appearance, and waved a huge fist at them in a very menacing way. "Off with ye! Go on now! Ye're not good fer me business, standing there like that! Go back t' Auld Reekie where ye belong!"

Gabrielle was too astounded at first to respond to the shopkeeper's callous dismissal of the children, but when they ceased singing and started to scoot quickly away, Gabrielle did not stop to exchange words with him, but hastily followed the children. The boys hadn't even flinched when the shopkeeper ordered them away, only looked disappointed, as if they were used to such treatment. But the poor little girl had trembled and hid behind one of her brothers when the shopkeeper shook his fist in the air, so frightened she snuffed out her candle by dropping it in the snow. During this process, the scarf she wore round her head fell back to reveal her hair.

Gabrielle's heart leaped to her throat. The little girl's hair was that rare shade of blond which, despite its pale color, was so bright and shiny it could rival the brilliance of the King's golden guineas. There was only one other person in the world that Gabrielle had ever seen whose thatch of yellow hair was so closely akin to sunbeams.

Zachary. His image loomed before her, snatching away her breath, filling all her senses with the remembered sight and sound of him. Tall, leanly muscular, nonchalantly aristocratic, and golden-eyed—like an African jungle cat. She could almost hear his voice and the nuance of comfortable familiarity and affectionate teasing which was part of his speech whenever he spoke to her. She could almost smell the heathery fragrance, mixed with soap and leather, that clung to him and tickled her nose whenever he used to pull her up on his dapple gray to share a gallop across Bodmin Moor.

That glimpse of gold had made Gabrielle long for Zachary with the same urgency she'd felt nearly a year ago when she'd been trundled off to London in Papa's stately traveling chaise, there to coyly and simperingly play her part in the age-old ritual of husband-catching ... and leaving behind the love of her life. Maybe to everyone else, maybe even to Zach, she was just a child, a pest of the little sister ilk, but she was determined to prove them absolutely wrong. Gabrielle suppressed the painful memories, the aching present, and found her voice. "Wait! Don't go! I've something for you!"

The children did not stop, but they looked back curiously. To convince them that she was quite earnest, Gabrielle took out her coin purse and waved it back and forth like a tolling bell. Too keenly hungry, too worldly-wise to ignore such a summons, the children stopped. They pressed and curled together like a four-fingered fist, almost intertwined in their close proximity to one another. As she approached, they stared at her, speechless, their enormous eyes as wary as they were hopeful.

"I enjoyed your singing very much," Gabrielle said, smiling kindly. "And I'm very sorry that ill-tempered man interrupted your performance. But you mustn't mind *him!* I daresay he doesn't feel the Christmas spirit like we do!" This bracing speech brought hesitant smiles to the children's lips, and the cautious looks in their eyes softened a little; but still they said nothing.

Gabrielle set down her parasol, leaning it against the wall of a confectioner's shop. She undid the ribbons that held together the closure of her embroidered and beaded purse and shook out several coins into the palm of her free hand. All four pair of eyes riveted to that glittery pile. Gabrielle extended her handful of money to the tallest boy, saying, "Here. I know you'll make good use of this." If possible, the boy's eyes widened still further. Gabrielle felt sure he did not trust good fortune that fell so easily within his grasp. He probably expected her to play a cruel trick on him by snatching back her hand if he dared to reach forth his own.

"Miss, ye dinna mean me t' take it all, do ye?"

"I do indeed!" Gabrielle assured him. "But I expect you to spend it wisely. Buy some warm mittens for your little sister and a pudding for your mum to boil on the morrow for Christmas dinner. I do not think it would be at all amiss if you made yourselves a little merry for the holidays!"

The boy's face lit up. "Mum's been sick. She said we'd not have a puddin' this year."

"Now you may!" Gabrielle said with cheerful insistence. "A good plum pudding after an excellent Christmas dinner will have your mum back in prime twig in no time. Take this money, young man, before I change my mind!"

Gabrielle's empty threat did the trick, and the boy darted out his cupped hands into which Gabrielle dumped her pile of coins. "What's your name, lad?"

"Will, miss. Will Tuttle's me name. Oh, miss, I dinna know how t' thank ye!" he stammered, looking down at the money, then up at Gabrielle with misty eyes, the corners of his mouth twitching with a manly effort to control his emotions.

"You already have thanked me," she assured him, her own eyes misting a little from the idea that the paltry amount of coinage she carried around as pin money could seem like such a fortune to someone else. She dropped her gaze to the girl, who was hanging on the coattail of one of the other boys and hiding her face behind his arm, one eye peeping through the triangle he'd made with his crooked elbow. "I'd like to give your little sister something for her very own, if you don't mind. What's her name?"

The boy smiled fondly at his sister and answered, "We call her Bella. Arabella's her Christian name."

Gabrielle stooped down, not minding that her skirt rested in the snow and would likely soak up a lot of dampness. She gently caught hold of the little girl's hand and pulled her round in front of her brother till she was face to face with Gabrielle. Bella was shy but unresisting. Gabrielle couldn't suppress the urge to reach out to test the softness of Bella's hair, to hold it just so and observe how the golden strands shone in the street lamp's pool of diffused illumination.

"I know someone who has hair just like yours, Bella," she said. "Hair as shiny and yellow as sunbeams." Gabrielle reached inside her purse and pulled out a last coin. "As bright as this new guinea, which is yours." She took Bella's hand, the fingertips still so pink from the cold, and pressed the money into her palm.

Bella just looked at the coin for a moment, then returned her wondering gaze to Gabrielle, her eyebrows and lips puckered in an endearingly bewildered expression. "Are ye a good fairy, miss?" she asked.

Gabrielle laughed. "No, Bella. I'm just another mortal such as you, but I'm not half so pretty as you because I haven't got such glorious golden hair. Do you want to know a secret?"

Bella nodded vigorously.

Gabrielle leaned close, so that they were cheek to cheek, then whispered, "I'm going to marry a man with hair the same color as yours, so that whenever I wake up in the morning and the sun's hidden behind a gray cloud, I'll have my very own sunshine right there beside me. Don't you think that's a good idea?"

Once again Bella responded with energetic headnodding.

"Gabrielle? What *are* you doing, my love?"

Gabrielle had expected to be interrupted eventually by Regina and Aunt Clarissa, who would have caught up with her by now, but not by Rory. He was supposed to be at Charlotte Square, waiting with the Murrays and a few guests for their return, after which the evening's festivities would commence. But his appearance was not unwelcome. She straightened up and turned about with a ready smile, immediately extending her hands, which were then just as immediately seized by a tall, mustachioed young man with glossy chestnut hair and blue eyes, dressed in a midnight blue, double-caped redingote. Behind him stood Aunt Clarissa and Regina and the servants, all of whom looked none too pleased with her for having wandered away.

Rory leaned forward and kissed her lightly on the cheek. "Done with your Christmas shopping, sweetheart? I hope you found something for me that will be just to my taste, or else I shall have to insist that you recompense me for my disappointment in some other way." He lifted one dark brow to a provocative arch.

Gabrielle laughed. "How do you expect me to find you a Christmas present if you do not allow me a little privacy?"

Still in possession of her hands and with no apparent intention of releasing them, he said, "You ought to have bought me something *days* ago, Gabrielle. Or doesn't your betrothed warrant such forethought?"

"Having never before been engaged, my lord, I don't know the proper amount of forethought one's betrothed is entitled to," she retorted with an impish grin.

"Oh, oodles, my love," he murmured. "Positively oodles!"

"Well, I'm still learning what to do and what not to do in this interesting contract called a betrothal," Gabrielle admitted with a tiny shrug of her shoulders. "You shall simply have to put up with me, Rory. But now, since it grows late, perhaps you had better help me pick something out for you which is *precisely* to your taste so that we won't be late for dinner."

Done with flirtatious sallies, Rory's attention strayed to a point beyond Gabrielle's shoulder where Bella and her brothers still stood. Gabrielle hoped the eldest boy, Will, had pocketed the money she'd given him, because she did not wish Rory to know that she'd just parted with the entire contents of her purse. She had no idea whether or not he would understand or approve of such an impetuous gesture of charity and she wasn't in the mood to defend herself.

She twirled round and was relieved to see that the coins were out of sight. She was actually rather surprised that the children had not already fled the scene of their unexpected rise to temporary prosperity in dread of their benefactress changing her mind. But rather like stray dogs that hung about after a stranger has deigned to pat them on the head or toss them a scrap of food, the children's devotion had been easily earned, and they seemed reluctant to go. To preserve her composure, which was minute by minute being jeopardized by the increase of compassion she felt for these urchins, she firmly bid them good-bye. "And have a happy Christmas!" she added with a special smile for Bella, who was staring at her perplexedly.

Somewhat chagrined, Gabrielle realized that Bella's puzzled stare must be the result of Rory's appearance being so inconsistent with the description she'd given the little girl of her husband-to-be. Unable at the moment to explain the inconsistency, Gabrielle took Rory's arm and briskly drew him down the street in the opposite direction. "By the way, Rory, my love, you'll have to loan me the money for your present. It seems I've overspent!"

While Rory laughed, Gabrielle glanced over her shoulder at the children. She saw Bella eyeing the golden guinea and twirling her finger in a lock of loose hair. Hair like Zach's.

CHAPTER ONE

Edinburgh
New Year's Eve, 1831

The carriage wobbled, swayed, and sometimes lurched over the mucky roads that wended through the Pentland Hills south of Edinburgh. Zach was afforded a bird's-eye view of the city when the road took a sharp turn westward to circumvent an especially large outcropping of basalt rock. The night was as black as the devil's soul, but gas lamps, torches, and candles lit up the shadowy vales and stark promontories of Edinburgh's hellishly uneven geography so that it shimmered like an oasis in the desert. Like a phantom lake on the Sahara, it was too beautiful, too incongruent a sight next to the surrounding solitude, to be real.

God help him if it weren't real, thought Zach, stretching out one long slim leg across the carriage to rest his foot on the opposite seat, taking care not to disturb his slumbering valet. He'd come from one end of Great Britain to the other to see Gabby, and if the next hour didn't herald the ending of his long journey, he'd very likely lose his mind. The walls of the carriage seemed, like the front lines of a relentless army, to be gaining on him inch by inch. Slow, steady, deadly.

No one but Bleader knew how he suffered from the phobia of being in too small or airless an enclosure, and he would take great care that no one ever would. On long trips such as this, he stopped the carriage frequently to stretch his legs and always kept one window slightly cracked to admit fresh air.

This fear of being trapped probably had its origins in the

incident of eleven years before when he and Alex had rescued Gabby from a collapsing tin mine. Zach's mouth twisted in a tiny ironic grin. Gabby had been looking for knackers—Cornish pixies who resided in underground caverns. Gabby was a dreamer, a fancier of the mystical and mysterious. But he sincerely hoped her betrothal to the Marquess of Lome was based on something real and substantial like love and respect, and not on some idealized conception of romance.

After leaving Alex's house in Surrey, where he'd stopped to spend Christmas Eve with his brother, Beth, and the children, Zach had intended to travel with all due haste to Edinburgh. From the moment he'd received Gabby's letter, he'd been aflame with curiosity to meet and—figuratively speaking—disassemble for inspection, piece by impossible piece, the paragon who had inspired her effusive praise.

But when Alex and Beth had intimated that he was reacting to Gabby's betrothal as if it was a catastrophe rather than a happy event, attributing that view of Gabby's impending nuptials as an indication that Zach's feelings for her were more than brotherly, Zach had forced himself to calm down and look at the situation objectively. The first thing he'd decided to do was spend a few more days in Surrey, rather than run after Gabby like a starving cur after the butcher's wagon, tongue hanging out, mouth frothing. But every time he read that damned letter...

Zach reached inside the pocket of his jacket and pulled out Gabby's letter. He kept it close at hand to refer to for precise directions to the Murrays' townhouse in Charlotte Square, where Gabby was staying. The weak puddle of light from the carriage lantern provided Zach with little illumination to read by, but what he couldn't make out by the lantern's glow, he could easily recall, having read the short missive innumerable times.

First, before trying to squint through the text of the letter, Zach lifted the parchment stationery to his nose and breathed in the delicate scent of orchids—no doubt the result of Gabby's London-learned notion of dousing her letters with Parisian toilet water. Zach frowned. The exotic scent in no way coincided with his mental image of Gabby. When he thought of his little friend, thirteen years his junior, he conjured up the smell of moor dirt, sea-salted breezes, and the pungent fragrance of damp bracken and heather after one of Cornwall's frequent rainfalls.

In thought, Gabby was Cornwall and Cornwall was Gabby, one and the same. Beloved, familiar… *familial.* She did not smell like orchids. Even when she'd gone off to London for her Season last spring, though she'd looked a bit like a stranger in her new toggery and self-conscious maturity—breasts and all—she had simply been Gabby rather awkwardly outfitted for some sort of fancy dress masquerade.

Now she was getting married, and he could hardly credit it. From the tone of her letter Zach surmised she was well and truly smitten with Rory Cameron. Zach bent to the irritating but curiously compelling exercise of rereading Gabby's letter.

> Dear Zach,
>
> Perhaps Mama has already told you the news, though I will mail this letter at the same time as I mail hers, but I have something truly *wonderful* to tell you! I'm getting married! Do close your mouth, dear friend, and find a chair in which you might collapse! It's true, I have finally decided to leg-shackle myself for life, even though my reluctance to entertain proposals from London beaux probably made you think my case a hopeless one. I suppose I was simply waiting for just the right man to come along! Mama will be ecstatic, I know, and I can't wait till she meets my dear, darling Rory!
>
> Oh, Zach, I hope I may not tire you with praise of him, but as my sister is married to your brother and you have stood almost as a paternal protector of sorts over the years, I feel a certain license in allowing myself to bore you silly with homage of dear, darling Rory…

Zach grunted cynically, as he invariably did whenever he got to this point in reading the letter. She was right about one thing: if he didn't love her and have a strong interest in her happiness, Zach wouldn't be able to tolerate such stomach-disordering encomiums about one mortal man who probably was just as riddled with imperfections as the next fellow. He continued reading.

> He's as tall as you, Zach, maybe even an inch or two taller. He's dark and handsome, like Alex, though not quite so gypsyish. Did you know I liked dark men, Zach? No, neither did I… till I met Rory! I will not mention Rory's title because that would be vulgar of me, but I imagine the distinction of being grandmother to a future marquess has made a favorable impression on Mama. You know I care nothing about such folderol. I would be happy married to a shopkeeper if he made me feel like a queen … like Rory does!

"Balderdash!" Zach said out loud to himself. "What high-flown romanticism is this? Fortunately no shopkeeper with such a talent for toadeating has come her way, the silly goose!"

> Did I mention that he's a bruising horseman and an excellent amateur pugilist?—talents I felt sure you would admire! He has a fine baritone singing voice, I might modestly add, and we've whiled away many evenings in the charming occupation of singing duets. Several of the songs we sing are poems Rory has written and later put to music.

"Gawd! I might lose my dinner yet! Not satisfied to awe the ordinary people with his physical prowess, he must needs be a singer and a poet, too!"

> Suffice it to say, my dear friend, Rory is everything a girl could want in a husband, too dear, too wonderful to be true!

"That is only too likely, Gabby!"

> I wish you could meet him. I'll be spending the Christmas holidays in Edinburgh with the Murrays. Naturally Rory will be in constant attendance. But

it is his wish to take me early in the new year to his ancestral home, Dunollie Castle in Perthshire, to meet his grandmother and to keep me as a "prisoner of love" till spring and the necessary removal to Cornwall to plan our wedding. I hope you may visit me at one or the other of these places and tell me what you think of my dear, darling Rory. But I do not tremble at the thought of the two most important men in my life meeting. I make no doubt you shall esteem him as highly as do I! The directions to the Murrays' townhouse are…

Zach refolded the letter and poked it viciously into his coat pocket. " 'Prisoner of love,' indeed! She does not mention that dear, darling Rory will find something in *me* that *he* might esteem, only the other way around! Gawd, it's enough to make me puke!"

"So you say, sir, every time you read that letter," came a sleepy, beleaguered voice from the dark carriage corner.

"Oh. Bleader. You're awake, then," muttered Zach, removing his foot from the opposite seat and sitting up a little straighter—gathering his dignity, as it were.

Bleader leaned over into the light, rubbing his eyes and yawning. "Yes, *now* I'm awake, sir." His straight brown hair was all on end, and he had a deep crease along his cheek from leaning too long against the corded edge of a carriage cushion.

"None too soon, either," Zach informed him briskly, still striving to recover his composure after being caught talking to himself. Then genuine amusement and appreciation for Bleader's disheveled appearance made him smile and say, "I can't imagine my consequence increasing with Miss Gabrielle's illustrious host and hostess if my valet were to alight from the carriage looking like a pugnacious tomcat lately emerged from an alley brawl."

Bleader grinned, the expression flattening his nose and transforming his eyes into narrow slits. Just so, thought Zach, he did look rather like a cat. Bleader's large, slightly pointed ears did not detract from this comparison, either.

My, how whimsical became his thoughts when he had rather not confront the more pressing and serious issues at hand, Zach reflected wryly. But while Bleader combed his hair and straightened his clothes, Zach mentally addressed those issues by attempting to nurture his objectivity in this matter of Gabby's betrothal. He did not for a minute believe Alex's hint that he had a secret *tendre* for Gabby. That was too absurd a notion to entertain for even a second. He was simply deeply interested in her happiness. She'd always been like a dear little sister to him, taking Beth's place as comforter and friend when Beth married Alex and left Cornwall.

True, there was a vast difference in their ages, but there had always been an affinity between Zach and Gabby—a kinship of souls. But never had he thought of Gabby in a romantic way. Even if he were inclined to think of her thus, he didn't deserve the love of such a wonderful girl. History told that story well and history often repeated itself. The fact was, Zach had never brought anything but grief and calamity to the women in his life. He would not play Gabby such a cruel trick by turning passionate toward her, but instead would keep her quite safe by loving her only as a little sister.

Suddenly the carriage jolted to an abrupt stop. Zach reached for the loaded pistol he kept in a compartment beneath his seat, ever on the alert for highwaymen. Clutching the stock of his gun, he looked warily through the carriage window into the black night. They had been steadily climbing for the last few minutes. Having visited Edinburgh before, Zach was well aware that they were on the edge of Old Town, the perimeter of which they must skirt before descending into the prosperous district of New Town.

"Auld Reekie," as the locals called the ancient area, meant "Old Smokey," and it was well named. The soot-covered, medieval city was crisscrossed with dark, narrow passageways towered over by many-storied dwellings with gothic turrets and crowstepped gables. The architecture was picturesque, but the stench and hopelessness of poverty, ignorance, and crime hung over the place, as tangible as the dark clouds of smoke coming from the chimneys.

Preserving an iron calm, despite his frayed nerves and Bleader's pale-face heaving panic just across the carriage, Zachary waited for some sign from his coachman that all was well, or to hear the belligerent bellow of a masked thief demanding all their money and possessions.

When his jowly coachman, Malcolm, appeared at the window, Zach released a pent-up breath. Malcolm didn't look terribly distressed, as would be the case if a highwayman were pointing a gun at the back of his head, but he did look a bit bothered. Zach guessed that there was a dead animal or a drunk obstructing their passage. He opened the window.

"What is it, Malcolm? Something we can help you with? Where's John?" John was the groom, a gaunt fellow who did not possess a great deal of physical strength, thereby necessitating Zach and Bleader having to lend a hand whenever the coach got stuck.

"John's givin' 'er a drink o' water, sir. Plum done-up, she is, sir!"

"*Who* is done-up, Malcolm?" Zachary asked, returning his pistol to its place of storage.

"A woman, sir. She was staggerin' alongside the road. She was likely to fall under the wheels if'n we jest passed 'er by, so's we stopped. Good thing, too. She's got a bun in the oven, sir. Belly's as big as a soup kettle. Looks sick an' tired. Young'un."

Zachary waited for no further description of this apparently wretched and unfortunate pregnant woman, but immediately stepped out of the carriage and walked swiftly round to the front of his fidgety team of chestnut horses. John was kneeling close to the ground, supporting a reclining woman and tilting a flask of water to her lips. She was blond and small, except for her ungainly stomach, the size of which could probably accommodate twins. She wore a rough woolen gown and cloak, but no bonnet or gloves, and her shoes were flimsy things filled with holes.

"Good God, what's she doing lying on the frozen ground like that?" Zach's voice was sharp, a reflex to the frustration that wrung his insides till they hurt. Zach had a special sort of empathy for pregnant women, particularly the friendless sort, and this one certainly looked as though she could use a friend.

"She swooned, sir," explained John, removing the flask from the girl's lips while she indulged in a fit of coughing. Hands on hips, legs slightly spread, Zach stood over the girl and watched and waited patiently till she was able to gain control over her ticklish throat. When she looked up at last with watery, red-rimmed eyes through a tangle of matted hair, her expression was one of bewilderment and fright.

"What's your name, lass?" he asked her, flinching inwardly at the fear in the girl's eyes. Why did he always feel so guilty? He'd seen that look a hundred times in the past years, and he was no more responsible for this poor girl's condition and desperation than he'd been for all the others, yet… He supposed all the guilt was somehow connected to sweet Tessy, dead now for more than ten years.

"Please dinna touch me." The plea was spoken so low and in such a raspy voice that Zach barely heard her. She seemed to shrink inside herself, pulling her legs up tight against her swollen belly, wrapping her skinny arms about her knees till she resembled a badly wound ball of yarn, smooth here, lumpy there.

"I'm not going to hurt you," he said kindly, though firmly. He suspected she was only partially aware of her surroundings. "When did you eat last?"

She did not reply, but stared glassy-eyed at him. He tried a different tack. "Where were you going? Do you have a family, a husband perhaps? Can we take you home?"

At the mention of a husband and home, whether from an aversion to them or perhaps the complete nonexistence of such a person and place, the girl finally responded, saying testily, *"Home?* Naw, I will'na go *home!"* She dug her feet into the ground and pushed back against John's narrow chest. She clutched his arm, never looking at him, but seeming in her disoriented state to think of John as an ally. Choosing one of them over the other, when the both of them were total strangers, did not bespeak a rational state of mind.

"She's cup-shot, sir," John said, his nostrils flaring and twitching. "Thought so at first, but now I know it fer a fact. Drinkin' 'ard all day long, I'd say, sir."

"That explains quite a lot. We had better put her in the coach," Zach said curtly.

"Where are we takin' 'er, sir?" Malcolm asked.

"Just where you might expect, Malcolm. To the shelter."

Malcolm nodded sagely.

Zach frowned down at the girl. "It is the logical thing to do till she recovers from her ... er ... state. Perhaps when she's feeling more the thing, she'll tell us something about herself."

Malcolm pushed a thumb under the brim of his three-cornered hat to scratch his scalp. "Should we tell 'er where she's goin', sir?"

"She'd likely not cooperate, but I don't care a fig whether she goes willingly or not. In such a condition, she can't be expected to know what's best for herself and the babe. Stand back, John," he ordered. "Malcolm, you take her feet. I'll heft her up from under the arms."

Zach positioned himself behind John, kneeling, tossing back the folds of his capacious redingote so that they were out of his way. He extended his hands, palms up, arms bent at the elbows, ready to take over as soon as John moved.

As the girl listened to the men's conversation with a befuddled scowl and obvious distrust, Zach was afraid she was rallying her strength for one last show of independence. She probably understood enough to know that they intended to take her somewhere, and speculating on her possible past experiences with the male sex, she might think Zach and his servants meant to ill-use her in some painful or humiliating way. She started screaming and kicking, flinging her arms about like a panicked child who had waded too far into the water.

John bolted, and Zach caught the girl, crisscrossing his arms just above her breasts. She yelled obscenities with such piercing stridency that Zach's ears buzzed. Her struggles reminded him of a beetle turned over on its back, the bulk of its weight all in the middle with legs and antennae writhing all about in an effort to regain a proper footing. He lifted her, dodging her flailing arms as best he could.

John and Malcolm were sharing the task at the other end, each of them wrestling with a single foot—in and out, back and forth. The girl's energy, spurred on no doubt by the conviction that she was being kidnapped for rape or some such thing, was Herculean. Once she managed to pull her foot from out of Malcolm's grasp and kicked him hard in the stomach. Malcolm's "Oomph!" and beet-red face made John's eyes widen and his grip on the young woman's foot tighten. John couldn't help but imagine how dreadful it would have been if the girl's aim had been just a few inches lower!

Zach held himself as far back as possible and kept his chin up to avoid a direct hit to the face. They finally got her to the carriage door and were maneuvering the breeding, wriggling, inebriated, profanity-spewing female inside. Zach was leaning over her in this process, trying very hard to be gentle and careful, when one of the girl's flinging fists found a mark—smack-dab in the middle of his right eye!

"Bloody hell!" he cursed beneath his breath, then laughed out loud. Still miles away from Gabby and the exasperating knack she had for attracting trouble and mischief, Zach nonetheless held his little friend entirely accountable for the injury to his eye. He had a strong feeling that this was just the beginning of an adventure that would likely leave him black and blue all over.

The Murray townhouse on Charlotte Square was lit up like Methuselah's birthday cake, with candles aglow on every available surface. The first-story salon was especially bright, and when new arrivals stepped through the arched entryway and into the midst of the New Year's Ball, they blinked and squinted till their eyes became accustomed to the visual melee of light, color, and movement.

Heavy crystal chandeliers hung from the ornate ceiling to bathe the dancers in lambency and upper-class, perfumed perspiration. The dipping, swaying convolution of bejeweled colorful damsels and their male partners—some in full Scottish regalia, and others rigged out in the more constrained elegance of an English gentleman's basic black—kept time to a lively waltz.

Gabrielle had begged exhaustion to spare herself a second awkward dance with the sweaty-palmed, obviously soused Captain Fitzwilliam of His Majesty's Royal Army. Now, sitting in surprising solitude and relative peace at the periphery of all the noise and gay confusion, she grew pensive. She glanced over at the cabinet clock, standing with polished dignity against the west wall, and observed that the new year was fast approaching. It was eleven-thirty.

Sitting in a chair just next to her was Aunt Clarissa, there in body but not in thought. She was fast asleep, her gray head lulling against the purple velvet of the chair back, a soft snore percolating between her pursed lips in little pops and whistles. Gabrielle sighed. She had hoped to start the new year with a somewhat more titillating companion.

She withdrew her fan from the folds of her aquamarine skirts to stir the air near her flushed face. Gabrielle couldn't seem to control the tiny prick of irritation she felt every time she snapped open the extremely expensive little gewgaw Rory had given her as a Christmas present. The fan was made of silk and feathers that exactly matched her gown. A score of tiny diamonds decorated the elaborately carved ivory handle. When she had opened the satin-bowed box on Christmas Eve and pushed aside the cream-colored vellum paper to find the beautiful fan, she'd felt absolutely wretched … and angry.

Knowing the delicate nature of the agreement between them, Rory should never have spent so much money on her. She had telegraphed her displeasure to him across a room full of people who were still exclaiming over the magnificence of his gift. Rory had paid her no heed at all, merely looking as innocent as he usually contrived to look in such situations.

The room was insufferably hot, and the fan wasn't helping. Gabrielle had stealthily stepped behind a curtain just moments before to press her cheek against the frosty windowpane, and she was thinking about doing it again. If Aunt Clarissa had seen her do such an unhealthy thing, Gabrielle would have been severely reprimanded. But it was easy to elude and delude Aunt Clarissa, just as it had been easy, so far, to delude everyone in Edinburgh into believing she and Rory Cameron were in love.

Just then Rory and Regina twirled by. He was flirting with her, as he always flirted with his dancing partners, and she was giggling behind one gloved hand, her fingertips pressed delicately against her mouth. Rory winked at Gabrielle over Regina's shoulder. Like Zach and Gabrielle, Regina and Rory had known each other since childhood, but their close friendship did not preclude that Rory abstain from flirting with her. It seemed he could not resist flirting with any woman, from the eldest dowager at any given function, to the greenest schoolroom miss.

It was understandable how everyone might easily believe Gabrielle to be in love with Rory, since there wasn't another man in the room who could compare with him in looks. He was as tall as Zach, but more stockily built. He had dark hair and blue eyes, and a very wicked charm and smile. He wore his kilt well, to say the least. If there was something especially attractive about Scotland, thought Gabrielle, besides its brooding, beautiful countryside and friendly people, it had to be the everyday sight of wellturned male calves below a richly colored tartan kilt.

Rory's amusements included a wide range of activities: womanizing, gambling, hunting, racing, singing, writing poetry—bad poetry, Gabrielle suspected, but then she was no literary genius—and taking every possible opportunity to indulge his penchant for the stage. It was this last characteristic of Rory's that had brought him to Gabrielle's notice. She shared Rory's passion for the theatre. As a child she had frequently repined that she was too well brought up to make a career treading the boards.

One rainy afternoon in November, Gabrielle and Rory had performed together in a comic pantomime for the enjoyment of some of the Murrays' guests. It was a spontaneous activity that proved most successful in entertaining the audience and diverting them from the sober, overcast day outside. In the process, Gabrielle and Rory, who had merely been polite acquaintances before, became fast friends. Three weeks later, much to the shock of Edinburgh's elite society, Rory Cameron, Marquess of Lorne, a confirmed bachelor of nine-and-twenty, announced himself besotted and betrothed to Gabrielle Tavistock.

Gabrielle smiled as she remembered the different reactions to their announcement. Most people probably wondered how she'd managed to bring to banns a notorious rake without the allure of either a remarkable amount of money or a remarkably stunning face and figure.

Gabrielle was well off, but not excessively wealthy. She believed she was quite pretty—she had been told as much all her life—but she knew she was not classically perfect in each feature or possessed of striking coloring. Her hair was a pleasant shade of medium blond, not flaxen or raven. Her eyes weren't icy blue or emerald green, they were hazel. She was neither petite nor the other current favored body type, tall and willowy. She was of medium height and slender, though perhaps a little too bosomy to suit her own notions of the ideal figure. The habit of fashionable ladies to wear bustles to make their skirts fuller, however, made her boyish hips look more in proportion with her generous bust.

She had "countenance." That's what everyone told her. People said she radiated an infectious liveliness. But at the moment, Gabrielle felt anything but lively. She didn't think she could keep up the facade of a sparkling, happily in love, soon-to-be-married young woman for the next four hours, which was very likely how much longer the party would continue.

She missed Zach dreadfully. She had counted on him being in Scotland by now and was confused and worried about his tardiness. She would much rather be in her bedchamber, puzzling about and missing Zach, than in a noisy, overbright, overheated room full of revelers. She had never felt so alone.

She could feign a headache. She'd already sat out one dance, hadn't she? But first she'd cool her cheeks by dashing one more time behind the curtains. She assessed the crowd. No one was looking. She didn't even see Regina's parents, Sir George Murray and Lady Grace, performing their perpetual hospitable rounds of the room. Perhaps they were seeing to another smattering of late arrivals. She stood up and side-stepped nonchalantly toward the draped window embrasure, then slipped behind the gold-tasseled, green damask curtains and into the welcoming draft of cool air.

Gabrielle propped her hands on the waist-high windowsill and rested her forehead against the icy glass. The dampness felt refreshing. Light snow fell, but the flakes melted as soon as they reached ground. She closed her eyes. There was a clatter of hooves on the street below, carriage wheels grinding to a slick halt in front of the house. Lazily, automatically, she opened one eye to see who the oh-so-fashionable latecomers were.

For a moment Gabrielle felt sure she was dreaming. She couldn't breathe. She felt as though her heart had swelled to incredible proportions and was flattening her poor, airless lungs against her ribs. Could it be? But whom had she met in Edinburgh who could possibly resemble Zach? A travel-worn Adonis stepped out of the carriage. She might be able to dream up such a gladsome sight, but the door that swung closed behind him sported the Wickham coat of arms and lent her dream the slap of reality it needed.

She finally forced her lungs to pull in a bit of air, then she immediately started to tremble. Two torches were lit at the bottom of the long flight of stairs outside and Zach moved into the fluctuating, wind-driven nimbus of light. Shadows pooled in the hollows of his cheeks and below his eyes. Orange accents flickered in the curl of longish, sunbeam-yellow hair that escaped the straight black lines of his hat.

She watched him stand at the bottom of the steps and speak to the footman at the top, no doubt explaining who he was and listening while his servants were given quick instructions. Zach always made sure his servants and the horses were well taken care of before seeing to his own comfort. Now he smiled, nodded his approval, and began to ascend the stairs.

As the light from the open door spilled over him, Gabrielle registered every detail of the man she loved. His incredibly long, well-shaped legs, snugly encased in dark pantaloons, propelled him up the stairs two at a time. One hand grasped the wrought-iron railing and the other swung free. He was as graceful as a tiger—and looked like one, too, with his odd golden eyes. How she longed for those eyes to rest on her as they used to do. "Zach..." she whispered, her breath creating a circle of condensation on the glass.

Suddenly Zach stopped midway up the stairs. He stood stock-still, balanced on one neatly booted foot, the other suspended above the step just below him. He hesitated, then looked to left and right, as if he had heard himself called by name but knew not from which direction he'd been summoned. Then he looked up. Gabrielle got her wish. They were eye to eye.

He smiled. She smiled back, foolishly, deliriously happy. Then she noticed it. A dark bruise ringed Zach's right eye. Her smile wavered. He'd been hurt!

As Gabrielle's expression changed, Zach's did, too, but not in the way she might have expected. Apparently comprehending that she was dismayed by his injured appearance, Zach raised both tawny brows, pointed to his purpled eye, then turned the finger back to her and shook it... as if *she* were somehow responsible for his injury! Gabrielle frowned in puzzlement, but Zach only threw back his head and laughed. Gabrielle's smile returned full force. Oh, how she loved him.

CHAPTER TWO

Rory preened in front of the oval mirror that hung on the wall of the small antechamber adjacent to the salon, straightening his cravat, pinching infinitesimal bits of lint off his brown velvet jacket. Gabrielle wrung her hands and watched impatiently. Music for a Scottish reel seeped through the walls like the strains of a ghostly orchestra, and Gabrielle's heart thumped in rhythm to each passing second of time.

Finally Rory had done with the straightening of his apparel and now pulled back his lips in a grimacing smile to inspect his teeth. Apparently satisfied with what he saw, he smoothed the ends of his mustache with a spit-dampened forefinger and turned round to face Gabrielle with a more natural grin.

"So, lass, how long do you think it will take to make ol' Zach mad with jealousy and ready to stick his neck in the marital noose?"

Gabrielle wrinkled her nose. "Rory, you do have *such* a way with words. You make me sound positively predatory!"

Rory shrugged one broad shoulder, saying, "Well, aren't you scheming and plotting to catch him? Looks like the hound chasing the fox to me."

Gabrielle crossed her arms and tapped an irritated rhythm against the rug with one satin slipper. "I thought you understood. I'm not trying to trap Zachary, I'm simply bringing him to his senses. He thinks of me as a child, you see—which I'm not, of course. I don't think he's ever imagined me married to anyone, least of all himself! Our pretend engagement will open his eyes to the fact that I'm a woman"—Gabriel lifted her chin—"and that he's in love with me. He just doesn't realize it yet!"

Rory snorted. "Poor devil!"

Gabrielle stamped her foot. "If you don't stop talking fustian, Rory, I'm likely to get a bit miffed with you!"

Rory laughed and slid his large hands about Gabrielle's waist, pulling her as close as her full skirts would allow, close enough that Gabrielle could smell the liquor on his breath and see the unnatural brightness of his blue eyes. Apparently he'd been making rather merry with the help of Sir George's good Highland whiskey. She held herself away from him with both hands pressed against his chest. "Don't take it personally, Gabrielle," he said. "You're a bonny lass, and if I were the marryin' sort, why you'd be right there at the top of my list of potential brides."

Gabrielle's lips curved in amusement. She reached down and tried to pry Rory's hands off her waist. "I'm deeply flattered, Rory. Now, if you don't mind—"

Rory held her firmly. He ducked his head till they were nearly nose to nose. "One way I'd reduce my list to final contenders would be to discover whose lips are the sweetest. Your hair's the color of honey, lass. Does that mean your lips taste like the nectar of the gods?"

Gabby wriggled out of Rory's grip with an agility that took him by surprise, leaving him with his lips puckered against empty air. "I've no intention of kissing anyone but Zach!"

Rory raised his brows and threw up his hands in a gesture of innocent acquiescence. "Then he's kissed you?"

Gabrielle felt herself blushing. For a moment she was tempted to lie, but she didn't. "No, we've never kissed. Well, at least not in *that* way. He kisses me—" She twirled her hand in the air as if searching for the right words, then in a deflated tone said, "On the head."

Rory *tsk-tsked* and moved to a rosewood table by the window. He flicked open a small enameled case, plucked out a cigarillo, and fit it between his lips. He lifted a three-tapered brace of candles and lit the cigarillo, leisurely puffing out a perfect circle of smoke before turning back to Gabrielle.

His insouciance annoyed her. Despite their friendship and collusion in this betrothal charade, Gabby felt certain that

Rory had no real understanding of how important the whole matter was to her. Besides putting off his matchmaking, nagging grandmother for a time, he probably saw their deception simply as an amusing lark to while away the dull winter months. His next words confirmed this suspicion.

"I've been waiting for this moment for a long time. Fooling the people hereabouts has been no test of my acting ability. Convincing this Wickham fellow—someone who's known you all your life—that I'm enamored of you, and you with me, presents a bit of a challenge, and I find challenges quite diverting. If the man's been pecking you on the crown like some doddering old uncle would do to his favorite niece, I'd say my work's cut out for me," he added with obvious satisfaction. "How long do you think he'll take to change his clothes and present himself in the salon?"

"Zachary never fusses over his appearance—" Gabrielle noticed Rory's slight sneer of pitying superiority and pointedly added, "Yet he still manages to look the very ideal of gentlemanly elegance. Some men are simply *quicker* at things than others."

"Being quicker at things is not always an attribute one strives for, Gabrielle," Rory suggested lazily, his blue eyes sparkling with bawdy humor. "For example, in the case of lovemaking..."

"You do not need to elaborate," Gabrielle informed him with a withering look. "Perhaps I chose the wrong word when I said Zach was quick. Perhaps I should rather have said that he is more *adept* at things than most men."

Rory laughed appreciatively. "You're loyal, I'll give you that!"

"Loyal and desperately in love, Rory," she said fervently, reaching out to trail a caressing hand along the plush texture of his jacket lapel. "I'm depending on you. My whole future— Zach's whole future—depends on you!"

Rory dropped his cigarillo into a porcelain dish on the table and lifted Gabrielle's hand to his lips, kissing the lacy back of her glove very tenderly. He was serious now, and Gabrielle felt relief flood through her. Rory could be an absolute dear when he was moved to honest emotion.

"No, Gabrielle," he advised her gently. "Yours and Zach's

future does not depend on me, but rather on you and Zach. If there's love between you, you must work through whatever is keeping you apart. I can't help but think Zach rather a fool, though, if the only thing that stands in the way of your happiness is the matter of a dozen or so years' difference in your ages."

Gabrielle felt her eyes filling with tears. She looked down, swallowing back the emotion that welled in her throat. "No. There's more to it than that, only I don't know exactly what. It has something to do with a woman he once loved. No one would ever tell me the details. I was very young when she died."

She lifted her gaze back to Rory's sympathetic, though unfortunately slightly befuddled expression. "For the past ten years, he's traveled a lot. He's gone all over England and Scotland, some say to lose himself in dissipation. But I don't believe it for a minute! When a person embraces a wild style of living to forget his troubles, his appearance shows it. Zach always returns from his trips looking younger, rejuvenated. But after a time the moroseness builds up again, and off he goes on another journey! I want to make it unnecessary for Zach to leave his home—which I know he loves—in order to be rid of this pain of his. I want to be Zach's … balm!"

"Lord, Gabrielle, that sounded straight out of a penny novel!" Rory complained, laughing. "His *balm?*"

Offended, Gabrielle sniffed. "Oh, just when I think you might be understanding a little!"

"I do understand, you minx, but you grow a trifle dramatic at times, which is exactly why I like you so much. I *love* high drama! Speaking of that, we had better get back to the salon before Zach makes his appearance, posing ourselves in a touching tableau which will make quite an impact on him the moment he enters the room."

Rory used his hands to frame an invisible square in the air, then stood gazing at the imagined scene. "By the fireplace, perhaps, with me looking soulfully into your eyes…" He squinted thoughtfully. "What do you think, lass?"

Gabrielle knitted her brows consideringly, staring at the same empty space. "Or sitting on the Egyptian couch in that one alcove, holding hands, of course." Her eyes brightened with sudden inspiration as he led her to the door. "I'll use my fan to flirt with you! Nothing could make me appear more mature and sophisticated, I daresay, then to use my fan!"

Rory grinned. "Ah, yes, the very thing," he murmured dryly. "But if that doesn't work, lass, there are other ways to make you look grown up!"

Gabrielle smiled uncertainly. She appreciated Rory's wholehearted participation and enthusiasm, but what could he possibly mean by *that?*

Rather like a wedding march, Zach kept a halting step-wait, step-wait rhythm as he walked behind the aging footman down the long hall to the salon. No escort was necessary, since he could have followed the noise and not gone amiss despite the large size of the Murrays' townhouse, but Sir George had insisted on leaving the servant standing outside Zach's door for just this purpose. It would probably offend the old fellow's dignity if Zach sped past him like a cocky hare kicking dust in the face of a persevering tortoise, so he endeavored to control his impatience. He pulled his watch from an inner waistcoat pocket and noted the time. Eleven-fifty-five. The new year was practically banging at the door. He wished the plodding footman would walk just a trifle faster!

Zach derived a great deal of pleasure from anticipating the maiden morning of 1832 in the company of Gabby, just as he'd felt an unexpectedly large burst of happiness to see her gazing down at him from an upper window when he'd arrived. It was almost too coincidental that she should be looking out just when he pulled up in front of the house, since he'd not written to announce when he might be expected, but what other explanation could there be for it except coincidence?

Zach had a silly notion that Gabby had somehow sensed his arrival, just as he'd felt an unaccountable, overwhelming urge to glance up toward the window. It had seemed as though he'd heard her call his name, but that was impossible since the window had been tightly shut against the cold winter night. Zach grunted derisively. Indeed, Gabby's fanciful imagination was finally rubbing off on him after all their years of friendship! He would not believe a bit of it!

To prod himself toward a more realistic train of thought, Zach looked down at his Wellington ankle boots and checked them for shine. As usual, Bleader had given them a brilliant luster. He needn't worry about the tidiness of any other article of his clothing, either. Bleader never allowed him out of his chamber unless he looked absolutely immaculate, even when, as tonight, Zach had hurried him through the usual routine.

Next to the colorful kilts of the Scots and a few bright holiday vests worn by the visiting Sassenach, he supposed he would fade into the background in his plain black toggery. So much the better, since anonymity suited him just fine. He only hoped he would not be so inconspicuous that he'd be unable to attract Gabby's attention. He had to find her before the clock chimed midnight.

Then another thought intruded on Zach's happy anticipation to see Gabby. Memories of that wretched girl he'd picked up outside Old Town continually cropped up. She'd swooned in the carriage on the way to the women's shelter and had been borne inside with considerably less trouble than when she'd been carried to the coach.

The woman looked ready to burst with child, and her drinking like a crusty sailor on a three-day leave did not bode well for the baby's health or the mother's. He supposed her heavy imbibing was a well-established habit. Zach hadn't had time to wait around for her to wake up so that he might ask her questions, so he left strict orders with Mr. Blake, the proprietor Zach had hired to oversee the charitable institution he'd established five years before, to keep her there till the morrow even if she must be restrained.

Zach suspected that the woman had been abused by her husband. Once they had gotten her into the light, he had seen bruises on her arms and face, and there were probably more elsewhere. Just thinking about it made his blood boil. He had been a rather peacekeeping fellow over the past ten years, but nothing made him feel angrier and more capable of violence than the thought of a man bullying and beating a defenseless woman.

There was that time when he'd actually seen such a despicable act taking place in the alley behind the shelter he owned in Liverpool. Zach rubbed the knuckles of his right hand, remembering how they'd been split open by the impact of his blow to the man's face. He'd nearly killed the bloody bastard, but Zach wasn't the least bit proud of the fact. Unfortunately the girl the man had been beating *did* die from her injuries.

Lord, when he thought of all the senseless misery and death he'd witnessed over the years! The three nonsectarian women's shelters he'd established and maintained with his own money, along with the contributions that eventually trickled in from the community, made only a small dent in all the suffering.

Zach lifted his hand to gingerly touch the swollen area round his eye. He hadn't yet considered how he would explain the injury to Gabby. Now that the doors to the salon were being opened for him and he was about to see her face to face, perhaps he had better think of something rather quickly!

Zach stood at the entryway and looked about the room. Busy, so busy. Like an anthill built on the remains of an extravagant picnic, there was food and activity everywhere. And the chattering! It grew louder by the moment, like the honking cacophony of a cloud of agitated geese flying over a marsh. The excitement, the expectation of the clock's chiming-in of the new year permeated the group—intensifying, building to a peak.

Fortunately the room was large, the ceilings high, the air circulating relatively well. Thank God someone had decided to keep open the doors that led into the gallery. Otherwise he'd be feeling the first stirrings of phobia: the sweaty palms, the trip-hammer heartbeat.

Eleven-fifty-eight. Zach felt a prick of uneasiness. Where was Gabby? Suddenly it was important to find her before midnight, to see the year out with her at his side, his only link to familial love and attachment in the relative strangeness of Edinburgh. He stood still, only his head and eyes moving as he surveyed the room. Then he saw her.

Sitting on a scroll-armed, exotic-looking couch in an alcove not twenty feet away, she batted her lashes above the crimped edge of a blue feathered fan. She was not alone. Sitting next to her, bending over her gloved hand as if he were about to bestow a kiss upon it, was a man. He was dark and handsome with a neat, fashionable mustache, rather burly, with good shoulders and muscular legs well suited for a kilt.

Zach's reaction to seeing Gabby with her betrothed hit him like a fist to the gullet. It shouldn't have been surprising to find her in the company of the marquess, yet Zach had not been thinking of sharing Gabby's company as they greeted the new year together. In Cornwall he was used to having her all to himself.

Zach sighed. Well, he would have to become accustomed to a different sort of relationship with Gabby now. The marquess probably would not look kindly on Zach monopolizing her attention. Though from the way she was gazing at her betrothed, Gabby's attention might not be as easily gained and kept by Zach as in the old days. Everything was different now. Where had the little girl gone?

Intellectually Zach had been aware of Gabby's budding womanhood for some time, but perhaps he'd tried to ignore it so that he could preserve the innocence of their relationship. He looked at her. Candlelight, like the touch of Midas, turned Gabby's hair to burnished gold. Her skin was tinted like ivory and roses, the delicate color and curve of her neck and shoulders set off by the low-sweeping neckline of her blue dress.

That neckline ... Something stirred in Zach at the sight of Gabby's breasts peeking above the silk ruching of her gown. He knew the feeling, though he would rather not recognize it for what it was. It was arousal. Good God in heaven, he was feeling the beginnings of passion for *Gabby!*

Zach was consumed with distressing emotions. First there was anger. How *dare* she grow up? By maturing into a beautiful, desirable woman she had effectively removed herself from the comfortable circle of their friendship. In essence, she had left him behind. He felt betrayed by the child who seemed suddenly, willfully, to have metamorphosed into a creature that he could not love for fear of destroying her. He dared to love the little girl she was, but he dared not love the woman she had become. After all, everyone knew that he brought nothing but unhappiness to the women in his life.

But what was he thinking of, anyway? She was engaged already to this Marquess of Lome fellow, and Zach wasn't here to speculate on his own feelings for Gabby—those were unimportant—but to ascertain whether or not the marquess was a suitable *parti* for his little Gabby.

His little Gabby, indeed! There was no one in the room who fit that description any longer. An overwhelming sadness enveloped Zach. He had lost her.

The clock began to strike the hour. A hush fell over the room. People were positioned in intimate little circles of friends and loved ones, ready to embrace and kiss on the echo of the last chime. Then Gabby turned, and her eyes met Zach's. He prayed she would not see the sadness he felt, for her face was alight with happiness. He pasted a smile on his lips and hoped it did not look as strained as it felt. She rose gracefully and strode quickly toward him, finally standing shamelessly in front of him in all her full-blown, ravishing, unrepentant womanhood. Gone was the little girl with heather sprigs tangled in her hair. Gone was the infantile scent of moor dirt and sunshine. Gabby smelled like ... orchids.

It had taken all Gabrielle's power of self-control to keep from flying off the couch the minute Zach entered the room. She had surreptitiously watched him as he stood straight and tall and calm, the eye of the storm in the middle of all the gay confusion. She knew the minute his gaze rested on her. She felt his scrutiny as surely as if he had been touching her. She wished he were touching her with those long tapered fingers of his...

She played her part, fluttering her fan and her eyelashes both. She flirted outrageously with Rory, coyly dimpling and simpering. Did Zach realize that while he stood there observing her, he was attracting the attention of everyone near him? In her peripheral vision, she saw the female heads turning, admiring— the male heads turning, envying, resenting. Did he know that the plain black elegance of his evening attire made his golden hair and eyes all the more striking?

Lord, she'd felt jealous: jealous of anyone who presumed to look at him while she was denying herself such a treat. Rory had kissed each finger of her hand with lingering devotion. Still Zach did not approach. Then, when the cabinet clock began to strike the hour, she could bear the distance between them no longer. She must join Zach in this momentous occasion of new beginnings, for she prayed the new year would portend the beginning of a new relationship between them. She snatched her hand from Rory and walked quickly toward Zach, but when she finally stood before him with the last seconds of the year passing irretrievably by, she felt a restraint in Zach, a sadness. In response, her own happiness dulled a little, and she felt shy and awkward.

He spoke first, a bittersweet smile curving his lips, a tender expression in his aureate eyes. "Hello, Gabby."

"Hello, my dear friend," she responded softly. The clock's chimes reverberated through the room. Should she extend her hand to him? Should she offer him her cheek to kiss? Wracked with indecision, she took the safe course. She did nothing. "I trust your journey was not too uncomfortable?"

"Certainly it was," he returned teasingly, lifting his hand to touch a forefinger to the bruised eye. "But it was well worth it to see you in all your blushing beauty as a bride-to-be."

She knew not how to respond to such a compliment. She was glad if she seemed in blushing beauty, but she was dismayed by the easy manner in which he could speak of her coming marriage. She had hoped he would act more ... well... *jealous!* Besides, she was blushing for *him,* the idiot!

Repressing her disappointment, she said, "How did you hurt yourself? I shall not believe it is my fault, unless you can prove it is." Then, in a desperate bid to lighten the moment, she suggested archly, "An unwilling damsel took objection to your wish to carry her away, perhaps?"

Zach's eyes crinkled in surprised amusement. "Just so, my dear Gabby. Just so!"

Gabrielle made herself laugh with him, supposing he was teasing her back, then prayed with every fiber of her being that he wasn't telling her the truth. "No, really, Zach?" She squeezed the question out through the gritted teeth of a forced smile.

Zach's expression sobered. He looked searchingly at her. "No, little friend, I'm not such a cad as that. Did you think me such a one? I'll tell you the truth." He leaned close to her ear and whispered, the warm breath tickling her cheek and making a chill run up her spine, "'Twas faeries, Gabby. I was attacked by wee folk like the sort we have in Cornwall, only these were meaner, and one of them possessed of a good right hook! See, it *was* your fault. Wherever you are, my dear, there's always some sort of enchanted chicanery going on!"

Gabrielle laughed delightedly as the twelfth chime of the clock resounded through the room. Pandemonium broke out. The orchestra began a jaunty tune, playing their instruments with loud and inexact enthusiasm, a fitting background to the shouts of merriment that filled the room.

Suddenly Gabrielle was seized by firm male hands, turned round, then pressed against a broad velvet-clad chest. Before she could emit even a feeble protest, Rory wrapped her in a smothering embrace and claimed her mouth in a hard, hot, thorough kiss that seemed to last for an eternity. She could not pull away, for she dare not show an aversion to her fiancé in front of Zach, but, oh, how she longed to box the scoundrel's ears good and proper! If this was Rory's idea of how to make her appear grown up he would soon be disabused of the notion!

Indignation clenched in Zach's chest like a balled-up fist. He needed all his strength of will to keep from physically wrenching Gabby out of her fiancé's embrace. Gawd, it looked as though he meant to swallow her whole, like some luscious fruit in ripe season to be smacked and slobbered over! Didn't he realize that he was making an embarrassing scene? Didn't he know that such conduct between a betrothed couple in public would only serve to encourage speculation about their conduct in private? *Did* he kiss her thus in private? Where was Aunt Clarissa? He had always known that woman had as much aptitude for chaperoning as a turkey did for flying!

The kiss lasted an eternity, a spleen-twisting, throat-burning, eye-bulging eternity. Zach could not vouch for his restraint if the man didn't pry his sucking lips off Gabby's face by the count of three. One … two …

Gabby was released. She weaved to and fro. Her eyes were glassy. She avoided looking at Zach. Her cheeks burned with anger… or was it passion? Either possibility did not sit well with Zach. She flicked open her fan and plied it through the tense air. "Goodness, Rory. *Goodness!*" she murmured faintly.

"Well, my little pigeon, what did you expect?" said the marquess in a tenderly remonstrative voice. "'Tis the new year, after all. Everybody was kissing *someone,* and who better to kiss than my betrothed? It was cruel of you to desert me at such a poignant moment!" The marquess twisted the end of his mustache and grinned down at Gabby.

"I'm … I'm sorry I left you, Rory," Gabby stammered, her thick lashes shielding her eyes from Zach's concerned inspection. "I saw my friend, Zachary, you see. He was standing quite alone and I thought it most proper and kind to…. to say hello. I've wanted very much for the two of you to meet—"

"So you're Zachary Wickham?"

Zachary found himself being addressed by the amorous marquess. He dragged his gaze from Gabby's flustered countenance and coolly—nay, coldly—fixed his eyes on her betrothed. Deigning to acknowledge the introduction by the merest inclination of his head, he answered, "Yes, I am. And I must conclude by the proceedings of the past few moments that you are Lord Lome?"

The marquess seemed completely unconscious of Zach's disapproval and frosty demeanor. "Yes, but you mustn't address me as such. Lord Lorne is such a tongue-twisting redundant name, don't you think? I had always thought it ill-done of my ancestors to inherit such an awkward title."

Zach had no reply to such an absurd statement. He could only suppose that his lordship was a bit of a rattle, addicted to nonsensical chattering. For Gabby's sake, he would humor him. He smiled. "Then what shall I call you, my lord?" If the marquess had no ready ideas, Zach could certainly think of a few fitting names.

"Rory, by all means. A friend of Gabrielle's is, by the natural way of things, a friend of mine."

"I'm honored," Zach lied smoothly.

Apparently somewhat recovered from her betrothed's assault upon her lips and her dignity, Gabby slipped her hand into the crook of Rory's elbow and looked at Zach. Her smile was wavering but determined. Was she displeased by Rory's conduct, or was she secretly pleased? Either emotion could account for her discomposure, made obvious by glowing eyes and cheeks. Yet if she were displeased, why would she cuddle up to him so? "I want you and Rory to become friends, Zach. I fancy you have a great deal in common. How long will you be staying?"

Zach tried to read Gabby's heart through her eyes, but for the first time since he could remember, those lovely hazel peepers were shuttered against him. "Not very long. Circumstances will dictate when I leave."

"Circumstances?" An ember of some sort of emotion sparked in her eyes, but it was quickly tamped down.

Zach made a dismissive gesture. "The climate. My mood." *Whether you have need of me, Gabby,* he added silently. *Whether it becomes necessary to extricate you from an ill-advised match.*

"There's good hunting in the winter, Zachary—I may call you Zachary?" Rory's self-assured smile suggested that he did not expect Zach to deny him. Again for Gabby's sake, Zach did not. He gave his consent for the use of his Christian name with another slight nod of his head.

"Do you like to bow-hunt?" Rory persisted cheerfully. "I

do. There's more of a challenge to the hunt when you use a bow instead of a gun. Primitive weapons put one on a more equal footing with the prey, so to speak. Have you an opinion on the subject, Zachary?"

"I do, but I think I'll keep it till we can discuss the matter at some other time," he said with a smile, but in a dampening tone. "Gabby cannot wish to listen to us prattle on about quivers and string and such the like, can you, Gabby?"

"Oh, I quite like to hear Rory talk about *anything*," she said sweetly. "He has a vast store of knowledge about a great many subjects." She turned an adoring gaze on her betrothed.

Zach studied her profile, the upturned, confiding look of devotion, and felt a twinge of guilt and … doubt. Was he being precisely fair toward Rory in coming to so swift a conclusion that he was an unfeeling brute? Could Gabby—his bright, perceptive, feisty, free-thinking Gabby—be so deceived by a person? Could all of her good sense have turned to mush simply by the influence of a pair of hairy legs in a kilt? He doubted that very much. And since she had never shown such admiration for any man before, perhaps there was something to this Rory Cameron, Marquess of Lome, besides his skirted swagger.

Upon first meeting, however, it seemed his lordship did not flaunt his good qualities on his shirt-sleeve. Zach realized he would probably have to spend time with the marquess in order to come to a fair reckoning of the man's caliber. He was willing to make the sacrifice for Gabby. He strove to dredge up more amiable feelings toward the man.

"I would be pleased to accompany you on a hunting excursion … er… Rory. I've visited the country before, but never hunted here. Besides, it will be an opportunity for us to get better acquainted. As you said, by our mutual connection to Gabby, we are automatically made friends."

A servant was passing with a tray of champagne. Zach stopped him, took a long-stemmed glass for Gabby, Rory, and himself, then raised his own in the air. "I propose a toast. To old friends." He paused and tipped his glass to Gabby, bowing over it. "To new friends." He paid the same tribute to Rory, then thrust his glass forward to collide with both of theirs, the crystal ringing melodically on impact. "And to the new year!"

Gabby tossed back the bubbly wine with festive abandon. "Yes, Zach," she said, licking the champagne from the corner of her mouth. "Good-bye to the old, hello to the new. Good-bye to childhood, and a hearty welcome to adulthood and all that comes with it!" Gabby's eyes glinted with heady determination. "I am ready!"

Zach barely registered the determination reflected in Gabby's eyes. He was looking at her champagne-moistened lips and remembering how sweet and pink her tongue had looked darting out to retrieve an errant drop. He swallowed hard. He tried to pull his eyes away, but he'd become intoxicated by the exotic scent of orchids. Gabby and orchids … did they really go together after all?

CHAPTER THREE

New Year's Day amongst the Edinburgh elite was given over to the custom of making social calls. Certain families traditionally opened their houses on this festive holiday to their friends and neighbors, providing buffet tables laden with food, genteel quartets of musicians playing background music, and throngs of people from their own set with whom they might compare and critique the previous evening's entertainments.

Gabrielle knew there would be no getting out of the necessity of accompanying the Murrays on their round of calls, and she was grateful that Zach had agreed to come along. She knew he was not much inclined to hobnob with strangers and to "do the pretty," but she hoped he was inspired to accept the Murrays' invitation not only out of politeness, but from a desire to be near her. She also hoped they'd find time for a little private conversation, something that had been so easy to do at home in Cornwall yet would be much more difficult in Edinburgh.

Everyone had gone to their rooms to fetch their winter accessories—hats, gloves, muffs, etcetera—and Gabrielle waited in the vestibule for Rory, to whom she'd given a firm message to meet her there well before the others were expected to come down. She'd sent Ralph, the burly footman who ordinarily kept sentry by the front door, into the adjoining parlor, telling him, with a sweet smile, that she'd ring when they needed assistance into their coats. She wanted to speak to Rory alone.

She tugged on her warm mittens, dyed to match her Devonshire brown pelisse trimmed with blond fur, and mentally rehearsed her lecture. She would make quite sure Rory understood that there would be no repeat of last night's unforeseen and most unwelcome kiss! She'd felt violated. She would only grant Zach such privileges, and Rory was going to be set straight on the matter before they embarked on another day of playacting as a betrothed couple.

"You summoned me, miss?"

Gabrielle turned at Rory's mocking voice. At the foot of the stairs he stood stiff and expressionless, obviously imitating the demeanor of a servant. Gabrielle gave a noisy sigh of exasperation. "You needn't be so silly. I simply wanted to talk to you before the others came down."

Rory relaxed from his servile pose and pursed his lips, sauntering across the few feet that separated them. He wore a kilt again, probably to impress Zach, because the chilly weather had compelled most Scots to wear trousers when they went out during the day. Rory certainly did look good in a kilt, but Gabrielle was sure Zach would look even better.

"It did not sound like a request to me, rather like an order," he said. His eyes glinted with mischief as he toyed with one of Gabrielle's bonnet ribbons. "You should know from the beginning that I'll not be a lap-pug sort of husband, heeling and fetching at your command." He caught her chin between thumb and forefinger, tilting her face and looking with exaggerated soulfulness into her eyes. "Have I kissed you good morning yet, lass?"

Gabrielle arched her chin free of Rory's grasp and caught his neatly arranged cravat in a tight fist, tugging on it till she and Rory were nose to nose. "That's exactly what I want to talk to you about, you scoundrel," she said, nearly hissing at him, her eyes darting round his wide shoulders to watch for people coming down the stairs. "Last night's kiss was the first, last, and *only* one you'll ever take from me!"

Rory frowned down at the small, strong fingers firmly clenching the easily wrinkled starched muslin of his cravat. "Gabrielle, in case you hadn't noticed, you're mussing my neckcloth. Billings spent at least a half-hour arranging the thing! Haven't you any remorse about sullying the purity of such a glorious creation?"

"Hang your neckcloth, Rory Cameron! What about my

lips? You had no scruples about sullying *them* last night! You took liberties you knew very well I didn't welcome! How dare you? How *dare* you?"

Rory sniffed, sliding his gaze past Gabrielle and staring instead at the unaccusing aspect of silk wall hangings. "You didn't pull away, I recall."

"How could I? Zach was standing right there. If he hadn't been, I'd have slapped you soundly!"

"Lord, settle down, you little tempest! I kissed you because I knew it would make Zach jealous. Isn't that what you want?"

"I want to make Zach jealous, but I don't want you kissing me. I want *him* kissing me! I was saving my lips for Zach!"

"Oh, fiddle-faddle, Gabrielle. You're getting mawkish again. Lips can't be put aside for someone, like Granny's wooden teeth in a crock, to be taken out when they're needed! It won't hurt you to kiss me till Zach steps in to take my place. Blether, let go, won't you? My neck's starting to hurt! Besides, what's in a kiss, you noodle?"

"That shows how little you know about true love, Rory," Gabrielle informed him severely. "When you're kissing someone you truly love, a kiss is much more than a physical thing. It's full of warmth and meaning and—"

"Humbug! What would you know about it? Do you really think that kissing Zach would be any different than kissing me? As a matter of fact, you might enjoy *my* kisses the better of the two! I'll have you know that I'm known hereabouts for being a first-rate kisser!"

Gabrielle let go of Rory's cravat. "If you like the sensation of being swallowed whole, perhaps."

Rory rubbed his neck, wincing. "What? Now wait just a minute, Gabrielle Tavistock—"

"I don't mean to be rude, Rory. Well, maybe I do… But I just want you to understand that I'll not tolerate you kissing me again, no matter who's watching!"

"Not even on the cheek?"

"Well, perhaps on the cheek it's all right, since I've always permitted you to do so, but nowhere else!"

"Not even on the forehead?"

Gabrielle crossed her arms. "You're being idiotish, Rory. You know exactly the point I'm trying to make, so don't play the dolt!"

Rory laughed and moved to the gilt-edged mirror hanging above the table where the butler neatly piled visitors' calling cards, but when he caught sight of his woefully disheveled neckcloth, his laugh died away, and he set to work rearranging the crumpled muslin. "You're a dangerous bit of fluff, Gabrielle. Could have choked me! If Zach's got a jot of sense, he'll stay well away from—"

"Hush! Someone's coming down the stairs!"

"'Tis only Regina. I'd know her step anywhere."

Rory was right. Regina, wearing a blush-colored redingote that complemented her auburn hair, appeared at the curve of the stairs, quickly skipping down the remaining steps. She frowned a remonstrance. "Anyone coming down could hear you squabbling and bickering like children! What's the to do?"

"She's miffed 'cause I kissed her, Reggie. Silly lass, ain't she? You'd not kick up such a dust over a nothing-meaning kiss, now would you? For revenge she's made my neckcloth not fit to be seen. I suppose I'll have to go back to my room and get a fresh one and put Billings to the task of doing it up again."

"I can fix your neckcloth, Rory," Regina told him, her face glowing with a maidenly blush brought on, no doubt, by Rory's opinions on kissing and Regina's hypothetical response. Rory turned dutifully round and spread his arms wide, allowing Regina full access to his person. She pressed her lips primly together, properly condemning by her demeanor the roguish way Rory was grinning down at her.

"If you don't want Zach to know what you're up to," she scolded, as she deftly twisted and tied the cravat into a pleasing shape, "you're both going to have to show a little restraint, in arguing and in kissing! Every day I ask myself why I consented to help you two in this ridiculous charade!"

Rory flicked her cheek with a careless finger, his grin widening. "'Cause you're a loyal lass, Reggie. As close to being man's best friend as a female can come!"

Regina's blush deepened, and her fingers fumbled a bit in their task of putting Rory to rights. "Now I'm to be compared to a devoted spaniel, eh?"

"Spaniels don't stammer and get a twitch in their eye when they're nervous or asked to tell a simple little untruth," Gabrielle reminded her. "I hope our charade doesn't put you in such a situation too often, for you're sure to give us away."

"I don't like telling lies!" Regina protested.

"Nor do I," said Gabrielle. "But in this case it's necessary and for a good cause."

"Spinning whiskers don't trouble me in the least," Rory confessed cheerfully. "It's really just acting, you know."

Gabrielle shook her head at Rory, then moved to the bottom of the stairs, peering up. "You don't think Zach heard us quarreling, do you?"

"There was no one in the gallery when I left my room," Regina reassured her, then added, "but you can't be too careful."

Gabrielle chewed nervously on her bottom lip. "You're right, of course." She looked at Rory, willing him to be serious. "Rory, we must work together on this. We mustn't fight. Promise me you'll be good!"

Regina patted the folds of the much-improved cravat, while Rory assumed his most demure pose. "I'm *always* good, lass."

"Oh, you devil... !"

"Lover's spat?"

Gabrielle froze at the sound of Zach's voice coming from behind her, not from the direction of the stairs as she'd expected. She pivoted and discovered him standing at the front of the hall that led to the library and the servants' stairs. Each time she saw him, it was as if she hadn't clapped eyes on him for ages. Each time she marveled at the effect he had on her senses—like a physical wrench. Today in a wine-colored jacket and black trousers close-fitted to his long shapely legs, and with his butter-yellow hair shining in the diffused morning light, he looked magnificent.

"Zach, where did you come from?" she blurted, worried

lest he'd heard the substance of their conversation.

Zach shrugged and smiled. "I came from my room, of course. I had a book I wanted to return to the library, so I came down the back way. Seemed the most logical approach. Why? Did I err?" he teased. "Miss Murray, am I not to use the servants' stairs?"

Regina forced a laugh. "Of course you may use any stairs you choose! And d-do call me R-Regina," she added. Regina's left eye began to twitch.

"You just surprised us, that's all, old man," Rory explained, stepping close to Gabrielle and draping his arm about her shoulders.

Zach raised a tawny brow, his gaze focused on Rory's arm, then fixed piercingly on Gabrielle's face. "Surprised you in the middle of a tiff?"

"Nonsense, Zach. Rory was just teasing me about something, and I called him a devil." Gabrielle gave a chirp of laughter. "You know me and my quick tongue!"

Zach's mouth twisted wryly. "Don't I, though." He peered at her from beneath slightly lowered lids, his golden eyes seeming to try to penetrate through her outer facade and into the hidden stores of thought and feeling. Gabrielle fidgeted under the scrutiny, a half-delicious sort of unease creeping along her spine. "At least I used to know you, Gabby," he added.

No one seemed capable of dredging up a fitting response to such a cryptic remark, but luckily they were all saved from the discomfort of an awkward silence when Sir George, Lady Grace, and Aunt Clarissa could be heard chattering their way down the stairs. The Murrays looked their usual polished selves, both tall, delicate-thin and silver-gray, aging elegantly, like an heirloom sterling tea set.

Aunt Clarissa, decked out in her uniform gray, looked like a dormouse, as usual. Waggling her fingers in front of her, she immediately attached herself to Zach and demanded to know how he'd got the black eye. Since she'd been asleep last night at the ball and hadn't had the opportunity to speak to him then, and had eaten breakfast at too early an hour to meet him in the dining parlor, he *must* tell her how dear Beth, Alex, and the children were! Amid several separate conversations and in the flurry of servant-assisted donnings of greatcoats and mantles, they left the house.

Zach squinted up at a cool white sun. Mother Nature had celebrated this first day of January 1832 by blessing the population with a cloudless sky as bright as a new penny, and with air as crisp as a pound note freshly printed from the London Mint. A fine powder of snow covered the roofs and laced the iron gates of Charlotte Square, and a grainy frost coated the walkways. Well-dressed ladies and gentlemen crunched along in their pattens and leather boots, laughing and talking and looking forward fearlessly to another prosperous year.

Zach found himself very much a part of this army of prosperity, headed for an address on Queen Street, though he would much rather have Gabby all to himself for the indulgence of private conversation. Grudgingly, politely smiling, he toed the line just behind her and the marquess, who were just behind Sir George and Lady Grace. Regina marched on one side of him, her gloved hand wedged in the crook of his elbow, a large mulberry-colored feather in her bonnet tickling his chin every time she turned to greet an acquaintance, and Aunt Clarissa marched on the other side.

Regina seemed a very likable young woman, appearing upon first impressions to be altogether artless and simple in her conversation and manners. She didn't try to impress him or flirt with him. She did not employ a single practiced feminine wile that he could discern, and, being a frequent target of females whose entire happiness was qualified by the admiration they inspired, Zach could spot the type clear across a room.

Regina, pretty, lithe, and auburn-haired, could certainly expect her fair share of admiration, yet she did not seem to feel the need to seek it out and store it up, like a squirrel gathering precious nuts for a barren winter. Zach could understand Gabby's friendship with such a modest, lively young woman, and he approved. But he still hadn't reckoned out what had attracted her to Rory Cameron! The marquess was certainly not in the least bit modest or shy. He seemed, in Zach's "objective" view, to be the male counterpart of the female type he'd just been pondering, ever needful of admiration and notice.

Just two steps ahead of them, Rory and Gabby were perfectly positioned so that Zach could watch and study them. Gabby seemed completely absorbed in her fiancé; however, Rory was not so oblivious to passers-by. He was especially cognizant of pretty young women who shyly nodded as they passed, dimpling and blushing in response to his bold look and sly grin. Then, when such diversions were gone, he turned back to Gabby, rewarding her devoted attention with intimate smiles, implying secrets and meanings that belonged to lovers; lengthy whisperings in her ear with his dark head bent close to hers; and the increased pressure of his large fingers round Gabby's waist, so neatly nipped in, as it was, by the tailored lines of her rich brown pelisse. Such a tiny waist, such big hands...

Zach felt his chest constricting, as so often happened when a fleeting memory of last night's ball came back to him. The one picture indelibly etched into his brain of the night before was of Gabby captured in the marquess's embrace, the large Scot's mouth moving over hers with the ravaging thoroughness of a love-starved inmate just escaped from gaol. Gawd, could there be a worse example of disrespect for one's betrothed than to compromise her in public? The worst of it, however, was that Gabby had not objected. And today they were as cozy and cooing as two turtledoves in a cote. Even after their tiff.

Though they'd tried to deny the existence of an argument between them, Zach knew that Rory and Gabby had had a disagreement that morning, but had deemed it best to hide the fact from him when he ventured into the vestibule on the echo of raised voices. Another odd happenstance was Regina's apparent willingness to help them hide the existence of an argument from Zach. Did Gabby care so much for Zach's good opinion of her fiancé that she would try to keep secret any unpleasantness attached to their engagement? Would she even involve Regina in this sort of subterfuge?

Zach shook his head, puzzled. To his mind, none of their

behavior seemed precisely genuine. Their adoration for each other seemed rather overwrought at times; Gabby's laughter too strident, Rory's lovemaking a bit too violent to be sincere. Certainly Zach had not been long enough in their joint company to have formed an unshakable opinion on the unsuitability of their match, but he had an odd, rather disjointed feeling that they weren't really a match at all... But it hardly seemed likely that Gabby and the marquess would impose on the Murrays' trust, her mother, and Rory's grandmother as well, by only *pretending* to be engaged ... or would they?

Zach pushed the thought aside. Such a suspicion was precipitant and only based on a feeling. He had often enough derided Gabby for placing too much emphasis on that whimsical non-substance called intuition. Besides, what motive would she have to do such a thing? Maybe he was simply jealous—in the unromantic sense, of course—that she'd supplanted him as best friend with this swaggering Scot. If only he felt Rory truly deserved her.

A brisk wind blew up from behind, lifting the tails of Zach's greatcoat and even momentarily penetrating the wool of his trousers, sending a shiver up his spine. He smiled with malicious satisfaction, imagining the effect such a breeze might have on a man wearing a kilt. He sincerely hoped that Rory was feeling the chill right up to his—

"Here, Regina, trade places with me," Gabby was saying suddenly, stopping to switch their positions. "I haven't had the chance to ask Zach about my sister and my dear little nieces and nephew." Regina moved with such alacrity that Zach was almost offended. Did all females find Rory's charm so irresistible?

"You, too, madam," Rory called back, offering his other elbow to Aunt Clarissa. "There's a shivery sort of *nirly*, as we Scots say, blowing down from the northern hills today, and I could use me another fetching female to cuddle up to!"

Aunt Clarissa giggled like a schoolgirl. "Posh, my lord, enough of your flummery!" But she accepted Rory's arm with nary a peep of demur.

As if by mutual consent, but without a word passing

between them, Gabby and Zach began to lag behind. His long strides shortened to match hers, and she perceptibly slowed down. Rory and the others appeared oblivious to the increasing distance growing between them and did not bother even to look back. Indeed, Rory seemed to have enthralled the two women with his conversation. Perhaps, Zach thought wryly, he was reciting one of his poems.

Suddenly Zach realized that he and Gabby hadn't spoken a word to each other in the interval. He was also abruptly aware of the almost too pleasurable sensation of having finally got her—relatively speaking—alone. Her arm was snugly tucked in the crook of his elbow, round and firm. His traitorous eyes flicked fleetingly over the curve of her bosom, also round and firm. He stared down at the crown of her bonnet and traced with his eyes the soft angle of her cheek and the downsweep of dark-brown lashes. She was looking at the ground in an unprecedented fit of shyness—if that's what it was that kept her gaze averted and her quick tongue silent.

She smelled so good. Orchids again, those damnable, exotic, intoxicating blooms.

Gabrielle was in a tremor. How many nights had she imagined being close to Zach, as now, their bodies touching, their movements in perfect harmony? She felt her face flush with heat. They hadn't been walking together in those vivid night fantasies, they'd been making love.

"They're all doing very well."

Gabrielle darted a surprised look at Zach, her blush warmed tenfold by the teasing slant of his mouth and the crinkled smile of his lionlike eyes. "What?"

"Beth and Alex and the children are fine, Gabby. Isn't that why you wanted to walk with me, to inquire after our mutual loved ones?"

"Oh, yes! I'm so glad that all is well in Surrey. And how did you leave my mother?"

Zach's brows puckered, but a ghost of a smile still curved his lips. "You'd probably be able to tell me more about your mother than I could tell you. Didn't you say last night that you'd just received a letter from her yesterday? I haven't heard from Mrs. Tavistock since I left Cornwall a fortnight ago."

"Oh." Gabrielle resumed her contemplation of the walkway. Her thoughts were muddled. The slight brushing of Zach's thigh against her skirt had snatched away her powers of concentration.

Zach chuckled softly. "Is it possible, Gabby, that we've nothing to say to each other? So long as we've been friends, I can't fathom this sudden dearth of subject matter."

Gabrielle lifted her eyes again, studying Zach's beautiful face. Yes, even with his bruised eye—which he'd offered several different tongue-in-cheek explanations for—he was still beautiful. He apparently felt the intensity of her gaze, and it made him uncomfortable to be studied so closely. His teasing expression faded away. He waited for her to speak, his features set in a tense mask of assumed pleasantry.

She took a breath and gathered her scattered thoughts. Hoping his discomposure was a good sign, she decided in a rush to make the point she most wanted him to concede. "Circumstances have changed. I've changed, Zach. I'm not a little girl anymore, you know."

"I know."

Her stomach flip-flopped. "You do?"

Zach's mouth thinned, then with an obvious effort he turned the corners up in a stiff smile. "You're betrothed, aren't you?"

Gabrielle gave a quick nod of her head. "Yes, but I grew up long before I met Rory. I was quite grown up before I ever left Cornwall. You just didn't notice."

"Ah, but that's a moot point, isn't it? Now that the fact seems beyond debate—your maturity, that is—does that mean we have nothing to say to each other?"

"No, of course not!" Gabrielle squeezed Zach's arm. She felt the lean muscles contract against her touch. His gaze dropped to her gloved hand, then lifted to her face. "I hope you will talk to me just as freely as you used to do! I'm only explaining that perhaps this reserve we're feeling between us has something to do with my growing up." She forced a laugh.

"Naturally it changes things a little. You do concede that I've grown up, don't you, Zach? You do see me as a woman now?"

Gabrielle looked hopefully into Zach's eyes. His casual facade slipped away entirely. He looked harassed; indeed, just as Rory had once suggested, he looked like a fox run to pieces by a pack of hounds. "I thought we'd settled that already," he said flatly.

Gabrielle continued to study the play of emotions over Zach's face, so familiar, yet so relentlessly stirring to her senses. She still rested her hand on his arm, and his muscles were still bunched and tense under her fingers. Watching him, feeling his reaction to her touch, she was struck with sudden insight. "Ah, now I understand!" she said, exultant. "You don't like it that I've grown up! And all along I'd thought you'd simply not noticed! Oh, I'm so glad you noticed! That means—"

"This is an odd subject to pursue, Gabby," Zach broke in, wedging a finger under the tight fit of his collar. "Only a pea-brain wouldn't have noticed. And why wouldn't I like you grown up? Why wouldn't I like you just as much as a woman as I liked you as a child?"

"Why, indeed," murmured Gabrielle, a thoughtful pucker forming between her brows. Zach kept his eyes fixed on some vista straight ahead. His mouth was drawn and slightly pinched, as though he had lately partaken of a sour piece of fruit. Another dawning revelation compelled Gabrielle to gently suggest, "Perhaps you don't wish to admit that you like me even better as a woman."

Zach never felt so trapped, nor so incapable of speech. The little scamp spoke freely, fearlessly, and had revealed the crux of the matter with disquieting astuteness. Not until that very moment had he fully admitted the truth of such a troublesome fact. He liked her as a woman, all right. He liked her too damned much for his own good—and hers. But what was her point in bringing up the matter? She was engaged to be married and ought not to care a smidgen about her old friend's opinion of her. Her fiancé's opinion should be sufficient, and judging by the way Rory had mauled her last night, there could be no doubt that he considered Gabby quite womanly.

That niggling, intuitive feeling returned. What if Gabby and the marquess weren't really engaged and this was some sort of a ruse to ... to do what? To make someone jealous? To make *him* jealous? It seemed an absurd idea, but Beth and Alex had hinted so broadly that Zach might have romantic feelings for Gabby, it was not beyond the range of possibility that Gabby might imagine herself to have romantic feelings for Zach! Gawd, could Gabby possibly think herself in love with *him!* The idea, coming upon him so unexpectedly, wrung from his soul a most unwelcome thrill of joy.

Zach suppressed the joy, scolded it, condemned it, and sent it ruthlessly back to the foolish heart that had given it birth. If Gabby thought she loved him, surely it was just a childish infatuation gone awry. For her own good, he would nip such misplaced and misunderstood ardor in the bud.

"Gabby, I—"

"Mr. Wickham, Gabrielle! Come along now, we've arrived at our first stop, the McLeods'!"

Aunt Clarissa, standing beneath a fan-shaped window at the steps of a house architecturally very similar to the Murrays' residence in Charlotte Square, beckoned to them. Apparently the others had already gone inside.

"Goodness, I had not thought she could see so far," said Gabby in a conversational tone, but Zach felt her arm shaking slightly against his side.

"I had not thought her capable of playing the part of chaperon so well, either," Zach said, paused, then pointedly and brutally added, "Though it hardly seems necessary for her to worry whilst you're in my company. I'm like an older brother to you, and, after all, you're engaged to the marquess."

Zach heard her faint, sharp intake of breath, then persevered in his quickly formed decision to clear the romantical cobwebs from her impressionable mind. He walked her firmly toward the house, patting her hand in a paternal manner. "Your aunt had ought to understand from whom she should be guarding you, eh, Gabby? Certainly not from an old family friend like myself!

No, certainly not from me!"

Gabby gave a brittle laugh. "Oh, no, not from you!" Then, in an almost belligerent voice and with a decidedly challenging look, she said, "Rory is very affectionate, however, and I have sometimes thought it unwise of her to leave us so often alone. You will forgive me for speaking so freely, Zach, but if I can't confide in you, who can I confide in?"

Zach suspected that Gabby was trying to discompose him, and, drat the little chit, she was succeeding! Whether or not she were actually engaged to Rory, maybe she was uncomfortable with Rory's amorous behavior. "What do you mean, Gabby? Does the marquess take liberties with you that you do not welcome? Do you want me to talk to him? I assure you, one hint from me, something to the point... like I shall twine his ears about his neck if he so much as touches—" Zach caught himself and looked up to see Gabby smiling in a secret, knowing, womanly way.

"Goodness, you two! Do hurry!" called Clarissa from the porch. "We've four more families to visit before we go home. We haven't the leisure to dawdle!"

Zach was only too happy to obey Clarissa. He had wished for the opportunity for private conversation with his sweet, comfortable Gabby; now there was nothing he wanted more than to be as far removed from her as possible. She had changed all right. She wasn't the least bit comforting. She was lethally provocative. And she was up to something.

The McLeods' small drawing room swarmed with people. Rory took Gabrielle's arm the minute she entered the stuffy chamber and escorted her around, leaving Zach in Regina's capable hands. Gabrielle and her two cohorts had earlier discussed the strategy for the afternoon, and it had been decided that Rory would display his devotion to Gabrielle at the McLeods' by reciting a poem. It would not be difficult to arrange for a reading, since Mrs. McLeod was one of the many females who had fallen under Rory's spell. All it would take would be a small hint to the lady, and that had been prearranged as Regina's duty.

Gabrielle looked about for Regina and Zach, but saw only Regina. She was already engaged in conversation with their hostess, and Mrs. McLeod was nodding her head, her round, florid face alight in animated agreement with whatever it was Regina was saying to her. Gabrielle believed it must be about Rory's poetry reading. Satisfied that all was going well in that quarter, she scanned the room for Zach.

The room was hot and smelled of firewood and wassail. After the subtle simplicity of winter's grays and whites outside, it was rather dizzying to look about a room so rich with color. The noise was deafening. It was hard to concentrate, to focus on finding Zach, though his golden hair stood out in most crowds. Come to think of it, however, back home she had rarely ever seen him in crowds. She pictured him much more naturally on the wide-open moors that surrounded their estates in Cornwall.

Ah, there he was, by a far window, practically plastered against the wall. He appeared to be trying to look interested in the conversation being shouted at him by Mr. McLeod, who made up for his near deafness by speaking in booming tones. Zach was decidedly whitish about the mouth, Gabrielle noticed, and his forehead glistened with perspiration. Occasionally he turned and took a long draw of air from the slightly opened window.

Gabrielle frowned, wondering if Zach were feeling ill. He'd been perfectly fine outside… in the sense of being physically well, that is. She knew she'd made him uncomfortable by forcing him to discuss the fact that she'd grown up. But she could not regret the pain she'd inflicted, because she'd learned something very important. She'd learned that Zach acknowledged that she'd passed into the realm of womanhood, but he was having difficulty adjusting to that fact.

Gabrielle's intuition also told her that the difficulty had its genesis in Zach's perfectly natural inclination to react to her as a man reacts to a woman. It must be awkward for him to readjust his feelings toward her. She didn't, however, believe that he shied away from a more intimate relationship between them exclusively, or even predominantly, because of their long friendship and family ties. She suspected that Zach's fear of intimacy went deeper than that. She knew she must find out more about Zach's past. That girl, Tessy, was part of the mystery that needed to be understood in order to get closer to the man she loved, the man she'd always loved. Gabrielle knew a secret lay hidden in the circumstances surrounding Zach's dead mistress.

Suddenly Mrs. McLeod was pushing through the crowd to stand near the fireplace under a sentimentalized plaster bust of Robert Burns holding a quill against his cheek, from which position she customarily made announcements. Her puce-colored silk dress rustled and billowed about her ample person as she majestically made an opening through the throngs of people. It could hardly go unnoticed that she'd made a grand march to her usual speaking-post, but she reinforced the obvious by lifting a crystal goblet from a nearby tray and tapping a spoon against it.

"Please, please, ladies and gentlemen," she called out, her face wreathed in a perfect hostess smile, her large bosom swelling with affable self-importance. "I'm delighted you're finding one another's company so stimulating. I daresay, if Mr. McLeod's hearing were better, he'd have thrown you all out long ago, so noisy as you are!"

Everyone laughed politely and turned to look at Mr. McLeod, who responded with a puzzled look, saying, "What? What d'ya say, m'dear?"

Mrs. McLeod, by long habit, ignored her husband and continued. "But you shan't begrudge me interrupting your conversations when you understand why I've presumed to do so." She set down the goblet and spoon and clasped her fat, beringed fingers together and fit them into the narrow space between her chins and her bust, smiling across the room at Rory. "Lord Lorne is here today, as you all can't have helped but noticed! And, in addition to gracing us with his presence, I'm hoping I can persuade him to read a poem he's just recently written in honor of his betrothal to the charming Miss Gabrielle Tavistock! Everyone join me, please, in encouraging his lordship to read!"

Zach watched, disbelieving, as the entire room broke out in appreciative murmurs and applause. Their readiness to listen to Rory's poetry was an irritation that almost made Zach forget how physically wretched he felt. The room was too small to hold so many warm-blooded, eating, talking, laughing people. It was all he could do to keep from bolting out the door to fling himself into the cool, quiet solitude of a snowbank.

Thank goodness he'd discovered the slightly opened window. Over the years he'd learned quickly to find a crowded room's source of fresh air, however meager and inadequate it proved for alleviating his phobic symptoms. But now, watching the scene before him, he could almost forget his rapid pulse and sweaty palms. Almost, but not quite.

"How did you know I'd written an ode to my betrothed, Mrs. McLeod?" Rory inquired, his expression one of humble surprise.

Mrs. McLeod trilled a laugh. "Do you expect me to expose my sources, foolish boy? Just read, won't you? I'm dying to hear your latest poetic masterpiece, my lord!"

Rory frowned, pulling on his chin with those grabby fingers of his. Gabby stood next to him, smiling like a religious devotee at her god! Zach felt another wave of nausea coming on, but this time it wasn't due to the closeness of the room.

"My latest poem was written expressly for my beautiful bride-to-be, Mrs. McLeod," Rory said with a sort of reverent modesty. He drew Gabby against his side and smiled down at her. Gabby snuggled obligingly. "I had not meant it to become public. I must ask Gabrielle's permission to read it. It might embarrass her!"

Zach was sure Gabby would have to get used to embarrassment if she married such an exhibitionist popinjay!

"Oh, do let him read it, Miss Tavistock!" Mrs. McLeod implored, extending her clasped hands in appeal.

"I should not mind," Gabby quietly assented, her adoring gaze never straying from her betrothed.

Zach gave a muted "humph!" of disgust, then covered it up with a cough.

Rory made a show of gracious acquiescence, then promptly

plucked a folded sheet of paper from his jacket pocket. Zach was appalled. Did the man carry around his private poetry for just such occasions as this? Did it take so little to persuade his lordship to expose his most cherished thoughts to inquisitive masses of strangers?

Rory moved through the crowd and took Mrs. McLeod's place beneath the bust of Robert Bums, a move so contrived Zach was surprised there weren't snickers from the crowd. He was hard-pressed himself not to laugh out loud! Rory cleared his throat, lifted his chin in an artistic pose, and, though the paper was open in his hand, he recited from memory. From the first syllable of the first word, Zach noticed that Rory's voice lowered an octave and increased in dramatic volume. How unpromising!

> "To the small rose of Scotland came a lass one day,
>   unequaled in beauty and grace,
>   I took but a look, I stole but a kiss,
>   and her memory I could not erase."

Rory paused while the crowd murmured appreciatively. Zach, withholding judgment, waited. So far the sonnet did nothing more remarkable than rhyme.

> "Befitting her maidenly mien,
>   she spoke not a come-hither word.
>   But her sighs and her smiles and her blushes,
>   spoke a language my heart quickly heard."

Zach inwardly groaned. Did these people like this mawkish pabulum? He could only suppose that the influence of Rory's charm and social status reconciled the Edinburgh elite to his awkward poetry.

> "Years of empty employments,
>   meaningless days and nights,
>   give way now to sweet expectation,
>   of eternal, connubial delights."

Rory bowed to enthusiastic applause. Zach moved through the crowd toward the door. He needed fresh air and plenty of it. Perhaps he could find it more easily in the dirty, choking atmosphere of Old Town. He remembered his latest charge, the drunken pregnant woman they'd nearly run over the night before. He didn't even know her name. Today, this very afternoon, he'd find out. He'd make his excuses to the Murrays and return to Charlotte Square, and from there he'd take his carriage to the women's shelter to wrap himself in the safe, soothing cloak of philanthropy.

He found the Murrays, politely and vaguely alluded to a pressing errand, and moved toward the entry hall. He glanced back where Gabby had been standing before, and caught her watching him. Their exchange of looks was fraught with unspoken challenge. Her eyes compelled him to stay. He looked away. He couldn't stay, he couldn't face the challenge she represented. He was suffocating. He needed air. He needed to escape from the closeness.

CHAPTER FOUR

As the carriage made its way through the crowded, narrow streets of Old Town toward Carruber's Close, Zach watched the unrestrained New Year's revelers through the window and compared them to the much more dignified carousers he'd left behind at Queen Street. He'd forgotten that the holiday was so well remembered in Edinburgh, particularly amongst the poor, who wanted nothing more than to believe that the new year would bring them the prosperity they needed.

Zach was trying to forget Gabby and the mute challenge she had conveyed with her eyes across the drawing room at the McLeods'. He was almost completely convinced now that Gabby was using Rory to make him jealous, but he wasn't sure yet whether or not Rory was part of the conspiracy. He would watch and listen and come to his own conclusions in due time. Then he would confront Gabby. But this afternoon he would relegate the matter to the back of his mind. As he had done over the years, he would forget his own troubles by immersing himself in the troubles of others.

Last night's snow had melted and then iced over on the steep walkways that were kept from the sun's direct rays by the multi-tiered *lands*, as the locals called their tall tenement buildings. These slick pavements perfectly accommodated the ragged children who used them for slides. Unfortunately, sometimes the icy surfaces turned the children into human projectiles, causing many a hack driver and coachman to nearly run over a slider who had flown into the way of their horses.

Zach had no desire to cripple some poor urchin under the wheels of his carriage, so he'd instructed Malcolm to progress slowly and pilot the team with great care. This admonition was necessary as well to avoid the many drunks—men and women both—who staggered onto the thoroughfare. It seemed that drinking was the main holiday amusement for many Old Town residents. All shops except for taverns, toy emporiums, and confectioners were closed, and, of the three, whiskey and other potent drinks were the cheapest commodity for merrymaking.

Currant loaves, Scotch buns, and circles of shortbread sprinkled with sugar were displayed in confectioners' windows and, judging by the many people going in and out through the doors of those sweet establishments, Zach could see that the bakers, as well as the tavernkeeps, were enjoying a brisk business day.

Up ahead there was a snowballing war going on between children based on opposite sides of the street. Zach did not begrudge the children their fun, but he sincerely hoped the horses would not be startled into a frenzy by an ill-directed throw. Zach's team was well-trained and used to the noise by now; however, he didn't think the horses would appreciate a hard, cold snowball biting into their hides.

They had but another length of building to pass before turning into Carruber's Close, where the women's shelter was located halfway up the tall structure on the third floor. He held his breath till they'd maneuvered past the snow-ballers, making it safely to the other side, due in part to Malcolm's shouting to the children, "Take a care, ye little rug-rats! No hittin' the cattle, or ye'll have me whip t' answer to!" Empty threats, of course, but perhaps an added inducement for the children to watch their aim.

The carriage stopped, and John jumped down from the box to open Zach's door. Zach stepped out and found himself standing no more than a foot from the entrance to the building, so close was the fit between *lands* in this particular section of the city. His head fell back as his gaze traversed the dingy stone facade, all the way up to the windows that belonged to the rented environs of the women's shelter.

He thought he caught a distorted glimpse of Mr. Blake's fleshy, habitually placid face outlined in the diamond-shaped window panes, then knew it for a certainty when the window opened and Mr. Blake stuck out his head. Today, however, the Quaker's face did not reflect his usual inner peace. Had the girl he'd brought last night caused trouble? Zach wondered. He wouldn't doubt it, as she'd "struck" him as being a feisty lass— pun intended!

"Good day, Friend Zachary," Mr. Blake called in his soft voice, using the Quaker form of address. "'Tis good to see thee. The young woman thou brought to us last night has proved to be rather… uncooperative. Come up and we'll warm thee with a spot of spiced cider, then we'd best discuss—"

But Mr. Blake was interrupted by a woman shouting from a floor above him, "Gardyloo, down there! Gardyloo!"

Mr. Blake's head immediately disappeared as a tubful of foul water cascaded through the air toward the street. Zach leapt out of the way of the airborne nastiness, but was unable to completely avoid the resulting splash. His right thigh was thoroughly baptized from crotch to knee.

"Gawd!" he shouted, standing stiff, his arms outstretched as he stared down at his ruined pants. He jerked his head upwards, hoping to discover the careless swill-flinger still in sight and within hearing. He'd a thing or two to say to the likes of—

"Tsk, tsk, friend," came Mr. Blake's plaintive voice from the window again. "That'll be a nasty stain to get out, and worse still, a dreadful odor to remove from thy pants. But, alas, 'tis a constant danger here to be caught in the midst of some housewife's disposing of the garbage. Do come in, and we'll see what we can do. Just another vexation to add to this day," he clucked, ducking back inside and shutting the window behind him.

"Return to Charlotte Square and fetch me another pair of trousers," said Zach to his wide-eyed coachman and groom, who could do nothing more than mutely sympathize with their fastidious master's plight. "And, John, when you enter the house, do try to be discreet!" Then Zach opened the door and began to ascend the steep stone stairs that led to the upper stories.

Each landing greeted him with a different noise: a baby's

puny cry, coughs, shrieks, laughter, and shouting. Each level added its own smell to the general dank mustiness that pervaded the building: fish frying, whiskey, wet dog, vomit. He had tried to avoid breathing through his nose, but running up three flights of stairs made this rather difficult. Finally he was outside the thick, paneled door, especially constructed for safe-keeping the shelter against irate relatives of the women seeking refuge there, and thieves and thugs in general. He knocked.

Zach heard the several chains and bolts being undone from the other side. The door opened, and a giant of a man, Charlie, the thirtyish, shaggy-blond guard hired to take care of anyone sly enough to get past the door and all its locks, greeted Zach with an ear-to-ear gap-toothed grin. He made a little bow and backed away, allowing Zach to enter, then closed the door and secured it again by redoing all the locks.

Charlie did not speak; in fact, he never spoke. But he appeared to be quite intelligent and perfectly understood everything going on around him. He had become an invaluable part of the organization. The root cause of Charlie's muteness, whether physically or emotionally induced, was never clear to Mr. Blake or to Zach. Charlie ignored and avoided any questions having to do with the subject.

It was safe to say, though, that Charlie's upbringing on the mean streets of Auld Reekie had been less than ideal, and had, perhaps, been somehow responsible for his being mute. The marvel was that he had evolved into such a good man, with the empathy and patience, as well as the size and strength, necessary for the sort of work he did at the shelter.

"Good New Year, Charlie," said Zach, smiling and pulling off his gloves. "Does the day bode well for the year ahead?"

Charlie shrugged, still grinning, then pointed to Zach's bruised eye, raising his brows in a question.

"It's feeling much better today, though I know it looks dreadful. I suppose it will turn all the colors of the rainbow before it's completely healed. The girl is a fighter."

Charlie's brows lowered, and he nodded with immediate understanding. Grimacing, he inclined his head toward the door leading from the receiving parlor where they stood to the back apartments. Zach could hear distant recriminations in a shrill female voice. At first he'd not been sure from whence the ruckus originated; the building resonated with varying levels of noise. The words were indistinct, but he would wager they were highly colorful terminology the girl had learned on the streets. Mr. Blake's tender ears and delicate sensibilities would be aflame with saintly umbrage. But even though Mr. Blake was extremely religious, he had a compassionate, tolerant nature, perfect for his guardian position at the shelter.

"Mrs. Stark is er… *helping* her bathe, is she?"

Charlie nodded again, his eyes wide.

"She must have slept all day then, and has the devil of a headache. Naturally she'd be a bit… peevish."

Charlie acknowledged the understatement with another grin, then his eyes narrowed and his nose twitched. He gazed down at Zach's wet pants.

"Aye. I could use a bath, too, or at least my pants could. I didn't jump fast enough to get altogether out of harm's way when a 'gardyloo' was called. Mr. Blake's head obstructed my view of the upper stories."

Charlie pursed his mouth knowingly.

"Where is Blake?" Zach shrugged out of his black redingote and tossed it onto a nearby chair. There was no butler here, no unnecessary servants whose salary would take away from the upkeep of the women in residence. Mr. Blake, Charlie, Mrs. Stark—the housekeeper, cook, and nurse—and a maid to assist Mrs. Stark, ran the shelter on a shoestring budget and performed a lot of hard, dedicated work. A physician was routinely called in to check the progress of the pregnant or the ill, or to follow and assist in the rehabilitation of women undergoing withdrawal from alcohol or opium addiction.

Charlie looked momentarily nonplussed by Zach's inquiry into Mr. Blake's whereabouts, seeming to indicate that he was surprised that the Quaker wasn't already present. He poked his chest with a thick, square thumb, gestured toward the door and left, presumably to fetch the absentee.

"Thank you, Charlie," said Zach to the giant's retreating back, then he sat down in a plain unupholstered chair near the modest peat fire burning in the grate. He dare not dampen the frayed brocade of the wing chair or the sofa with his soiled trousers, because the stench would be difficult to be rid of and they couldn't afford new furniture.

The screaming down the hall at the end of the house where the bathing room was located continued. Aye, she was a feisty lass, and probably as slippery and hard to keep in the tin tub as a fat, wriggly worm in a bucket. But, as vivid memory recalled, she desperately needed a bath. Unfortunate that she should kick up such a dust over it, like a willful child.

Comparing the bathing woman to a child brought Zach's mind back to his earlier thoughts about Gabby's maturity. This memory led, in a somewhat baffling line of logic, to imagining Gabby sea-bathing. She used to bathe in Dozmary Cove on the Cornish coast. He remembered her compact, slim little figure as she slapped in the waves, the sun glinting off her burnished hair, her bathing gown clinging to her like a second skin. He superimposed Gabby's womanly figure into the same scenario and was appalled by the way his stomach gnawed with a distinctly non-avuncular hunger. He put her out of his mind, erasing the fantasy of her wet bathing gown clinging to the full round curves of her breasts. He determinedly looked about the room for diversion.

It was a tasteful room, neat as a pin as always, but rather worn. Before the "Great Flitting," the abandonment of Old Town by the upper crust for the clean, Georgian elegance of New Town, these high-stacked tenements were inhabited by all ranks of society. The garret and the basement were rented to the hoi polloi, and the middle reaches were given at high rents to the Quality.

This particular house once belonged to Lord Elphinstone, and the elaborately painted ceiling, plasterwork, and carved fireplaces bespoke better times. The furnishings, however, were plain and old, standing in the glorious rooms like bourgeoisie— cheeky and defiant in the midst of aristocratic grandeur.

Suddenly another sound was added to the litany of female curses—a male voice. It obviously belonged to Mr. Blake, and Zach knew that something out of the ordinary was afoot if the gentle Quaker was compelled to raise his voice. He stood up, but was hesitant to intrude if he wasn't really needed. After all, Mr. Blake capably oversaw the shelter 365 days a year without Zach's assistance. When he heard Charlie's heavy footsteps coming quickly down the hall, however, Zach opened the door and looked out.

Charlie's face was eloquent with meaning. Something was terribly wrong. Charlie did an abrupt about-face, and Zach followed, moving past the several curious women who'd stuck their heads through the opened doors that lined the hall. He vaguely noted that the shelter was full. He'd counted at least eight heads, and there were probably other women too sick, too pregnant, or too apathetic to investigate the source of excitement.

They'd reached the bathing room, a small, snug enclosure kept well heated by a substantial fireplace in the corner. Zach's eyes first fell on the large tin tub in the middle of the room, empty, but with its foamy water rocking from a recent disturbance.

The pregnant girl, her blond hair slicked back from a delousing shampoo, had backed against the wall. A bathing sheet tucked around her barely preserved her modesty. Her breathing was fast and shallow, her ludicrously large stomach pushing rhythmically against the damp sheet with each exhalation.

She had blue eyes, the striking color of cornflowers. Zach felt a jolt of painful nostalgia. Tessy's eyes had been deep blue, too. The girl's face was as pale as the sheet around her, but there were blotches of high color on both cheekbones. She held a shaving blade against an extended wrist.

Mr. Blake, Mrs. Stark, and the maid stood in a semicircle around the girl, frozen in startled, wary indecision. The girl darted a furtive look at Zach and Charlie as they entered the small chamber, then she lifted her chin and placed the blade closer to the delicate blue veins of her wrist. Her voice was clear and steady. "Come one step more and I'll slash meself. Dinna doubt, I'll do it sure enough, muckin' up yer clean room with blood puddles as wide and deep as Duddingston Loch!"

Zach became as immobile as the others, but forced his body to assume a relaxed pose, as if he dealt with suicidal women on a regular basis. Her calm manner in announcing her intentions was ominous. Calm people succeeded much more often in killing themselves than did the hysterical sort. He slowly, ever so slowly, lifted his hands, palms up, in a reasoning gesture. "What do you want?"

Her face contorted, an anguished crumpling of small features. "I want to die!"

"I don't think you do. I think—"

"Who gives a bloody hell what *you* think?" she spat, her eyes narrowed viciously, her mouth stretched in a sneer. "A prissy swell like you canna know anythin' about my life!"

"You'd be surprised what I know." Zach dropped his hands and clasped them loosely behind his back in a non-threatening gesture.

"Ha! What a crock o' horse dung!" She shifted her weight, wincing. Her cumbersome belly probably played the very devil with her back.

"I know that you drink too much, and right now your head is ringing like the Sabbath bells of St. Giles from the pint of whiskey you drank last night."

She sniffed, undenying but defensive. "I drink t' keep me man company, not fer the pleasure of it."

"Your husband?"

The girl raised her brows imperiously. Her mood changed with manic abruptness. "I'm married right and proper afore God." She poked the blade at her belly. "This ain't no bastard if'n that's what ye're implyin'!"

Zach avoided directly answering most of her assertions and questions. He had plenty of questions of his own. "What's your name?"

"Dinna ye know it already, Mr. Smart-Arse?"

"Please … Your name?"

The girl seemed momentarily surprised and mollified by his

politeness. "Kate, I'm called."

Zach smiled. She glared back. Her grip on the handle of the shaving blade had become a little lax, but he knew it was still far from safe to approach the girl. He hoped the others realized this, too. "Kate, why don't you get dressed, and then we'll talk."

Her lip curled. "What about? You and the likes o' me dinna have nothin' to talk about."

"We can talk about those bruises on your arms and neck—"

Her eyes flashed with anger. "Ain't none o' yer business how I got these marks—" She stopped herself and looked suddenly enlightened, as if an idea had come to her that would discompose her keepers and gain her the upper hand. "What if I told ye that the men what brung me here last night misused me, beat me … raped me?"

"I'd say you were lying through your teeth."

"How would ye know?"

"*I* brought you here last night, and the only person who sustained an injury while transporting you was me." He pointed to his eye.

"I did that?" She seemed pleased.

"My coachman has a rather tender stomach this morning, too, from where you kicked him."

"Good!" She gloated, standing a little straighter, her prideful pose losing something, however, in the face of her nakedness, her vulnerable belly, the bruises. Zach's heart ached for her.

"Your husband beats you, doesn't he?"

Up came the chin again. "I love me Douglas, he's a good lad! Dinna speak ill of 'im!"

"I want you to stay at the shelter, Kate, till you have the baby. If he beats you again, he could harm the baby, too."

Kate's hand splayed in a protective gesture over her stomach, the fingers looking sadly small and inadequate as protection for so large a target. "I would'na let no one hurt me babe!"

"Is that why you left him, Kate? Is that why you were leaving the city last night on foot? Were you afraid for the baby?"

Kate's brows furrowed. "I dinna remember much about last night. I dinna remember you." There was a long pause, while she appeared to be sifting through her disjointed memories. "Douglas and me, we fought…" As her recollections cleared and became more cohesive, her face pinched with sadness. Sudden tears rolled from her unblinking, unfocused eyes. "'Tis a wicked world to bring a babe into."

"We want to help thee, friend," Mr. Blake said, his voice full of sincere compassion.

The girl's gaze sharpened as it shifted to Mr. Blake. She wet her dry lips with a quick swipe of her tongue. "Then fetch me some whiskey."

"No," he said sorrowfully. "Strong drink is thine enemy, friend, and the child's burden, too, when thou taketh it into thy body."

She lifted the blade and held it again to her wrist. She grit her teeth. "Fetch me some whiskey!"

"Thou wilt not take thy life," said Mr. Blake, "because thou cannot in good conscience take thy child's life with thee. The world is a wicked place, but good can be found in it." Earnestly he repeated, "Let us help thee, friend."

The girl stood for what seemed an eternity, her trembling hand grasping the blade, holding it to her wrist, the tears streaming down her face. There was no sobbing, no outward sound of inner pain. But she hurt. Zach could see how much she hurt.

Finally her hand dropped to her side, the blade thudding dully against the bare wood floor. She dropped her head against the wall and closed her eyes. "If I canna drink and I canna die, then let me sleep. I'm sick and I'm tired." She slumped, and her legs buckled; she was about to swoon. Zach stepped quickly forward and caught her under the knees and about the shoulders, lifting her. She rested her head against his chest and gave a sigh of relieved surrender.

Charlie blocked the way as Zach tottered toward the door, poking his massive chest with his thumb, frowning.

"I can carry her, Charlie. Just move," Zach said impatiently. Kate wasn't so much heavy as she was terribly awkward, the weight being so unevenly distributed. Zach knew he could get her to the bedchamber, if only this giant would move. But Charlie shook his head.

"Let him do it, friend," persuaded Mr. Blake with a significant look and nod. "We need Charlie for just these sorts of jobs. He's very strong."

Zach was feeling just stubborn enough to resist. He stood, braced, irresolute. His grip tightened. He wanted to help this girl, and he'd start by carrying her to the chamber she'd share with two or three other women. How else could he ease the pain in his own chest, the pain that throbbed and twisted each time he met a girl like Kate, a girl abused and hurt by the man who supposedly loved her?

"She is unwieldy. Thou might drop her," Mr. Blake added with succinct good sense.

Kate wriggled a little in his arms. "Let Charlie carry me," she said with a sleepy sigh. "No offense meant, sir, but fer a gentry cove, ye smell like bloody hell."

Zach felt the tension inside him ease away. He smiled and let Charlie take the girl. "She'll be all right," he said to Mr. Blake as they watched her being carried out with Mrs. Stark and the maid following behind. "She has spirit."

"If my guess is correct, she also has twins," Mr. Blake said gravely.

"I wondered if she might," said Zach. "She's huge, isn't she, for so small a lass? Have you sent for the doctor?"

Mr. Blake nodded. "He's coming tonight. I thought it best to clean her up a bit first. She's going to have a difficult time of it. I expect she's due within a matter of days. We may have to ease her off the whiskey bit by bit, dashing a little in her tea now and then. An abrupt withdrawal from the alcohol might be too severe a shock to her system and harm the child … or children."

"I'll be in Edinburgh for a while. I can check on her progress every day."

Mr. Blake gave Zach a keen look. "That's kind of thee, friend. Thou art taking a particular interest in the lass."

Zach waved a hand dismissively. "I'll want to know about the others, too. Have you time this afternoon to fill me in?"

Mr. Blake nodded. "I've the ledgers for thee to look at, as well. But if we are to be closeted together in the office, might I ask thee … ?" The Quaker's face grew crimson.

"What, Blake?" Zach prompted, perplexed and a little amused by Mr. Blake's sudden embarrassment.

"Wilt thou—forgive me, friend—but wilt thou allow me to lend thee a pair of my breeches whilst thine own are being laundered?"

Zach laughed, clapping the man on the back. "I've sent for a change, but with the streets so crowded, it may take my servants a while to return. Certainly, Blake, I'll borrow a pair from you. As Kate said, I smell like—"

Mr. Blake raised an admonishing finger. "—A trifle ripe. To say thou smelleth a trifle ripe is description enough, friend. We have to work on purifying the girl's language, don't we? And how better to do that than by our own example?"

From her bedchamber, Gabrielle heard Zach's carriage rattling over the cobbles in the small courtyard adjacent to the mews behind the Murrays' townhouse. That would mean that Zach was probably already ascending the stairs from the front hall, having relieved himself of his hat, coat, and cane in the vestibule. She'd been waiting and watching for him for over an hour, ever since they'd returned from their New Year's round of social calls.

Gabrielle quickly assessed her appearance in the mirror over the dressing table, patting an errant curl into place. She picked up from the table a small silver-foiled box, ornamented with a black satin bow, and moved to the door, going out into the hall.

It was dusk and the servants had not, as yet, lit all the candles in the large house, though they were undoubtedly in the process of doing so. The hall was dim; gray-gold shadows obscured the corners, all the sharp angles of wall, ceiling, and floor merging together like a seamless backdrop brushed onto canvas, as if prepared for the portrait artist's vivid rendering of his subject.

At the top of the stairs, the subject appeared—Zach, looking tired and a little sad. Gabrielle clutched her gaily wrapped box and waited for him to see her. She'd not strayed more than a foot from the threshold of her door. Her stomach fluttered so at the sight of him, it would take more courage and composure than she had at her immediate command to step forward and address him.

His progress down the gallery was slow, the bend of his head implying deep thought. She began to imagine that he might walk right past without even noticing her—and her struck dumb with shyness and unable to make her presence known! Things had changed between them, and Gabrielle wasn't so sure at times that all of the changes were good ones.

Suddenly, from the opposite end of the hall where the servants' stairs were located, a shaft of light from a chambermaid's tallow work candle speared the shadows and reflected against Gabrielle's brightly papered box. Zach's head lifted. His first response in seeing Gabrielle was a smile, which made her heart sing with happiness. But then a wary, guarded expression crept over his features, a reaction not unlike the result of a half-forgotten, infelicitous memory abruptly recalled. Gabrielle knew what that memory was. Their last conversation.

Nonetheless, the smile, slightly subdued at the corners, remained. He moved to stand in front of her, while in the background the hall began to brighten as the chambermaid quietly went about lighting wall sconces along the length of it.

"Hello, Gabby. I'd have thought you'd be napping after your arduous afternoon of calls. And isn't there another party tonight?"

Gabrielle's fingers nervously stroked the black satin ribbon. "Almost every night there's a party somewhere. It gets a trifle boring."

Zach looked surprised. "I'd think the company of your betrothed would enliven things a bit. He seems a general favorite."

"Oh, yes! Rory's very popular!" She bowed her head. "Only..."

Gabrielle could sense the shifting of Zach's shoulders as he bent to look into her face. She could hear the faint static swish of linen against muslin, she could smell the scents of chimney smoke and the crisp wintry smell that clung to his clothes. "Only what?"

"Only sometimes I miss Cornwall." *I miss you,* she added to herself. She lifted her head and was disconcerted to find his face so close to hers. "Don't you miss home, Zach?" she asked him on a caught breath. *Don't you miss me?*

Zach straightened, putting space between them. "Everywhere I go, I miss Cornwall. I can never stay away too long."

"But you leave Cornwall frequently," she felt bound to remind him.

"I never said I didn't like to travel. I just don't like staying away from home too long, that's all."

"I hope you aren't leaving Edinburgh very soon?"

"I haven't decided about that yet." He paused, studying her. "You will have to grow accustomed to being away from Cornwall, you know. After all, you're going to make your home in Perthshire."

Gabrielle shrugged. "Rory says it's beautiful there."

"I'm sure it is."

Another pause. Zach's eyes fixed on the gift she'd nearly forgotten. Perhaps to have something to say, he tapped his finger on the lid of the shiny box and said, "Is this a present for the marquess?"

"No, as a matter of fact, it's for you." She thrust the gift toward him with an awkward little jerk of her arms.

"For me? What's the occasion?" He took the box, balancing it in his long fingers as he examined its shiny contours. "Not a Christmas gift, I hope, since you already sent to Ockley Hall the slippers you'd knitted for me. Did I never thank you for them? They're wonderful. Warm and soft. I don't need another gift."

"Thank you, I'm glad you liked the slippers, but this is not another Christmas gift, it's a *handsel.* A token of good luck for the coming year."

"Ah!" Zach nodded his understanding. "We don't do that in Cornwall, but I keep forgetting how much the Scots like New Year's. Do you want me to open it now?"

Excitement was beginning to well up in Gabrielle. She was feeling more comfortable, more natural with Zach. Perhaps they'd only needed time alone together. Even the chambermaid had finished her task and was gone now. "Yes, do open it," she said, then clasped her hands behind her and rocked on her heels.

Zach pulled on the bow, and the satin easily slipped from its decorative knot. He shoved the ribbon into his coat pocket. He lifted the lid of the box and looked inside, staring for what Gabrielle deemed an inordinate amount of time. Doubt crept into her heart.

"Don't you like it?"

Zach reached inside the box and drew out the large, flat, fan-shaped seashell. Its pinks and pale yellows, streaks of oyster-white and silver-gray, lustered in the candlelight.

"Is it from Dozmary Cove?" His voice seemed odd, rather strangled.

"Of course! Where else? I cleaned it and spent hours polishing it. Beautiful, isn't it?"

"Yes."

Gabrielle heard the sincerity in Zach's tone, and her doubts vanished. Relieved, she laughed. "I thought it might make you think of Cornwall and miss it a little less when you're away from there. It makes me think of all our fun excursions in the cove, swimming and burying each other in the sand. Do you remember?"

Zach looked up abruptly. "Of course I do. In fact, just today I was remembering—" Zach cut himself off. It would not do to explain that he'd fondly remembered her as a child in a dripping-wet bathing gown, then with much different feelings—warm, aroused feelings—he'd vividly imagined her as a woman in a dripping-wet bathing gown. Oddly, Gabby did not press him to complete his thought. But maybe she knew what he was thinking. He darted her a nervous look, but she only seemed happy to have pleased him with the gift.

"Where did you go today, Zach?"

"I toured the town."

"My abigail said your servants returned to fetch you a fresh pair of trousers."

Zach made a mental note to ask John and Malcolm if they understood the word discreet. "I had an accident."

"You've been having a lot of those lately."

Gabby grinned, and Zach couldn't help but grin back. "I'm in your general vicinity, aren't I?"

"You never did adequately or consistently explain how you blackened your eye," she persisted.

"One of the explanations I gave was strictly the truth. I leave it up to you to decide which one, Gabby. You like riddles, don't you?"

Gabby sniffed. "At least tell me what happened to your pants."

"A woman dumped her garbage on me from an upper window."

Gabby's brows furrowed. "Truly?"

Zach nodded.

"I heard they still do that in Old Town, but not around here. Who do you know in Old Town?"

"No one," he lied. "I was admiring the sights."

Gabby's frown deepened, and she looked troubled. "I've never been to Old Town. Lady Grace forbids me to go there."

"You want to go there?"

"Yes. There's a family of children I met on Christmas Eve—very poor and ragged. They were caroling, and they weren't very well received by Princes Street merchants. I'd like to pay them a visit, but whenever I broach the subject to Lady Grace, she reads me a discourse on the perfidy of mankind. She says perfidy runs rampant in Old Town."

Besides her fears for Gabrielle's safety, Lady Grace had distinct opinions about poor people in general. Gabrielle remembered her saying, *You can't trust them. You can never tell the deserving from the undeserving. I've heard of men who became quite well off from begging on street corners, making more money than an honest man at his honest job. And what do they do with the money, I ask you? Buy whiskey. Do as I do, Gabrielle. Give your mite to the church and let them disperse it properly amongst the poor. There is no need to fraternize with them, after all. 'Tis not safe or healthy or conducive to one's delicacy of mind.*

And thus the subject had been swept under the rug. Upon contemplation, however, Gabrielle couldn't help but strongly disagree with her kind host, but she felt her hands were tied. Unless …

Zach was impressed by Gabby's compassion for the children, and, yes, a little surprised. She'd always shown a charitable disposition in Cornwall, but he'd thought that perhaps she'd been too self-absorbed lately to pay much attention to the plight of others. Besides, women of her social standing were insulated by their guardians from much of the harsh realities of life. "Auld Reekie is a rough place, Gabby."

Gabby grudgingly mumbled agreement to this fact, then her face brightened. "But I would be safe if I went with you!"

Zach grunted. He'd seen this one coming, yet he'd still blundered into it with the adeptness of a born fool. "Do you know the name and the address of these children?"

"I know their name. Tuttle."

"Thousands of people live in Old Town, Gabby. The layout of the town is a hopeless maze of narrow streets and wynds. There's little chance you'd locate these Tuttles."

Gabby sighed heavily. "I've been worried about them. Their mother was sick, they said. I wish I'd thought to ask them their directions." She chuckled self-consciously. "I've even dreamed about the little girl. She had hair like …" Gabby's voice trailed off.

"Don't fret," Zach said, moved by her sincere concern. "I've business in Old Town for the next few days, and I'll see what I can find out about this family of carolers."

"But I thought you said you didn't know anyone in Old Town?"

Zach gave a hiss of exasperation. "Do you want my help, Gabby?"

"Well, yes, but I still want to know—"

"If you do want my help, then you'll have to stifle your damnable curiosity for once and quit plaguing me with questions!"

When he saw Gabby flinch, Zach realized that he'd sounded

harsh. He didn't want to hurt her; no, never that. Impulsively he reached out and cupped the back of her head with his splayed fingers. "I'm sorry, sweeting. I didn't mean to snarl."

Gabby turned her head and pressed her cheek into the cradle of Zach's large palm. He would have pulled back, but she reached up and held his hand against her face. Her eyes drifted shut. The softness and warmth of her skin made his pulse accelerate. Heaven help him, she might detect the throbbing pace of his heart through the thin, fluttering skin at his wrist! Then she'd know! She'd know how she affected him! But he couldn't pull away.

She opened her eyes. How could a woman look so innocent, yet so sultry? "You haven't called me 'sweeting' since we last saw each other in Cornwall." Her voice was breathy, reverent.

Zach tried to swallow past his dry throat. "Haven't I?"

Her lips made a small pout. "And you've never even kissed me 'hello' as you used to do." She tilted her face. "Won't you kiss me, Zach?"

CHAPTER FIVE

Zach stared down at the beautiful candle-lit face angled up to him so trustingly. Gabby's dark-amber lashes fanned against delicate skin, her lips parted slightly, and her mouth ever so barely curved in an expectant smile, with now and then a little quiver at the corners. She was hopeful but nervous, brave but braced for disappointment. She was adorable.

Zach's thumb rested just to the side of her mouth, and he could faintly feel the passage of her breath. All was silent, except for the thunder in his ears from the harsh, insistent pounding of his heart.

He was too aware of her—all of her. The soft but solid reality of her. The living, breathing, pleasing shape of her. And she wanted him to kiss her. Not on the head, he'd wager. No, not there, not where he used to plant a brotherly peck. And he wanted to oblige her in the worst way.

Yet he did not want to stop with a kiss on those tentatively upturned lips. He wanted to crush her against him till there was nothing left of her but a powdery, magical essence he could mix up and drink like a potion. He wanted to absorb her, mesh her soul with his, become one. This fierce possessive urge frightened him. He must guard against it. He must keep their physical relationship as platonic as it had ever been.

He leaned down and touched his lips briefly to her forehead. Coming so close to Gabby was a test of his strength, because her softness, her orchid scent, her lacy ribbons, and silky sensuality tempted him to make that pure salute only a prerequisite to a thorough tactile exploration of every feature of her face. Yet he managed to pull away ...

Until her eyes opened and she looked at him. Again she

challenged him with her half-reproachful, half-daring look, just as she'd so effectively done across the McLeods' crowded drawing room. Zach felt as though he'd been issued an invitation to duel at twenty paces; the glove had been thrown down, his honor at stake. So stupid of him to react in a knee-jerk fashion, as if her taunting, teasing look somehow challenged his courage, his manhood! Yet he could not resist the age-old lure. One kiss on the lips, that's all he would permit himself. Perhaps he could prove to Gabby and to himself that just as it had been with her sister, Beth, there was nothing between them but the sort of affection he'd show a sibling. He bent his head and touched his lips to hers.

Gabrielle was totally unprepared for the sensation of Zach's lips against hers. She'd imagined this moment a thousand times, the image filling every thought that wasn't specifically assigned to the rational processes of day-to-day living. At night she fell asleep thinking of him, priming her dreams to complete the fantasy of lovemaking she was too naive and too well brought up to dare to complete in the daylight hours. But she'd never imagined that kissing Zach could feel like this.

Her whole body warmed, every inch of her skin aflame with new awareness. A weakness seeped into her legs, yet an overwhelming strength of feeling permeated her. How odd, this seesaw of weakness and strength, and how utterly delicious. She strained toward Zach. She let go of the hand he still held against her cheek, and twined both arms around his neck. She needed to be next to him, as close as two people could come.

Somewhere in the distance, Zach heard the box drop to the floor, releasing his hands to do what they most wanted to do—hold Gabby as close to him as possible. The kiss had started out so chaste, so well rationalized, but the jolt that surged through him as their lips touched gave every reasonable objection to kissing Gabby as little impact as a pebble flung into the sea.

She gave a small moan, a throaty purr of pleasure that not even the most expert Cyprian could imitate with the same results. Her honest enjoyment of being kissed, of being held by him, was the most powerful aphrodisiac Zach could imagine.

He was immediately aroused to the point that he could have flung her to the ground on the spot and taken her with the gusto of a sailor just returned from months at sea. And he had the most tantalizing, the most frightening suspicion that Gabby—his curious, intrepid, life-loving Gabby—would fully participate.

Each passing second deepened the kiss, Gabrielle eagerly opening to Zach's graceful, forceful exploration of her mouth. Smooth, sharp, moist textures of tongue and teeth. It was so intimate, yet she knew that it was only the beginning of even greater intimacy, an act of love that her body was preparing for. She felt it in the stirring in her stomach, the aching heaviness of her breasts. She wanted him to touch her in all the spots that suddenly tingled with needy anticipation. Rory was wrong. There was a difference between kissing one's friend—even though he was an acclaimed kisser—and kissing the one person you'd loved and waited for your whole life. Zach.

He was losing control. Zach felt his rational thoughts pushed aside, replaced by erotic images of Gabby beneath him, her back arched, her breasts bare and white. He wasn't sure if he ever consciously made the decision to maneuver her into the embrasure of her bedchamber door, but they were there, and he had her pressed against the panels, her light weight entirely supported by his own body. Every curve Gabby owned—and these were considerable—were molded against him. He couldn't get enough of her mouth. She intoxicated him. He was drunk with wanting her. He reached down and around to her breast, cupping and squeezing the firm shape of her, and she gasped.

Then they heard voices. Someone was coming up the servants' stairs. Gabrielle didn't care who saw them, but apparently Zach did. He took her by the shoulders and put her firmly at arm's length, backing away. Gabrielle caught a brief look at Zach's face before he turned and stooped to pick up the box. His expression was confused, distraught, almost panicked. She looked down at his bent head and beyond to the floor where the box lay on its side, the lid off. The seashell was scattered on the polished wood floor, broken in three clean pieces.

"God, Gabby, I've broken it."

It took a moment for Gabrielle to register everything. The butler, Mr. Phipps, was quietly chastising a meek chambermaid who'd neglected to dust her ladyship's jewelry casket. They glanced toward Zach and Gabrielle, gave quick, slight bows of respect, then turned down the hall the other way. Gabrielle wondered that they didn't stand gaping at her, for surely she'd changed outwardly to reflect her inner transformation. She was dazed; she felt like she was fighting through clouds to regain an earthly footing. Zach's next words brought her back to reality with a thud.

"I break everything." Gabrielle looked down again at the back of Zach's head. He was holding the three broken pieces of the seashell in a cup he'd made with his hands. He looked up at her. His eyes were glassy with anguish. "Don't you understand, Gabby? I break everything."

"It can be fixed. The edges are neat. I can glue it for you." She kneeled, balancing herself with a hand on Zach's raised knee. He flinched. She looked into his face and was frightened by the depth of remorse she thought she saw there. "Don't be so upset. It's nothing. Just an accident." She tried to cajole him with a smile. "You're being much too hard on yourself."

Zach laid the pieces carefully back in the box. He stood up. Gabrielle stood up, too, peering into his face, trying to catch his eye. But he successfully avoided her gaze. "You'd better go to your room now, Gabby."

Gabrielle gave a nervous laugh. "That's it? That's all you have to say to me after what happened just now?"

Zach sighed, rubbing his eyes with a thumb and forefinger. In an expressionless voice, and as if he were reciting from rote, he said, "It would be best if we both forgot what happened, but if you mean I should apologize, you're absolutely right. I'm sorry I took advantage of the situation. I should have kissed you on the head, as I've always done before. Forgive me, Gabby. I completely lost control of myself. I shouldn't have touched you so... but never mind! If you feel duty-bound to tell Rory what a cad I've been, I'll understand." Zach finally met her eyes briefly, mugging a self-derisive smile. "I just hope he lets me choose the weapon. I'm not good with bow and arrow."

Disbelieving, infuriated, Gabrielle stamped her foot. "Oh, Zachary Wickham, how can you be so *stupid?* How can you make jokes?"

Zach fixed her with a straight-on, piercing look. "Doesn't Rory have a right to be angry if you kiss another man? He *is* your betrothed, isn't he?"

Gabrielle could see that Zach wasn't going to be a bit cooperative. Even when it was obvious that the sparks between them could light the darkest dungeon, chasing out all the past ghosts and demons that kept him from committing to a new course of happiness, he remained stubbornly opposed. The charade was not over. The contest was not won. He loved her— she knew it, she felt it to her bones! But he wouldn't admit it. Not yet, anyway. But she wasn't about to give up.

"Of course Rory would be furious," Gabrielle said, accommodating Zach in his penchant for misery, deliberately, obligingly pouring salt in the wound. "You've seen how possessive he is, how demonstrative."

Zach gritted his teeth. Drat the baggage, she still wouldn't admit the whole thing was a farce! "Yes, I've noticed his devotion to you. The sonnet he recited today was most... touching, wasn't it?"

Gabby nodded assent, saying nothing, looking like royalty miffed at a peon. Rory's poetry wasn't the issue, she said with her eyes. Don't you recognize quality when you see it, taste it? her look said. Don't you recognize love?

The walls were closing in. Zach had never noticed before how narrow the hall was, how low the ceilings, how the heat rising from the kitchen parched his throat with dryness. He had to leave before panic made him the fool. "I need a bath before dinner, Gabby, so if you'll excuse me..." He turned and left her.

"Are you frightened of me, Zach?"

The plaintive voice, devoid of anger now, carried across the hall and hit him in the gut like the broad end of a sword, leaving him breathless. With his hand on the cut-glass knob of his bedchamber door, he looked over his shoulder, saying sadly, "No, Gabby, I'm frightened *for* you." Then he went inside.

• • • •

For a week Gabrielle saw Zach only when in the company of others. No matter how much she contrived a chance encounter, he consistently foiled her designs. Even at parties, when private conversation together might be obscured by the noise of a hundred other conversations, Zach always managed to pull someone else into the huddle, the subject matter relegated to idle chitchat. His manners toward her were punctiliously polite, remote and odiously proper. He never touched her. He barely looked at her, even when directing a comment to her. He was pretending as though nothing had happened between them, and by his odd behavior proving just the opposite.

Gabrielle had glued together the broken shell and sent it to Zach's room, but even that he acknowledged with only a brief, banal expression of polite gratitude. This was too much. She had to get him to open up to her. After what happened in the hall, she was encouraged to be more forward in convincing him they were meant to be together. She couldn't forget how wonderful it felt to be held and kissed and caressed by Zach. The memory haunted her.

At the end of this torturous week, as Gabrielle was beginning to feel rather desperate, the Murrays decided to spend a quiet evening at home. Due to the holiday season, their social schedule for the past several weeks had been more hectic than usual, and Lady Grace felt the need for a respite. Tonight she had a headache and retired to her bedchamber directly after dinner. The rest of the party settled in the drawing room for tea and conversation. Gabrielle was hoping that the intimacy of their gathering would at last present her with an opportunity to speak to Zach alone.

He was not cooperating, however. Probably having decided that it would be rude if he quit their company at too early an hour, he nevertheless avoided a tête-à-tête with Gabrielle by sitting in a chair by Sir George and Aunt Clarissa, politely dividing his attention between the two elders and leaving Gabrielle, Rory, and Regina to their own devices.

"Correct me if I'm wrong," whispered Rory into Gabrielle's ear as he stretched an arm behind her on the sofa the three of them shared, "but I don't think Zach is rising to the bait, as it were. Do you think I ought to try wooing you a little more … er… aggressively?"

Regina, sitting on Gabrielle's other side, leaned close, scolding, "Short of tossing her onto the carpet and making mad love to her, I don't know how you could be much more aggressive."

Rory winked at her. "Jealous, Reggie? You and I used to wrestle on the carpet when we were younger, but ever since you came back from that fancy girls' academy I didn't think you'd oblige me if I challenged you to a tussle."

Regina blushed, trying hard to frown and failing miserably. "For shame, Rory!"

Gabrielle sighed. "I don't think Zach would respond even if I writhed through a houri's dance with a sapphire in my navel. He's too stubborn."

"Why doesn't he join us?" said Regina. "It's got to be slow going talking to Papa and your aunt! He's obviously avoiding you, Gabrielle. What did you do to make him so skittish?"

"I got too close to him, that's what. And, first chance I get, I'm going to get even closer."

"That's the spirit, lass!" Rory said approvingly. "And here's your chance! He's gone to fetch your aunt her nightly dose of sherry. How obliging of him. Quick, Gabrielle! Go!"

Gabrielle was indeed beginning to feel like a predator who'd caught the scent of her dinner and was running it down. But she had no time to lose. She rose from the sofa, smoothing down the front of her daisy-sprigged skirt and trying to look nonchalant as she followed Zach to a distant corner of the room where Sir George kept his liquor cabinet. Zach was dressed in a deep blue jacket tonight, and his back looked very broad and his legs, in fawn-colored trousers, very slim and muscled.

Zach heard her coming. Every muscle in his body bunched and every nerve hummed with expectation. He steeled himself against the sensory assault he knew he would feel the minute she was within grabbing distance. He wished he completely understood her situation with Rory, but he still felt the need to bide his time for a spell, just watching and forming opinions. But he was only human, after all, and how was he expected to keep resisting what she promised with her sweet, eager kisses? Ever since their encounter at the threshold of her bedchamber door, he was too aware of the tenuousness of his self-control.

Her scent was in the air; she'd arrived. He kept his back resolutely turned toward her.

"Zach?"

"Hmm?" He opened the cabinet and searched for the decanter of sherry.

"Don't grunt at me! Turn around and speak to me like a gentleman."

Zach couldn't seem to find the dratted sherry decanter. He gritted his teeth and turned his head, glancing at Gabby over his shoulder. "Did you want some sherry, too, Gabby?" Her eyes were wide and appealing. Her lips were pursed in a slight pout. Damned kissable-looking, they were. Of course, he didn't have to guess about that. He knew how kissable her lips were. He hadn't slept well for a week thinking about the warm, firm texture of her mouth and the incredible taste of it.

"You know I don't want sherry. I want to talk to you."

Zach returned to his task, viewing the various crystal containers with unseeing eyes. He saw Gabby's reflection in the polished glass of the cabinet door. She was dressed in yellow and white, the fresh, delicate colors making her look like a bloomy dairy maid. "We talk all the time, Gabby."

"I don't mean about the amount of snow we've got this year, Zach, or what's up with good King William. Weather and politics are things polite acquaintances talk about, and we're much more than that!" She had been speaking in a whisper, but now she lowered her voice still further and caught his arm, leaning into him. "What about the other day? You enjoyed that kiss as much as I did. And ever since you've been treating me as though I have the plague! I'd like an explanation."

He could feel the curve of her breast against his arm. Warmth emanated from her. He swallowed hard. He stared determinedly into the liquor cabinet, willing himself to concentrate. At last he spied the sherry decanter and, relieved, reached for it, gently pulling his arm free of Gabby's grasp. "Your aunt is waiting for her sherry. She says she shan't sleep a wink unless she has her usual dose." He removed the lid of the decanter and reached for a small wineglass. His hands were shaking as he poured a generous helping. Perhaps he was responding to his own inclination for a calming drink.

"I don't think my aunt will have a bit of trouble falling asleep tonight. In fact—"

"Nevertheless, she's waiting for me."

"She's asleep right now, Zach!"

Zach turned and was dismayed to see that this was true. Aunt Clarissa was in her customary position for napping, head back, mouth open. Sir George had happily immersed himself in the *Times,* and Rory and Regina had their heads together as they conversed. No one would mind their absence even if they left the room. Damn.

"Why don't we go into the parlor across the hall, Zach, and you can settle this awkwardness between us once and for all."

"And how am I to do that, Gabby?"

"By explaining to me how it is you can kiss me so passionately and then pretend nothing happened. I want to know your true feelings, Zach."

Zach was prepared to lie. If it would keep Gabby safe from his own desires, he would blame his conduct in the hall last week on something as base and basic as ... lust. Love, he would say, had nothing to do with it. "All right," he said. "We'll clear the air, Gabby." Then he tossed back the sherry meant for Aunt Clarissa and led Gabby out of the room, lighting a candelabra in the hall under the interested eye of Ralph the footman, and then on into the adjoining parlor. There was no fire, and the room was cold.

"Shall we ring for wood?" Gabby suggested.

"No," said Zach. He set the candelabra on a low table, then sat down in a large wing chair by the fireplace and faced her. "We won't be here that long."

"We won't?" She had hovered near the door for the first moment or two, and now she approached slowly, her hands clasped behind her. He found this pose rather disturbing, as it caused the fabric of her gown to stretch taut across her breasts.

"No. I've decided that you are quite right in demanding an explanation for the other day and clearing up the misunderstanding once and for all."

She stopped just inches away, looking at him with a confused expression. "Misunderstanding?"

Zach flourished a hand through the air, a gesture of summary dismissal. "Lust, Gabby, that's all it was. Because of the few kisses we shared, you imagined that I felt romantically toward you. But the sad truth that I have striven to keep from you is this: When a comely young woman allows a man to kiss her in an intimate manner, he responds automatically. It's man's nature to do so. I would have responded the same way if, say, Regina had made herself as willing as you did that day."

All during his breezy speech, he'd watched Gabby's reaction. She didn't look a bit miffed by his implication that she'd been forward and therefore had mechanized his frail male, knee-jerk reaction of flattening her against the wall and kissing her with demented abandon. No, not a bit. And judging by the determined expression on her face, he greatly feared she meant to call his bluff somehow.

She arched a brow. "Why don't we call Regina in here and test out that theory?"

He choked out a cursory laugh. "Don't be absurd."

"I won't, if you won't."

"I'm not being—"

She sat down on the arm of the chair, her hand resting on his shoulder. Her slim thigh hovered just above his lap. He had an almost uncontrollable urge to pull her down on top of him and read her bedtime stories. Then take her to bed. Her breasts were at eye level. "Admit it, Zach. You do have romantic feelings for me."

He clenched his jaw. "Admit it, Gabby. You and Rory aren't engaged."

She reached across and ran her hand along his lapel, caressing the smooth blue superfine with light strokes that Zach registered in every nerve in his body. "I asked first," she taunted, lifting her chin and looking down at him through half-closed eyes.

He caught her hand and held it still against his chest. "This isn't a game, Gabby."

Gabby's face changed suddenly. She looked dead earnest. "No, I know it isn't," she agreed. "Kiss me, Zach. Just like last week. Kiss me."

Zach was beginning to wish that lust *was* all he felt for Gabby. If it were just lust, he could slide her off the chair arm, set her on her feet, and send her out of the room in a state of humiliation. Teach her a lesson, as it were. Then he'd leave the house and find a willing Cyprian to cool the fire that Gabby had started with an orgy of unrestrained sex. But it wasn't that simple.

He loved Gabby. He didn't want to hurt her. And, as well, he wouldn't get her out of his system simply by copulating with a courtesan. His connection to Gabby was as spiritual as it was physical. Right now the fine line between these two components was so faint as to be indistinguishable. Hell, he wanted her and he wanted her now.

He groaned and pulled her onto his lap, burying his face in the warm scented dip of her cleavage. She responded immediately by plunging her fingers into his hair and holding him closer. Her firm round bottom felt rather too good in his lap. His hands pressed into the dip of her small waist and followed the outward curve of ribs and bosom. He pushed up and flicked his tongue into the deepening crease between her breasts. Gabby moaned and tugged his hair in rhythm with each swipe of his tongue.

My God... What am I doing? With a mammoth surge of willpower, Zach lifted his head and stared into Gabby's flushed, ecstatic face. She bent to kiss him, and he turned away. He avoided looking at her as he lifted her gently and set her on her feet, just as he should have done five minutes before, before he completely lost all sense of right or wrong. He stood up and walked toward the door.

"No, Zach. Not again!" cried Gabby, hurrying along right behind him. "You're running away! You're running away from me and from the truth!"

Zach turned at the door, his hand on the knob. "You're one to talk, Gabby. Maybe when you're ready to tell the truth, we'll talk again." He left her and, ignoring Ralph's covertly curious expression, took the stairs two at a time to his bedchamber to spend another sleepless night grappling with his conscience and his desire.

Every afternoon, while everyone else rested from their morning calls and prepared for the evening's entertainments, Zach left the premises in his carriage. He said he had business in Old Town, and Gabrielle was dying of curiosity as to exactly what that business was. She was afraid it might be a woman. She was afraid it might be someone who put no demands on Zach's heart, someone who didn't scare the living daylights out of him the way she did.

It was the day after Zach had run out on her again, and, despite Lady Grace's strictures, Gabrielle decided to follow Zach to Old Town. She was going to find out what drew him there day after day, as religiously devoted to the outing as a novice to prayer. She slipped out of the house right after the others went to their various chambers to repose; she left a note on her bed, just in case she didn't return before time to dress for dinner. She hailed a hack disgorging passengers on the corner and paid the driver to let her simply sit inside the cab until Zach's carriage drove by. Then they followed at a discreet distance.

They were in the midst of Old Town now, and Gabrielle was practically gawking out the window at the fascinating, dreary, historical wonder of the place. She felt dizzy just trying to glimpse the gables of the rooftops, so high were the tenements. The people moved in diverse droves of humanity; some sharp-eyed, some dingily clothed, some in flashy attire and slightly improper, some prim, neat, and businesslike. Some appeared jovial, others grim, angry, pathetic, sick, maimed, or even—she suspected after viewing one body in the gutter—dead. More likely, though, it was a drunk she'd seen. At least she hoped that was the case.

There was a continuity in the masses of people simply because of their diversity. It was a thrilling, bustling, frightening place, the scape of the buildings a hodgepodge of cubbyholes, alleys, and dark serpentine roads running steeply down into parts unknown. No wonder Lady Grace forbade her to go there. But Gabrielle was quite sure she could take care of herself. She'd been in enough scrapes in her lifetime, and she'd managed to survive them all. A niggling voice reminded her that Zach had usually been the one to pluck her out of her messes in the past. But then he *was* nearby, wasn't he?

The carriage stopped, the portal in the roof opened, and the hack driver's whiskered face appeared. "The carriage is stopped in Carruber's Close, miss, and the gentleman 'as stepped out and gone in the buildin'. I'll be wantin' my two pence, miss."

Gabrielle hurriedly gave the driver his due and stepped out of the carriage. She must find a hiding place out of view of Zach's servants, then try to ascertain exactly what sort of place he was visiting. The hack drove off, and Gabrielle was grateful to discover that the tiny alley the driver had called Carruber's Close was not so well trod by the throngs of pedestrians. Only an occasional person emerged from its shadows now and then.

Conveniently, and much to her surprise, Malcolm backed the carriage out of the close and drove off. Now she needn't worry that she'd be caught spying on Zach, but the leaving of the carriage indicated that Zach routinely spent considerable time in this one spot, not allocating his afternoon to several different locations.

Gabrielle stood peering up at the building, at all the many windows, wondering which apartment Zach was in. It looked like a common dwelling tenement, not a place of any sort of business. At least not a legitimate business. Suddenly she realized that she was being stared at by a small, dirty boy of about five years old. He was carrying a bucket of peat, apparently on an errand. She smiled and said, "Hello. Do you live around here?"

He shook his head. "Not in this part o' town. I jest work 'ere. I can tell ye dinna live round 'ere either, miss." He smiled, displaying several badly stained teeth, then went on his way, whistling.

Gabrielle looked down at her emerald green, erminelined pelisse, her favorite winter garb. She *tsked* to herself. Indeed, she'd not dressed very appropriately for this venture. She looked much too grand. She glanced nervously about. If a small child could make such a remark, she obviously stuck out like a sore thumb. She could easily be made a target by the criminally inclined. She clutched her reticule against her side, shrugging the braided carrying strap higher up on her shoulder. She hastily looked about for some place to sit or stand that would minimize her conspicuousness.

She saw a boarded-up door to an abandoned building behind her. The overhang and the steps leading into the basement-like entryway would shield her a little from passersby, yet still allow her a good view of the building Zach had gone into. She supposed that she'd just have to wait for him to come out now, since she'd not discovered anything by the outward appearance of the place.

She stepped down into the cubicle of rough stone that passed for the porch and threshold of the doorway. A half inch of water and a layer of dead leaves coated the bottom. A sour smell pervaded the small area, and Gabrielle was sure she wasn't going to enjoy the time she'd be spending there. She gingerly settled her bottom on the cold slab of the top step and watched the door of the opposite building. What was he doing? she wondered. Who was he with?

CHAPTER SIX

"How are you today, Kate?" Zach stood just inside the parlor, delighted to find Kate sitting in the chair by the fire, busily knitting. She wore a neat round dress of blue cambric, and her shiny blond hair was pulled into a tidy bun atop her head, but with a few pretty curls bouncing over onto her forehead and down her neck. Her bruises had nearly healed and, clean and sober, Kate was a fetching lass, with delicate features and a rosebud mouth. Her arms and legs were slim and shapely, indicating that she'd had a small waist before the onset of her pregnancy. In looks she bore an uncanny resemblance to Tessy.

It was a little unnerving for Zach each time he saw Kate, as each day the ravages of her hard living subsided a bit more, allowing her fine-boned beauty to show through. Kate's personality was very different than Tessy's had been, however. Kate was a spitfire, her temper easily ignited, her rights fought for with zeal, although in the past couple of days she'd been behaving with admirable restraint. She must have finally figured out that they were only trying to help her.

Kate smiled, her face alight with cheerful welcome. "Wickham! Ye're late, ye scoundrel! Dinna ye remember that ye promised me a ride in the carriage today? I'm cravin' me some fresh air."

Zach laughed easily, glad to forget for a time the thoughts and doubts that plagued him continually at Charlotte Square. *Gabby.* He felt a pang of longing, of regret. He squelched it. He looked at Kate, drawing a measure of cheerfulness from her own high spirits. He removed his hat and gloves and laid them on the table by the door. Charlie, who'd stood by and looked on with mild interest up till then, yawned and left them alone.

"Yes, I remember," Zach said. "I'm still a little leery of taking you out in public, though. Blake said it's rumored your husband's been asking about town for you. It's only a matter of time before he comes here. He wouldn't get in, of course, unless we want him in. But we want to avoid a disruptive scene."

Kate grimaced. "Naw, he will'na come here. He dinna know 'bout the place. *I dinna* know 'bout it afore you brung me here."

"But others know about it, and eventually someone will tell him you might have sought refuge here."

Kate made a glum face and looked hard at her knitting. "I will'na go with him if he comes. Not yet, anyway."

"You've changed your tune since that first day."

"I'm thinkin' much clearer now. I've my babe—" She beamed with unabashed pride. "My *babes* to worry about."

"And are you missing your whiskey very much?"

"Certain, I do. But, though I know Blake tries t' hide the fact from me, he's told Mrs. Stark t' slip some in my tea, a wee bit less of it every day, so's I won't go into fits."

"You were near to fits those first days."

"It was hellish, sure as sh…" Kate stopped herself from saying a most unfeminine word. "Pardon." She grinned self-consciously. "'Tis hard to break old habits, but I'm bound t' try fer Blake's sake. He cringes so when I use me colorful language."

Zach sat down on the sofa and crossed his legs. He liked his conversations with Kate. They were always refreshingly honest. He liked to watch her improving day by day, and he was dreading the time when she'd return to her husband, Douglas McKeen. As Kate said, old habits were hard to break, and her husband had probably been beating her for a long time. Kate's stay at the shelter might simply be a temporary respite from her misery. Zach didn't want that to happen, and the only way to stop it from happening was to work with Kate on a solution that included her husband's cooperation. So far, though she was honest to a fault on all subjects, her husband was one subject she refused to discuss.

"How badly do you want that carriage ride, Kate?" Zach tried to appear casual, flicking a bit of lint from the nap of his trousers, pulled taut across his bent knee.

Kate eyed him suspiciously, setting down her yellow ball of yarn and needles on the handy platform her stomach made. "I'm suspectin' that ye're tryin' t' wheedle some promises out o' me, Wickham. There's—how do ye say it?—stumpulations attached to this treat ye're givin' me, is there?"

"No, there are no stipulations, Kate, though I'm tempted to resort to bribery and blackmail to get you to talk about your husband."

Kate took up her knitting again, so busy. Too busy to talk, apparently. Her mouth compressed into a pucker, a declaration of noncooperation.

"If you plan to make a home with this man again, Kate, if you mean to allow him to help raise your children, you must talk about him. There's no guarantee that he'll have been softened by your leaving, or that he'll treat you any better when you go back to him. He may be angry and treat you even worse. He may harm the children."

"Dinna ye talk so, Wickham!" She tossed her ball of yarn at him, unraveling several knots she'd made in the little blanket. She crossed her arms, resting them on her stomach. She scowled at him.

Zach sighed, picked up the ball, and automatically began to rewind it. "Whatever made him drink and be abusive toward you before won't magically remedy itself while you're gone. Don't be fool enough to think he'll be so enchanted by the babies, either, that he'll turn into an angel overnight."

"Douglas has had a hard time of it, Wickham. His troubles ain't nothin' like you've ever knowed in yer pretty little life."

"Don't be snide. I may be a flash cove, as you say, but I do have a modicum of intelligence and compassion. I think I might strive to understand Douglas's problems."

Kate's face crumpled. "I'm sorry, Wickham. But I feel disloyal-like, talkin' 'bout Douglas."

"I'm not making judgments. God knows I'd be the last man justified to throw stones! I just want to help you work things out for when you leave here. Or do you want to separate from

Douglas? We can help you find a position somewhere. We've trained women for many different situations, though I'd think you'd rather be home with your babies if at all possible."

"I dinna want t' leave Douglas forever. I told ye, I love 'im!"

"Then talk." Zach handed her the rewound ball of yarn.

Kate heaved a long sigh, taking the yarn and staring at it listlessly. "He lost 'is job as a smithy 'bout three months ago."

"Why?"

"He was drinkin' on the job. He bungled some things and made some blokes mad at 'im fer harming their cattle. He's done odd jobs since, but they dinna pay much."

"So the source of Douglas's employment problem is not a lack of skills, but his inability to control his drinking?"

"Douglas drinks all day and all night, if'n he can get 'is hands on the stuff. He's sold every decent thing we owned t' buy liquor, even me mum's weddin' ring she left me." Kate made a grim face. "I was fumin' fer some time after he pilfered me mum's ring right out o' me special keepsake box. But when he can't drink, he beats me. Without it, he gets mean." She shrugged. "With it, he gets mean, too. There's never a good time no more." Kate turned pleading eyes to Zach. "Before he got the habit, Wickham, there *were* good times. Douglas was a good man. As good as they come." She blushed. "As good as you."

Zach winced. "I'm not sure that's such a compliment, but I'm willing to believe your Douglas has redeeming qualities. He'll have to break the habit before he's safe to live with again, Kate."

"How's he t' do it, Wickham?" Kate spread her arms, her eyes widening to match her gesture. "Who's t' help him? Is there such a place as this for men?"

Zach pressed his lips together, thinking, wishing he could come up with something he'd never considered before in all his long ponderings of the problem. "Not that I know of." He saw what she was thinking, and though he knew she'd be disappointed, he explained, "It would be impossible to bring him here. We're not equipped at the shelter to deal properly with Douglas's problems. We have to consider the women, too. They are our first priority. But, don't worry, we'll work something out, Kate."

He assumed a bracing tone. "In the meantime, I won't allow you to get overly upset. We'll forget the matter for now and go on that carriage ride. If I'm not mistaken, that's Malcolm I hear tooling the horses into the close. I sent him to the confectioner's for some fresh sticky buns." He stood up and extended Kate a hand, helping her to her feet. This was not an easy task. She pushed from the back, he pulled from the front, and finally she stood.

She frowned at him. "Sticky buns, Wickham?"

He raised a brow. "I thought you liked them. Craved I think was the actual word you used to describe your affinity for those sweets."

"Sure and I do crave 'em. Even now my mouth's waterin' at the thought of 'em! But I'll be big as a house 'fore the babes come!"

Zach laughed. "Get a wrap. It's nippy out. We'll drive down by Duddingston Loch and watch the skaters."

Kate clapped her hands, looking like a schoolgirl—at least from the neck up. Zach watched her go, a hard knot of pain twisting in his chest. If only he could turn back time and bring the same sort of happiness and hope to another pregnant girl— to Tessy. But the child Kate carried wasn't his, thank God. At least he didn't have that burden of guilt, and had never had again since Tessy's pregnancy.

His unruly mind, prone lately to unrelated images popping up suddenly, conjured a picture of Gabby, her belly as round as a grapefruit, but much larger. Gabby, appealingly gravid, wonderfully big with child. His child. Zach shook his head, dispelling the image, suppressing the desire.

Gray clouds had gathered in the last half hour and snow began to fall again, but just a smattering, the flakes more ice than snow. Gabrielle's fingertips were starting to ache from the cold. She pushed back into the shadows when she saw the carriage return. She was at an angle that allowed her a clear view of the front of the building.

A few minutes passed, then the door opened, and Zach appeared. He was in the way as his companion walked out, and all Gabrielle could see of her was a voluminous brown greatcoat and a blue skirt swishing around small ankles as she stepped into Zach's carriage. They were laughing and talking about something, something that Gabrielle couldn't hear well enough to make sense of. But how could she concentrate on what they were saying when her heart pounded in her ears and her eyes stung with tears? Her worst suspicions had been confirmed. Zach had a mistress.

She waited till the carriage was gone, then she stiffly stood up, climbing out of the scummy little hole she'd sat in to spy on Zach. And all for what? To discover that he was meeting a woman every day, taking her out in his carriage, laughing and talking with her like *they* used to do?

Gabrielle moved to stand in the middle of the narrow lane, staring in the direction that the carriage had gone, though there was nothing left to see. She felt a stinging dampness on her cheeks and looked up at the sky. The intermittent clouds drifted quickly over the rooftops, dropping snowflakes into gusts of wind that dashed against her face. Were her cheeks damp with snow or tears? She couldn't tell the difference anymore.

She started to walk. She would find another hack to drive her safely down the hill to New Town, but she couldn't seem to organize her thoughts well enough yet to provide the needed motivation for such rational action. She was disbelieving and hurt. Maybe Zach traveled from town to town for the purpose of visiting different mistresses. Maybe he *did* lead a life of debauchery when he was away from Pencarrow, as many of the gossips back home had suggested. But for whatever reasons Zach was visiting this woman—though to Gabrielle it seemed pretty clear what those reasons were—there was obviously a side of Zach that she didn't know. Zach had secrets, secrets that excluded her.

• • •

Douglas McKeen watched from the shadows of a low-hanging roof, his lean, wiry body pressed against the outside wall of the building, his dirty brown coat and trousers blending into the background. He'd been standing there since before that dandified, yellow-haired, good-looking, slick-talking swell had shown up in his fancy rig, then gone inside the building to the shelter.

The shelter. Douglas made a face, screwed his mouth sideways, and spat a mouthful of tobacco onto the cobbled street. Who the hell did this bloke Wickham think he was, paying lease on a place to keep women away from their rightful duties, from their spouses, for Christ's sake? Damned criminal, it was. Who knew what the man's real purpose was in being so philanthropic? And where the hell had he taken his Kate?

Douglas had searched for his wife for five days, then finally got a lead from a taverner nearby. For a coin—one he could scarce afford to part with—he'd been told everything the man knew about the women's shelter and its founder and chief patron, Zachary Wickham, an "odd'un" who took it upon himself to save downtrodden women from self-destructive, vile habits and sometimes from destructive, vile men.

He'd been told that it was useless to try to storm the place, demanding Kate's release. Wickham kept a Goliath type as a watchdog, and a goody buckle-shoed Quaker as overall manager and guardian. Since yesterday, all Douglas had done was watch the place and its comings and goings, impotent to do anything more active than prod his whiskey-befuddled brain to come up with a plan.

Douglas smiled to himself. Today he had a plan. He'd been seething with anger as he'd watched fancy-pants Wickham drive off with his Kate, and her all beaming with happiness, her face freshly scrubbed, her walk the straight, unwobbling gait of a sober woman. His heart had given a lurch at the sight of her. He was relieved to see her so well, then furious to find her existing so happily without him!

Then he'd seen the girl in the green, fur-trimmed coat. Quality, every inch of her. Pretty, too, even with her nose pink and her eyes runny from the cold and … tears. She stared after the carriage, long since disappeared round the corner, in the melancholy manner of the deeply besotted.

Ah, yes. Barter. That's the ticket. He'd offer this little royalty type in exchange for his Kate. Yes, she looked like a princess in her plush toggery. Obviously she knew Wickham and had feelings for him. And Wickham, bleeding heart that he was, would be obliged to cooperate even if he didn't care a button for the lass. Quality always claimed precedence over poor little street rats like his Kate.

Douglas reached inside his coat pocket and pulled out a flask. The moment demanded a celebratory toast. He lifted the flask briefly in the air, then took a long swig, never taking his eyes off the stylish figure of the princess who left Carruber's Close, never knowing she was being followed.

Just steps from Carruber's Close, Gabrielle found herself in the midst of a crowd, being jostled, elbowed, and pushed into the general flow of traffic. People stared directly at her, most hostile and envious, others pitying, as if she were a pigeon destined for somebody's pie. Discomposed, she clutched her reticule close to her and peered through and around the crowd to try to find an unoccupied hack. So far she'd seen none at all.

The cords in her neck felt tight; her muscles were knotting from rising panic. She tried to stop and get her bearings, to remember the way the hack driver had taken her to the shelter, and then endeavor to retrace her way down the hill to New Town, on foot if necessary. But standing still in the crowd was difficult and drew more attention than seemed prudent. She decided that it was best to keep moving, even if she didn't have a clue where she was headed, and to try to look as though she felt perfectly at home in her surroundings instead of rapidly becoming more and more frightened and disoriented.

Then it happened. Someone snatched her reticule, at the same time nearly pulling her shoulder out of its socket. Thrown off balance, she lurched to the side, skidding in a puddle of sludge. She would have fallen, but someone caught her arm and righted her with a tug, setting her solidly on her feet again.

"The lad's gettin' off with yer purse, miss."

Gabrielle looked up into a pair of bloodshot blue eyes, set in the rather grimy face of a thin, dark-haired man of medium height in a brown coat. His breath reeked of liquor and tobacco. He was standing much too close.

"If you were a gentleman, sir," Gabrielle informed him, reduced to uncharacteristic testiness by utter frustration, "you'd have run after him and retrieved my purse!"

"And let ye fall, miss?"

Gabrielle rubbed her shoulder. The man still held her arm, but the gesture wasn't reassuring. Though he had lent a helping hand, she mistrusted him. Perhaps she was being ungrateful, but she couldn't seem to stop herself from remarking petulantly, "I assure you I couldn't feel much worse than I do already, so you might as well have let me fall!" Tears blurred her vision. She turned and blinked at the throngs of people still milling past her. "You said it was a boy who stole it? Oh, there he goes!"

Gabrielle saw her black beaded reticule rounding a corner clutched under the skinny arm of an ill-clothed boy. A part of her felt instinctive pity for the child. She knew he probably needed the money much worse than she did, but another part of her rankled at the indignity of having it taken from her so roughly and without her consent! Everything in her life seemed so out of control, so out of step with the way she'd planned it! First Zach, now this...

Gabrielle gathered her skirts in her fists, of half a mind to push her way through the crowd and risk life and limb pursuing the child. Even if she didn't catch him, she'd have tried her best to, and that alone would make her feel much better. And if she did catch him, she'd just give him a severe lecture, then a portion of her purse.

"'Tis no use, miss. Ye'd never catch 'im," said the man, his strong fingers biting into her flesh where he still held on to her arm. "Why dinna ye jest come with me, and I'll find ye a hack t' fetch ye home—"

Gabrielle pulled herself free of the man's grip. Being told that she couldn't do something always made her all the more determined to do it! She gritted her teeth and hurtled herself through the crowd, now and then throwing out a "pardon me" with such ferocity, a few surprised people voluntarily stepped aside. She headed straight for the corner around which the lad had disappeared. Inconsequentially she noticed that "Jem loves Ethel" had been scribbled in coal in large letters on the wall. She took the turn sharply, only to see the boy turning another corner, and then another, till she had followed him deep inside a lonely section of wynds far from the main thoroughfare.

Gabrielle stopped and caught her breath for a moment, craning her neck to try to glimpse a small piece of sky above the gothic, towering tenements. The closeness of the buildings was stifling. And the smell was worse. Human waste, stagnant water, and rancid cooking odors made the bile rise in her throat. She covered her mouth with her hand and tried to ward off the horrid smells with the wool of her mittens.

Gabrielle was sure now that the boy had outrun her, but she needed to stand perfectly still for a moment until the nausea passed, then retrace her steps to the main road. But as she stood there, with only the persistent pattering of snow melting off the gables and plunging into puddles in the street, she heard another sound. It was the sound of someone breathing hard. Was it the boy catching his breath? If so, he was just around the corner! But if she could hear him, surely he must be able to hear her, too? But perhaps he didn't know he'd been followed all this time....

Gabrielle moved quickly to the edge of the building, then, hoping to surprise the boy, she swiftly rounded the corner, unfortunately landing on a patch of black ice. She slid, her feet flying out from under her. She fell on her bottom with an "oomph!," her hands and elbows scraping painfully against the ice as she braced herself.

Gabrielle's bonnet fell forward, for a moment obscuring her view. She let out a hiss of frustration, straightened to a sitting position, and pushed back her bonnet with her forearm.

She fully expected the child to have run away by then, as she obviously had not made a stealthy approach! But there he was, hunched over on a doorstep not ten feet away, rummaging through the contents of her reticule, his blond head bent to the absorbing task.

"You!" she shouted. "What's the idea of taking something I'd gladly have given you if only you'd—"

Belatedly the lad looked up, his face reflecting the shocked fear of an apprehended criminal. He clambered to his feet.

Gabrielle couldn't believe her eyes. "Will? Will Tuttle, is that you?" She'd wanted to see the boy again. She'd wanted to see his whole family, his little sister particularly. But she'd not expected their reunion to be like this!

He recognized her immediately. His face reflected myriad emotions, the most prominent being shame. Gabrielle stared back at him, her anger rapidly dissipating. His face was thin and pale. There were dark smudges of fatigue under his eyes. He looked sick and hungry.

Gabrielle moved to stand up. Everything hurt, and it took some rather graceless maneuvering to heave herself from the ice to an upright position. Finally she managed to stand, her fingers gripping a brick for support that stuck out from the adjacent wall. When she lifted her eyes, her reticule lay on the ground, but Will was gone.

"Will? Will, come back! I'm not angry!" she called, pivoting to scan the dark corners of the alley. But except for the persistent dripping from the roofs, all was once again silent.

A heaviness fell over Gabrielle, a depression as dark as that which she'd felt when she'd witnessed Zach driving away with his ladybird. The poor boy, she lamented silently, her heart twisting with pity, her thoughts filled with self-reproach. Logically she'd had every reason to be upset and angry at Will for taking her purse, but after catching a good look at him, she knew he must have been driven to commit the theft out of desperation. But he was gone, and she'd probably never find him again. The brief encounter had been a quirk of coincidence, and she had lost the opportunity now to ask him about his mother and Bella and the other boys, and to try to help them through their difficulties.

Gabrielle picked up her reticule, a sharp pain stabbing the small of her back as she bent over. She straightened carefully, rubbing the tender spot. Her coin purse was still in the reticule, still full to bursting with the generous amount of pin money her mother sent regularly for incidental spending. It could have fed the Turtles for a month at least. Tears welled in her eyes again, but this time she wasn't crying for herself. If only she'd not yelled at him. If only she'd—

"Lookin' fer the lad, are ye, miss?"

Gabrielle whirled around and found herself facing a woman her own height, but considerably heavier and older. Even in the late afternoon shadows Gabrielle could see that the woman's face was thickly coated with cosmetics. Rouge and powder filled the deep creases on each side of her bright red lips and was also unattractively settled in the numerous lines that fanned out from her eyes. Her hair was piled high atop her head, though not very neatly, and the untidy tresses were the most unlikely shade of carrot red that Gabrielle could imagine.

CHAPTER SEVEN

"Did ye hear me, miss, or are ye deaf like the lad?"

This stirred Gabrielle out of her reverie. She wiped the tears from her eyes with two quick swipes. "Like the lad? Will is … deaf?" This would explain how she'd snuck up on him so easily, why he'd seemed not to have been aware of being followed.

"He was'na born that way, but he's been sickly all winter, and he seems t' hear less and less each day." The woman grinned, an inappropriate accompaniment to the sad news. Her teeth were dingy yellow against the garish red of her painted lips.

"You know Will, then?" Gabrielle couldn't help snatching a glimpse of the woman's clothes, though she'd been taught better manners than to gape at someone, particularly if she was not as well dressed as herself. But this woman gave Gabrielle an unsettled feeling that had nothing to do with the embarrassment of wealth face to face with poverty. The woman's clothes were in much better condition than Gabrielle had expected. The material from which her gown was made appeared costly, and the shawl hanging over her arms was of a finely worked lace. But the impression altogether was slatternly and immodest. The gown was tight, the bodice revealing a generous amount of bosom. The woman smelled as though she hadn't bathed for a fortnight.

"Done with summin' me up, have ye, miss?" Gabrielle's eyes clashed guiltily with the woman's. She bit her lip and shifted her eyes to settle on a door behind the woman which stood slightly ajar, a beam of light from the room beyond spilling into the dim alley. She thought she saw movement through the crack, as if someone were there—perhaps even watching them. Gooseflesh erupted on her arms and down her back.

"I beg your pardon, madam," Gabrielle mumbled, then hastily added, "You obviously are acquainted with the Tuttles, and I would consider it a great favor if you would give me their directions." Fumbling through the process, Gabrielle reached into her reticule, dug a shilling out of her purse, and offered it to the woman. "I will gladly recompense you for your trouble."

Gabrielle's fingers shook. She tried to compose herself, since it would not do to appear frightened and vulnerable. The woman might decide to throttle her and take the reticule from her, claiming the entire contents for herself. In such a case, she'd much rather have had Will succeed with the original theft!

The woman eyed the coin for some time, then darted out a hand to grab it, the sudden movement making Gabrielle flinch. She looked up at the woman, who was smiling again, as though frightening her had given some sort of perverse pleasure. "How is it ye're all alone in this part o' town, miss?"

Too quickly Gabrielle blurted, "Oh, I'm not alone! Not at all! My carriage is just—" She motioned vaguely in the direction she'd come from, knowing full well that even if a carriage were waiting for her, it would be too far away to serve as any sort of deterrent to crime. "Just 'round the corner."

The woman raised her kohl-darkened brows. "I see."

Gabrielle felt her cheeks suffuse with color. She was quite sure the woman did see—right through her miserable attempt at impromptu lying. And she was sure the woman had noticed she'd been crying. Gabrielle could still feel the tracks of tears on her cheeks, icy and stinging in the dropping temperature.

"Come this way, miss," the woman said, turning and gesturing toward the door behind her.

Gabrielle didn't move. "Will lives here? I thought this was your house?"

The woman nodded. "Aye, miss, 'tis my house, but this is the back entrance. The front opens onto a square where the lad lives. 'Tis the fastest, safest way to get there. Otherwise ye'll have t' backtrack."

"I'm Gabrielle Tavistock. What's your name, madam?" Gabrielle was stalling, or maybe some desperate part of her

JOURNEY OF THE HEART

thought that if they were on terms of polite acquaintance, the woman wouldn't seem as menacing to her.

"What does it matter, miss?" said the woman, sneering. "It's not likely we'll be meetin' fer tea sometime in the future, now is it? But I'll tell ye anyway. 'Tis Mrs. Henn."

Still Gabrielle hesitated. The woman turned again, her look impatient, indignant. "Do ye want me t' help ye or not, miss? I've no' got all day and night t' dally wi' ye."

The alley grew darker and darker. Gabrielle knew it must be nigh onto five o'clock by now. Soon it would be pitch black, and she'd never find her way out of the confusing maze of back streets. A vision of her lifeless body in the gutter, like the body she'd seen earlier that day, flitted through her mind. After visiting with the Tuttles, Will could surely guide her to the main thoroughfare and help her catch the attention of a hack driver. She had no choice but to trust this strange woman. The alternative, the idea of facing unknown dangers alone in the dark, was even more frightening.

Gabrielle took a step forward. Mrs. Henn cackled her approval—not a reassuring sound—then turned and walked into the house. Gabrielle followed. She had just stepped inside the room, registering for a brief moment the candle-lit interior decorated in faux splendor—secondhand facsimiles of Georgian drawing room accoutrements, red velvet swags clashing with purple brocade chairs—when a hand holding a foul-smelling cloth clamped over her mouth and nose.

Gabrielle struggled, but strong arms held her fast against a hard, flat chest obviously not belonging to the busty Mrs. Henn. The room spun. Gabrielle was falling ... falling ... *Zach, where are you?* she wondered silently, desperately. *You're always there for me when I need you. I need you now!* Over the edge of the cloth pressed so painfully against her face, Mrs. Henn's clownish face reappeared, grinning. It was the last thing Gabrielle saw before darkness engulfed her.

• • •

Douglas McKeen watched with mixed emotions. Hidden in the shadows, he'd seen and heard everything. The princess, this Gabrielle Tavistock, was as green as grass, and as ripe as a nicely rounded peach ready for picking. And now "Mother" Henn had her. Soon a man would be sent to High Street for the purpose of spreading the news to well-paying customers that Mother Henn had a Quality virgin for sale and would be taking bids for the privilege of bedding her.

Mother Henn could see a hapless female a mile off, most of her victims being new lasses in town, fresh from the country. But this naive little idiot had walked straight into the beastie's lair. Mother Henn was probably gleefully blessing Lady Luck and deciding on a high sum as barter for the lass's "company." She would bring a pretty penny, that one, so bonny as she was.

Well practiced at packing up and moving on to another spot to avoid the police, Mother Henn harbored no worries about despoiling a lass of obvious Quality like this one, with parents undoubtedly on the lookout for her. She'd make use of the girl, then release her into the street, reeling from the aftereffects of drugs and rape. Once returned home, the girl's family would then take great pains to ensure that nobody ever found out about their daughter's scandalous misfortune.

Douglas shook his head. His conscience was picking at him. But his designs for the girl hadn't been well-intended, either. He thought he'd nearly caught the princess when he'd saved her from falling. He'd planned to take her back to his place and arrange an exchange for Kate, but she was a feisty one with a will of her own. He'd let her get away, and now his plan was no longer feasible. After Mother Henn was through with her, the lass would not be seen in Old Town again. She'd not be so feisty, either, he'd wager.

Douglas felt another twinge of conscience. Reflexively, he took a swig of whiskey, the warmth seeming to go straight to his head, dulling honorable urges, rationalizing revenge. After all, the lass was connected to that Wickham fellow, the man who was keeping him away from his Kate. If the lass didn't precisely deserve her fate, Wickham, at least, deserved the suffering he would endure because of what would happen to her. Douglas shrugged his sloped shoulders and staggered out of the alley toward home.

As Zach's carriage rattled over the cobbles through Old Town, dusk fell. Zach kept the carriage lantern burning low, the light from it just bright enough to illuminate the pleasing picture of Kate, fast asleep and nestled in the opposite corner under two blankets. He didn't want to disturb her rest till absolutely necessary, for though their excursion had been quite enjoyable, it had also been most fatiguing for a young girl breeding with twins.

Kate had wanted to stay till dark so that they could watch the torches lighting up and the skaters making designs on the ice with their bright, shining beacons held overhead. That was a nightly sight during the winter in Edinburgh, but Kate had been well and truly trapped in Auld Reekie for so long, and so continuously under the influence of strong drink, she'd not been able to enjoy much of anything.

Zach smiled, remembering how much she'd relished the sticky buns. She'd eaten three, the little glutton, explaining coyly that one was for her and that the two others were for each of the twins. There was a tiny, glittery spot of sugar glaze in the middle of her left cheek, and a thin strand of hair stuck to it. He leaned forward, lifting the strand, each hair separating individually from her cheek. She opened her eyes.

"That tickles, Wickham," she said with a sleepy smile. "Why dinna ye tell me that my face was dirty?"

"A gentleman never tells a lady such a thing," he teased, settling back into his side of the carriage.

Kate straightened up. "I'm a lady, am I? Not exactly, Wickham, and dinna ye argue wi' me!" She waggled an admonishing finger. "I've had enough of that fer one day."

"As you say, madam," Zach acquiesced with a smile.

Kate wet the three middle fingers of one hand with her tongue and wiped away the sticky spot. She gave him a sly look.

"I'm always suspicious when ye're so agreeable—Oh!"

Zach leaned forward, watching anxiously as Kate pushed back against the carriage squabs, a grimace on her face. "What is it, Kate? Are you having a pain?"

"No, not a pain exactly, but near enough." She chuckled, pressing both hands to her stomach. "Sometimes these babes get to kicking both at the same time, and in opposite directions. I feel as though I'm being stretched out like a too-small pair o' boots, so's the little angels can have more room fer themselves!"

Zach laughed, relieved. "Boys, I'll bet. They'll lead you a merry chase once they've got legs under them. Ah, we're here."

As the carriage jerked to a stop, Zach was surprised to discover Blake waiting at the curb, lantern in hand. "What is it, Blake? Is something wrong?" he asked as John opened the door.

"Yes, friend, something is terribly wrong. It's happened before, but this time with thy help perhaps the worst can be avoided."

Zach frowned. "What do you mean?"

Blake flickered a glance behind him, and Charlie moved into the light of the lantern. "Charlie, take Mrs. McKeen upstairs." Blake handed him the lantern. "'Tis far too cold for her to wait outside while friend Zachary and I talk."

"Dinna ye fret, Blake," said Kate with a little grunt as she maneuvered her stomach through the carriage door, "I ken that ye're wantin't' talk t' Wickham private-like." She turned to Zach and assumed an outrageously accurate pose of a simpering debutante. "Thank you, Wickham. I've had a lovely day." Then she extended her fingers to be kissed. Diverted by her liveliness, Zach complied, returning her saucy gaze over the top of her hand.

"Good night, Kate," he called to her as Charlie escorted her through the door. "Take the steps slow, Charlie, and let her lean on you." Charlie and Kate glanced over their shoulders, both throwing him looks of amused exasperation that implied that they were perfectly capable of exerting common sense without Zach's fussy interference.

When they were out of sight, he turned back to Blake.

"Now, Blake, come inside the carriage and get cozy, then tell me what's the to-do." Mr. Blake hesitated. He seemed restive, worried. Perhaps he thought the comfort of the carriage would offend his Quaker's preference for plainness and even minimize the urgency of his news. But there were shadowed figures creeping up and down the street, and Zach knew that their business would be best discussed and dispatched from the relative safety of his carriage. "There are a few people about, Blake," he said in a low voice. "Inside they won't hear what we're saying."

Mr. Blake nodded and gave a tired sigh, his breath showing in the frosty air like a miniature cloud, then he stepped into the carriage. Once they were both settled inside, Blake spoke. "A boy, who resides nearby, came to the shelter not an hour ago. At present there is a house of ill-repute operating in the boy's immediate neighborhood. There are, of course, many such despicable establishments in Old Town, but this particular one is run by the most unscrupulous woman of any of the hardened Cyprians who ply such a trade in all of Scotland, I'd wager."

"Why is she worse than the rest?"

"She is not satisfied to lure gullible girls into the profession with fantastic lies, but she actually kidnaps and drugs those who are unwilling. Some of these unfortunate girls continue on with the sordid life, but this woman—Mother Henn, she's called— kidnaps young women of Quality with parents, as well as the unprotected and orphaned. She is compelled to return the Quality sorts to the streets. They are eventually found by their families, but they are scarred emotionally and sometimes physically."

"Good God, how does she manage to get her hands on such protected chits? And what have the police to say about such goings-on?"

"'Tis a rare opportunity when Mother Henn can snaffle a Quality girl to put up for auction to her customers, since, as thou sayeth, they are hard to get hold of. She has been too wily to be caught by the police, and thus far they've been unable to produce enough evidence to arrest her for kidnapping. That's why it's important, friend Zachary, that thou will agree to interfere in this case."

"The boy you spoke of witnessed a kidnapping?"

"Yes, he did."

"Is he a reliable source of information?"

"He's a good boy, though lately his family has fallen on hard times—at least, harder than usual. I suspect he's been … But never mind that now! He did not need to come tell me what he saw, but he seemed most upset. He said the girl was young, pretty, and well dressed. Almost certainly—pardon my bluntness, friend—a … er… virgin. Mother Henn will conduct an auction. Thou must go there and bid for the girl. If thou biddest enough money, they will allow thee … er… access to her, and thou may contrive to somehow get her out of the house before harm is done her. I don't dare try to alert the police. They are watched for with such assiduity by Mother Henn's hirelings, the police would not be successful, I'm afraid, and the girl would end up somewhere quite out of our reach."

"Gawd! The girl must be a complete simpleton to be in such a situation! What was she doing in Old Town alone, I wonder? Where are her parents, her friends? But never mind! That, I suppose, is a moot point now. The lass needs rescuing." Zach shook his head, a small rueful smile suddenly curving his lips.

Mr. Blake raised his brows. "Something amuses thee?"

"No, it's only that this poor girl's situation reminds me of just the sort of scrape a friend of mine—a female I've known since she was in leading strings—would fall into. I would be half mad with worry if I didn't know exactiy where Gabby was right now! Thank God, she's safe home at Charlotte Square resting for her next party!"

"Indeed, friend," Mr. Blake said, nodding gravely, "thank God!"

Gabrielle was awakened by a distinct feeling of discomfort. She blinked her eyes open and found herself staring up at a crimson-colored bed canopy. Where was she? Her own bed at Charlotte Square was overhung by a pale yellow canopy and floral drapes.

There was a dull thud in her right temple. Her mouth hurt, too, and her wrist and ankles. ...

Memory swarmed back like a lethal cloud of killer bees. That woman—that Mrs. Henn—had drugged her! Gabrielle tried to scream, but her mouth was gagged with a strip of linen. She tried to sit up, but her wrists were tied together with rope, and so were her ankles! She was shackled like some criminal, or a slave! Her heart beating wildly, Gabrielle strained forward, her eyes darting about the room—lit by a single candle at her bedside—for her kidnapper. Out of the shadows a shape emerged—a man's shape! Two hands clamped her shoulders and pinned her back against the pillow. A face came into view, one side eclipsed in shadows, the other side garishly lit by the flickering candle.

"And where d' ye think yer goin', lassy?"

The hard, cold voice fit the face perfectly. The man looked to be middle-aged, was unshaven, and had greasy dark hair that fell forward into his eyes. His breath was vile. Gabrielle fought the urge to vomit.

He snickered. "Dinna ye fancy the gag? Well, it'll be comin' off soon enough. 'Tis time fer yer medicine, lassy." He moved back a bit and his gaze shifted from her face to the front of her gown. Gabrielle looked down, too, and was horrified to discover that she no longer was wearing the modest dress she'd left home in, but had on a white diaphanous nightgown that dipped low across her bosom, barely covering her nipples. Filled with indignation, she squirmed, wishing with all her heart that she could slap the man's face till his ears rang.

"Oh, I've made ye mad, have I?" he sneered, catching and correctly deciphering the furious expression in her eyes. "But I would'na be so high and mighty, miss. What makes ye think I dinna do a lot more than look at ye when ye was sleepin' so sound?"

Gabrielle felt a spasm of fear, of shame. Had this man touched her? He was grinning down at her, his gaze trailing lasciviously from her face to her breasts and back again. The filthy bent of his thoughts was obvious. He leaned closer.

Gabrielle squeezed her eyes shut and squirmed harder. At least if he was compelled to hold her down with both hands, he wouldn't have those hands free to do as they pleased. She could smell his breath, feel its heat against her neck.

"Jasper, get off the lass now or I'll kill ye!"

The mattress sprang up under her as Jasper lifted his weight from the bed. Gabrielle opened her eyes and saw a slit of light from the hall disappearing as the door to the chamber closed and Mrs. Henn walked quickly to the bedside. She stared down at Gabrielle for a moment, scanning the length of her, then switched her piercing gaze to Jasper. He stood at the end of the bed, nervously rubbing his jaw and shifting from foot to foot.

"Fool!" spat Mrs. Henn. "Canna I leave ye alone with the chits fer even a minute? Where's Bob?"

"G-gone t' fetch supper, Mother. She just woke up, and she was squirmin' like, and I jest thought I'd best—"

"Hold her down, Jasper? And with yer bare arse in the air 'tween her legs, I s'pose?"

Jasper gave a violent shake to his head. "No, Mother! No, I'd never—"

"Ye've sullied the merchandise afore, Jasper. And ye'd have done it again if'n I had'na come back when I did. You and Bob—idiot that he is, leavin' ye alone with 'er—will get one shillin' less this week in yer wages."

"Mother, I never touched 'er! I dinna say that I was'na tempted to, 'cause she's as fair a chit as ye've caught in many a month, but I would' na have—"

"Spare me yer speeches! I jest count meself lucky I come in when I did." She looked down at Gabrielle, her eyes alight with greedy speculation. "She's a fair one, all right, and I've got the price fer her up to a hundred pounds already, and coves still comin' in off the street with bulgin' purses, jest slatherin' at the mouth fer a taste o' Mother Henn's latest piece of purity."

"Are ye goin' t' dose her now, Mother?"

"Aye. Then we'll untie her and arrange her fittin'-like on the bed, with her fair white hands under her cheek, lookin' as sweet and unspoiled as an angel." Mrs. Henn leaned down, pushing her face close to Gabrielle's. "Dinna worry, lass," she said with a leer, "by the time ye wake up, the worst'll be over. Then whatever else the gent does t' ye will'na matter. My advice t' ye is t' lay back and enjoy it."

Gabrielle narrowed her eyes, trying to convey to this despicable Mother Henn person that she'd no intention of letting any man have his way with her without one devil of a fight! Mother Henn had apparently seen the look before. She smiled knowingly. "Yes, lass, I ken what yer sayin'. 'Tis good ye've got spunk. The gents like a chit with spirit, but I would'na push 'im too far, or else he'll backhand ye 'cross the room. He'll have paid for ye, lass, and if'n ye prove too tetchy, we'll jest dose ye again. Yer not the first, nor will ye be the last. I've not failed t' deliver to me customers yet, and dinna think ye're goin' t' be an exception to the rule."

Gabrielle wanted to be brave. She wanted to glare back at Mother Henn with undiminished scorn and determination. But it was hard to feel brave and strong when her feet and hands were trussed like a chicken for the plucking, and a gag bit into her tongue and the corners of her mouth so that she couldn't shout back a single word of rebuttal or protest. Gabrielle felt her eyes welling with tears. *Zach, where are you?*

Through a salty sheen she saw Mother Henn measuring out a generous dose of what appeared to be laudanum. She wondered if it would be possible to pretend to swallow the drug and somehow store it in the corner of her mouth and allow it to dribble out later when they posed her "fittin'-like" on the bed. She'd still not have much defense against her rapist, but she would at least be able to fight him without the disadvantage of being drugged. And if she lost her struggle, she'd make sure he hurt in sensitive places for days to come!

"Come here, Jasper, and lift 'er up so's she dinna choke."

Once again Gabrielle was compelled to tolerate the touch of that vile man and feel his hot breath on her skin, as he propped her upright with one hand spread in the middle of her back and the other curving round her neck. She had a feeling that if she struggled, those fingers wouldn't hesitate to encourage her cooperation by nearly strangling her. Mother Henn fit the large soup spoon fiill of liquid into Gabrielle's mouth, just under the gag, and tipped it.

The taste and feel of laudanum spilled over Gabrielle's tongue. She moved her tongue to the side, trying to divert most of the opiate into the pocket of her cheek.

"Swallow it, lassy," said Mother Henn, giving Gabrielle's shoulder a shake. "Ye canna hold it in yer mouth forever."

Gabrielle made a swallowing motion with the muscles of her jaw and throat, but managed to retain at least half of the dose inside her mouth. She fluttered her eyes shut, hoping to convince them that she was beaten, that she had given up and was ready to sleep her way through the worst of the situation.

In another moment, they lay her back against the pillows. She kept her eyes closed as, for several more minutes, they watched her. Neither Mother Henn nor the man touched her, nor did they speak, but she could feel their presence and could hear their breathing in the silent room.

"Ye think she's far enough under that she'll not put up a fight, Mother?"

"Aye. She's sleepin' like a babe. Take the ropes off, Jasper."

Gabrielle kept herself as limp and heavy as a sack of potatoes as Jasper undid the ropes that bound her and removed the gag. She inwardly cringed when his hands wandered from their task, touching her unnecessarily, but she dared not stir. All her hopes of escape, of defending herself against the man who'd be entering the room shortly, depended on convincing her captors that she was unconscious and helpless.

"Now then, let's push her legs up just so—"

They arranged her as she customarily slept, on her side with her knees bent and her arms flexed at the elbows. They added a bit of contrived coquetry by placing her hands palm to palm, resting her cheek against them in a pose of childish innocence.

"Go down t' the kitchen, Jasper, and eat yer supper. I will'na leave ye alone wi' th' lass, and I've got to return to the parlor to settle on a bid. Judgin' by the buzz comin' from downstairs, the gents are gettin' a trifle impatient. She'll lay still till the gent comes up, and long after that, I'll wager. Once she has her senses back, the gent what bought her will know how t' make her as biddable as he pleases."

Jasper snorted. "If'n I were the gent, I'd not mind a bit of a fight from the lass."

Mother Henn echoed his mirth with one of her grating cackles. "Aye, and if he stays till she's got her wits back, I'm sure he'll get a fight from this one!"

Finally Gabrielle heard their feet scuffling against the carpet as they exited the room, the door closing with a soft *whoosh* behind them, and a key scraping in the lock. Gabrielle immediately pushed herself to the edge of the bed, sat up, and spit out the laudanum into a large vase on the bedside table. She rubbed her wrists where the rope had left red indentations. She felt woozy from the amount of laudanum she'd swallowed, but not sleepy. Not yet, anyway.

She must think now, think about how she was going to get out of that place with her virginity intact. Her gaze darted in a desperate quest about the room and rested, again, on the vase on the bedside table. She lifted it, considering its suitability as a weapon. It had a long narrow neck and a heavy bowl-shaped base. A small smile curved her lips. Yes, it would do. It would do excellently.

CHAPTER EIGHT

"I'm sure ye'll no' be disappointed, sir."

Zach eyed Mother Henn with undisguised distaste. He was safe in doing so, because her own gaze was downcast in an assumed pose of servile deference. She sickened him, but he mustn't reveal his revulsion. After all, he was the grateful and eager customer—the high bidder for the imprisoned virginal sacrifice awaiting him upstairs. Or, at least he was playing the part of such a debauched cad in order to secure the girl's safety. He couldn't resist baiting the old witch just a little, though.

"If I *am* disappointed, Mother, I'll know just who to blame, won't I?"

Mother Henn's eyes lifted to his. He saw a flicker of fear in the jaded blue orbs, then a brazen standoff. "There'll be no blame to fix," she said. "She's a virgin, right enough. The maidenhead's intact I made sure of it meself."

With that, Zach had no stomach for baiting the woman into further assurances and guarantees. The sooner he could get the girl out of that place, and both of them out of the whole sordid mess, the better. "You said you had a key for me?"

"Aye, and you a purse for me?" Mother Henn held the key in one hand and extended her other hand, the plump upturned palm curved and waiting.

Zach took a pouch of coins from his jacket pocket. Since he didn't ordinarily carry two hundred pounds in cash around with him, he'd had to borrow money from the shelter's small-valuables box. Thank goodness the bidding had not gone beyond the sum he'd had in his keeping, though the amount was still well beyond what he'd expected to pay. The girl must be a prize, indeed, to embolden Mother Henn to demand so much shiny chicken feed.

"Here." He dropped the pouch into her cupped hand. "Don't insult me by counting it, or at least wait till I've left the room, if you please. I'm most anxious to get on with things."

Mother Henn immediately tucked the pouch into a large pocket hidden in the seam of her skirt, cackling softly. "Aye, I'm sure ye are, sir. Here's the key. Second floor, first door on the right."

Zach took the key. "I trust I'll not be disturbed?"

"Not till dawn, no matter what noise comes out the room. Ye know the rules 'bout not causin' the lass serious injuries. But the deal's fer the night, that's all. Then ye'll be on yer way, or Bob and Jasper'll have t' ... *help* ye out."

Zach favored Mother Henn with one of his most withering looks and had the satisfaction of seeing her wince. "Bob's and Jasper's assistance in my departure won't be necessary. I keep to the terms of my business arrangements, and I expect you to do the same. If my time with the girl is disturbed, I'll have my money back in full." He wanted to make sure that no one interrupted while he and the girl made good their escape.

Mother Henn shrugged. "Like I said, we dinna pay no heed to the sounds comin' out of that room, but she's a feisty lass, so's ye'd better watch yerself. If'n ye want more laudanum, jest stick yer head out the door and holler fer Jasper."

Zach sniffed dismissively at Mother Henn's spurious concern and coolly turned his back on her to walk up the stairs. He took pains to appear uninterested and disdainful of his surroundings, but he surreptitiously took in every detail as he ascended to the upper floor. He'd already taken the measure of Bob and Jasper, and though they appeared dull-witted, both of them looked vicious enough, if provoked, to tear him apart like two stray curs fighting over a piece of meat. And they both carried pistols.

This fact, and the appearance of other lackeys he'd seen ducking in and out of the room, convinced him that he'd been correct in deciding to take the girl out of the building through a window. Even with Malcolm and John's help, they'd have been woefully outnumbered, and it was obvious that the other more daring plan he'd considered to force their way through the main rooms to the front door had been wisely scrapped. He had no intention of endangering the lives of his servants or the girl when another more prudent course of action was available.

Before entering the building, he and John had stealthily studied the two outside entries and all the windows, while Malcolm stayed with the carriage, parked inconspicuously in a nearby alley. Zach hoped there was a window in the chamber he was being sent to, preferably facing the back of the building and with some means of descending to the narrow wynd below. John was on the watch, waiting—albeit nervously—in the cobbled square onto which Mother Henn's front door opened. It was through the square that Zach planned their escape route.

Apparently the "regulars" inhabited the first floor. Glancing down the hall from the landing, two of the idle damsels, all pout, powder, and perfume, rolled their hips and batted their lashes, hoping, he supposed, to divert him into a side trip. He assumed a look of apologetic regret and continued on to the next floor. It was quieter there, and he suspected that Mother Henn's bedchamber was on this floor along with a couple of rooms kept for special occasions such as this one.

He inserted the key into the lock of the door he'd been directed to and turned it. He entered the room, closing the door quietly behind him, then leaned against it as his eyes adjusted to the dimly lit chamber. A small fire burned in the grate of a low-manteled fireplace, and a single candle flickered on the bedside stand. The girl lay on the bed, facing away.

All in white, her reclining figure appeared as a snow-covered slope of hill and dale—slim hips and a small uncorseted waist creating an undulating human landscape. Dark-gold unbound hair cascaded over her shoulders and down her back, and a faint floral scent mingled with the earthy smoke smell of a peat fire...

Oh, Gawd Orchids!

Dread, mixed with a slightly delirious impression of impending laughter, descended on Zach. It was impossible, wasn't it? Other women had hair like hers and used a floral scent.

It couldn't be Gabby! He'd left her safe and sound at Charlotte Square! But she had expressed an earnest wish to visit that family she'd met on Christmas Eve, and Zach had made no secret out of the fact that he frequented Old Town on business. Knowing Gabby, knowing her curiosity and her stubborn refusal to be deterred by conventions or prudence, she might have ventured into Old Town to try to find the Tuttles. Or she might have even followed him that afternoon and somehow got lost, later to be found and tricked into such a dangerous situation by the devious Mother Henn. Leave it to Gabby…

Zach still stood with his back pressed against the door, beads of sweat forming on his brow. He had only to walk a few feet into the room to discover if his suspicions had any validity. He might be surprised and relieved to find a strange face belonging to the alarmingly familiar shape on the bed. But somehow he knew that that would not be the case. He knew it was Gabby, but he was reluctant to confirm that fact.

Suddenly she moaned and moved on the bed, one arm falling over the edge, her body perilously close to following in a slow and heavy roll. Zach was spurred to action, pushing away from the door. She might hurt herself tumbling off the bed, the little shatterbrain! Then, as he moved toward her, all the implications of Gabby's situation flooded his mind. A fall off the bed was nothing compared to what she might have already endured! Of a certainty, Mother Henn and her goons had humiliated and manhandled her. But if they'd done more than that to her, Zach vowed that he'd kill the bloody bastards!

Zach was at the bedside now, bending over Gabby, reaching out to pull her away from the edge. Her face was hidden by a thick veil of hair, but it was Gabby, all right. He'd never before seen a woman with such boyish hips and a small waist have so generous a bosom. He tried not to look, but her rosy nipples showed through the nearly transparent dressing gown.

Zach's momentary distraction proved unfortunate. Suddenly Gabby reared up, the hand that had fallen over the side of the bed reappeared—in possession of a large vase! Zach had time only to register the irony of it and shout Gabby's name, before the vase hit him squarely on the crown, sending him reeling to the floor. Blasts of color exploded behind his fluttering eyelids. Just before darkness enveloped him, he saw through a blur the horrified expression on Gabby's face as she stood over him. He smiled grimly, then passed into blessed oblivion.

"Oh, what have I done?"

Gabrielle was stunned. She'd wished for Zach with such fervor, yet it was beyond the range of reasonable possibilities that he could have been alerted to her situation! No one knew where she was, so how did Zach get there? What was he doing at a house of ill repute?

The blood trickling down Zach's scalp forced Gabrielle out of her state of shock. Now was not the time for speculation! She placed the shattered remains of the vase on the bedside stand and moved to the dressing table, which held a pewter basin, a pitcher of water, and a single washcloth. She poured some water into the basin and soaked the cloth in it, wringing it well. She dropped to her knees beside Zach's inert body and gingerly dabbed at the wound.

He lay perfectly still. He was flat on his back, his long legs slightly bent at the knees and turned to the side, his arms flung wide of his body. Panic mounted inside her, but Gabrielle recalled that their family physician once told her that head wounds, even minor ones, always bled profusely. Surely she'd not inflicted a mortal wound! Just to reassure herself, however, she pressed her palm against Zach's chest and felt it rise and fall in deep breathing, and also detected the strong, steady rhythm of his heart. This calmed her a little, and she focused on the tasks at hand; she must stem the flow of blood and help Zach return to consciousness.

The first proved to be easier than she thought it would be. She grew braver and wiped at the blood with a firmer hand, finding that the cut, once cleaned and visible, was not more than a half-inch wide. A large knot formed beneath it, however. She pushed carefully against the cloth and hoped the pressure would suffice in stopping the blood flow, since she doubted there were materials for bandages in the room. And she certainly could not summon Mother Henn for help! After a few moments, she could see that her efforts were paying off; the blood was coagulating and forming a seal.

The task of helping him to regain consciousness would not be so easily accomplished. Without her reticule, she had no smelling salts at hand. How soon he woke up on his own would depend on how badly injured he was. Gabrielle shook her head as tears sprung to her eyes. She couldn't believe she'd actually whacked Zach over the head with a vase! She had once again managed to involve the poor man in one of her scrapes and placed him in danger. Her mother always said she attracted trouble like bees to honey, and poor Zach always managed to get caught in the resulting stickiness. Maybe he'd be better off if she did marry someone like Rory and moved far away from Pencarrow!

"Gabby?"

Gabrielle's heart skipped a beat. She blinked through the tears and looked down at Zach. "Zach? Are you all right?" He was peering at her from beneath half-closed lids, his golden eyes glowing like candlelight spilling out of a window with the shade half down. Oh, what a welcome sight!

"Am I all right?" he repeated, as if she'd asked an idiotic question. "I very much doubt it, Gabby." He groaned and lifted a hand toward his head in an instinctive, self-protective gesture.

She caught his hand. "Don't touch, Zach. I'm trying to stop the bleeding."

His hand dropped to his side and he closed his eyes again. "Trying to stop what you started?"

Gabrielle felt her cheeks grow hot. "I didn't know it was you. I was defending myself against—" She couldn't say it. Rape was such a detestable word, and now that Zach was there, now that she was safe, the horror of what would certainly have happened to her—despite her determined resistance—nearly overpowered Gabrielle.

Zach's eyes opened. "I know, Gabby."

The understanding in Zach's voice and look both soothed and agitated her. Gabrielle swallowed the lump of emotion swelling in her throat and averted her eyes. "How did you know I was here?"

Zach grimaced. "I didn't. In fact, not long ago I was thanking God you weren't the poor girl I was sent to rescue. Believe me, I'm as surprised to see you as you are to see me!"

"What do you mean? Who sent you?"

Zach moved restlessly, finally crossing his arms across his chest as though to keep them still until Gabrielle was through with her ministration. "I was alerted by Mr. Blake, the proprietor of a women's shelter nearby, that Mother Henn had snaffled herself a young woman of Quality. He suggested, and I agreed, that the only way to rescue the girl was by posing as a customer. In the past, the police have been ineffectual in this sort of matter."

"How did Mr. Blake know?"

"A boy told him he saw Mother Henn lure you inside this place."

"Ah, that would be Will—bless him! But how do you know Mr. Blake, Zach?"

"Full of questions as usual, I see," he grumbled.

Gabrielle clicked her tongue with exasperation. "Unless you have something to hide, I don't know why you should object to my questions!" But he did have something to hide. In her mind's eye, she saw that blond woman in the brown mantle stepping into Zach's carriage, her trill of laughter a sharp contrast to Gabrielle's misery as she'd watched them drive off together. It was on the tip of her tongue to ask Zach about her, but she dared not.

Maybe the girl was somehow connected to this Mr. Blake. His daughter, perhaps. But if Mr. Blake was a respectable man, his daughter would be respectable, too, and then Gabrielle would have to conclude that the girl was not Zach's mistress. The girl would be something much more threatening to Gabrielle's happiness—a bona fide romantic interest. Gabrielle was dying to know, but she remained silent. Now was not the most propitious time to ask.

"I have questions, too," Zach asserted harshly, his narrowed eyes now more like piercing lightning than warm candlelight. He propped his head slightly off the floor with one bent arm, glaring at her. "What were you doing in Old Town by yourself? And who in Hades is Will?"

Gabrielle felt a shiver of gratification run through her. He was angry. That meant he cared. "Will is one of the Tuttle children I told you. about, the family of urchins I met on Christmas Eve."

Zach's eyes widened. "Lord, you don't say? You found them, then, in all this hodgepodge of buildings and people? How did you accomplish that?"

"Well, I didn't, actually. Will found me. He stole my reticule, and I chased him. Next thing I knew, I was deep inside a maze of streets and being offered assistance by Mother Henn."

"So you came to Old Town to find the Tuttles? That was foolish of you, Gabby, as well you know."

"You were supposed to make inquiries for me."

Zach looked pained. "I forgot all about that. I'm sorry."

Gabrielle fell silent. He had supplied a reason for her being in Old Town, and she would not contradict him, though he was dead wrong. She'd wanted to find the Tuttles, but she wasn't so short of a sheet that she didn't realize that it would be well-nigh impossible to do it without assistance, and it was Zach's assistance she'd waited for. But it was no wonder he'd forgotten all about his offer to nose about amongst his connections in Old Town for news of the Tuttles. She and Zach had hardly been speaking for a week now. He'd apparently had other things on his mind.

And so had she. Her search for the impoverished family had been set aside till she could thaw the icy attitude Zach had assumed after their encounter in the hall. Her first step in accomplishing this was to try to discover what attracted him to Old Town day after day. Now that she thought she knew what that attraction was, she must discover how formidable the blond girl was in terms of competition. Gabrielle had been hurt and discouraged when she'd seen Zach with the girl, but she had not given up. No, never that.

"It's stopped bleeding. I think you can sit up now, if you'd like," she said, after lifting the cloth and examining the wound.

"If I'd like, she says," muttered Zach. "As if I'd prefer lying flat on my back in some..." Zach's voice trailed off as he levered himself to a sitting position, swaying a bit from his head's diminished ability to make smooth transitions from one altitude to another.

Gabrielle caught his shoulders, steadying him. "You moved too suddenly," she scolded. "Your head may have stopped bleeding, but you're bound to be dizzy for a while. It will pass eventually."

Zach pulled his knees up and propped his elbows on them, cradling his head in his hands. "I haven't the leisure to wait for my dizziness to pass. The Murrays and Clarissa will be frantic with worry, not to mention Rory—"

"Oh, they think I'm with you."

Zach lifted his head, a grimace born of pain and incredulity distorting his handsome features. "What?"

"I left a note telling the Murrays I had gone out driving and touring with you. They trust you, Zach, and I thought it an excellent way to keep them from worrying if I didn't happen to get back before I was discovered missing. Of course, I'm sure by now they know I'm gone, and as late as it is, even knowing I'm with you won't lend them much comfort."

"No. In fact, I'm sure they're furious with me! We'll have to think of some farradiddle to protect your reputation and keep them from knowing the real reason you've been gone all afternoon. But all that can be addressed—of necessity, in a brief fashion!—en route to New Town. Our first concern is to get out of here, Gabby. We'll have to go out through the window since Mother Henn and her brutish hirelings won't allow me to simply take you out the front door, you know, and in my present condition I don't expect I'd win in a match of fisticuffs against the two of them, or be able to outshoot them, either."

"Oh, I don't know. You're quite athletic, Zach, and a crack shot. I could help! I'm rather good at swinging vases and other such domestic things laying about the house."

Despite the dull throbbing he felt in every inch of his skull, Zach was gratified and amused by Gabby's faith in his abilities and her matter-of-fact statement concerning her own powers of resourceful battling. A half-smile had formed on his lips, but it quickly disappeared when, for the first time since she'd hit him with the vase, he really looked at her.

She sat back on her heels, her night rail puddled about her knees. Her hands rested in her lap; small fingers curled knuckle against knuckle. Her gown had no sleeves, and her slim white arms had the look of lustrous porcelain in the firelight. The neckline of her gown was naturally low-cut, but in the hectic activity of the past few moments it had gone askew and was draped even lower over her ample bust. Her nipples pressed against the thin material, as rosy ... and rigid ... as rubies. Despite their warm color, everyone knew that rubies were cold to the touch. But Gabby's nipples wouldn't be cold. Against his tongue, they'd be warm and taut....

Alarmed by this titillating comparison springing so easily to his mind, Zach shifted his gaze to her face, but if he'd hoped he could dam up the rising tide of desire by only looking at her from the neck up, he was quite wrong. Her face was framed by that luxurious tumble of honey-blond hair she possessed, the beauty of it when unbound he'd nearly, and mercifully, forgotten. Covered by a bonnet or a flower spray, or coiled and tucked into a fashionable coiffure, the real magnificence of Gabby's hair was usually hidden from view. He hadn't seen it down since she was an awkward, coltish girl of thirteen, and even then it had made him catch his breath. "Zach?"

Zach met Gabby's gaze. Her eyes were luminous and dewy, the pupils slightly dilated. There also was a question there, but no fear, and her lack of fear frightened Zach more than any bugbears or villains ever could. Then a challenge crept into her expression, and he was petrified. He'd been goaded by that look before, and he'd met the challenge with a kiss. But that kiss in the hall a week ago had tormented him through six restless nights, making him yearn for something he could never allow himself—Gabby's love.

"You're taking all this in surprising stride, Gabby," he remarked hesitantly, biding his time while he stifled his urge to pull her into his arms.

Gabby bit her lower lip and furrowed her brows consideringly. She had wonderful, full, kissable lips. "I am quite relaxed. It must be the small amount of laudanum I swallowed. If I'd swallowed the whole of it they'd given me, I'd be unconscious. As it is, I actually feel rather—" She smiled, a slow, sensuous tilt of those luscious lips. "*Carefree*." She cocked her head to the side. "And rather brave. Yes, brave. But then, just having you here, Zach, has made all my fears disappear."

"Now I know you're dizzy," he said tersely. "We're still in a great deal of danger, Gabby. Get some clothes on."

"I don't know where they are."

Zach stood up—still a little dizzy himself—and braced himself by catching hold of the bedpost, then inclined his head toward the armoire resting against the opposite wall. "Did you look in there?"

Gabby raised her brows. "Well, no, up till now I've been either in a drugged stupor or fighting for my virtue and life. I promised myself, however, that as soon as I had a free moment I'd check to see if the room had an armoire, then ascertain whether or not it held my clothes!"

Zach frowned at Gabby's dry—and what he considered inappropriate—humor. He supposed he could fault the laudanum for this, too. "You ought to put something on. It's cold in here. You might catch your death in that flimsy thing." He shifted his gaze away from Gabby's candid, disbelieving look.

"I'm not cold. And you don't look cold, either. In fact—"

"Oh, for Christ's sake, Gabby, do it for the sake of modesty, then!" Zach turned away and walked to the armoire, flinging open the doors with an excess of force, making them bang against the wood. "Look, there are plenty of things in here! If we can't find your clothes, then surely one of these—" Zach's voice trailed off. The armoire was filled with clothing, but nothing a woman would wear on the street. Dressing gowns and bloomers, corsets and chemises hung suggestively as if for consideration by the lascivious peruser of armoires, and, conveniently, in a variety of colors and sizes.

"I hardly think I'd be warmer in one of those," Gabby remarked, still in that wry tone, her voice coming from much too close for Zach's tenuous comfort. He turned quickly and discovered his tormenter not six inches away. At such a minimal distance and from the perspective of his considerable height, he could look right down the front of Gabby's gown. *Rubies.* He shrugged past her and walked to the window, yanking open the drapes and pushing up the sill two inches. He closed his eyes and breathed the crisp, cold air.

"I thought you said it was chilly in here?"

Zach gritted his teeth, willing his body to relax, his heartbeat to slow to a normal rhythm. "Pour me some water, Gabby."

"What?"

"Some fresh water in the basin, if you please. I need to wash. The sight of blood will alarm your aunt and the Murrays and will not put them in the proper frame of mind to believe our story, whatever it will be." He felt her hesitation, and sighed tiredly. "Please, Gabby, just do as I ask."

He could hear her moving behind him, pouring the water. He forced himself to concentrate on the important matter of their escape. He looked out the window and, just as he'd hoped, they were facing the back, the narrow wynd below them. And, as he'd ascertained earlier while studying the building, the chamber's window was situated above a decorative ledge. Since the building was quite old, the ledge could possibly be a bit decrepit and unstable. He would have to be very careful about testing each step as they moved along the ledge to the neighboring building, where they would then enter a window of some unsuspecting and possibly irate tenement dweller. But it seemed the only way to get them out of there.

"'Tis done. What else would you have me do?"

There was a note of resignation in Gabby's voice. Perhaps she finally understood how dangerous their situation was. And he wasn't just thinking of Mother Henn and her two goons.

He was thinking of them alone together in that room with her half-dressed and him half-mad with wanting her. Tersely he said, "Get under the covers and pull them up to your chin."

He heard the bed squeak as she climbed into it, and the rustle of bedclothes. "Well, I'm covered now. It's safe to look."

He turned. She had the counterpane pulled up, her fingers clutching the crimson material in a wad just beneath her chin. Her eyes bespoke her annoyance, however, and her lips were slanted in a petulant frown. He pointed a warning finger at her. "After I've cleaned myself up a bit, we're going to get out of here, Gabby. But in the meantime, you will stay in that bed and you will not move an inch!"

He watched her a moment, his finger still pointing a warning, and waited for a rebellious reply. When none came, he lowered his hand and turned toward the dressing table, hazarding a look at himself in the mirror hanging on the wall above it. There was blood matted in his hair, but really very little on his face. He dipped his head in the basin and rinsed the stickiness from his hair, then wrung the excess water out and stood up. He extracted a pair of muslin bloomers from the armoire and toweled his hair nearly dry. Then he took a small brush from an inner waistcoat pocket and arranged his thick, straight locks, avoiding the wound and the tender goose-egg sized bump beneath it as best he could. All the while, he could feel Gabby watching him.

"You surprise me."

He turned and glanced at her. Her arms lay on top of the covers now. Not usually considered objects of lust, he couldn't imagine why the sight of her smooth white arms excited him. Apparently all of her excited him. He looked quickly away and busied himself with straightening his neckcloth. "What do you mean, Gabby?"

"You're such a prude."

Zach felt his jaw tighten. "Just because I don't think it seemly that you should be prancing about the room with practically nothing on? *You* surprise *me*, Gabby. I should think you'd feel compelled by your proper upbringing to behave in a more ladylike fashion and demonstrate a little modesty."

Gabby sighed. "I suppose you're right. But the thing is, when I'm around you, Zach, I don't feel I'm doing something wrong if I'm not quite dressed."

Zach's busy, nervous fingers froze in their efforts for a moment, while a shiver coursed through him. "You don't know what you're saying, Gabby. As you're so fond of remarking, you're not a child anymore and you shouldn't—"

"And I don't think there's anything wrong with kissing you, either. What happened the other day was wonderful, Zach. I've been sleepless every night this week from thinking about it. And I'm quite sure I'd not feel a bit of guilt even if we … made love."

Zach could feel the sweat forming again on his brow. Her honesty had a most devastating effect on his body temperature and his nerves. Gooseflesh rippled its way down his back, his arms, his legs.

Yet she was not so honest about all things. He shifted slightly till he caught her reflection in the mirror, but without allowing her the same view of him. "Strange words coming from someone who is betrothed to marry."

He watched the play of emotions on her face: indecision, resolution, and finally sincerity. "Rory and I are not betrothed. 'Tis nothing but a sham. I hoped to make you jealous enough that you would realize that you and I are meant to be together. But now I realize that I should have been honest with you all along." She paused, tilting her chin higher, gathering courage. "I love you, Zach."

Zach swiveled, the momentary triumph of extracting the truth from her diminished by the impact that selfsame truth was having on his composure. He took recourse in denial, flippantly remarking, "Laudanum is not a reliable truth serum, I see. Only part of what you say is the truth."

"What part don't you believe? I assure you, Rory and I agreed from the beginning that our engagement was only—"

"No. I don't mean the engagement." Zach's palms were coated with icy perspiration. The room seemed suddenly too confining. "I… I discerned a certain falseness about that from the beginning. He's not your type, Gabby."

Gabby leaned forward, the counterpane falling away from the front of her, the sweet seductiveness of her once again in clear view. "*You're* my type. And you know I'm being truthful when I say I love you, Zach. I've always loved you. And you love me. Why can't you admit it? Why won't you let me get close to you? Why can't you let yourself be happy? Is it because of that woman who died when I was very young? Tell me about her, Zach. Maybe it would help us both understand things better if you talked about her."

The room was small, but not so close and airless that he should be having phobic symptoms. But he was. Even with the window open, Zach was feeling trapped and suffocated. The stimulant of sheer panic raced through his bloodstream and urged his heart to a frenetic speed. He was cold and clammy, light-headed and itching to break free of that room to the freedom of the outdoors. Outside where there was no wanting, no wishful yearning, no painful confrontations with the past, the present, and the truth. No Gabby…

"Zach, what is it? You don't look well." Gabby scrambled out of the bed. Zach could only watch, unable to move, unable to think clearly. He had to marshal every ounce of resolution to keep himself from bolting out the door. *What a coward*, he derided himself. *What a craven milksop!*

Gabby stood in front of him now, holding his hands, rubbing warmth and sensation into his frozen fingers. The room spun around them, everything too bright, too sharply focused. "I think you must be having a delayed reaction to that hit on your head, Zach. Come, sit on the bed."

Zach went unresisting to the bed and sat down, then immediately began shivering convulsively. Gabby watched him with fear in her eyes. "You're freezing! I'm going to close the window." Gabby turned, but Zach caught her wrist.

"No! Don't!"

She stared at him, puzzlement and alarm written plainly on her face. "I won't, then, but you're so cold. Here, get under the covers."

Feeling like a complete idiot—the errant knight in the ludicrous position of being mollycoddled by the damsel in distress—Zach allowed Gabby to take off his boots and jacket and assist him into the bed and under the covers. He was still shaking rather violently and could do nothing till the episode passed. What had brought it on? he wondered. If it wasn't the environment he found himself in, what was it? Was it Gabby's confession of love, or his own feelings of love and desire for her that threatened to spin completely out of control? Was it her insistence that he face the past and confront the fears that still haunted him today because of Tessy's death?

Zach sighed through chattering teeth. It was too complicated, too damned hard! He'd rather avoid the whole ordeal of sorting out his feelings for Gabby. He was much more comfortable with his feelings for, and the resulting good works attached to, the poor and downtrodden. Those feelings were pleasantly distant, while his feelings for Gabby were uncomfortably ... close.

The reality of the situation was that he did love her, just as much as she claimed to love him. In fact, he cared too much for her to subject her to his particular brand of destructive affection. The only way to keep her from harm, then, was to convince her that she didn't really love him, and, as well, never admit to loving her. If he admitted his feelings, there would be no stopping the girl and no way to resist her.

Then the unexpected happened. Apparently Gabby was unstoppable even without the added ammunition of admitting he loved her. She climbed into bed beside him, wrapped an arm over his chest, and nestled her warm body against his. "There, Zach. Now you shan't be cold."

CHAPTER NINE

For as long as Gabrielle had known him, Zach had never shown fear of any kind. Caution and common sense he had in abundance, and he'd frequently lectured her over the years about her apparent lack of these estimable qualities. But when it came down to being brave, there was no one who could top Zach. After all, he was always the one who rescued her from the scrapes her curiosity and intrepidness continually got her into.

He'd saved her from that crumbling tin mine she'd been lost in years ago, a happenstance that had secured her eternal devotion to Zach—at least all the devotion she hadn't already given him. He was nearly killed in that mine, but he had never considered the danger to himself. His only thoughts had been to find her.

Maybe that's why it was so frightening to Gabrielle to see Zach in an apparent state of terror. She knew he wasn't just sick, or in shock from his injury. He was petrified. But Zach's vulnerability didn't lessen him in Gabrielle's eyes in the least. She knew his fears had nothing to do with goons like Jasper and Bob, or trepidation over the necessity of climbing out on a second-story ledge to rescue his shatterbrained sister-in-law from the clutches of an amoral mistress of a bawdy house. His fears were internalized and emotion-driven, and therefore deeper, more complex, and much harder to resolve. And until he quit shaking, till his complexion returned to a healthy color and the dazed look of panic left his expression, she would do what instinct and love told her to do. She would hold him.

Except for Zach's quick, shallow breathing, and the crackle of the fire, the room was silent. Muffled sounds from the lower two stories, however, drifted up the stairs and through the floorboards—a woman's coy laughter, a man's low, rumbling voice, the rhythmic squeak of a bed, followed by a female's ecstatic cry. Naive as she was, Gabrielle realized that, given the circumstances, the woman's outcry was probably false and performed for the benefit of her customer's sense of manly pride.

It was an odd sensation lying there, listening to the sounds of commercialized sex—bought and paid for, dehumanized copulation—while at the same time, glorying in the bliss that was finally hers by being in Zach's arms. The surroundings were not in the least romantic or sacred, but the sense of knowing she belonged exactly where she was, with Zach, was overwhelmingly satisfying to Gabrielle. Even if she'd found herself compelled to share a bed of nails with Zach, she told herself, she'd happily have lain there with him forever.

After a time, Zach's breathing slowed and deepened. He no longer shook. Her head rested on his shoulder and her arm was draped across his chest. She moved her hand to place it over Zach's heart. She was relieved to discover the frenetic rhythm had slowed to a reasonable pace, though it still seemed to beat harder and faster than normal.

She liked the feel of his chest beneath the sensitive pads of her palm. With just the thin material of his muslin shirt between her skin and his, the heat of his body radiated through. She found a gap between the buttons of his shirt and slid a finger between, testing the texture of his chest. She felt a tremor run through him, but she knew that what he experienced now was much different from the shaking of before, and came from a different source. She had inadvertently pleasured him, and she liked how that made her feel.

From an accidental peek of Zach in the midst of dressing for a Pencarrow party many years before, Gabrielle remembered that his chest was smooth, the muscles and sinew well-defined. As a child she had been entranced by the beauty of the man, her infantile admiration approaching something akin to worship. As a woman, she still appreciated Zach's masculine beauty, but today she wanted to experience it on a less aesthetic, less lofty plane, and on a more basic level. She wanted to enjoy him as a mortal woman enjoys a mortal man. She wanted to touch and kiss every inch of him.

She began to stroke his chest, prepared at any moment for the probability of his hand darting up to stop her. But it didn't. He just lay there, breathing deeply. She didn't speak. She didn't want the mood broken by ill-judged words, or to inadvertently repeat the things that might have precipitated Zach's strange attack of panic.

She grew braver, extending her hesitant strokes over a wider area of Zach's chest. When she felt Zach's nipple beneath her fingers, she lingered over the hard nub, finding the exploration of his anatomy a pleasing, engrossing process. When he gave a little gasp and covered her hand with his, Gabrielle knew Zach found the process just as pleasing. Maybe too pleasing.

"Gabby, what are you doing?" His voice was a rasp.

"I'm touching you. Don't you like it, Zach?" Gabrielle was surprised at the huskiness she detected in her own voice.

"I—" He didn't finish what he was about to say, and he didn't move. Gabrielle took this as encouragement. After a moment, she pulled her hand from beneath his—he made a token show of resistance, nothing to signify—and began to unbutton Zach's shirt. One-handed, this was a time-consuming task, but despite the very real probability of a houseful of people worrying about her and wondering where she was, Gabrielle was in no hurry. She had been waiting for this her whole life.

Finally the shirt fell open, and she pushed aside the muslin, sliding her hand over the contours of his bare chest, the shock of flesh on flesh almost unbearably thrilling. Zach moaned and pulled Gabrielle on top of him. Her breasts were flush against his chest, her legs tangled with his. And they were eye to eye.

Zach felt intoxicated. Holding Gabby this closely worked on him like a drug. Even though her confrontational words had, most curiously, been the cause of his phobic attack, the comfort she extended to him afterward was apparently the cure. A languid sense of well-being had stole over him as she'd snuggled close, the symptoms of his disorder easing away like the sting of a burn after bathing it in cool water, every passing second bringing more relief.

Then he'd felt drowsy, content, almost post-orgasmic. He also felt grateful. In Gabby's arms, he'd recovered from his attack without feeling a smidgen of embarrassment. Bleader was the only other living person to have witnessed one of Zach's attacks. And, though Bleader was as loyal, devoted, and compassionate a servant as a man could hope for, afterward Zach had felt considerable embarrassment.

So he'd continued to repose on the bed with Gabby, allowing her gentle caresses, hardly expecting the aroused shudder that went through him as it became obvious that Gabby's designs in touching him had changed from the comforting ministrations of a friend to the sexual inquisitiveness of a lover.

Now he had pulled her atop him, her weight evenly and delightfully distributed over the length of him. He could feel her nipples against his bare chest, knotted like hard pebbles. One of her legs had slid between his, and the other was pressed tight against his thigh. He was breathing fast, and so was she, and they hadn't even kissed. Zach felt as though he were under the influence of an aphrodisiac, awash in stuporous pleasure that took away his ability to reason.

The rise of her mons lay against his erection. He moved his hands slowly down her back, down the smooth slim curves, till they rested on her buttocks. He cupped her and pulled her hard against him. Her lips parted, her eyelids fluttered, and she gasped. Zach bit his lip, the same intensity of arousal making it very hard for him to do what he knew he must—stop. Still he didn't move. He just held her against him, not as yet able to sever the contact, but unwilling to ignore his conscience and take Gabby on to the next step, and, inevitably, toward consummation.

Gabby had no similar qualms. She settled the matter by pressing her lips to his. The contact was searing. Zach groaned and opened his mouth against hers, kissing her hard and long. He felt her fingers in his hair, tugging him closer. He rolled over and pinned her neatly beneath him, parting her legs with a nudge of his knee, running his hand up her calf, all along the inside of her smooth, warm thigh.

He covered her face, neck, and shoulders with kisses, her flimsy nightdress working its way down from the neckline and up from the hem. There was just a narrow swath of fabric covering Gabby's torso, and the silky texture of it chafed against Zach's chest erotically. But he was sure her completely naked body would feel even better...

"Oh, Zach," Gabby whispered in his ear. "I'm so glad, so glad you want me..."

Gabby's words relocated Zach's wandering conscience. He pulled back and looked into Gabby's flushed face. In her eyes Zach saw infinite trust and sensual need. Coupled like two disparate entities was the child he knew and the woman he feared. If he made love to her, would he be abusing the trust of the child? Or would he be committing himself to the expectations of the woman? Either way, Gabby would be the loser. He was not marriage material. He'd been a jinx, really, to every woman he'd loved. Therefore he would not compromise Gabby into the necessity of what would amount to yet another sham betrothal.

Quickly he rolled off her, then got up from the bed. He walked to the armoire and began rifling through the clothes hanging inside. "There's got to be something in here you can put on! We need to leave immediately, Gabby."

No sound came from the bed. Gabby was either shocked into silence by his abrupt departure, or too angry—or hurt—to speak to him. Or all three. He refused to turn and look at her. He busied himself with searching through the armoire, till he finally discovered something in the very back. A man's heavy velvet dressing robe. He snatched at it, thinking it would at least adequately cover her and keep her warm in the carriage until they were able to return to Charlotte Square. How he was going to explain Gabby's state of undress to the Murrays, however, was a puzzle!

Then luck favored Zach. Hidden beneath the robe was Gabby's green ermine-lined mantle, and a green-and-pinksprigged morning gown that must be hers, too. Even her shift and corset were there, as well as her rice-straw bonnet. "Thank God, I've found your clothes, Gabby! We might actually see this thing through without jeopardizing your reputation!"

In his relief, he turned impetuously to look at her, an exultant smile tilting his lips. But Gabby did not return his smile, nor should he expect her to, he supposed. She sat on the bed, the coverlets pulled up and around her shoulders. She stared back at him accusingly. In such a pose, with such an angry, petulant slant to her full lips, but with such obvious hurt in her eyes, she looked more the child he knew than the woman he feared. He felt himself softening.

Zach took Gabby's clothes from the armoire and laid them at the foot of the bed, avoiding looking at her. "I'm sorry, Gabby. Sweeting, you just don't understand. You may love me, but I think your feelings are confused. We've been friends for a long time. A childish infatuation doesn't serve well as a solid basis for a marriage—"

"Oh, Zach, do stop with the Banbury tale, if you please!" she said sharply, causing Zach to turn and stare at her. Her eyes were flashing with emotion. "You know very well that's not what's keeping us apart! What I feel for you is not infatuation. Any fool watching us for the past ten minutes could see how much I love you! There's something else that's coming between us, although admittedly something that I don't understand. Something you won't tell me! But never fear, Zach, I *will* find out what that something is. Because there's nothing and no one—not even you—that's going to keep us from being happy together." Gabby lifted her chin and gave Zach an imperious look from beneath haughtily lowered lids. "Not even the blond woman I saw you with today will keep us apart."

Zach raked a hand through his hair. "Gawd, Gabby, how did you manage to be in so many places in one day? Just get dressed!"

"Aren't you going to tell me who she is?" she demanded.

"No, I'm not! It's none of your business." Explaining Kate would necessitate explaining the women's shelter, too, and he wasn't prepared to do that. His charities had been his saving grace during the past years, and he had a superstitious notion that if he told his family and friends about them, the good works done at each shelter would no longer … well, *count*.

"I'm not leaving here till you tell me, Zach."

Zach sat down on the bed and tugged on his boots. "I should have expected such an attitude, Gabby. It clearly shows me just what a child you really are," he said coolly, standing and buttoning his shirt. "You're being selfish not thinking of the Murrays and your aunt, who are undoubtedly sick with worry about you. Malcolm and John await us outside in the cold, as well. But, then, children are notoriously selfish."

Gabrielle knew he was right. She was hardly displaying maturity by delaying their return to Charlotte Square. She might even be jeopardizing their safety by resisting Zach's urgings to hurry and dress. And as far as making romantic headway with Zach, certainly staying where they were was accomplishing nothing. He was putting on his jacket.

As Gabrielle threw off the covers and climbed out of the bed, Zach moved to stand by the window, his back turned to her. Zach's deliberate removal and the show of his back had a twofold reason, she was sure. First, he was studying the escape route and concocting a believable story to excuse their long absence. Second, he was being a perfect gentleman by allowing her to dress without the embarrassment of being watched.

How noble, she thought, pulling her shift over her head. And how unnecessary. As she'd truthfully told Zach, she didn't feel the least unnatural or uncomfortable about being slightly, or even completely, undressed in front of him. A self-satisfied smile curved her lips. It apparently made *him* deuced uncomfortable, and that was very good news to her.

As she completed dressing, Gabrielle relived her moments in the bed with Zach. Because of the monumental importance of what had happened in that room, their time there had seemed longer than the actual half hour that had passed. She also contemplated asking Zach about his attack of panic, but she didn't want to embarrass him or make a to-do over it. If he wanted to discuss it, he'd bring up the subject himself. She felt sure that the attack had something to do with Zach's past, and was probably tangled in with the other conflicts that kept him from making a commitment to her. Now was not the time, but she definitely would find out what troubled Zach so much.

Finally she stood before the mirror and straightened her hair as best she could, then put on her bonnet. "There," she said, turning toward Zach. "Will I do?"

Zach swiveled and looked at her, taking in her appearance from head to toe. "Yes, you'll do. A bit of disarray won't hurt, either, since I've decided to tell the Murrays that our carriage broke a wheel while we tooled 'round Duddingston Loch. Then we walked to an inn to seek shelter and refreshment while the smithy made repairs."

Gabrielle raised her brows. "And we didn't send them word?"

"Oh, we *did* send word," Zach returned, obviously having thought through all the possible hitches in his plan. "But the fellow I sent with the note apparently wasn't a reliable messenger. Mayhap he took the coin I gave him and bought a bottle of Blue Ruin. Naturally neither of us will know the fellow had failed to fulfill his commission till we reach Charlotte Square. Then we must act terribly surprised that they never received our missive. You like to act, Gabby. This will be a perfect opportunity for you."

"That was not very nice of you to say," Gabrielle informed him matter-of-factly.

Zach grimaced. "I know. Actually I never intended it to come out 'nice.' I'm sorry, Gabby. I think I'm punishing you a little. Personally I find lying distasteful, but in this case, if we told the truth your reputation would be in shambles and the Murrays and Clarissa would hold themselves responsible. We'd better lie convincingly."

"Like I did about Rory?"

Zach shrugged. "Well, didn't you? Everyone believes you are truly besotted with and betrothed to the man. All of Edinburgh, it seems. Even your mother in distant Cornwall is looking forward to your spring nuptials." Zach gave a self-derisive laugh. "Lord, when I think of that letter you sent me, I—"

"It did the trick, didn't it? I made you jealous, didn't I?"

Zach's mouth clamped shut, and he let his eyelids droop over his eyes in that lordly pose he assumed when he was miffed and wanted to deliver a setdown to an encroacher. Gabrielle sighed. "Don't use your setdown stare on me, Zach. I'll tell the Murrays and Mama the truth about my betrothal to Rory."

"When?"

Gabrielle couldn't resist. "When you tell me who that blond woman is."

"You're impossible!" Zach exploded, turning away to yank open the window. "We won't discuss this anymore today, Gabby, because you are driving me mad! We still have to get down to the street without breaking our necks. We'll need to concentrate, and squabbling our way along the ledge might alert Mother Henn or one of her lackeys. If we die, poor Malcolm and John will bear the burden of carrying the real truth of this folly to Charlotte Square, and I'm sure they wouldn't relish such a chore! Now, come here!"

Zach held out his hand, and Gabrielle obediently took it, then he drew her to the window. She tried to ignore how his proximity made her heart race. They both bent to look outside. She was grateful to note that the light flurry of snow had passed, and the sky was clear and brightly lit by a three-quarter moon.

"At least we shouldn't have any problem seeing where we're going," she remarked.

"Nor would anyone have the least trouble seeing us, either, if they should happen to be looking up."

"At least I don't think anyone downstairs is paying much attention to what we're doing."

"They're probably making merry over the extra money your abduction contributed to the coffers of this lovely establishment."

Gabrielle turned her head to look at him. Their noses were practically touching. "How much *did* I contribute?"

Zach swallowed and drew back, frowning. "I can't believe you'd even want to know. The whole thing is rather sordid," he said dampeningly.

Gabrielle was undaunted. She leaned toward him, tilting her chin so her lips were invitingly close. "You should know me better than that, Zach. Of course I'm curious. How much?"

His gaze was riveted to her mouth. "You'd only puff up with pride if I told you, so I'm not going to tell you." She saw his jaw tighten as he determinedly looked away. He'd resisted temptation and, as well, had dropped the subject of her price. She admired and loathed his willpower. He angled a finger outside, all business now. "We're going to scoot along this ledge till we get next to that other building. It doesn't have a ledge we can balance on, but there's a window close enough to climb into. I just pray it's not secured somehow from the other side. I expect, however, that the residents don't worry overly much about burglars breaking in from two stories up. Then once we're in, I hope there are no dogs to attack us, or a bloke with a gun bent on defending his home. The element of surprise is on our side. I can't see any light inside, so possibly they're not even at home. But if they are, we'll dash through before they know what's happening. John is waiting near the entrance of the building, and Malcolm is with the carriage a few streets away."

Gabrielle paid close attention while Zach explained things, and now she looked once again at the ledge, which was perhaps a foot wide. She'd seen much narrower ledges, so she supposed she ought to be grateful for the generous size of this one, but still... She swallowed nervously. "I understand, but I must tell you, I'm awfully frightened. Are you sure this is the best way to go?"

"Mother Henn's hirelings are armed. The house is full of people. We'd never get out without a confrontation, and that's too risky." Zach gave her hand a squeeze. "Being frightened is nothing to be ashamed of. It only shows a proper amount of respect for danger. If you weren't frightened, I'd think you were an idiot. Besides, I'll go before you. You just must do exactly as I do—"

"Unless you fall." Gabrielle smiled nervously.

Zach gave her a rueful grin, acknowledging his appreciation of her humor under such unnerving circumstances. "Yes, unless I fall."

Her smile fell away. She felt a sharp pang of fear. "But you won't, will you? You aren't still dizzy from that topknot I gave you, are you?"

"Of course not. What about you? The laudanum hasn't made you feel tipsy, has it?"

"No, I'm quite sober. The cold air is bracing."

"Good. Don't worry. There's plenty of room on this ledge. You've crossed the creek at Brookmoor on logs half this width. You must just lean back against the building."

Suddenly the discussion was over. There was nothing left to talk about, no more instructions and reassurances; it was time to move. Zach lifted a leg and hiked it through the open window, setting a foot down carefully on the ledge. He tested the strength of the ledge by bouncing on the heel of his boot several times, then pulled his other leg through, ducked his head, and stood up. Gabrielle held her breath as she watched him turn and face away from the building.

He looked down at her, a triumphant, slightly twitchy smile spread over his handsome face. "Simple as pie. Come along, sweeting. Take my hand."

"You know I make terrible pie, Zach," Gabrielle demurred, but she did as she was bid. After all, what was the alternative? She'd rather risk life and limb than remain a living, breathing victim of Mrs. Henn's. Exactly imitating Zach's movements, soon Gabrielle was standing beside him on the ledge.

It was a curious sensation, standing spread-legged and with her arms stretched against the cold stone of the building, the icy winter air stinging her cheeks. She was high above the street— one quick dizzying look down confirmed that—and yet not so high that the stars should by contrast seem so much closer. She gazed past the crown of her bonnet at the sky, past the wind-driven curls of smoke that emanated from the hundreds of chimneys. The stars *did* look closer. Though the stimulant pumping through her veins was three parts fear, Gabrielle felt buoyed and exhilarated from seemingly rubbing elbows with the constellations. For a brief, crazed moment, she almost felt as though if she leapt off the building, she'd fly.

"Don't look down, Gabby, nor up for that matter. Look at me, and as I take a step, you take a step. Do you understand?"

Gabrielle shook her head, clearing away the glittering pixy dust of imagination that sometimes cluttered her brain, then turned to Zach. They still held hands, and, since she was too agitated to speak, she squeezed his fingers to relay her understanding. Zach nodded, gave her another smile to encourage her, then led the way.

Step by slow, excruciating step, they made their way along the ledge. They were required to pass one window of the apartments belonging to Mother Henn. The room appeared unlit, but that didn't necessarily mean it was empty. Gabrielle imagined that Mother Henn liked keeping all her rooms as full and busy as possible. She held her breath as they went by, releasing it only when they were both past the window. Now they were within easy distance of the neighboring building.

"I've got to let go of your hand, Gabby," Zach whispered. "I have to open the window."

Even from such a precarious perch, holding on to Zach made Gabrielle feel safe. It was one of the hardest things she'd ever done, but she made herself loosen her grip, slide her fingers free, and press her hand against the building.

It was too shadowy where they stood to be sure of it, but Gabrielle thought Zach gave her a reassuring smile. She felt it like an energy that vibrated between them. "That's right. Keep leaning back. It'll take me just a minute." Then Zach very slowly squatted down, balancing on the balls of his feet, his inside shoulder pressed to the building, his outside hand braced against the edge of the ledge.

There were about eighteen inches between the buildings, and the window they hoped to enter through was a step down from the ledge, so Zach had to lean down to grab hold of the sash and pull it up. Naturally there was no handle on the outside, so he must exert pressure on the frame itself. And he would have to do it as quietly as possible, just in case there was someone inside the darkened room.

Gabrielle noticed that the curtains hanging in the window were tattered and threadbare, barely covering the glass. She wondered if the Tuttles lived in a similarly impoverished apartment. She shivered, thinking about how cold she was and how cold Will and his family must be continuously if they didn't have the wherewithal to buy fuel for their fires.

There was a sharp splintering sound—cold, damp wood grudgingly separating. He'd opened the window. Now he kept very still, probably listening for noise from inside. Apparently relieved that the first crack of the window had not prompted a guard dog or a brawny head of the household to investigate, Zach slowly pushed up the sash till it was high enough to allow them entry.

Zach turned and looked at Gabrielle. "I'll go first. Don't move till I tell you to. Understand?"

Gabrielle nodded. Her exhilaration had been ebbing away with the increasingly numb state of her fingers and toes. She was freezing. Her teeth were chattering, the convulsive reaction made all the more violent by the state of her nerves.

Zach climbed in, lithely stepping over the abyss between the buildings and easily fitting himself through the window opening. Though most incongruent to the tensely dangerous situation, Gabrielle couldn't seem to help herself from admiring Zach's narrow hips and long, slim legs as he so adeptly accomplished what would have been a chore for someone less athletic. Like herself, for example.

She lost sight of him for a moment, then his face reappeared. Light from an overhead window filtered over him like a pale, pearlescent veil, making him look almost ghostly. He smiled, dispelling the gloomy aspect, and extended his arms. "We're in luck, Gabby. The room's empty. Now listen carefully, and do exactly as I say. Keeping your back against the wall, slowly, ever so slowly, bend your knees and lower yourself till your bottom is touching the ledge. Then sit down."

She looked down at the dark crack between the buildings, the black chasm that separated her from Zach's waiting arms.

"Don't look down, sweeting. Look at me. And don't worry,

I'll catch you if you start to fall." He gave her a teasing grin. "Though I'd rather not be put to the trouble. Might wrench my back, you know."

Zach's easy manner and tone of voice were soothing. Gabrielle looked at him, and he held her gaze with the intensity of his own. He may be trying to break the tension by teasing her, but she knew he was dead earnest about making sure she made it across to safety. She did what he'd instructed her to do, but as she bent her knees she thought they seemed remarkably weak. She prayed they wouldn't buckle under her and send her teetering off the side of the building.

"That's my girl," Zach crooned. "Perfect, Gabby, perfect."

Sitting at last, Gabrielle hissed a relieved breath through her chattering teeth.

"Now put your feet on the window sill—There, that's right! Lean over and put your hands on my forearms, while I catch hold of your waist. Then as you lift off from the ledge, I'll heft you through the window on the count of three. Ready?"

Positioned in the manner in which Zach had instructed her, with her legs stretched across the gap between the buildings and her hands clutching Zach's forearms, Gabrielle once again nodded her head. His strong hands encircling her waist would give her whatever courage was required to propel herself off the ledge and into his arms.

She heard him count off the numbers, then felt herself practically airborne for an instant. She wasn't aware of it at the time, but she'd had her eyes closed throughout the entire maneuver. When she opened them, she was standing in a dark chamber, with Zach's arms wrapped around her and her face pressed against his chest. Naturally she could see nothing beyond his lapel. But she didn't care. She was still cold, but her teeth weren't chattering anymore. She was safe. She was with Zach. And he was holding her as though he didn't intend to release her in the foreseeable future.

"Thank God, Gabby." Suddenly, disappointingly, he clasped her shoulders and put her at arms' length. "Let's get out of here before the owner comes back." Then he took her by the hand and pulled her along toward the door. At least, she assumed that was where they were headed. Frankly she was having difficulty seeing anything in the dark room. She received definite impressions, however, from her other senses. Like so many places she'd been that day, the apartment was stale and malodorous. It was cold, too, there being very little difference inside from the temperature outside. The ever-present noise of tenement life that surrounded them vibrated from the walls, the floors, and the ceiling.

They had gained the door, but it was locked. Zach moved his hand over the adjacent wall, looking for a key hanging there, she supposed. By his grunt of satisfaction, she deduced that he'd found one. The key grated in the lock, and the knob turned. Zach threw the key on the floor, opened the door and went out, tugging Gabrielle behind him as she tried to keep pace with his long-legged strides.

A surge of relieved joy swelled in Gabrielle as she blinked against the relative brightness of the gallery. They'd done it. They were free! But her mood of happiness was precipitant. Before they'd had a chance to close the door behind them, a voice called out, "Hey, you there! What d' ye think ye're doin' comin' out me chum's place?"

Gabrielle looked up and into the scowling countenance of a huge bearded man with arms the size of ale barrels.

CHAPTER TEN

Zach wasn't the least surprised to discover that the challenges of the evening weren't over. After all, he was in the company of Gabby, wasn't he? The bruise on his eye had faded a few days before, so he supposed that the gods had convened in their celestial conference chamber and decreed that it was Zach's fate to reacquire a little color. What would it be this time? he wondered. A broken nose in shades of delicate fuchsia, a tomato-red swollen lip, or perhaps another black eye?

"I'm talkin' ye, ye arsehole."

Zach scuttled Gabby behind him and faced the man with as much sangfroid as he could muster. "That's not a very pleasant name to call your chum's cousin."

The man looked taken aback for a moment, then recovered, saying churlishly, "I ain't no chawbacon, guv'nor. I reckon Pete's no relation to a nob like you."

Zach cleared his throat and smiled engagingly. "I'll take that as a compliment, though I don't expect Peter would appreciate you doubting his genealogy."

The man's brow furrowed in deep multiple lines, like the loose-skinned head of a basset hound. "*Peter,* eh?" The man held a basket of groceries under one furry arm, and with his free hand he pulled thoughtfully on his bewhiskered jaw, carefully studying Zach from head to toe. "Cousins, ye say?" He peered over Zach's shoulder at Gabby. "And what about the chit?"

"My sister," Zach lied smoothly.

The man continued to frown. "What be the two of ye called?"

To Zach's utmost irritation, Gabby sidled around him and smiled demurely at the ruffian. "I'm Anastasia, and my brother is Demetri. We're from Cumbria. And, if I might be so bold as to inquire, sir, what are you called?" She batted her lashes. Gawd, what was the little nodcock about? Did she think she could charm the venom out of this snake with a few coy flutterings of her lashes and an exchange of names? And where the devil had she got those sissified names? Straight out of a Radcliffe novel, he'd wager!

The man's brow did clear a little, however, and his next question was put forth in a much less surly tone, and directed to Gabby. "So where's Pete?"

"Did I catch your name, sir?" Zach asked him, employing Gabby's tactics of cajolery despite his criticism of them.

"Lem," he muttered grudgingly. Zach noticed that the man had spoken much more agreeably to Gabby. Perhaps there was something to batting one's lashes, though he doubted that Lem would be similarly charmed if Zach did it. "Now what about Pete?"

"I… we … don't really know where he is, er … Lem. We were supposed to meet him here a half hour ago." Zach started sidestepping, hoping to work their way cautiously toward the stairs. "Since he's obviously been held up, we thought we'd find a pub and buy old Pete a nice splash of whiskey to bring home."

Suddenly Lem's face darkened, the blood boiling up under his skin like molten lava. "Pete dinna drink whiskey. He's pure fer gin, and anyone what know's 'im, know's that fer a fact! You ain't his cousin. I expect ye're one of those gentlemen thieves, is what I think!" He gouged the air, pointing a thick finger toward Gabby. "And she's yer distractin' wench! Hand over whatever ye took from Pete's place, or I'll turn ye upside down and shake ye till yer teeth rattle and yer pockets are empty! The chit, too!"

Zach had been averse to making a sudden move. Large men were frequently much quicker with their "bunches of five" than people suspected. And he'd Gabby to think of, too. But it appeared that time had run out for thinking. Pete's chum had set his basket of food on the floor and was pulling back his fist to deliver Zach a stunning blow to one of those facial features he had moments earlier been imagining in different colors.

"Duck, Gabby!" Zach shouted, just before he made the necessary dip himself. Lem's arm whistled through the air just above Zach's head as he took his swing. Zach slipped past Lem, pulling Gabby along with him. And they ran. They ran down the stairs as if the very hounds of hell were nipping at their heels.

Comparing the loyal Lem to a hound again seemed appropriate, because the large, furry fellow appeared to enjoy the chase as much as any baying canine might. Lem even growled and snarled as he thudded heavily behind them, and such animalistic noises issuing forth from the hairy—albeit two-legged—species pursuing them so purposefully was not conducive to Zach's peace of mind.

They had gained the door leading to the outside. Zach burst through and skidded to a stop at the front of the building, causing Gabby to bump into him by the sheer momentum of their flight and the abrupt stop. There were a few people in the small cobbled square, and Zach scanned the shadowed faces for John. He did not know where Malcolm had finally parked the carriage, and without John to guide them, they'd never find it. But with Lem hot on their tail, Zach had no leisure to stay put in one spot till John noticed them. Behind them, Lem was just coming through the door, and Zach was trying to decide which direction to go. Then he saw John. He was standing just across the way with his mouth gaping open and his eyes agog.

Zach supposed John must be excused for his inability to move. It must be a shock to see Gabby and to deduce by slow and painful mental rumination that she was the abducted girl Mr. Blake had sent him to rescue from a nunnery. But there was no time for the indulgence of incredulity. "John!" he called, pulling a wide-eyed Gabby out of the way of the lunging Lem just in time.

John was finally made to realize how dire the situation was, and nudged into movement. "This way, sir!" he called, swooping a skinny arm through the air to show their direction. Then he took off running down one of the many narrow wynds that were offshoots of the little courtlike square they presently stood in, and Zach and Gabby followed.

Weaving through the people traversing the passageways was an intricate business and took a bit of agility. Zach was glad John was guiding them through to the carriage instead of Malcolm, because John's thin frame was much more conducive to the maneuvers required, such as dodging the occasional unsuspecting pedestrian.

John had an odd way of running, with his arms bent tight at the elbows, tucked close to his sides, and lifted chesthigh. His long fingers were curled into fists, his knees bobbed up and down in straight vertical thrusts, and he pivoted his scrawny neck around at intervals to make sure Zach and Gabby were still close behind. John had never had much upper-body strength, but judging by the evidence presented this day, Zach had to conclude—with much admiration—that John was a first-rate runner. So first-rate that Zach had a little difficulty keeping up with him, especially since Gabby slowed him down. He could hear Gabby's labored breathing, but he couldn't stop and allow them both to catch their wind, because he could still hear Lem in heated pursuit.

For such a big man, Lem had remarkable staying power. Zach was beginning to wonder if they'd be driving down the hill to New Town with Lem's considerable bulk attached to the carriage in some way—perhaps dragging from the back, Lem's fingers curled tightly around the wheel axles.

Suddenly Zach heard a large thud behind them and painful grunts, like air being expelled from lungs by an outside force. Zach craned his neck and saw Lem sprawled on the ground with some poor sucker in a heap just opposite, obviously having been ploughed down by the lumbering Lem. Zach pitied the fellow who had unwittingly ambled into Lem's path, but at least now they needn't worry about him attaching himself to the carriage, and they could slow down.

"John!" After catching his attention, Zach indicated to his sprinting servant that speed was no longer vital to their escape, and then he pulled Gabby to his side and put his arm around her waist, supporting her as they quickly walked the remaining distance to the carriage.

Gabrielle huddled in the carriage under a lap rug and two thick woolen blankets, waiting while Zach gave Malcolm and John brief instructions for compliance with their made up story about what had happened that day. They would support Zach's farradiddle, she was sure of it. Zach treated his servants so well that they would do anything to repay his many kindnesses.

Gabrielle felt dazed. In the past few minutes since they'd escaped from Mother Henn's brothel, she hadn't had time to do much of anything besides catch her breath and keep up with Zach without falling. She found it remarkable that she'd managed to do both, though her legs ached and her lungs and throat felt raw and burning from the icy air she'd been sucking in at such a rate.

Presently Zach got in the carriage, and Gabrielle lifted the ends of the blankets so he could scoot beneath them and share their warmth with her. He hesitated a moment, then accepted the mute invitation, settling himself close to Gabrielle and pulling her against his side. Gabrielle smiled to herself and happily nestled under his arm, resting her head on his chest.

"Does this mean you're not angry with me?" She loved the sound of his heart so close to her ear, the feel of its rhythm against her cheek.

He sighed, the chill air making his breath fog. "How can you dare ask me that? Of course I'm angry with you. You might have been killed."

She toyed with the buttons of his vest. "But you forgive me?" His heart was beating faster.

"I'll take that under consideration."

"What must I do?" She poked a finger through the front closure of the vest, feeling the cool muslin of his shirt underneath, remembering the warm skin under the muslin.

He covered her hand with his, holding the curious fingers in a firm grip that made movement impossible. "You must stay out of trouble, to begin with." She suspected his warning had a double meaning. "And you must tell the Murrays about your false engagement."

She pulled her hand free and rested it in her lap. Her

cheek remained where it was, against his chest where she could continue to enjoy listening to the rapid beat of his heart. "You're not going to tell them?"

"No, I shall leave that to you."

"Will you also leave it to me to decide on the proper time and place to do it?"

There was a pause. "Are you stalling, Gabby? What's the point in prolonging this travesty?"

Gabrielle did not reply at once. She was afraid that if Zach thought things resolved in Edinburgh, he might leave. Unless, of course, that woman in Old Town had some sort of hold on him. But she knew Zach was jealous of Rory, and she was reluctant to relinquish her last trump.

"You have said you're not the marriageable sort, Zach, though I have told you straight out that I'm in love with you."

"I explained that, Gabby," he began, trying to express his reasoning. "I don't think you love me in the manner—"

"Let's not argue, Zach," Gabrielle interrupted him in a soothing voice. She casually laid her hand on Zach's knee. His heart immediately beat faster. "I think Rory's in love with me, and perhaps, since you don't want me, I should reconsider and take Rory's proposal seriously."

Zach stiffened, perhaps as much in response to the hand on his knee as to Gabrielle's words. "I thought Rory understood that the betrothal was just a farce."

"That has always been the understanding, but I... er ... suspect that he would like to make it a genuine promise to marry. Perhaps until I make up my mind I hadn't ought to cause a to-do by confessing everything to the Murrays. If Rory and I decide to wed after all, no one will be the wiser, and therefore no one will be upset." Gabrielle traced circles on the taut fabric covering Zach's knee.

Again he caught her hand and held it firm. Sounding more than a little exasperated, he said, "I thought you said Rory wasn't your type."

"No, *you* said that. Besides, Zach, if I can't have the man I love, I may as well have another man. Someone attractive and fun."

"He's a womanizer!"

"As long as he comes home to me, I don't care how many women he ogles and flirts with."

"Then you assuredly don't love him!"

"I never said I did. You know who I love. But I want children, Zach. Lots and lots of children. And, as you know, there's only one way to get them."

His heart was thudding furiously. She knew she was twisting the knife, but she didn't know any other way to communicate to Zach the absurdity and tragedy of marriage to someone other than the love of her life. She wanted children, all right, but not with Rory or anyone else but Zach. Little towheaded boys with amber eyes...

"It's getting stuffy in here," he said at last in a grim, constrained voice. He threw off the covers, gently pushed Gabrielle away and moved to the opposite end of the seat they shared, cracked open the window just a tad, and drew deep breaths.

She let him be. They were both tired and they still had an ordeal to face once they reached Charlotte Square. Tomorrow was another day.

The Murrays had been understandably worried by Gabrielle's and Zach's protracted absence, Regina and Rory included, but Aunt Clarissa, stripped by worry of her usual complacence, was fit to be tied. As soon as Gabrielle and Zach reached the house and played out their broken wheel scenario, displaying the proper amount of astonishment and indignation over their messenger's failure to deliver the note, Aunt Clarissa descended on Gabrielle like a ruffled, clucking hen—shooing her upstairs to her room and ordering a hot bath and a throat elixir, certain that Gabrielle's cold walk to the inn at Duddingston had given her an inflammation of the vocal cords. Gabrielle's voice was a bit raspy, and she was certainly in need of a bone-warming, soothing bath, so she allowed her aunt to fuss over her and finally to tuck her into bed.

Interaction with the rest of the family had been minimal, but Gabrielle was glad of the reprieve. No doubt, poor Zach was still downstairs, deeply immersed in the distasteful task of lying, guiltily accepting the Murrays' kind thanks for taking care of their charge, and wincing at the knowledge that they completely believed every word he'd uttered. At that very moment, he was probably trying to ease out of the room and up to his bedchamber where he could be miserable by himself.

As Gabrielle drifted off to an exhausted sleep, she had a sad, wistful feeling that maybe Zach would be better off if she simply left him alone and married someone else. And why not Rory? She knew he liked her and was physically attracted to her. As she'd told Zach, Rory had hinted that if he had the urge to marry, she'd be his first consideration. After all, if you couldn't have the man you loved ...

Gabrielle had slept late, but when she paused at the arched entrance to the breakfast parlor and looked in, everyone was still there, except Zach. Despite her disappointment, Gabrielle couldn't help but be cheered by the bright winter snowscape as seen through the large bow window just opposite the dining table. Streams of sunshine fell on the crisp white tablecloth set with gleaming blue and white china. A vase of hothouse salmon-colored cabbage roses stood in the center. The smell of bacon and kippers and fragrant freshly brewed coffee drifted from the sideboard. Since she hadn't eaten much the day before, she was hungry.

As she entered the room, the conversation stopped, and everyone looked at her. She was feeling guilty this morning for making them worry, and she was ever so grateful when all of them smiled at her and caroled, "Good morning."

As Rory pulled out a chair for Gabrielle to be seated, she turned to Sir George, smiling. "I'm surprised to discover all of you still sitting about the table. I slept later than usual this morning."

Sir George smiled back, nodding his head. "That's understandable, lass. You had a tiring time of it yesterday."

"Sir George and I wanted to make sure you were feeling quite the thing before we went about our scheduled activities," Lady Grace said in her smooth, modulated voice. "And I believe Regina and Rory have an excursion in mind about which they wish to speak to you."

Gabrielle feigned interest with another polite smile, then casually inquired, "But where's Zach? Isn't he to be included in this excursion?" A servant poured Gabrielle a steaming cup of coffee, which she immediately doctored with a large dollop of cream and three shavings of sugar.

"Zach's gone off already," Rory told her with a significant look. "Business, as usual."

"I dare say I haven't the slightest idea what business Zachary has in Edinburgh," commented Aunt Clarissa, peering myopically through her spectacles down the length of the table.

"Women aren't required to understand the range and intricacies of a man's business, madam," Sir George informed her in a kindly patronizing tone. "So I would not trouble myself, if I were you. No need to cudgel your brain about it."

"Thank you, Sir George, for the advice," returned Aunt Clarissa meekly, not in the least offended. "And I will be about *my* business now and insist that Gabrielle eat something before another word is said! No one can be expected to hold a conversation on an empty stomach." When Gabrielle started to rise to fill her plate from the sideboard, Clarissa popped up from her seat, exclaiming, "I'll do it!

You sit." So Gabrielle sat and thought about Zach, wondering if he was with the blond woman again.

"Eat, Gabrielle!" Regina's voice interrupted Gabrielle's thoughts and drew her attention to the plate of savory-smelling food Aunt Clarissa had set before her. "If your aunt won't let us talk to you till you've got something in your stomach, you'd better hurry up, because Rory and I are bursting." Rory and Regina were sitting next to each other, and she was looking fresh-faced and chirpy this morning. She slid a bright look at

Rory, which he returned, along with a wide grin.

"You don't have to urge me," Gabrielle said, chuckling. "I'm starved! But do talk while I eat. I don't think Aunt Clarissa will object to that! Besides, I'm dying to know all about this proposed excursion."

Gabrielle had to force animation into her voice and a few bites of food down her throat. Despite what she'd said, suddenly she was no longer hungry. Contemplating Zach's visit to Old Town had diminished her appetite.

Rory folded his arms on the table and leaned forward. "Reggie and I were waltzing about the drawing room last night, whiling away the time till word came of you, when it occurred to us that dancing without music is rather like skating."

"And neither of us have gone skating for an age," continued Regina enthusiastically. "What about you, Gabrielle?"

"In Cornwall we don't skate much," admitted Gabrielle. "It rains much more than it snows. And there are more streams and rivers than lakes. There's really no place to skate, unless some farmer's duck pond freezes up."

Rory's eyes widened questioningly. "Have you *ever* skated, Gabrielle?"

Gabrielle pushed her bits of poached egg around the plate, hoping by strategic placement of her food to make it appear as though she'd eaten more than she had. They wanted her to go skating, and ordinarily she would jump at the idea. She liked new experiences, new challenges. And it was a beautiful day, perfect for doing something outside. So why didn't the skating excursion appeal to her?

Last night, worn out from her adventures and discouraged by Zach's persistence in pushing her away, she had thought the unthinkable. She had imagined herself actually marrying someone other than Zach. In the clear light of day, rested and rational, however, she knew she'd rather die a spinster than marry anyone else. And she didn't anticipate much pleasure in an outing that did not include him.

During the last couple of weeks since he'd arrived, even if she wasn't talking to him or dancing with him, Zach's mere presence in a room had given each social event an edge, a pleasant tension that made her happier, brighter, wittier, because there was always the sweet possibility of a talk with him or a dance coming up. She even derived considerable pleasure from just looking at him as he talked and danced with others! What a sad case she'd become, indeed!

"If you're nervous, I'll help you till you're sure on your blades, Gabrielle." Rory arched one of his wicked brows. "I've helped many an inexperienced lass 'round the pond."

"I don't doubt it," Gabrielle replied, throwing him a rueful grin as she pushed her plate away.

"Mayhap Gabrielle is not up to skating," Aunt Clarissa suggested worriedly. "She was chilled to the bone last night."

"You know I have the constitution of a workhorse, Auntie," Gabrielle refuted her mildly, deciding to do something—anything—to divert her mind from Zach. "I'm fine. And I'd love to go."

Regina clapped her hands and leaned into Rory's shoulder, smiling delightedly at him.

Aunt Clarissa's mouth formed a button of disapproval. "You didn't eat enough this morning to keep a bird alive, Gabrielle. How do you expect to have the energy to skate, pray tell me?"

Gabrielle chuckled indulgently. "Goodness, Aunt Clarissa, you're becoming such a fusspot!"

Clarissa waggled her fingers. "Just doing my duty by you, my dear, that's all. I'll go to the kitchen and order us a nuncheon to take along. I don't want you swooning on the ice." Aunt Clarissa got up and moved with alacrity to the door leading through the pantry and down to the kitchen.

Sir George got up, too, pulling out his lady's chair. "Since everything is settled amongst you young people, Lady Grace and I will leave you. We're promised to the Willbys for luncheon and an afternoon of whist and piquet."

Lady Grace dropped her napkin on the table and stood as well. "Dress warmly, dears—particularly you, Regina. You know how the cold wind makes you cough. And do return in time to rest before dinner. We're engaged for a musical evening at the Garrisons tonight, and you don't want to be droopish during the performances, do you? Good-bye."

They bid the Murrays good-bye, and as soon as they were conceivably out of earshot, Rory leaned across the table toward Gabrielle, demanding, "Well? Tell us! We're perishing to know! What *really* happened last night?"

Gabrielle laughed self-consciously, averting her eyes, fingering her napkin. "What makes you so sure we didn't actually have a broken wheel?"

"Because we know you, Gabrielle," said Regina. "And we know how frustratingly distant Zach's been lately. He didn't ask you to go for a drive, did he? You followed Zach to Old Town."

"Yes, I did," she admitted.

"And what did you discover?" prompted Rory, watching Gabrielle keenly "What sort of business does Zach have in Old Town?"

Gabrielle sighed. "I saw him with a woman."

Rory slammed his open palm on the table, making the china rattle. "I knew it! Sorry, Gabrielle, but I just knew there was a woman involved!"

Gabrielle felt a decided twinge of irritation. "What do you mean?"

"Well, you don't suppose he's been celibate all these years, do you?"

Gabrielle took great pains in arranging her napkin in precise folds, her face warning. "No, I never supposed he was. But 1 did think that he could ... get by for the short time he'll be in Edinburgh without having to ..."

Rory shrugged his broad shoulders. "A man does what a man's got to do."

Regina clipped Rory's shoulder. "Oh, hush! Can't you see how you're making her feel?"

"Actually," said Gabrielle, giving them a sheepish look, "if I knew for sure she was his mistress, I'd feel much better."

Regina's eyes widened. "You don't mean...?"

"Yes, there's a possibility that she could be a respectable

female."

Rory sat back in his chair. "Gabrielle, you'd better explain."

Gabrielle took a deep breath and briefly described her experiences of the day before, leaving out the parts about Zach's panic attack and their intimacies in Mother Henn's bedchamber.

"Lord!" exclaimed Rory at the end of her recital. "A bawdy house? You really are a handful, ain't you, lass? And you came right out and told Zach you loved him, and he still insists it's nothing but a childish infatuation? There's more than meets the eye here, Gabrielle."

"That I'm sure of."

"Did you really tell him that our betrothal was a sham? I'd hate to think our lark is over already! My grandmother will be breathing down my neck again, demanding that I produce an heir before she sticks her spoon in the wall! Blether, I begin to think it would be worth it to marry just to get Grandmother to leave me be!"

"Nevertheless, Rory, I believe telling Zach the truth was probably a very wise thing to do," said Regina with a decided nod.

Rory shook his head. "I'm not so sure."

"Neither am I, Rory," said Gabrielle, glad to know he felt the same way about it as she did. "Making Zach feel a little insecure can't hurt. That's why I told him last night that while you and I had entered into the betrothal with the idea of making him jealous, you actually had expressed a bona fide romantic interest in me."

Regina sat up straight, her head turning side to side as she looked at both of them. "What? Is... is this true?" she said faintly.

"Well, actually, Rory's never—"

Rory reached across the table and snatched Gabrielle's hand. "I did say you'd be at the top of my list if I got the notion to tie the nuptial knot, Gabrielle. And, of late, I've had the notion." He chuckled self-consciously. "Can't say why, really. Maybe it's all this talk of marriage. Maybe acting like a besotted mooncalf all day has given me a taste for the real thing."

Gabrielle gently pulled free her hand, then patted Rory's as it lay on the table between them. "You know I love Zach, Rory, and if you don't choose to help me any longer, I'll understand."

"I'm having a fine frolic, Gabrielle. And if you don't mind, I don't mind waiting in the wings just in case you realize that I'm the better man of the two. After all, as you know, I'm a first-rate kisser."

Gabrielle laughed and turned toward Regina to share her amusement over Rory's silliness. She was surprised to catch a sober expression on her friend's face as she stared unaccountably at her empty teacup, and with a pinched border of white circling her mouth.

"Regina, dear, what's wrong? You look ill."

Regina started, flicked a glance at Gabrielle, and abruptly stood up. She would have tipped her chair backwards onto the floor if Rory hadn't handily caught it just in time.

"I d-do feel rather ill," she admitted in a reedy little voice and with a twitchy eye. "I-I don't think I shall be going with you."

Rory looked incredulous. "But Reggie, you were fine—"

"It came on s-suddenly." Regina fixed her gaze on the table, looking at neither of them. "Probably just a slight stomach disorder, but it shouldn't do at all if I c-cascaded all over the ice, w-would it?" She gave a thin laugh. "Forgive me, but I really m-must lie down."

Gabrielle stared after her friend, flabbergasted by the sudden turnabout in her health. She frowned. More likely it was Regina's mood that had changed rather than her state of health. Gabrielle had not missed the stuttering or the eye twitching. "Be sure and ring for your abigail, dear," Gabrielle called after her, "and I'll come see you as soon as we return."

Regina threw Gabrielle a weak smile over her shoulder and was gone.

"Well, that's deuced strange," Rory declared in a bewildered voice. "She was mad to go skating!" He frowned at the door through which she'd vanished. "And now it shan't be half as fun!"

CHAPTER ELEVEN

Douglas McKeen had the very devil of a headache. He sat in the Spotted Dog Pub at a battered table shoved in the darkest corner, sipping coffee so black and thick he could practically chew it. But he was used to the bitter, murky beverage, and to the routine. He went through several mugs every morning before he could face the day, before he could face the prospect of flinging slop for a pittance at Craggen's piggery in the village of Duddingston.

Craggen paid Douglas by the hour, since, as he'd explained, he never knew if Douglas would show up, or whether or not he'd be sober when he did show up. And every afternoon when his filthy job was done, Douglas would take his coins and buy whiskey. With the shock of Kate's leaving him, he'd disciplined himself to drinking only after working hours, though this was only accomplished with considerable difficulty and physical discomfort. He'd still start drinking by four o'clock, however, and the rest of the day was pretty much a blur. He remembered only fragments of his nights.

Douglas set down his mug and rubbed his temples with strong strokes of his lean fingers. Kate used to rub his head for him. She used to do a lot of wonderful, wifely things. When he was working as a smithy and bringing in decent wages, he'd come home to a tidy apartment and a bird cooking on the spit, cabbage soup in the kettle, and Kate's winsome smile.

In those days, he wouldn't start drinking till he'd had his dinner and maybe a little pillow-play with Kate. She was always willing, as feisty in bed as she was in everything else. Remembering those happier times, Douglas smiled, even though that minimal stretching of muscles made his head throb even more. When they discovered Kate was breeding, they were both happy and looking forward to an addition to their little family.

But then Douglas got to drinking earlier and earlier in the day, till he was snitching drinks at work. He started making mistakes, and the next thing he knew he was out of a job. Jobs were hard to come by, and Douglas quickly got discouraged. Soon he was drinking every waking hour and selling everything they owned to pay for the liquor. Kate was drinking with him, too, at first by his insistence and later because she craved it as much as he did.

They lost the lease on their humble but decent apartment and were forced to move to a dingy, rodent-infested garret in a worse section of town. Douglas remembered feeling worthless and desperate all the time. One night, when Kate's feisty tongue had been loosened by the whiskey and she'd upbraided him for selling her dead mother's wedding ring, even though he'd flatly refused to sell his grandfather's pocket watch, he'd slapped her hard across the mouth. Shocked and hurt, she'd cried, and he'd cried too, hating himself. They'd kissed and made up. But then it happened again, and again...

Douglas's insides twisted with self-loathing and remorse whenever he thought about his hands on Kate—not loving her as they used to do, but shaking her and pushing her and knocking her against the wall. He never expected to hurt her, and he never meant to do it again. But it always did happen again. He reckoned it was the combination of the whiskey and the rage, and Kate was always there to take the brunt. His wee, bonny Kate. But understanding why he abused her didn't stop him. When he drank the whiskey, the dark, cruel side of him took over.

That was over now, he told himself firmly. Somehow he had to get Kate back, had to convince her that he was a changed man, that he could confine his drinking to the sociable hours. That he loved her and would never, ever hurt her again...

"Hey, Douglas, me man. How are ye?"

Douglas looked up through the blurred vision of bloodshot eyes. The figure of a tall, ragged, broomstick-thin man was oudined against the puny amount of sunshine that seeped through the small, grimy windows. "Donovan." He acknowledged the man's presence with an unenthusiastic nod. Donovan was deep into flimflammery, ready and willing to cheat the trews off even his best chum if he needed a pair. And he was keen on gossip.

Donovan pulled up a chair, straddled it backwards and rested his arms on the top rail. "Did ye hear 'bout what happened at Mother Henn's roost last night, Douglas?"

Douglas rubbed one eye with the heel of his hand. The last thing he wanted to hear about was the brutal despoiling of that wistful-eyed pretty little wench in the green mantle. The princess. This morning he was sure he shouldn't have allowed the lass to suffer just to punish Wickham. Here was another reason to hate himself. He assumed a disinterested pose, shrugging his shoulders. "I heard that she'd another virgin fer sale. 'Tis hardly worth mentionin'."

Donovan grinned. "Aye, ifn that were the whole story."

"I heard she was Quality. But I dinna think that worth mentionin', either."

"From what I'm hearin', she might still be a virgin."

Douglas sat up straighter. "What do ye mean?"

"Jasper told me all about it this mornin'. Mother's in a pelter, 'cause the lass was a fair one, and she dinna get all what she could off the chit."

"The lass went fer a small purse, then?"

"Naw, the first bloke was a well-breeched gent—good-lookin', too, or so says Jasper. He paid two hundred pounds fer the pleasure o' beddin' her."

"As much as that, eh?"

"But ye know Mother Henn keeps her bits o' Quality fluff fer a day or two and makes as much blunt as she can off the chits till the freshness 'as worn off."

Douglas felt disgust churning his already acid-filled stomach. But he was as disgusting as Mother Henn, because under the influence of his alcohol-induced dark side, and out of jealousy and rancor, he'd left the lass to her fate when he knew he could have alerted Wickham and perhaps saved her. But maybe someone else had saved her. That would be a good thing for her, and maybe a good thing for him, too. Maybe he could still use her as barter. He'd not hurt the girl, just keep her prisoner till Wickham gave him back his Kate.

"Ye're beatin' round the bush, Donovan. Why dinna Mother Henn get the chit's worth out o' her?"

"At daybreak, when Jasper went to t' tell the bloke 'twas time t' be shovin' off, the chamber was empty. They'd climbed out the window and escaped by way of the ledge and through a window in the next buildin'."

Douglas raised his brows, impressed. "Blether, that'd be a risky way t' go!"

"But not as risky as through the front door, with Jasper and Bob's barkin' irons at the ready." Donovan leaned closer, his sharp black eyes snapping with eagerness to tell all. "The bed was barely mussed, and there was no blood t' be found. So, 'twasn't a case of the bloke findin' the lass so tight and sweet that he wanted more of 'er. Seems as though he knew her already and had come special t' fetch 'er. Interestin', eh? And a bit discomfortin't' Mother Henn. Jasper says she's been thinkin' that she might not bother with the Quality again. Too much trouble. She's moved out o' her roost, too, and gone into hidin' fer a spell."

Despite the strain it caused on such a shriveled bit of his morning-after brain, Douglas considered the facts Donovan had obligingly supplied him. He rubbed his chin. "Did Jasper say what the bloke looked like, besides that he was'na hard t' look on?"

"Aye, he did," Donovan said, glad to be a further source of information and therefore being paid some rapt attention.

"Tall and yellow-haired, wearin' a wine-red coat, and with cat eyes. Dinna 'specially know what he meant by that, but there it is."

Douglas didn't know either, but he had a strong suspicion that if he met Wickham face to face, he'd know exactly what Jasper meant by cat eyes. So, Wickham had somehow found out about the lass's capture and got her out! An extraordinary accomplishment that filled Douglas with grudging respect... and jealous hatred.

Wickham was everything Douglas wanted to be, everything Kate deserved in a man. Wickham was daunting competition, but Douglas wouldn't cry craven and give up, because Kate belonged to him, and the child she carried was his. He would get her back if it killed him. But with the help of that little princess in the green mantle, Douglas was hoping he'd not have to resort to such drastic measures.

The sky was a pristine, pellucid blue above the snow-powdered silver birch and larch that bordered Duddingston Loch. Bramble thickets encrusted with tiny starlike icicles crimped the shoreline. The tree branches were full of noisy rooks, cawing abuses at the encroaching humans gliding over the glassy surface of the loch, and building fires to toast their hands and roast buttered apple wedges and bits of ham for nuncheon.

There were lots of children on the ice, too, some of them obviously poor, dressed in ragged clothes inadequate to ward off the penetrating cold and the icy wind from the firth. After watching a small group of them for a while, Gabrielle realized that they were taking turns with a single pair of skates, the others warming themselves by a fire while they waited and watched. She decided then and there that when she and Rory were done skating she'd leave her skates—just purchased that morning— with the group, thereby doubling their time on the ice.

These children also reminded her of her resolve to make a visit to the Tuttles. Especially after learning that Will was losing his hearing, probably because of an untreated illness, she was doubly determined to do something to help the impoverished family. Besides that, Gabrielle wanted to thank Will for having done her a monumental service in alerting Mr. Blake to her incarceration in Mother Henn's brothel.

Now that she knew their general neighborhood, it shouldn't be that difficult to locate the Tuttles' home. The trouble was, their neighborhood was the same as Mother Henn's, unless the horrid woman, out of fear of reprisal for her abduction of Gabrielle, had already moved on to another location.

Gabrielle was still hoping she could get Zach to help her with the Tuttles, because she was afraid to go alone. So far today she hadn't even had an opportunity to speak to Zach, however, and, fearing that Will's hearing would be permanently damaged, she didn't want to wait too long to give the Tuttles the money they'd need to consult a physician. She sighed. Somehow she must find a way to get to Old Town no later than tomorrow, with or without Zach's help.

A curlew swooped overhead, its mournful cry drawing Gabrielle's attention. She looked up again at the blue sky and around at the snow-covered, iron-hard fields, crisscrossed with small dry stone dikes. Even in the harshness of winter, Scotland was breathtaking to behold. Whenever confronted with natural beauty of such magnitude, Gabrielle's heart stirred with appreciation. But her heart ached a little, too. She wanted to share her delight with Zach.

"Here, Gabrielle, sit down and I'll strap on your skates for you." While Gabrielle had been standing amongst the small rocks and scree scattered at the shore of the loch, Rory had dusted the snow off a tree stump and placed a thick piece of huckaback on it for her to sit on so she'd be well protected from the damp. The stump was very close to where the carriage stood, and Gabrielle could see that Aunt Clarissa had not as yet alighted.

She walked back, calling, "Aunt Clarissa, aren't you getting out?"

Aunt Clarissa tried to make herself heard through the glass, but when it became apparent that Gabrielle wasn't catching a word, she opened the door. "I'm staying inside till the servants light a fire. I've a warm brick 'neath my feet and am quite cozy and warm." She smiled and closed the window, pulling the carriage blankets up to her chin. Gabrielle did not doubt that her aunt would be asleep within minutes. She walked over to the stump, her sturdy Wellingtons crunching in the snow.

"Well, so much for your chaperon," said Rory with a

chuckle, extending a hand to help Gabrielle to her seat.

"Perhaps she doesn't imagine that you'll try to compromise me on the ice."

"Then she doesn't have much imagination," Rory retorted with a gleam in his eye. "And she must not have noticed how fetching you look today, lass."

Gabrielle smiled faintly at Rory's compliment and uttered a polite "thank you." She was grateful to Rory for trying, but she didn't think flummery was going to lift her spirits today. She'd hoped that by dressing in the mantle her mother had sent her for Christmas she'd somehow feel special and less depressed. But even the lively peacock blues, jade greens, and wine reds of her "Ali Baba" mantle, and the smart ostrich plume in her bonnet—dyed all three colors to match her mantle—could make up for Zach's absence. And if she wasn't mistaken, she believed that Rory's spirits were lagging a little, too.

It wasn't that he didn't look quite smashing, because he did. She'd no doubt he'd attract his usual share of attention once they were seen on the ice. His redingote was a deep brown with sleeved capes trimmed with black astrakhan, which, as he'd explained to her, was a blend of Persian lamb's wool. He wore a black velvet cravat, a Neapolitan top hat, and black kid gloves. For once he'd compromised his preference for kilts by wearing a pair of practical, though fashionable, checked trousers.

"You're quite fetching yourself today, Rory," she told him.

He had kneeled on one knee to strap on her skates, another square of huckaback folded several times and used to shield his trousers from the snow. Having secured one skate, he looked up from his task and smiled at her, his fingers still wrapped most unnecessarily around her ankle. "I say we forget all about Zach, and you and I get married, Gabrielle. We make a handsome pair."

She dimpled, squirming her ankle out of Rory's grip. "You're an incorrigible flirt, Rory Cameron!"

Suddenly he sobered and concentrated on her other skate. "Once I'm married, Gabrielle, I don't intend to keep up the flirting, you know."

Gabrielle looked down at his crisp brown curls, laughing

uncertainly. "My, you're being very serious!"

"Yes."

Gabrielle grew serious, too. "You do seem much more receptive to the idea of marriage lately, Rory. Why do you suppose——?"

Her skates strapped on, he looked up, his eyes as blue as the sky, sincerity shining through like rays of sunshine. "I can't say for sure. I can only suppose it's because of you."

Flustered, Gabrielle stood up. "Well, I'm not so sure of that. We ought to forget about marriage today, however, and think of nothing else but the beauty of this afternoon and the jolly fun we're going to have skating!" This was all said with a great deal of enthusiasm, and then her ankles buckled, her knees bent, and she fell hard on her bottom.

"Blether, Gabrielle," shouted Rory, laughing. "Can't you even wait till you're on the ice?"

Zach watched from his carriage window. When he had spied Gabby and Rory by the shore, Zach had signaled to Malcolm to interrupt their leisurely perambulations around the loch and stop the carriage just across the way, hidden partially from view by a clump of high rhododendron bushes. From this inconspicuous position he could observe Gabby and Rory while they weren't aware they were being observed. Perhaps by doing so, he could make a valid judgment about their relationship.

Gabby had confused him considerably on that score. All along, Zach thought he was only interested in Gabby's happiness. But now he didn't know what he wanted for her.

The only thing he knew for sure was that he wanted her for himself, and if he were a truly good man, he'd squelch that idea under his boot like an obnoxious little bug.

"Why are we stopping, Wickham?"

A comfortable silence had settled between Kate and Zach during the course of their drive, and she'd almost dozed. Now she was wide awake. He turned and gave her a quick smile. "I thought you might enjoy just sitting here for a few moments, taking in the view."

He immediately returned his gaze to the spot where Rory and Gabby were, just in time to see her fall on her bottom. He gave a little snort of amusement.

Kate stirred in her seat, sticking her face close to the glass. "What are ye snortin' 'bout, Wickham?"

"Nothing, really. Someone just fell down, that's all."

Kate settled back in her seat. "Well, that's kind of mean of ye, dinna ye think?"

"No harm was done." Gabby and Rory were on the ice now. He had one of his large paws wrapped around her small waist. She was quite wobbly. They were both laughing very hard.

"Now ye're frownin', Wickham. I'm beginnin' to suspicion that it's not trees and water and hills ye're lookin' at, but somethin' female." Kate leaned forward, rearranging her stomach as best she could, and looked where Zach was looking. "'Tis that blond lass there, ain't it—the one in the mantle like Joseph's coat from the Bible? Ye ken what I mean, the 'coat of many colors'? Do ye know 'er, Wickham? She's a bonny lass, and he's a braw lad, too. Are ye jealous, Wickham?"

Zach hardly knew which question to avoid first. Kate had progressed from one assumption to another with mind-boggling rapidity. And she was right about them all. But all he had to do to put her off was say, "I don't know which blond girl you mean," then rap on the ceiling with his cane, and they'd be off. But instead he turned to Kate and opened his mouth, but nothing came out at all.

He didn't know how he looked to her. Probably like an idiot. But he knew how he felt. He loved Gabby so damn much, and it killed him to see her enjoying herself with Rory when she hadn't a clue she was being watched by him. Their pleasure was not an act. It was real.

Kate's face melted into soft lines of sympathy and understanding. "Oh, Wickham ... ye love 'er, dinna ye?"

Usually Zach hated sympathy. It made him feel vulnerable and foolish. But for some reason, sitting there so comfortably with Kate, he didn't mind. Maybe he was just so tired of denying his feelings to himself and to everyone else, the idea of telling someone the truth for once was a compelling temptation. He sighed heavily. "Yes, God help me, I love her."

"Is she in love with that fellow she's skatin' with, then?"

"I don't think so."

Kate shook her head, confused. "Then what's the to-do? Ye're a braw fellow, too, Wickham, if'n ye dinna mind me sayin' so. Make her love ye back!"

"She says she does already."

Kate gave a hiss of exasperation. "I dinna understand you Quality types. If'n ye love her and she loves you, why dinna ye jest get married?"

Zach continued to watch Gabby, not just because he was mesmerized by the rainbow-cloaked nymph on skates, but because he was about to make what he considered an emasculating confession. "It's not so simple as that, Kate. I'm ... afraid."

To his relief, Kate's voice remained perfectiy normal, her approach characteristically straightforward. "Of what are ye afraid, pray tell? She dinna look dangerous t' me!"

This made Zach laugh. Turning to Kate, he exclaimed, "You don't know Gabby! She's dangerous, all right!" Then his smile faded "The truth is, I'm afraid I'll hurt her."

There was a pause, then in a small voice, she said, "Ye dinna mean like Douglas hurts me?"

Zach turned and took her hand, chafing it between his two. "No, not in that way. I'd love to get my hands on the little minx, but not to—" He turned back to the window, still holding Kate's hand. "I can't even explain my fear, Kate. I think I know where it comes from, though." Zach considered the appropriateness of telling Kate everything that was burdening his heart, then decided with a sudden surge of impetuousness to quit weighing his words and simply speak the truth. "You see, there was a woman in my life many years ago when Gabby was just a little girl—"

"The blond lass—her name is Gabby?"

"Yes. Gabrielle's her given name, but I call her Gabby. I

was engaged to her sister, but I also had a mistress named Tess. I thought I was in love with Gabby's sister, but in reality I was in love with Tess. It's a very complicated thing to explain, and I don't want to bore you—"

Kate squeezed Zach's hand. "Please, Wickham, bore me!"

Zach smiled gratefully. Now that he'd begun, he didn't want to stop. "You see, my brother Alex and I had been separated for many years—seventeen, to be exact. My father had sent me away to live with my maternal grandfather when I was just five and Alex was thirteen."

"Why?"

"Because he hated me. My mother died giving me life, and he never forgave me for that." Zach felt the bitter bile burning his throat. "Father never minced words. Even at the age of five, I knew exactly what a horrendous thing I'd done."

"Wickham, you couldn't help it if your mother died!"

"I know that. But while I could believe that with my head, I could never reconcile the situation in my heart. I always felt desperately guilty."

Kate shook her head, saying nothing.

"Finally he couldn't stand the sight of me any longer and trundled me off to Cornwall, stipulating to my grandfather that if he wanted to raise me, he must intercept any correspondence between me and Alex. Grandfather kept honorably to this agreement, and Alex and I both believed the other responsible for our estrangement. At Grandfather's funeral, we were reunited and the misunderstanding cleared up." Zach smiled, remembering. "It was wonderful having my brother back. We became fast friends. But then things got more complicated."

"How so, Wickham?"

"My betrothed, Beth, Gabby's older sister by some eleven years, fell in love with my brother and she with him."

"Oh, dear. That must have hurt very much."

Zach smiled bitterly. "Not in the way you might suppose, Kate. In truth, I wasn't in love with Beth. I cared for her like a sister. It was my mistress, Tessy, that I was truly in love with. But I was too blinded by the rules of society to admit or accept my love for her. When I was nearly killed in a tin-mine collapse, and in my darkest hours my thoughts had been for Tess, I knew I'd gone beyond the bounds of acceptability. I knew that if I continued to see her, I'd marry her. And I was too prideful to do that. I severed my relationship with Tess and at the same time learned she was pregnant with my child."

"Lor', Wickham!"

"I left her anyway, told her I would support the child. When I returned to my estate, Pencarrow, I found Beth and Alex in his bedchamber. They'd just made love. I wanted to kill him, Kate. And all over stupid pride for Beth's cuckolding me, and anger at Tess for nearly duping me, as I saw it, into marriage. My brother and I have made up, of course. We're closer than ever, and Beth's like a dear sister to me. Their children are like … my own."

Lost in the painful memories, Zach was almost startled when Kate spoke again. "What happened to Tess and the baby?"

"The selfsame day I severed my ties with Tessy, she bore the babe. It was two and a half months early. Something went wrong. Tess died."

Kate drew a sharp breath. "Oh, Wickham, I'm so sorry. But what about the babe?"

Zach had told Gabby that he hated lying. He did hate it, but in the case of Tessy's daughter—his daughter—he'd already lied to half of England. And he would continue to do so till he'd breathed his last rattled gulp of air, and without feeling the least smidgen of guilt. He'd do anything to protect Tessy's child from becoming the sort of social outcast her mother had been due to her inadequate bloodlines. Alex and Beth were raising his child, Torie, as their own, as their firstborn. But he told Kate the usual lie. "The baby died and was buried with Tess."

Silence once again settled between them. But it wasn't a cozy, comfortable silence. It was a quiet reverence for the shadows of things past and unchangeable, a time for regrets. Zach knew Kate had her own share of problems and regrets, and he suddenly felt guilty for burdening her with his. He took one last lingering look at Gabby, who was now capably sailing over the ice like a graceful, exotic bird with multicolored feathers, then tapped his cane against the ceiling. The carriage immediately jerked into motion.

"Wickham," said Kate, leaning back now into her side of the carriage, "I hope I can say somethin' to ye and ye will'na take it amiss."

Zach gave Kate a tender, teasing smile. "I've trusted you with things I've not told anyone these eleven years and more. I think I can stand a little advice, if that's what you're hinting at, Kate. You've borne with me putting my oar in where it's not wanted—forcing you to talk about Douglas. I'll forgive you for doing the same."

"It was good fer me to talk 'bout Douglas, and I think it's been good fer you, Wickham, to speak to me about yer fears. Only I think it'd be better if'n ye'd told Gabby 'stead of me."

"I can't—"

"Yes, I know ye're afraid. I ken what ye're sayin'!" Kate poked her forehead with her finger. "In yer head ye know ye dinna kill yer mum or Tess—though to Tess ye may have been a bit hard." She spread her hand, palm down, on her chest. Her voice gentled and lowered. "But in yer heart, ye've always blamed yerself, and ye're afraid ye're goin' t' hurt Gabby, too, in some roundabout way that dinna make a jot o' sense."

"I know it doesn't make sense," Zach admitted. "But I can't seem to help it."

Kate leaned back and crossed her arms, her voice changing once again, this time into tones of authority. "Well, it seems t' me, Wickham, that what ye canna work out in yer head, ye got t' work out in yer heart! But ye canna do it by yerself. Ye've got t' let Gabby help ye. I'm not a romantical miss. I've had me eyes open since I was no higher than me da's boots. But by my way o' thinkin', Wickham, love is the cure fer what ails ye. And it'd be a damned shame if'n ye lost another woman ye love 'cause o' fears, when all ye'd need t' do is let 'er help ye face 'em. Now I've said all I'm goin' t' say."

Kate's words profoundly stirred Zach, and it was a good thing she didn't seem to expect a response to her little speech, so ably delivered, because he was unable to speak a word. She leaned back against the soft squabs of the carriage and eyed him for a minute or two, then sighed softly and turned her head as if settling to sleep. She slept a lot, but Blake had assured Zach that it was perfectly normal for a girl in Kate's condition to require naps during the day, as well as several sound hours of sleep each night.

He watched her eyes drift shut and her lips part slightly in a dainty snore. He thought of Kate's husband and pitied him for losing her, though he hoped mightily that the loss was not permanent, that Douglas McKeen could be cured of his weakness for drink and the resulting erosion of his finer character traits—the traits that could keep him from beating his wife when he wanted to lash out at life. He hoped Douglas could be reunited with his family.

The carriage traces jingled as they climbed their way up the Mound to High Street, past St. Giles to Carruber's Close. Zach thought about everything Kate had said. She was wise in her way, her wisdom earned harum-scarum on the streets of Auld Reekie. She'd said that love was the cure. He remembered how he'd felt that night at the brothel when Gabby had first brought on a phobic attack, then soothed it away with her loving caresses. *Love was the cure.* She'd also said that it would be a shame if Zach lost another woman because of his fears. Yes, maybe he'd not lost Tessy through death. Maybe he'd lost her long before that. Maybe Kate was right about a lot of things...

CHAPTER TWELVE

The Murrays and their guests were invited for the evening to a musical soirée at the Garrisons' townhouse at Heriot Row, and Gabrielle was in the process of dressing for it. Her abigail had just finished Gabrielle's coiffure and been dismissed. Now, all alone in her bedchamber, Gabrielle studied her appearance in the mirror above her dressing table. It was vitally important that she look her best tonight, because she doubted that she had much time left to try to break through Zach's wall of emotional resistance before he went flying back to the safety of Cornwall, or, worse still, got himself leg-shackled to someone quite unsuitable, someone who was not the love of his life—which meant anyone who was not Gabrielle Tavistock.

Gabrielle had seen him with the mystery girl again today at Duddingston Loch. She was sure he didn't know that she'd spied his carriage partially hidden by that overgrown clump of rhododendron bushes. Where Zach was concerned, Gabrielle had an uncanny way of sensing his nearness. Never mind that she'd failed miserably at detecting his nearness when she'd hit him over the head with a vase at Mother Henn's brothel! She supposed she could blame that little slipup on dulled senses, due to the small dose of laudanum she'd swallowed. But tonight there must be no slipups. She wanted to look beautiful. She wanted to make Zach ache to hold her, as much as she ached to be held by him.

She and Rory had agreed to continue the engagement charade and to act besotted with each other. After all, though she had admitted to Zach that she and Rory had entered into the engagement without intending to see it through, she'd also told him that there was a chance that Rory might want to make the engagement a bona fide betrothal. Since Zach had been watching them at the loch, he was probably wondering about their relationship and maybe even feeling jealous. Tonight Gabrielle meant to reinforce that jealousy.

Gabrielle had chosen a most becoming gown of white tulle, trimmed with gold embroidered flowers at the hem, a gold rose at the center of her bodice where it made a provocative dip above the full mounds of her breasts, gold trim on the off-the-shoulder sleeves, and with a gold tasseled rope tied around her cinched-in waist. She wore white gloves, white slippers, and gold earrings with pearl teardrops.

She'd parted her hair in the center and wound two thick braids around her head in a simple, elegant style. As a finishing touch, she'd had her abigail artistically arrange a string of pearls on her crown, something like a halo that had slipped a bit and was skimming her forehead. It was a rather sophisticated style she'd seen in a French fashion magazine. She thought it made her look decidedly grown up.

Pinching her cheeks to encourage a blooming complexion and biting her lips to redden them, she took up her fan and a small pearl-seeded reticule and moved toward the door with a determined stride. She'd tried telling the truth to get through to Zach, but since that hadn't worked, she wasn't above resorting once again to deceit. She would do anything to convince Zach that their love was worth fighting for.

Two carriages were required to transport the party to the Garrisons. Aunt Clarissa rode with Rory and Gabrielle, and Zach and Regina rode with Lady Grace and Sir George.

Due to this arrangement, and because Zach didn't come down till the last minute to board the coach, Gabrielle still had not exchanged one word with him since the night before. The memory of their closeness, both emotionally and physically, made Gabrielle long to see him, speak to him, and touch him again.

The drive to Heriot Row was filled with inconsequential chatter, but fortunately for Gabrielle's burning impatience to see Zach the drive was short, and in less than ten minutes they were alighting from the carriage and walking up the steps to the Garrisons' front door. The Murrays had arrived just before their own carriage, and the two couples had already been relieved of their winter wraps and were making their way into the drawing room to mingle with the other guests. Gabrielle could see the back of Zach's golden hair and his broad shoulders as he escorted Regina through the moderate-sized crowd.

The Garrisons were very select about whom they invited to their musical evenings, and therefore this social event would not be a crush like so many other parties. Gabrielle was familiar with the routine; they would talk a little, drink a little sherry, eat a little cake, then at precisely ten o'clock, they would be politely invited to be seated in a semicircle round a dais, occupied by a pianoforte and with room to hold other instruments and the musicians who played them. During the evening, the Garrisons' guests would be entertained by the various compositions of such luminaries as Bach, Mozart, and Vivaldi.

The Garrisons were working their way around the room, welcoming and chitchatting briefly with everyone. Presently they were talking to the Murrays, Zach, and Regina. Much like the Murrays, the Garrisons were a distinguished pair. They were gracious hosts and, though Mr. Garrison held no titles and was only related distantly to peerage, both sides of the family were impeccably pedigreed. The couple were considered artiters of good *ton* in Edinburgh, and held this lofty position without being snobbish. In fact, the Garrisons frequently sponsored poor fledgling musicians and, by inviting them to perform at their soirees, provided them with the exposure they needed to promote their careers.

Ordinarily Gabrielle looked forward to these musical evenings because she liked the Garrisons and she loved the music. But tonight she was distracted from her usual anticipation of pleasure because she was consumed with wondering how Zach would react when they were finally face to face. She hoped he would admire her. In fact, she wished he would admire her so much that he would lose control, sweep her off her feet, and—

"Gabrielle, would you like some sherry?" Gabrielle hadn't

noticed that a servant had been standing—possibly for a long time—at her elbow with a tray of crystal glasses filled with the delicate nutty-flavored Spanish wine. Rory was smiling down at her with a wrinkle between his eyebrows and an arch in one brow which could only mean he was amused. She must have been obviously lost in a world of fantasy.

"Yes, thank you, Rory," she finally managed to say, lifting a glass from the silver tray and taking a sip of the warming liquid.

As the servant walked away, Rory whispered teasingly, "I don't think we're going to convince anyone that we're in love with each other if you stand about in a daze, lass. You're supposed to be paying rapt attention to everything I say!"

Gabrielle smiled nervously. "I know. But I haven't spoken to Zach since last night, and I'm dying to—"

Rory was looking past Gabrielle's shoulder. Still whispering, he said, "Well, here's your chance."

Gabrielle turned and saw Mr. Garrison and Zach approaching them. Quickly she caught hold of Rory's arm and trilled a laugh, as if Rory had just said something immensely diverting. Though he was holding conversation with Mr. Garrison, Zach's eyes were on Gabrielle. She felt that familiar thrill of awareness, of anticipation, of yearning.

Even while standing next to one of the best-dressed, most distinguished men in Scotland, Zach did not suffer by comparison. He wore a jacket in the fashionable new color of night green. It wasn't precisely green, nor was it nearly dark enough to be labeled black, but it was somewhere in between the two. His cravat was simply tied, but blindingly white. His trousers were a smooth fit of black fabric that all too perfectly accentuated the lean strength of his long legs. Due to his abundance of hair, the knot she'd given him with the vase was hidden from view. And his eyes were warm, lucid, amber-bright.

"Miss Tavistock, Lord Lome, how do you do?" said Mr. Garrison. Bows and the usual polite inquiries were exchanged. "Meeting Mr. Wickham has pricked my memory, Miss Tavistock. I knew your father."

Gabrielle smiled. "Indeed, sir?" She darted a flustered

glance at Zach. She'd loved her papa dearly, but with Zach so near, it was hard to concentrate even during conversation about her father. "H-has Zachary been talking of Cornwall, then?"

"Aye, he has. Tavistock is a common enough name, but when he mentioned you were family friends, that his estate, Pencarrow, marched with yours—Brookmoor—I instantly made the connection to my old school chum, Benjamin Tavistock. He was a good lad. 'Tis a shame we never met again after the wedding. Mr. Wickham thought you might enjoy hearing something about our experiences together at Eton."

Gabrielle felt gratified by Mr. Garrison's kindness, and equally pleased that Zach had initiated such kindness. "Thank you, sir. I was very young when he died. I would truly enjoy hearing anything about Papa." Mr. Garrison smiled and touched Gabrielle's elbow, guiding her to a quiet corner of the room where a settee and two armchairs were grouped for conversation.

Gabrielle threw a look over her shoulder at Zach that was half reproach and half gratitude. She wanted to hear Mr. Garrison's stories about her papa, but she also wanted to talk to Zach. She threw him a mute appeal. *Won't you join us?* But he ignored her, shifting his gaze to Rory. Aunt Clarissa, who'd had her nose quite close to a Constable landscape which hung on the wall, in rapt inspection of the verdant colors, noticed that Gabrielle had sat down with Mr. Garrison and dutifully joined them.

As soon as she was out of earshot, Gabrielle saw that Zach immediately engaged Rory in conversation. A few unsmiling words were exchanged, then they walked away together, out of the room. Gabrielle's curiosity was enormously aroused. Somehow she didn't think they were retiring to a private location to finally fix a date for their proposed bow-hunting excursion. It was all she could do to sit still and make the proper responses while Mr. Garrison related a half-dozen anecdotes about her father's schoolboy antics.

Fifteen minutes later Mr. Garrison regretfully excused himself, saying he'd neglected his other guests far too long and that Mrs. Garrison would be in a pucker, particularly since he had abandoned her for such a lovely young woman as Gabrielle. Gabrielle smiled and thanked him for sharing memories of her father. He bowed gracefully over her hand, then took himself off to do his duty as host and to placate his wife.

Gabrielle looked across at Aunt Clarissa. The sherry and the soothing baritone voice of Mr. Garrison had put her aunt to sleep. Gabrielle saw this as an opportunity to get away to look for Zach and Rory. She quickly exited through the same door Zach had led Rory through and found herself in the main hall. The two footmen standing sentry there gave her cool glances, but did not presume to ask her if she needed anything.

Trying to appear as though she knew exactly where she was going, she started down the hall. As soon as she was out of sight of the footmen, Gabrielle began testing doors and peeking inside. So far the rooms had been dark and the fires unlit. Finally, after she'd rounded a corner and was at the very end of the hall, she opened the door to candlelight. There wasn't much of it, but enough to faintly illuminate the figure of a tall Adonis in a night-green jacket as he stood with his back to her, gazing out a tall window. It was just one of many windows that took up the entire east wall of the room. Zach stood in a small conservatory surrounded by potted palms, hyacinths, and geraniums.

Gabrielle closed the door behind her and walked a few steps into the leafy, loamy-smelling interior, her skirts swishing noisily, before Zach turned and looked at her. A three-tapered brace of lighted candles had been placed on the mantle of a large rock-hewn fireplace. There was no fire, and the chamber was cold. Gabrielle registered the chill, but she didn't actually feel it. She was too caught up in the thrilling novelty of being alone with Zach.

"What are you doing here, Gabby?" His voice was as chill as the room. "Where's your aunt?"

Gabrielle put her hands behind her, where Zach couldn't see them, and squeezed her fingers tightly together. She attempted a light tone of voice, saying, "My aunt's asleep. 'Tis impossible for her to unlearn the habits and disposition of a lifetime simply because she is suddenly my chaperon."

Zach grunted, resigned to the truth of what she said.

"As for myself," she continued, "I saw you and Rory leave together. I thought you might have gone off to play billiards, and I wanted to watch."

He moved into the nebulous circle of candlelight. Her breath caught when she saw his eyes. She couldn't decipher the essence of that look; she didn't know which passion or passions might have created such intensity of expression. Hate? Jealousy? Love? Desire? Patent disapproval? All five? She couldn't tell.

"You're lying again, and you know how I hate lies."

Instinctively she defended herself with a counterattack, childish but effective. "Then you're being hypocritical, Zach. *You* tell lies all the time!"

His mouth twitched. She saw his jaw tighten, become more square and sharp-angled with the strength of his anger. "If you are referring to our adventure in Old Town, I had to lie about that to protect your reputation."

She took another step closer. His gaze dropped to where her slight advance had stirred her noisy skirt. They were separated now by about six feet. "I'm not talking about that. I'm talking about all the secrets you keep and all the lies you tell yourself every day."

He lifted his chin slightly, peering warily from under drooping eyelids. "I don't know what you're talking about."

Another step, another swish of tulle skirt and taffeta petticoats. "I'm talking about that woman you spend time with in Old Town. That's a secret you've kept."

"And will continue to keep. She's none of your concern."

"And what about your 'business' there? Why won't you talk about it?"

"Again … none of your concern."

"I can accept that, but——"

"Ha! That's a clanker! You have to know everything! Your curiosity is appalling and has caused us both a deal of grief!"

Gabrielle bit her lip, feeling the heat creep into her cheeks. "It's a failing of mine, I know. I control my curiosity better now that I'm older, but everything about you interests me, Zach."

He remained silent, watching her with the same wary expression.

"Isn't it my concern to know whether or not you love me?" she blurted out.

"This is a threadbare topic, Gabby," he said sternly. "Of course I love you, but not the same way you imagine you love me."

Up went Gabrielle's chin, defiant. "That's a lie."

He blew a huff of exasperation. "If it's a lie, why should I feel bound to tell the truth, when you don't feel similarly impelled?"

"Because you don't like it when I tell the truth!" she shot back.

Zach raked a hand through his hair and began pacing, his shoulder stirring the fronds of a large fern. "You're wrong, Gabby! I hate the way you dally with Rory, thinking it's a way to get to me. I hate your sham betrothal. I hate your lies to the Murrays, to your mother, and to all of Edinburgh. And as for Rory, I know you don't love him, and since you don't, marrying him would be just another huge, colossal lie! And during my conversation with him just now, I realized that if you were willing, he would marry you, which would be the biggest mistake of his life!"

"Why, Zach?" she demanded, frustrated, close to tears. "Because I would bring him a 'deal of grief'?"

Zach strode quickly over and gripped her arms, bending to look straight into her eyes. "Because, you little idiot, Regina's in love with him!" He let go of her and resumed pacing. "Can't you see the torture you're putting her through with this stupid charade? If you left him alone, quit dangling that tantalizing carrot of 'will she or won't she,' I know Rory would realize that he loves her, too. But to help enlighten the fellow, I told him what a dolt I thought he was, dancing after you when he'd a woman so devoted to him as Regina. I've given him something to ponder, I'll wager."

He turned back to her, his hands upheld in supplication. "God, Gabby, if you want to be perceived as an adult, you have to act like one! And blinding yourself to the people around you, the hurts you may be inflicting on them, is the height of selfishness. And if that's not childish, I don't know what is." He turned away and walked to the window, once again staring out into the pearly black and white of a moonlit winter nightscape.

Gabrielle was stunned. How could she have been so blind? Everything began to fall neatly into place now, to make eminent sense. Regina's blushes when Rory teased her, the absence of animation when he wasn't in the room, her laughter and excitement when he was. Of course Regina loved Rory. She behaved around Rory exactly as Gabrielle behaved around Zach. Now Gabrielle's tears fell in earnest. Tears of shame.

"Zach, I didn't know. I swear I didn't know."

Zach heard the tears in Gabby's voice and her watery remorse. He tried to blot out the image of her standing there in her white dress, trimmed with gold to match her hair—regal and lovely—reduced now to misery. Her cheeks would be streaked and damp because he couldn't stop himself from flinging hurtful words. His behavior was as childish as hers. But seeing her tonight, looking so beautiful and so obviously bent on making him jealous by flirting with Rory, was more than he could bear.

He'd thought about what Kate had said that afternoon. He'd even gone so far as to consider confessing all to Gabby and asking her to help him heal. To heal. To be whole again, unafraid. To be able to love her. *To love her!* But he was still fighting it, still so afraid. Still pushing her away with angry, hurtful words.

Even without the telltale swish of skirts, he'd known she had moved closer to him. Her orchid scent drifted on the cool air. He felt his whole body stiffen, tension pulsating through every nerve. Like an automaton, he turned, steeling himself for the impact of seeing her, of seeing what he'd done to her.

The tears had been wiped away. All that was left were cheeks pinker than usual, eyes that glistened with spent grief, lashes stuck together in thick wet spikes. Her manner was composed, contrite, resigned. "I'm sorry, Zach. I hope you'll forgive me." Then she turned and walked toward the door.

Terror gripped Zach. Suddenly he knew there would be

no more lies from Gabby, no more make-believe betrothals, no more naive seductive advances to try to convince him that she was a grown-up woman and that he loved her. He had finally wrung the last bit of hope out of Gabby's tender heart. He was a fool! He needed her and he had pushed her away. He couldn't let her go. No, he wouldn't let it happen again!

"Gabby!"

With her hand on the cut-glass knob of the door, she turned. She wore an anxious expression, and he knew she didn't know what to expect. Another lecture, perhaps. To dispel the anxiety, he spoke quickly. "I'm the one who should be asking forgiveness, Gabby. You're right. You're right about so many things."

She stood there, waiting for more explanations, but he'd run out of words. There was so much that needed to be said, but he didn't know where to begin. Maybe he should begin by holding her... He lifted one arm and extended it, his hand upturned in a mute invitation.

After a moment's hesitation, she came. He wasn't sure he should be allowing himself this sheer indulgence, this gift of giving in to what he wanted most in the world. But she was in his arms, and he would forget, for now, everything else but that.

He held her fast against him, her head tucked beneath his chin. Her hair was fragrant, the pearls she'd used as decoration rolled against his cheek. Her arms were like bands around his waist, so strong and possessive. Her voluminous skirt swathed both their legs. He rocked her in silent joy, back and forth, the swishing tulle and taffeta keeping rhythm. They were one. Like two jigsaw pieces, they fit perfectly.

She stirred, pulling slightly back, lifting her face to look at him. She glowed like a Rembrandt painting, all light and vibrant softness. He bent his head and kissed her smiling mouth.

The other times he'd kissed Gabby, Zach had held his emotions in check. Now, like a reservoir dam cracking and giving way under the strain of flood waters, he was allowing himself to feel everything he'd been suppressing. It was terrifying how right she felt in his arms, how good she tasted, how much he wanted her.

Gabrielle slid her hands from around Zach's waist, slowly up his hard, broad back. Every nuance of muscle and bone delighted her. Her fingers tangled in the thick, straight hair at the nape of his neck. It felt like silk, like something Rumpelstiltskin would spin at his magic wheel. Spun gold.

Zach gasped, and their lips parted for a moment, just long enough for him to drift feather-light kisses over her face—each feature duly given its share of affectionate notice. Then he bent his head and nuzzled her neck with his mouth. Her head fell back instinctively, allowing him full access, conveying with her deep breathing and closed eyes all the encouragement a man could possibly want.

Desire imploded in Zach, catching him unaware. But he was only a man, after all, and the pent-up need for Gabby had been denied for too long. He kissed her again, but this time his mouth closed over hers with a reckless, brutal force. His tongue swirled and danced with hers. Her fingers convulsed in his hair, then splayed over his shoulders, holding him to her, apparently as disinclined to end the kiss as he was.

Her breasts were pressed against his chest. He could imagine the nipples rosy and turgid, as they'd been at Mother Henn's. Then he cursed himself for putting Gabby and Mother Henn together in the same thought. His hands moved up from her narrow waist along the side seam of her gown, around to the front, cupping her breasts. She moaned into his mouth, arching her body against his open palms.

Just like in her dreams, Zach's lean, beautiful hands were caressing her, making her feel warm and womanly, powerless and powerful at the same time. Gabrielle didn't want the lovemaking to stop. She wanted more…

Still cupping her breasts, Zach kissed her bare collarbone all along the sensitive ridge. Then he went lower, tasting the skin just above her bodice where her breasts plumped up like firm pillows.

Gabrielle was in heaven. She held onto his shoulders like a drowning woman to a piece of driftwood, clinging, fighting against complete submersion. Zach pushed down the sleeves of her gown, taking the upper portion of her bodice with them, till her breasts were exposed. She felt the cool air against her nipples, then warm hands covering them, clever fingers kneading them to hard, sensitive nubs.

Zach couldn't believe how beautiful she was. Her breasts were like alabaster marble, cool, white, the skin almost transparent with tiny blue veins showing through here and there. But the nipples were bold red, like rubies. He bent his head and took one in his mouth, pushing and pulling with his tongue and teeth till Gabby groaned, her fingers curling and clutching in his hair.

Zach was losing control. Somewhere in the back of his consciousness he knew that what they were doing was dangerous. By now they'd be missed. By now Clarissa might have been roused from slumber by some viola player tuning and plucking his instrument. She might be looking for them, opening each door along the hall, just as Gabby had done, till she found them.

He was about to pull away when Gabby's curious hands began exploring again, this time starting at the backs of his thighs and moving slowly up till her palms lay flat and firm on his buttocks. Instinctively he did the same to her, pulling her against him, against the hard, hot swelling in his groin.

Gabrielle's eyes blinked open, her lips parting in a shudder of unexpected, overwhelming pleasure. She never knew she could feel this way. Every inch of her throbbed with an unfulfilled need. And that most sensitive and private part of her felt it most of all. She could feel Zach's hardness against her. Since her mother grew faint and queasy at the mere mention of such a forbidden subject, Gabrielle had learned about the anatomy and function of male parts from her sister, Beth. And because of that candid conversation, Gabrielle knew that Zach was ready to make love.

Fascinated, curious, her hands drifted around to the front placket of his trousers, her fingers closing over the hard ridge of his manhood. Zach's breath drew in sharply. Yes, he was ready, and so was she.

"Make love to me, Zach," she begged him. "Make love to me right now!"

CHAPTER THIRTEEN

Zach could hardly believe that he'd allowed the situation to progress this far. He'd obviously underestimated Gabby. He'd had a feeling she'd be a passionate woman, ready and eager to indulge in all the diverse delights of lovemaking, but he didn't think she'd be ready and eager in the conservatory of one of the pillars of Edinburgh society! If they were caught, she'd be the grist of drawing room gossip for time ad infinitum. He couldn't allow that, no matter how hard it was to resist her innocent seductiveness.

Garnering all his strength of will, he caught her wrists and gently pulled her hands away from the front of his trousers. She looked confused at first, then, as he carefully pulled her bodice up to cover her breasts, her face flushed with humiliation. As he fumbled with her sleeves, she turned away. "Thank you, but I can dress myself."

"Gabby," he began in a reasoning tone, his voice still rough-timbred with passion, "they'll have missed us by now. What if someone walked in on us with you looking so... compromised?"

Gabby turned to face him, her dress now pulled modestly into place. "I expect you'd be bound to marry me, and that wouldn't do at all, would it, Zachary?" She grabbed handfuls of her skirt and walked majestically toward the door.

Zach followed. "Gabby, sweeting, you don't understand. It's not that I don't—Oh, hell! We need to talk, not make love in the Garrisons' conservatory, for Christ's sake!"

"I'm done with throwing myself at you, Zachary Wickham," she told him in a voice that strived to be brisk but couldn't hide an underlying tremor. "You're always running away from me! It's lowering to one's pride to be constantly ... rebuffed." She stumbled on that last word. Her huffiness was all an act to hide her hurt. He wanted to beat his head against the wall out of pure frustration. He'd hurt her again, damn it!

"Gabby, don't go. Let's talk."

"Talking doesn't seem to get us anywhere. You just lecture, accuse, and deny."

She was right, but Zach was ready to change that. "Gabby, I promise—"

But she had reached the door, opened it, and was already half running down the hall, her skirts swishing and swinging out behind her like a great, fancy whisk broom. Feeling powerless and frustrated by the situation, Zach watched as she disappeared around the corner. He stood there, knowing he dare not insult his host by going back to the conservatory and shutting himself in for the evening to sort things out. He did not, however, look forward a bit to returning to the drawing room and putting on a social face for all those people.

He sighed and moved slowly down the hall. The musicians had arrived and were tuning their instruments. He would try to finagle a seat by someone who was not an inveterate chin-wag. Perhaps if left alone to enjoy the music, he could unscramble his brain to the soothing cadence of a pastorale. With his luck, however, the musicians the Garrisons had secured for the evening's entertainment would be the tortured, romantic type, with a decided preference for similar music. Then he'd be too stirred up to think of anything other than what had occurred in the conservatory. Even now he had difficulty removing the images and sensations from the forefront of his mind.

Finally he stood at the entry of the drawing room. People were filling the chairs placed round the musicians. Gabby was already seated in the front row between Rory and Regina. Mr. Garrison glanced Zach's way, smiled, and waved him over. Zach returned his smile politely and cast about for someone to sit by who looked as though they would not annoy him with constant jabbering.

Ah, the perfect choice. Aunt Clarissa was, incredibly, still nodding in the chair where she'd been sitting a half hour ago as he'd exited the room with Rory. He would wake her up and insist that she sit by him during the performances. No doubt she would sleep like a babe, leaving Zach with plenty of uninterrupted time to think. For both their sakes—his and Gabby's—he had to decide what to do about this love, this passion, they had for each other. Yes, he knew now that something had to be done.

Somehow the evening passed. Gabrielle sat through each musical selection with her face arranged in a pleasant, smiling mask which said much indeed for her acting abilities. She felt horrid. Each lyrical, evocative piece melded into the other, her rankled, wretched thoughts never far away, and her inherent appreciation for music dulled by more pressing considerations. There was much to think about, not the least of which were Zach's revelations about Rory and Regina.

There was a restraint in Rory that hadn't been there before, presumably brought on by his conversation with Zach. And if Gabrielle had been paying attention, she would have noticed that ever since their conversation that morning in the breakfast room, Regina had been unusually quiet and withdrawn. At first she supposed that Regina had truly been unwell when she'd cried off going on the skating excursion and was still suffering from a lack of energy, but now she knew that Rory's flirtatious comments about making their engagement official had plunged Regina into gloom.

Now, seated between them, Gabrielle felt the veriest fool. Zach was right; she'd been so caught up in her own affairs that she'd blinded herself to the people around her, people she cared about and who had always treated her with the utmost kindness. This group of victims included Sir George and Lady Grace, Aunt Clarissa, Rory's grandmother, and her own mother, who was whiling away the long, windy, winter nights in Cornwall by blissfully anticipating Gabrielle's spring nuptials.

Well, as for that, Gabrielle was going to waste no further time in telling everyone the truth. As she drove home with Rory that night, she'd convince him that the time had come to tell the truth, and together fix on an hour on the morrow to meet with the Murrays to do the disagreeable deed of telling the whole story. It would probably be ill-advised to break the news that night, since Gabrielle knew Lady Grace grew rather fragile and fatigued after the clock had struck midnight, and she didn't think Lady Grace would appreciate such a confession being sprung upon her at such an odd hour. No, she'd let her enjoy a sound sleep tonight. Tomorrow would be soon enough to out with it, just after Gabrielle had returned from visiting the Tuttles.

Yes, that was another thing Gabrielle wasn't going to delay another moment, because once she'd made her confession to the Murrays, she would make plans to return to Brookmoor immediately. There were two reasons for this expediency. First of all, once she knew the truth, her mother would be beside herself with disappointment and resentment toward Gabrielle, and would fancy herself ill. Gabrielle should be there to soothe and nurse her mother through the worst of it.

Secondly—and Gabrielle knew this was selfish—she couldn't bear the idea of facing all of Edinburgh once her broken engagement had been circulated by the capable machinations of the gossip mill. The end of a much-talked-about engagement was a dicey affair in the first place, but if the truth got out, that they had been pulling the wool over the eyes of the Edinburgh elite for their own nefarious purposes, Rory and Gabrielle would be decidedly *de trop*, an embarrassment to the Murrays as well as themselves.

Gabrielle couldn't imagine why she hadn't thought of all this before. She had been single-minded in her efforts to somehow get through to Zach, and she supposed she had thought that everything could be smoothed over in the end by her engagement to him.

Zach. Gabrielle ought to be heartened by his obvious desire for her, as illustrated by his ardent behavior in the conservatory. Just thinking about what had transpired there made Gabrielle's arms and legs go rough with gooseflesh. But they'd started out the encounter in an argument, with Zach still guarding his feelings and his secrets as if they were the Queen's jewels. Physically he'd let down his guard, and for a blissful few moments they'd shared the sort of intimacies Gabrielle had dreamed about. But, though he'd expressed a desire to talk after he'd abruptly stopped their lovemaking, she knew that chances were he'd pull himself into his shell again like a cantankerous clam.

Gabrielle sighed. She needed more patience. But she was beginning to wonder if her self-respect could allow her the leisure of more patience. She'd frightened herself that night because she'd realized how desperately besotted she was with Zach and to what lengths she was prepared to go to prove herself to him and to convince him that they were meant to be together! After all, what self-respecting woman could beg a man to make love to her in total disregard of the fact that they were in an unlocked chamber in the respectable lodgings of perhaps the most respected family in all of Edinburgh?

But the truth was, there had been no conscious decision-making going on at the time. She had not thought to prove herself, or seduce him, or any such nonsense. She had been, quite frankly, swept away by passion. Even if he left for Cornwall in the morning, if they'd made love she'd not have considered it a shameful thing or a wasted endeavor. She would have cherished it forever. She loved him that much.

This was the frightening part of it. For Gabrielle, this was the straw that broke the camel's back. She couldn't keep up the facade. She couldn't be patient anymore. She loved him to the point of abandoning prudence and pride. This would never do. Now the time had come for Zach to make his decision without any further interference and promptings from her. If he truly wanted to talk, tomorrow, in the sanity and safety of the parlor in Charlotte Square, he must be the instigator.

Having thought all this through, Gabrielle was filled with a sense of peace. Suddenly the comforting strains of Beethoven's *Pastoral* broke through her troubled preoccupation. Deep within her she felt her spirit stir as if revivified with hope. She would share this new optimism with the Tuttles, leaving to find them first thing in the morning with Ralph the burly footman in tow. Ralph could handily carry her bundles and fight off whatever ruffian might happen to be lurking in the dark alleys of Old Town. With Ralph she'd be safe. She didn't need Zach this time. Surely she could do this one thing without his help.

The dawn broke with an exceptional display of pink and yellow streaks against the cloudless, blue-gray sky above Arthur's Seat. Gabrielle watched it from her bedchamber window, fully dressed and draped in a brown mantle she seldom wore because of its somber color. She much preferred her green mantle or her Ali Baba, but this one, kept primarily for the dirty exigencies of travel, would be much more nondescript and, she hoped, help her to blend in better with the populace of Old Town.

She also wore a brown velvet bonnet, from the band of which she'd plucked the scarlet pheasant feathers serving as decoration. She pulled on her mittens and tucked her reticule under her arm. She left the room, closing the door very quietly behind her, and tiptoed down the hall past Regina's door and the Murrays', secure in the knowledge that they'd not be up before ten or eleven, thereby giving her plenty of time to pay her visit to the Tuttles and be back in time for breakfast. She descended the back stairs to the kitchen where Ralph waited for her with the bundles, a troubled frown marring his usual stolid visage.

Two of the scullery maids were about, stoking the fire and arranging pots for cooking, eyeing the pair of travelers but saying nothing, and Gabrielle knew that other servants were creeping about as well, preparing the house for the eventual appearance of the Murrays. Gabrielle wasn't so much concerned that she be undetected in leaving the house, however, just that she be undeterred. She hoped to carry it off by acting not at all secretive in the servants' presence, just as though the Murrays wouldn't care a fig that she was going on such an early morning mission of mercy, and with her only escort being Ralph.

She could tell that Ralph was uncomfortable, and had been since the moment she'd solicited his help last night before retiring to her bedchamber. He'd stood there in the hall, stalwart as ever, as she'd handed him the note more or less ordering him to put together two bundles of blankets and food articles, as per her list, and be waiting for her at the back door precisely at dawn. He'd never think to gainsay a genteel young lady's instructions, however ill-advised he thought they were. And it had been too late last night, and too early this morning, to confide in and seek advice from Phipps, the majordomo, or Flossie, the cook. He had no recourse but to do as the young lady asked and hope all went well, and that, in the end, he wouldn't be relieved of his job.

Gabrielle smiled reassuringly at Ralph, hoping to put him at ease. "Thank you, Ralph, for collecting the contents of these bundles for me. I wouldn't have had a clue where to look for these items myself. I would have asked Lady Grace or the housekeeper where to find them yesterday, but I didn't decide to go till the last minute and didn't want to disturb them, late as it was."

Ralph, a young man with a black beard and piercing black eyes, still looked unconvinced, though he made a little cursory nod with his head by way of acknowledging his deference to her, however grudging.

Gabrielle, pitying his predicament, reached out a hand and laid it on his muscular forearm. "Don't worry, Ralph. I intend to have us back by no later than Sir George's usual breakfasting hour, and I will explain everything to both him and Lady Grace at that time. I also plan to have the housekeeper replace these items at my expense. I wouldn't be setting out at such an ungodly hour except that I have a great deal of other things to do today, and this family we're visiting is in dire need of help. I simply can't put it off any longer."

She had told him the truth. Never mind that Lady Grace would also be flatly opposed to her venturing into Old Town at all, especially with only Ralph to lend her countenance and protection. But that couldn't be helped. She had to go and see the Tuttles before the household was thrown into confusion later that morning by her confession. Then, if all went as planned, she'd be overseeing the packing of her trunks and arranging for transportation back to Brookmoor. No, the visit to the Tuttles had to be done this morning.

"Then let's be off, miss," said Ralph, the grim set of his jaw softened a little by her assurances. "I walked t' Princes Street and fetched a hack. 'Tis waitin' outside."

Gabrielle smiled her approval and thanks, Ralph hefted the bundles under both his arms, and they went outside to board the rented coach. Ralph asked her for directions, in order to convey them to the hack driver. His disapproving and worried expression returned when she admitted that she didn't know the exact address, but was quite sure of the neighborhood. Gabrielle told him to go to Carruber's Close, and from there she'd backtrack her way to the street that led to the Tuttles' home.

Ralph looked skeptical, as well he might, since Gabrielle wasn't positive she could find her way back to the correct neighborhood, either. She only hoped she'd not run into Mother Henn or one of her lackeys, though Ralph looked strong enough to hold his own if such a necessity arose.

At such an early hour, the streets of Old Town were not as crowded, and their journey was unimpeded and timely. Spying an open bakery, Gabrielle had the driver stop and wait while she went inside and bought a basket of warm scones. Their raisin-sweet odor filled the carriage and made Gabrielle's mouth water. At Carruber's Close they alighted, and Gabrielle paid the driver.

With just a glance at the tall building where Zach's mystery woman resided, and the attendant pang of jealousy she felt at the thought of the two of them together, Gabrielle led Ralph down High Street, watching for the corner with the building that had scrawled on it with coal, "Jem loves Ethel." It was fortunate that she'd noticed this seemingly unimportant detail during her adventures of the previous day, because otherwise she didn't think she'd have had a ghost of a chance finding the right street.

Douglas McKeen leaned against the building opposite the shelter, his hat pulled low over his brow, watching the princess and her burly servant alight from the rented coach. He had been waiting for this opportunity for a long time. Besotted little fool that she apparently was, he'd expected the lass to return to

Carruber's Close eventually, and, after her run-in with Mother Henn, he reckoned she'd not come alone. He hadn't expected her to bring such a monstrous large fellow as this one, however.

Douglas sighed. Never mind. He'd deal with the fellow simply by taking him by surprise and delivering him a stunner to the back of his skull with any handy, weighty object that might be lying about. He certainly wasn't fool enough to take the black-haired bloke on face to face. He'd other things to worry about, like tricking the princess into a hack with him and down the hill to the McSwains' holiday cottage.

Rich folk from the border, the McSwains used their cottage just outside the village of Dirleton for summer holidays with the family and frequent hunting parties. Douglas used to shoe McSwain's horses and, now and again, did odd jobs about the place when the family was in residence. Douglas knew Mr. McSwain had been up just last week with a few cronies, fishing for trout in the stream and shooting wild geese. The place was deserted now till the next hunting party, and Douglas planned to take Wickham's lass there and lock her up in the small servants' loft above the stable. Then he'd send word to Wickham that he'd exchange her for Kate.

The whole ordeal was a strain on Douglas, both to his conscience and his purse. In fact, he'd finally sold his father's pocket watch to pay the ready for such an out-of-the-ordinary expense as the hack. Lord knew, he never enjoyed such a luxury as being tooled about town in a coach instead of pounding the ground on foot, as was his usual mode of transportation. But it was the best and most secretive way to snare the princess and get her safely out of town without a visible struggle. He'd hired a horse, too, to heave his poor, wee pregnant Kate atop and trot her ceremoniously home after Wickham relinquished her into Douglas's rightful, husbandly care.

Douglas thought it ironic that, given his love of liquor, he'd never sold his da's watch to quench his ungodly thirst, but, instead, had pawned the cherished timepiece to finance a plan to get Kate back. Lord, that possibly meant he loved Kate more than his da's watch—more than liquor, too. It was a sobering realization.

Douglas had chosen the McSwain cottage as the spot for exchange of the women because in Auld Reekie there were too many nooks and crannies where Wickham's possible cohorts might hide. At the cottage, it would be just him and Wickham. He'd be able to see him and Kate coming from a mile off, and if Wickham were so unwise as to disregard his instructive note, warning him against bringing anyone along besides Kate, he'd just have to use threats against the princess to make Wickham see sense.

Douglas stuck his hand inside the large pocket of his ragged redingote. His fingers slid over the smooth, cold barrel of his newly acquired pistol. He wasn't a killer, and he prayed to God he wouldn't have to use the gun for anything more than a threat, a means of exercising power. But he'd do whatever was necessary to get his Kate back.

Douglas's now ever-present, niggling voice of conscience suggested that the thing most conducive to getting Kate back and keeping her was to stop his drinking, which would also stop his fits of physical rage. He hated the rages. He hated himself for hurting Kate, and he was determined never again to lay a hand on her. He knew to help insure this he ought to quit drinking, but he didn't know if it was possible to stop something that had become more necessary to him than food. Which, he wondered, did he love the most? Kate or the bottle?

Never mind. First he'd get her back, then he'd work through and around all this other aggravation. As the princess and her servant left Carruber's Close, Douglas followed at a discreet distance.

CHAPTER FOURTEEN

Gabrielle found the "Jem and Ethel" corner and, turning down it, led Ralph away from the bustle of High Street. There were the familiar moldering, disagreeable smells, and the sound of melting snow dripping from the eaves. Ralph's eyes shifted back and forth, peering into the shadows as they walked down the narrow wynd. "How far is th' place, miss?" he asked.

"Not much farther, I think." Gabrielle remembered that when she'd chased Will, though the wynds had curved endlessly, she'd not taken any sharp corners till the very last. Once she and Ralph rounded that corner, they'd be in Mother Henn's territory. But as soon as they'd gone that far, she'd see if there was a way to get through to the parallel street where Will lived without having to actually pass by the brothel. Then they could stop people on the Tuttles' street and inquire about them, or, if necessary, they could knock on doors.

For all her brave front, Gabrielle was very uneasy. Beneath her skirts, her knees shook. The alleys were understandably dark because of the high buildings close in on both sides, but, with the sun climbing higher in the sky as the morning progressed, it wasn't nearly as dark as on that stormy dusk of two days before. Nevertheless, because of her horrid experiences then, the atmosphere felt sinister to Gabrielle. Whenever someone passed, she ducked her head, in constant dread that Jasper or Bob or even Mother Henn might be on some unlikely, unlucky early morning errand. So if any of the passers-by happened to smile at her or look friendly, she wasn't aware and was therefore unable to eke even a little comfort from the possibility that decent people traveled these alleys as well as scoundrels and thieves.

Ralph did not speak. She suspected he was too disgruntled,

and feeling too alarmed and guarded, to do anything but walk and watch. Finally they reached the corner, and Gabrielle stopped abruptly.

"Is this it?" Ralph inquired with a definite note of hope in his voice.

Gabrielle looked around her. Mother Henn had told her that finding the direct way to Will's apartment required some backtracking. "We want the little square on the other side of these buildings, Ralph. I think we'll need to go back some."

Ralph jerked his head in the direction of the corner, round which Gabrielle knew was Mother Henn's brothel. "Canna we go this way, miss? It might be closer."

Gabrielle tried not to sound nervous. "No, Ralph. Now that I have my bearings, I know just how to get there."

Ralph frowned, obviously unconvinced. "Ye've been there afore, then, miss?"

"Once, with Mr. Wickham."

Ralph nodded, marginally relieved to hear a man's name juxtaposed with Miss Tavistock's line of reasoning. She turned and walked to an alley she'd seen a few yards back, desperately hoping that it did not meander away in the opposite direction from where they needed to go. Hefting his bundles, Ralph trudged behind.

For once, Gabrielle was in luck. The alley opened up onto a small square that she suspected was the very same one she and Zach had escaped into from the building next to Mother Henn's. This also meant that Mother Henn could be close at hand. That possible danger couldn't be helped, though, and now that they'd come so far, Gabrielle wasn't about to cry craven and turn back.

"This is it," she told Ralph. "The family lives in this square. All we have to do now is find someone who knows them and ask for the correct building and apartment."

Again Ralph nodded, immediately looking for a likely person to approach to ask about the Tuttles. There was an old man practically smothered in a thick woolen scarf up to his nose, with a small, shaggy dog on the end of a short rope, shuffling—or so it appeared—in a circle round the perimeter of the little square. Their morning exercise, Gabrielle suspected. The man looked harmless enough, and so did the dog. She and Ralph exchanged glances, communicated without saying a word, and walked toward the pair.

The man saw them coming, eyeing them thoroughly as they drew up beside him, but he did not stop. The dog paid no attention to them whatsoever, keeping his nose to the ground as he investigated the various smells and squirming insect life that flourished in the muddy cracks between the cobbles.

"Excuse me, sir," Gabrielle began, "but I believe you may be able to help us."

The old man turned to Gabrielle and raised his brows, saying wryly, "Do ye think so, miss?" He didn't miss a step in his walk, but it was easy to keep up with him and hold conversation simultaneously. His slow, shuffling gait reminded Gabrielle of how an extremely ancient Chinese man might take his exercise.

"We're looking for a family called Tuttle. I believe they live in this square, but I don't know which building. Do you know them?"

The man's keen eyes narrowed. "And what would ye be wantin' with the Tuttles?"

Gabrielle hurriedly explained. She'd rather spend as little time as possible in the open square, perhaps in full view of one of Mother Henn's windows. "I met the children on Christmas Eve. They were caroling in New Town. I've learned since then that Will is sick, and the mother, too. Recently Will did me a great service, and I want to thank him and help them all with a few creature comforts and a little money to pay a physician—"

"Say no more, lass," the man interrupted her, smiling on her this time with genuine warmth. With a gnarled, arthritic finger, he pointed to a building. "It's there. Ground floor, first door on the left as ye go in."

"Oh, thank you, sir! Thank you very much!" Gabrielle was thrilled and immensely relieved. At last she was going to see Will and Bella and the other children! She hoped they wouldn't be embarrassed by her visit, or refuse to allow her to help them. She knew Will, especially, might feel uncomfortable after the incident with her reticule. But if any objections happened to surface, she was ready and determined to override them.

Ralph dutifully followed her as she walked quickly to the building and through the drab brown outer door, all splintery and weather-beaten. Like the other buildings, this one had probably once been the home of a well-to-do merchant, or a solicitor, or even a magistrate. The main structure of the building had been added onto, the top three floors obviously not part of the original house plan. It made for an interesting facade.

The building's ground floor vestibule was very dirty. The stairs going to the upper floors looked much mended. Gabrielle found herself thankful that Bella and the other children didn't have to use the stairs to reach their apartment. They walked to the door purported to belong to the Tuttles, and Gabrielle knocked. Her heart was beating hard and fast. She was excited to see them, but nervous and unsure of her reception. She was also worried about what she might find behind the well-scrubbed panels of the door. Yes, both the door and the threshold looked very clean. This was encouraging. Apparently someone was healthy enough, and full of enough pride of ownership, to have vigorously wielded a scrub brush.

The door opened. It was Will. Gabrielle smiled, but he only stood there, apparently dumbfounded at first, then shamefaced.

"Won't you invite me in, Will? I assure you, I'm not angry. I've brought you some things, and then we must talk."

Will had been watching her lips intently while she was speaking, and her heart twisted with pity. Even at such close proximity, he couldn't hear her well enough without also having to read her lips. He hesitated, still unsmiling, but finally pulled the door open and stepped aside. "Come in, miss."

Gabrielle walked into the small, windowless chamber, and Ralph followed. Once her eyes adjusted to the dark interior, she noticed that the room was long and narrow, with a fireplace at one end and a threadbare blanket strung across the other end on a rope, probably to section off the sleeping area. Though a few meager twigs for kindling and a lump of coal were laid ready to spark, there was no fire on the grate, and the room was quite cold. The bare floors were rough-planked wood, clean but devoid of an oil polishing for some time. The furnishings were sparse and shabby. A line of wash hung across a section of wall, and the clothes were stiff with cold.

No one was about, and Gabrielle thought perhaps they'd stayed in bed late to keep warm. This theory seemed even more likely when she heard murmurings from behind the blanket, and then one of the other boys appeared, peeking round the makeshift privacy curtain, his eyes enormous.

"Tell Mum we've company, Danus," ordered Will, whereupon the boy disappeared, and more murmurs and movement could be heard behind the blanket.

Gabrielle touched Will's shoulder. "Is your mother well enough to get up? I don't wish to cause any inconvenience. I just wanted to help where I could."

Will blushed. "Me mum's doin' better. She's gone t' work at the bakery the last three days. But it's been hard comin' up with the blunt fer food."

Gabrielle looked earnestly into his face. "But you're doing worse, aren't you? Your ears are bothering you? You can't hear very well."

If possible, Will blushed an even deeper shade of red. "'Twill get better."

"Maybe not, Will, unless a doctor is consulted. Do your ears give you pain?"

Will acknowledged this with a glum nod.

"Poor boy," said Gabrielle, but probably too low for Will to hear, and it was just as well he didn't. He was proud. He was embarrassed just having her standing there in the midst of their poverty, in her somber but well-to-do clothes. He was staring down, digging the floor with the ragged toe of his boot. She touched his shoulder again. He looked up shyly. "I want to thank you for sending help the other night."

His gaze shifted abruptly, embarrassment overcoming him once again, this time more for her than for himself. After all, she'd been in a whorehouse, for goodness' sake. She bent close to his ear and said in low, succinct syllables, "You saved me from a terrible fate. I escaped with my friend with nary a scratch." The same couldn't be said of Zach, poor dear.

Relieved and gratified, Will looked up and smiled genuinely. "I'm glad of it, miss." Then, screwing up his courage, he added, "She's moved on, ye know. Mother Henn's gone t' who knows where, and we're more'n glad t' be rid o' her. Ye needn't worry 'bout seein' the likes o' her 'round here."

Gabrielle breathed a relieved sigh. "Well, that's good news!"

"Aye. Some say Blake and Wickham, them blokes what run the women's shelter, met with the police and put a scare in 'er. But no one's mentioned yer name, miss. No one knows it."

Gabrielle's brows knitted together. Surely she couldn't have heard Will correctly. "What did you say, Will, about Mr. Wickham? He's the friend who helped me escape from Mother Henn, you know. Did you say he *runs* the women's shelter?"

"Well, not 'xactly, miss."

"I thought not—"

"He owns it. Comes t' visit now and then, so we hear."

Gabrielle was incredulous. "Zach *owns* the women's shelter?"

Will cocked his head, puzzled. "I thought ye said Mr. Wickham was yer friend, miss? Dinna ye know that he owned the shelter?"

"May I sit down, Will?"

Suddenly Mrs. Tuttle appeared from behind the tattered screen, tucking back her hair with one hand and smoothing her clean apron with the other. "Yes, miss, do sit down. Sorry t' keep ye waitin', but we stay abed till near time fer me t' go t' the bakery. Saves the fire. Will, where's yer manners, son? Sit down, miss, here by the hearth, and I'll light the wood." Mrs. Tuttle bent to the task.

Gabrielle sat down in a narrow reed-backed chair by the fireplace, flabbergasted by this unexpected news concerning Zach. He *owned* the women's shelter? That must be at least part of what comprised his business in Old Town. Was it located in Carubber's Close? Was that woman Zach squired about in his carriage an inmate of the women's shelter? What sort of a shelter was it, anyway? This was all very intriguing.

After Mrs. Tuttle had got the tiny fire started, she turned to Will. "Dinna ye think ye ought t' introduce me to the lady, Will?"

"I dinna know her name, Mum," Will confessed.

Mrs. Tuttle, a small, youngish woman with dark brown hair and a pinched, tired look about the eyes, seemed nonplussed by this pronouncement, standing, waiting, wiping her hands on her apron.

"Don't worry, Mrs. Tuttle," said Gabrielle, putting her thoughts of Zach aside to concentrate on the Tuttles. "I do know the children, though I've never introduced myself to them." She stood up and extended her hand, smiling. "I'm Gabrielle Tavistock."

Mrs. Tuttle diffidently shook hands, her pale lips tilted in a nervous smile. Gabrielle could see that Mrs. Tuttle was a pretty woman beneath her tired exterior.

"I met the children on Christmas Eve when they caroled on Princes Street."

Mrs. Tuttle's eyes lit up. "Oh, now I know ye! Yer generosity got us through the worst of times! I was knocked up in bed fer the longest spell, too sick t' go t' work, too sick t' even feed the bairns. But Will did the cookin', with wee Bella helpin' out."

"Where is Bella?" asked Gabrielle, glancing toward the curtain. "I hope she isn't sick?"

"Feelin' shy, I expect. Would ye like to see the lot of 'em?"

"If I may," Gabrielle admitted. "I see you haven't started breakfast yet, so perhaps they'd enjoy having some warm scones I fetched at the bakery on my way. The smell of them has been teasing my nose for some time."

Mrs. Tuttle's face turned pink, and her eyes misted with gratitude. "Ye're so kind, Miss Tavistock. I'll put on a kettle and we'll have tea. I'm afraid I dinna have any milk to go with the scones."

Gabrielle suspected that she didn't have much of anything in her larder, judging by the thinness of her. "I brought some milk," Gabrielle told her, "but I'd still enjoy some tea." Gabrielle wanted Mrs. Tuttle to feel as though she were contributing to the breakfast, and requesting tea seemed a good way to accomplish this. Mrs. Tuttle nodded and smiled and bustled about, filling the kettle from a bucket and hanging it from a hook over the fire. There were no handy conveniences in this home.

"Now I'll fetch the bairns. Bella will want me t' comb her hair afore ye see her, fine lady that ye are and so lovely. She said ye was a fairy princess, miss, and I begin to think so meself." She smiled, then hurried away, disappearing behind the curtain. Will followed, probably too shy to stay and talk.

Suddenly Gabrielle remembered Ralph, who had been standing all this time by the door. He had set down the bundles and was leaning against the wall, his legs crossed at the ankles and his arms folded over his wide chest. He no longer looked disgruntled, but rather bemused.

"Oh, Ralph, forgive me," said Gabrielle, shaking her head and throwing up her hands in apology. "I didn't mean to completely ignore you. I should have introduced you, too, but I was quite rudely caught up in my own thoughts. You will come and have a scone and some tea with us, as I am certain you didn't get a bit of breakfast this morning, so early did I drag you from your bed!"

Ralph pushed away from the wall, surprised and clearly embarrassed. "Miss Tavistock, there's no need t' introduce me, as I'm only the servant come along to tote fer ye."

"Stuff and nonsense, Ralph!" Gabrielle retorted briskly. "I'm sure the Tuttles feel as strongly averse to the idea of you standing there starving while we eat as I do."

Still Ralph frowned, shifting from foot to foot. "Miss, it ain't proper-like fer you and me t' sit down t'gether t' break bread—"

"If you must be stubborn, Ralph, I shall simply have to pull rank. I order you to join us for breakfast. Do you understand?"

Ralph scowled, and Gabrielle smiled. It was a standoff till the other children emerged from behind the curtain. Just like the first time she'd seen them, they stood in order of age, one blond head bobbing down to the next. Mrs. Tuttle recited their names. Will, Robby, Danus, and Bella. Her clothes were shabby, she was thin as a lamppost, but Bella's face was scrubbed clean and her guinea-gold hair was pulled back in a shiny braid. Bella's head was down, her eyes averted, but she was smiling.

"Hello, children," said Gabrielle, her gaze irresistibly drawn to the little girl.

Nudged by her mother, Bella stepped forward and made a curtsy. "Good morning miss." Then she turned and bobbed another curtsy in Ralph's general direction, saying, "Please, sir, will you take breakfast with us?" After this remarkable bit of bravery, Bella ran back to her mother and hung on her skirt, hiding her face in its folds.

Gabrielle looked at Ralph, smiling triumphantly. No one could resist such an invitation. Ralph grinned back, his broad face glowing with pleasure mixed with acute embarrassment. He shrugged, the slight roll of his hefty shoulders acknowledging his defeat as no words could. "I'd be pleased, little miss," he told Bella, then gave her the merest ghost of a wink and disposed his considerable bulk in the chair next to Gabrielle.

CHAPTER FIFTEEN

From one of the heavily laden baskets, Gabrielle produced sweet butter, gooseberry jam, and a corked bottle of milk to go with the scones. She also instructed Ralph to build up the fire with a few pieces of coal they'd included in their bounty. Presently the fire crackled cheerily, the tiny apartment filled with warmth, and the tea kettle sang. There wasn't room enough for everyone to sit around the small square eating table, so Ralph returned to his perch by the fire. When the tea was passed, he balanced the chipped dish on his knee and lifted the handleless cup to his mouth to down its contents in one lusty gulp. Gabrielle supposed he did this in order to eat his scone more easily without the worry of scalding himself with spilt tea.

"We've no' had such a fire fer the whole of winter," Robby commented solemnly, his eyes fixed on the healthy blaze, his cheeks pink with reflected heat. The other children stared at the flames, too, as if they hadn't remembered how good a brisk fire could feel. And they ate and ate, not a crumb left for a mouse by the time they were through, or a drop of milk or a dab of jam. Gabrielle loved to watch them, and she encouraged them, between bites, to talk. The children chatted genially about the things children are most likely to be interested in: their chums, the dog upstairs that danced on his back legs for a nip of cheese, and the funny man down the street who told stories.

"Did you know that Ralph tells stories?" Gabrielle interjected. All four of the children turned their wide-eyed gazes on Ralph, who had been caught in mid-chew and appeared frozen with alarm. "Isn't that right, Ralph?" Gabrielle prompted.

Ralph hastily swallowed. "Well, miss, I—"

"It would be such a treat for the children if you told them

a story while Mrs. Tuttle and I had a comfortable chat on our own." She raised her brows and leveled Ralph a significant look he couldn't possibly misunderstand. His mouth clamped shut in stubborn refusal. He looked about as likely to sprout feathers and fly as he was to tell a story.

Gabrielle knew she could only push the fellow so far, and was cudgeling her brain for an alternate way of achieving a private conversation with Mrs. Tuttle before she left for work at the bakery, when Bella climbed off her chair and moved to stand by Ralph, placing her hand on his knee. "I'd like a story very much, sir," she said in a voice just above a whisper, and so sweetly she might easily melt Ralph's heart, which Gabrielle suspected was pretty soft to begin with.

As soon as the children were settled around Ralph, full of food and feeling toasty-warm for a change, Gabrielle and Mrs. Tuttle, by tacit unspoken agreement, moved to a far corner of the room.

"I canna tell ye how much I appreciate all ye've done, Miss Tavistock," Mrs. Tuttle began fervently. "Yer generous gift at Christmas paid our rent through January and bought the bairns clothes they needed badly, and kept food on the table whilst I was too sick t' work. And then all ye've brought t'day—"

"But it's not enough, Mrs. Tuttle," said Gabrielle. "Somehow I don't think what they pay you at the bakery can possibly cover all the needs of your growing brood." She hesitated, then pushed on. "I hope you don't think I'm indelicate, but I want to help, and I need to know how matters stand. If you don't mind telling me ... are you married?"

Mrs. Tuttle did not seem to take umbrage. "I am. But me husband left several months ago."

"Left?"

"Aye. He just up and left one day, and we've not seen hide ner hair of 'im since," she continued, not at all in a self-pitying voice.

"Do the children miss him?"

"No, nor do I," was her simple but significant reply. She did not elaborate, and Gabrielle did not pry.

"But without a man about the house to help with money, you're going to have the devil of a time making ends meet. Is there nothing else you can do?"

Mrs. Tuttle shook her head. "I'm not sure what ye mean, miss. I canna do much 'cept cook and clean, like I do at the bakery shop, back in the scullery. Will sometimes finds a bit o' work t' do, here and there."

Gabrielle did not tell her that he also sometimes snatched reticules. He should be in school. This brought to Gabrielle's mind another of the worrisome consequences of the Tuttles' poverty.

"Since you can't afford to send the children to school or hire a tutor, the boys' abilities to pursue worthwhile vocations will be seriously hampered. It also certainly lessens Bella's chances of marrying into a desirable situation. This concerns me."

Mrs. Tuttle clicked her tongue. "Dinna ye think, miss, that it concerns me, as well? But I'm no' about t' bring another man into the place jest t' help with the money. He's got t' be a good man, and I've got t' love 'im. I'm no' about t' make *that* mistake again! Besides which, in the eyes o' the kirk, I'm still married to the bairns' father—God rot 'is soul!"

Gabby was glad to see Mrs. Tuttle had some pepper in her, as made evident by her flashing brown eyes as she expressed her heartfelt wishes for her husband's eternal condition. "Actually I hadn't meant to suggest that you remarry. I was wondering if you have family, in the country perhaps?"

"No. I come from the country, though. I was raised by me da on a wee, sweet croft just outside the village of Aberlady. But he's gone now and the croft, too."

Gabrielle smiled. "You like the country."

Mrs. Tuttle returned her smile. "I crave it—the clean air, the flowers, the grass, the burns gurglin' down the hillsides, the sheep and the cows. Aye, Miss Tavistock, I like the country considerable. I wish I could raise me bairns there, 'stead of here in Auld Reekie. But 'tis no use wishin' fer what's never t' be. I'm a practical woman, miss, and not a flibbertigibbet with me head in the clouds. And now, if'n ye'll forgive me, I have t' be goin't' work." Mrs. Tuttle stood up.

Gabrielle stood, too. "One last thing, Mrs. Tuttle. About Will's hearing…"

Mrs. Tuttle nodded gravely. "I'm worried sick about 'im."

"I suspect he just needs to be seen by a physician. He probably has a bad infection that requires a particular treatment. I want you to summon a doctor for Will today." She reached inside her reticule, found her purse and opened it, extracting several heavy coins. "This ought to pay for the doctor's visit, the medicine, and a scuttle full of coal."

As Will had done on Christmas Eve, Mrs. Tuttle just stared at the money being offered her and seemed incapable of holding out her hand to receive it. So Gabrielle put the coins in Mrs. Tuttle's hand, folding her nerveless fingers carefully over the little cache of coins so she'd not drop them. Gradually Mrs. Tuttle regained her wits. "Miss Tavistock," she said earnestly, "we canna keep takin' yer money like this. Ye dinna even know us. Why are ye bein' so kind?"

Gabrielle smiled. "I like your children. I like you, Mrs. Tuttle. You seem a deserving family that could use a little help. Besides, Will did me a huge favor the other day, and this is just one way of expressing my thanks."

Mrs. Tuttle glanced over at Will, sitting with his elbows propped on his knees, as absorbed in the story as the younger children. Her eyes were loving, her voice soft with affection. "Did he, now?"

"Yes, but I shan't tell you what he did. It was embarrassing for me. He helped extricate me from a very awkward situation. And as for the money, I don't expect I shall have to be helping you forever, though I'd not mind doing so. You'd never allow me, however, and—"

"Aye, ye're right 'bout that, miss!"

"—I fully expect we shall come up with a plan so that you can earn a better living and make enough money to comfortably support your little family. Now I'll leave so you can go to work, but I shall be in touch … one way or the other."

Mrs. Tuttle probably thought Gabrielle was being overly optimistic, but she shook Gabrielle's hand—her eyes bright with unshed tears—and thanked her again before disappearing behind the curtain to ready herself for work.

Gabrielle joined the group by the fire. Ralph had apparently risen to the occasion. He was even using exaggerated gestures and changing the pitch and volume of his voice for the different characters in his drama. It certainly was a drama, too, all about a bunch of hunters in the woods and a particularly large and vicious wolf. The hero of the story was a brave, cunning fellow named Ralph, of course, and the other hunters hadn't the brain of a pea amongst the lot of them. The children were rapt, hanging on to every word.

Having noticed that Gabrielle was ready to go, and perhaps feeling a trifle self-conscious with an adult in the audience, Ralph hurriedly tied up the story by blowing a hole with a blunderbuss through the poor wolf's head, then concluded with a moral, which, of course, was necessary to the ending of any self-respecting children's tale. As Ralph's explanation was rather convoluted, Gabrielle wasn't sure exactly what the moral of the story was. Her best guess was this: don't go into the woods with a parcel of fools.

Notwithstanding the vague moralism, the children seemed well pleased with the story and were very disappointed when Gabrielle announced that she and Ralph must leave. In a desperate effort to detain them, Bella threw herself onto Ralph's leg, wrapping her skinny limbs around him like a monkey about to climb a coconut tree. Surprised, but flattered and pleased as well, Ralph gave a great, deep shout of laughter. The children all goggled at him at first, alarmed by the unexpected explosion of mirth that had rumbled up from his massive chest like lava from a volcano. Then they joined him, laughing at they knew not what, but laughing still the same.

"If I promise t' come back and visit ye again, will ye let me go?" Ralph asked them. "Miss Tavistock will sit with ye fer a mite while I fetch her a hack t' carry 'er home. Ye dinna want poor old Ralph t' lose 'is position now, do ye?"

The children finally reluctantly agreed that Ralph must go, but only if he promised to come back for a visit very soon.

Ralph still had to peel Bella off his leg, however, and hand her to Gabrielle, who, feeling like second best, tried to divert the child till Ralph could make good his escape. Gabrielle was delighted that the children had taken to Ralph, but she was a little nervous about his promise to return for another visit. Since she would be returning to Cornwall, he'd have to come on his own. She hoped he had been sincere, or else the children would be very disappointed. She imagined that they desperately craved a man's attention and influence in their lives.

Gabrielle petted Bella and stroked her beautiful golden hair till the little girl's bottom lip quit quivering. She said good-bye to each of them in turn—Will, Robby, Danus, and Bella—and finally moved to the door, confident that Ralph would have found a hack by then and that they would be able to leave immediately for Charlotte Square. Her mind was already racing ahead to her next task, which would not be so pleasant as the one she'd just concluded. She must tell the Murrays about her false engagement.

She was also thinking about what Will had told her, that Zach owned the women's shelter. She'd made a promise to herself to allow Zach the initiative in their relationship from then on, and had also vowed to curb her rampant curiosity. Therefore Gabrielle knew she wouldn't ask Zach anything about the shelter. There was no harm done, however, in indulging in her own speculations. Was the mystery girl an inmate of the shelter, or perhaps Mr. Blake's daughter?

Tying her bonnet, Mrs. Tuttle came out from behind the curtain and bade Gabrielle good-bye as well, and Gabrielle left feeling much relieved about the family and their circumstances. She knew she'd so far made only temporary improvements in their living conditions, but she was going to speak with Sir George about the Tuttles and hopefully arouse his sympathies and solicit his help to find Mrs. Tuttle better employment, in the country, perhaps. She realized that he might not be much in sympathy with her once she had made her confession, but surely he could put such resentments aside to consider a genuine case of charity.

Gabrielle knew Lady Grace was a bit ambivalent and squeamish about directly helping the poor, but even she, if she met the deserving Tuttles, would certainly change her policy of noninvolvement.

Thinking hard all the while, Gabrielle left the apartment and the building and stood outside in the square. She did not see Ralph anywhere, but she did see a hack waiting just a few yards away with the passenger door standing open and a piebald horse tethered to the back of it. The extra horse was unusual, though probably perfectly explainable.

She wondered why Ralph didn't have the driver pull up in front of the Tuttles' building, but perhaps he'd encountered a recalcitrant driver who chose to park his coach precisely where he pleased. She also thought it odd that Ralph wasn't standing outside the vehicle, prepared in his usual way to help her board. Perhaps he'd grown tired of waiting for her and had decided to sit down.

She shrugged her shoulders and walked to the open door of the coach and, head down, gathered and lifted her skirts to step inside. "Well, now, Ralph, that wasn't so bad, was it? I rather think you enjoyed—"

Gabrielle had sat down and closed the door behind her before she realized that the man sitting opposite her wasn't Ralph. He was a tall, wiry man, grubbily dressed, with intense blue eyes and a two-day beard. Where had she seen him before? But she had no time to ponder the matter before the coach began to move. "Oh, you must excuse me, sir! Tell the driver to stop! I thought the coach was for me. My servant—"

"'Tis fer you, miss," said the man. "And if'n ye care fer that servant of yers, or fer Wickham fer that matter, ye'd better not scream ner try t' leap out the coach. Jest sit still."

Gabrielle's heart was gripped with icy dread. Now she recognized the man. Like that other time, he smelled of liquor and tobacco, and looked as if he hadn't slept, shaved, or bathed for days. He'd kept her from falling down after Will had yanked her purse away and run off with it. He'd offered to find her a hack, and she'd refused him, chasing after her purse instead.

"Don't say you hold a grudge against me, sir, for refusing your assistance the other day? Or is this the hack you wanted to fetch me, only a bit late?" She tried to sound light and unafraid, but she was really very alarmed. She didn't dare make a dash for the door and fling herself out, as the man had made threats against Zach and Ralph.

"This ain't no joke," he said in grim tones that did nothing to diminish Gabrielle's growing fear.

"What have you done with Ralph?" she demanded to know. "And why do you mention Wickham as if you mean to do him harm?"

The coach had trundled slowly through a narrow street that led away from the square, but now, on the main thoroughfare, it moved much more swiftly. Gabrielle couldn't imagine where the man was taking her. She couldn't imagine, either, how she'd somehow got herself deep in the suds again.

"Ralph's a hearty bloke. He'll come 'round."

Gabrielle was filled with indignation. "I suppose that means you clouted him over the head while he wasn't looking. How very brave of you!"

The man raised his brows. "A sassy lass, ain't ye? Ye dinna expect me to play fisticuffs with such a giant, now did ye?"

"What about Zach? Have you hurt him, as well?"

The man's jaw tightened as he turned and stared out of the carriage window. They were descending the Mound now, headed either for New Town or the open country. "I'd sure as hell like t' hurt 'im."

The anger in the man's voice sent a chill up Gabrielle's spine. "Why? Who are you? What has Zach ever done to hurt you?"

He turned back, his blue eyes glinting pale and silvery. "Me name's Douglas McKeen. Does the name ring a bell?"

Gabrielle shook her head. "Should it?"

Douglas shrugged. "No, he'd have hid it all from ye, I suspect. Wickham's got me wife at his damned shelter, and I canna get near 'er. She belongs with me, not with the high-and-mighty likes o' him!"

Good heavens, could this man possibly be husband to the

woman she'd seen with Zach in his carriage? "Who is your wife, sir? Why would Zach have taken her into the shelter in the first place? What... er... sort of shelter is it?"

The man eyed her, cautiously speculative. "Are ye tryin' t' tell me, miss, that ye dinna know *nothin'?* Dinna ye even know 'bout the shelter and what it's fer? I thought you and Wickham was friendly-like?"

Gabrielle flushed. "Indeed, I don't wonder that you are surprised, but I assure you I know less about this shelter than you do. And I know nothing about your wife."

The man gave a bark of rude laughter. "Poor little princess! Thrown over fer a scurvy little chit like me Kate!"

"Kate?"

"Aye, and her 'bout t' burst with child."

Gabrielle shook her head confusedly. With child? The woman was *pregnant?* Her mouth was dry, her nerves frazzled. She glanced out of the window and noticed that they were indeed turning in a northerly direction instead of toward New Town. Her hands felt clammy. She twined her fingers tightly together, but hid them in the full folds of her mantle so McKeen wouldn't see the evidence of her fear. Trying to appear haughty, she lifted her chin. "What you say intrigues me, I admit. But before another word is spoken, I demand that you tell me where we're going and what you intend to do with me once we arrive."

"Ye're in no position t' demand anything, princess," drawled the man, giving her a slow, scathing once-over. "But I'll tell ye this much. We're goin' to a little cottage used by a southern gent who comes up fer holidays and hunting. Locked up and deserted, fer now."

"Then how——?"

"I'll be puttin' you in the loft above the stable, and there ye'll stay till Wickham does exactly as I tell 'im to."

"And that is?"

"Give me Kate back."

"I'm to be used as a sort of barter, then?"

"Aye."

"Why do you need a hostage? Why doesn't Kate come back

to you of her own accord?"

"He's filled her head with nonsense, that's why! He's dazzled 'er with 'is pretty airs and ways, and she dinna know what's right ner wrong, no more."

Gabrielle swallowed with difficulty. "Are you inferring that he's made her fall in love with him?"

"What do ye think? You saw the two o' them laughin' and talkin' the other day."

Gabrielle flinched.

He smiled grimly. "Aye, I saw ye hidin' and waitin' in the alley. I saw yer tears whilst they drove off together! Like two cooin' doves, they were! Tell me ye dinna think it's true what I'm sayin'!"

"I didn't know your Kate was with child. I only caught a snatch of her. I misunderstood the situation. There's another explanation besides the one you're so set on! Zach would never willingly lure a pregnant woman away from her husband." Gabrielle tried to sound indignant, even while her own heart was filled with doubt. There were so many unanswered questions! "And, as owner of this shelter, which I assume exists for the benefit of needy women, he wouldn't abuse his position to take advantage of Kate, or any woman, for that matter."

"Ye think he's a blessed saint, do ye?" he sneered.

Gabrielle did not reply. Douglas McKeen was obviously unhappy with Zach. More to the point, he was jealous. He continued to gaze at her balefully as he reached inside his jacket pocket and pulled out a small flask. This he lifted to his lips, never taking his eyes off her, and took a long swig.

"A little early in the day for liquor, isn't it?"

He grimaced, wiped his chin with the back of his wrist, then put the flask away. He curled his lips into a smirk. "Medicinal."

"And what pain do you suffer, sir?" she taunted him, then wished she hadn't. She ought to mind her tongue. She'd no idea what this man was capable of.

"Wickham's what pains me, princess," he told her. "But I've got 'im over a barrel now, what with you in wraps."

"What's to keep me from screaming when the driver stops the hack?"

"Sold me da's watch. Paid the driver well. And he's no fool. 'E'd be just as guilty as me if the police got wise. Now shut up. I'm gettin' tired of listenin' to yer proper Sassenach gibberish and all yer infernal questions." He leaned back against the shabby squabs of the coach and turned his gaze to the window.

Gabrielle watched him for a minute, then the realization of what had probably happened to Kate struck her forcefully. She spoke without thinking. "She ran away! Kate left you, didn't she?"

She saw how his jaw tightened with anger. "I said shut up."

Why couldn't she keep quiet? Why was she so impelled to antagonize him? But, as always, she was hungry for the truth. "She ran away because of your drinking."

With a suddenness that stunned her, he lurched forward, his face within inches of hers. He'd pulled back one hand as if to strike her. His eyes were startling pinpoints of blue wrath, his teeth clenched together in a fierce grimace. "I tol' ye t' shut up!" he ground out with slow deliberation, enunciating and emphasizing each word. "Shut up or else I'll shut ye up in me own way!"

Gabrielle shrunk back in her seat, ready at last to still her willful tongue. She had never been hit by a man in her life. From what she remembered of her father, he'd been a gentle man, and he'd treated her and her sister, Beth, and her mother as if they were precious works of art, to be treasured and handled with care. Just so was the way Alex treated Beth, and the way Zach had always treated her, too. Being threatened with violence was something foreign to Gabrielle, something more frightening than anything else. And degrading. Just as degrading as the treatment she'd endured at Mother Henn's whorehouse.

But it must be hell itself to be beaten by someone who supposedly loved you. Now she knew exactly why Kate left Douglas.

Gabrielle watched him as he took another drink. His thoughts were cankerous, eating his soul like worms on a corpse. She could see how the liquor fed his sense of ill-usage, self-pity, and envious hate. It was the liquor that made him ugly. It was the liquor that made Douglas McKeen the villain he was ... and the loser.

CHAPTER SIXTEEN

Zach had left Charlotte Square that morning, just before the usual breakfast hour. He wasn't avoiding Gabby. On the contrary, he truly meant to speak to her, to unravel the complicated weave of their relationship. He'd lain awake half the night thinking about her, about their love, about his own misgivings. He was ready to talk, ready to face the bogeys, those nebulous fears that had been haunting him for eleven years. But first he wanted to pay one more visit to Kate. She'd helped him make sense of things the other day, and he could use another dose of her insightful, down-to-earth logic.

It was a warm day for January. Snow was melting in steady rivulets off the roofs. The atmosphere was still and heavy with expectation. Zach recognized the signs. It was the lull before the storm. Iron-gray clouds were brewing off the coast. Soon the wind would pick up, blowing the moisture inland.

Much to his dismay, when Zach arrived at the shelter things were at sixes and sevens. Mrs. Stark had taken a sudden notion to do a New Year's cleaning of the place, from ceiling to floor and everything washable in between. Charlie had answered the door as usual, then stood alongside Zach, observing in companionable commiseration the chaos that surrounded them. His sympathetic expression and slightly rueful smile told Zach that he understood completely how out of place a man might feel amidst so much domestic hustle-bustle.

Like a lieutenant in the army, Mrs. Stark had recruited every able-bodied female in the house and put her to work. All the rugs were up, undoubtedly well beaten, and now pegged on the drying line outside the window to be aired. The windows themselves were denuded of their usual cheery curtains and being wiped to squeaky transparency. Furniture was being polished, floors and walls scrubbed, fireplaces swept. The place was redolent with soap, beeswax, and the fresh, cool air breezing in from the open window by the drying line. Disturbed from nooks and crannies, dust motes floated in the thin sunshine that filled the room.

Many of the women were humming, too, as they went about their chores, each their own tune. The place thrummed like a hive of musical bees.

"Gawd!" Zach muttered. "Where's Blake?"

Charlie angled his head toward the door.

"Gone out, has he?"

Charlie nodded and sighed.

"Can't say I blame him. No place to sit in comfort and peace in the entire apartment, I daresay. But you're stuck here, eh, Charlie?"

Another nod, another sigh.

Zach clapped him on the back. "You're indispensable, old fellow. We really ought to get another man about the place to help out, give you a little holiday now and again. Do you ever just leave and stretch your legs, so to speak, Charlie?"

Charlie shrugged, gave a tentative half-nod, looked glum.

"Not often enough, I'll wager. And when you do go out you feel as though you're leaving the place unprotected, even with all those locks." Zach gestured toward the fortress-like chains and bolts on the door.

Charlie shifted his gaze, as if embarrassed to be so well understood.

Zach shook his head. "I'm sorry, Charlie. It should have occurred to me that you'd begin to feel like a prisoner with so many people depending on you."

Charlie suddenly looked troubled, lifting his hands in an impotent gesture, as if he wished for once to be able to explain in a babble of words.

"I know," said Zach, instantly recognizing Charlie's frustration. "You don't want me to think you're unhappy. You enjoy your work here."

Much relieved, Charlie gave an emphatic nod.

"But you could use a holiday," Zach said decisively. "I'll have a chat with Blake to see about hiring another man to cover your duties while you're absent."

Charlie agreed with this, but again looked concerned.

"Don't worry," Zach reassured him. "We'll be very careful about who we hire for the position. We wouldn't want anything to happen to our lasses, would we?"

Charlie smiled at Zach, then, benignly, at the lasses, some of whom were covertly sliding appreciative glances in Zach's direction. If he happened to catch one of them looking at him, Zach smiled, saying a friendly "good morning" to those who persistently stared. Admiration embarrassed Zach and always took him by surprise. Besides, he'd no time for such nonsense. He was looking for Kate. He didn't suppose Mrs. Stark had given Kate anything strenuous to do, as she was too near delivering those twins.

"Speaking of the lasses, where's our most pregnant one? Where's Kate?"

Charlie curled a forefinger at Zach, bidding him to follow. He led him to the kitchen, then turned and left.

Kate stood at the scrubbed preparation table that stood in the middle of the room. The table was powdered with flour that settled in the nicks and nubs of its uneven, rough, wood surface. She was kneading a large mound of yeasty-smelling bread dough. Her hair was tucked beneath a muslin scarf, which was knotted neatly at the nape of her neck. She had on a voluminous apron, loosely tied behind her and covered in the front with flour. To accommodate her stomach, she stood well back from the table, her arms just reaching her task. Her brows were knitted in concentration. She wasn't even aware that he was watching her.

For a small lass, she molded the dough with considerable power. Slap, slap, pound, pound … roll, knead, and turn. Slap, slap, pound, pound… roll, knead, and turn. Very rhythmic, she was.

"What can you be thinking of, Kate, to put such energy into your kneading?"

She looked up, a smile instantly lighting her face. There was flour on her chin and on the eyelashes of her right eye. "I was thinkin' of you, Wickham, and how I'd like t' slap some sense into ye."

"My, how domestic you sound! Just like a wife!"

She made a pout. "I am a wife. And I begin t' wish I could see me Douglas."

Zach walked to the table and began to idly trace letters in the flour. "I thought we agreed that it would be best if you waited till after the babies were born. Then he'd be invited here to see you—provided he's sober and Charlie stands guard during the interview—whereupon you'd deliver him an ultimatum. He must sober up, or you won't go back to him."

"Aye, but how's he t' do it on 'is own? He needs help, Wickham, just like I did when I first come here. Who's goin' t' help me Douglas?"

Kate's voice shook with emotion. Zach looked up and saw the tears in her eyes, ready to fall. She started to reach for the apron hem to wipe them away, but he pulled out his clean handkerchief and gave it to her. "Here. You'll get flour in your eyes if you use that apron."

She dabbed her eyes and stuffed away the handkerchief in her pocket, to be laundered, pressed, and returned at a later date. Besides, she might need it again. As Zach had learned over the years, pregnant women were apt to be emotional. "Well, Wickham, what d' ye say?" she prompted, resuming her vigorous kneading. "Ye said ye'd think about it. Have ye reckoned a way t' help me Douglas? Is there such a place like this in Edinburgh where Douglas could go?"

"I've looked into the matter and have come to only one conclusion. It's against my usual policies," Zach began, having also returned to his previous employment—tracing letters in the flour. "But perhaps we could bring him… here."

"What?" Kate stopped kneading, a disbelieving frown lining her usually smooth forehead. "*Here*, Wickham? But ye said the shelter was'na meant fer men, jest fer women. Ye said—"

"Yes, I know what I said. Mind you, we'd only be able to

keep him here through the first bad days. From the start he'd have to fully understand how wretched and miserable he's going to feel while he goes through withdrawal, then he'd have to consent to giving himself completely into our care and under our authority, enduring whatever we are forced to do to keep him from drinking.

"We'd have to lock him in a room for a time, and Charlie and Blake would be the only people allowed in to bring him food, clean up his sick messes, and all, because I've no doubt he'll grow rather desperate and wild. It will be a disturbance to the other women, but Blake and I will have a chat with them and ask them to tolerate the situation for your sake. You've made friends here, Kate. They'll support you."

He looked up again, but this time the tears weren't just standing in Kate's eyes, they were streaming down her face, making wet stripes in the light film of flour on her cheeks. Zach smiled. "Don't say I've left you speechless for once?"

"Why, Wickham?" she asked him in a hoarse whisper. "Why are ye bein' so good t' me?"

"Do I have to have a reason? I care about you." He felt a bittersweet rush of memory. *And you remind me of someone I used to know.*

"Oh, Wickham! Thank you! Thank you so much!" Kate skipped around the table and flung herself into Zach's arms, squeezing her large stomach between them. Because of that very prominent part of her anatomy, she couldn't get quite close enough for a satisfactory hug. Her hands barely met behind his neck. She couldn't rest her cheek against his waistcoat, so made do, instead, with pressing the kerchiefed crown of her head against him. It was a laughable, touching moment that culminated when one of the twins decided to object to being crowded in such a manner, and gave Kate a stout kick in the ribs.

Zach also felt the movement of the unborn child, stirring up all sorts of yearnings. He wanted to get Gabby with child, as big in incipient pregnancy as Kate was. Bursting with child. His child.

Despite the uncomfortable treatment of her ribs, Kate

continued in good spirits and was full of conversation as she fixed a late breakfast for Zach and got all the bread dough in pans, covered and set out near the fire to rise. Mrs. Stark and some of the women came in and out, and Zach asked them about themselves and listened to what they said, occasionally throwing in a word of praise or encouragement. An hour and a half passed in this manner, and Zach was just about to bring up his own concerns when Charlie once again entered the kitchen. He held out a scrolled-up square of dirty parchment, tied with a bit of string.

"What's this, Charlie? Something for me?" Zach took the odd-looking missive and undid the string, shaking out the parchment so it could be read. "Did it come just now?"

Charlie nodded.

"Who brought it?"

Charlie indicated the size of the messenger by lowering a hand to the height of his hip.

"A child who was paid a penny to run it up the stairs, I expect." Zach bent to the task of perusing the note, which would have been difficult to read even if the paper it was written on had been clean and of better quality, because the writing and grammar were crude, the ink uneven and blotched. But the manner in which it was written become unimportant as Zach deciphered the substance of the message. He felt the blood drain from his head as if it pooled in the very soles of his boots. *Oh, dear God, Gabby...*

Kate watched as Zachary Wickham grew pale as a ghost. Her smile fell away. "What is it, Wickham? Who's the note from?"

He hastily stuffed the parchment scroll into an inner waistcoat pocket. She watched him arrange his face into a neutral non-expression. "I have to go." His voice was edged with urgency.

Kate's heart flip-flopped with fear. "No one's died, have they, Wickham?"

"No," he said, moving toward the door. "Don't worry, Kate. It's nothing I can't handle. I'll see you tomorrow." He turned and threw her a vague, unconvincing smile, his mind obviously occupied with sober thoughts.

With a few quick strides down the hall he reached the parlor. She heard the brassy sound of locks being briskly and efficiently undone and the slam of the door echoing through the apartment. He was gone. She and Charlie looked at each other, one worried face reflecting the other. Then Charlie went and rehooked the chains and redid the bolts and locks.

The house still smelled clean and freshly scrubbed. The other women still hummed like contented bees. But fear replaced the happiness in Kate's heart. She had an awful feeling that Douglas was involved in this note business. He was up to something. She couldn't imagine what, but she couldn't dismiss the uneasy feeling, either. She'd heard that he was seen frequently in Carruber's Close. She'd even seen him herself once from the window, their eyes meeting for an instant before she drew back, overcome with mixed feelings of love and fear. But he'd never actually come to the door. Maybe he'd heard about Charlie.

Kate knew Douglas must be furious with her. She knew he was probably consumed with rage at her audacity in actually consenting to be locked up and kept away from him.

Kate leaned against the table as an achy pressure in her lower stomach made her legs go weak as water. She braced herself with her hands on the tabletop and waited for the sensation to pass. She busied her mind by remembering how she and Douglas used to be. Oh, how she'd loved him! How she wished him back the way he used to be! Wickham said he'd help, but Douglas would have to be willing to help himself, too. Without Douglas's complete cooperation, any attempts to change his destructive habits would be doomed to failure.

Poor Wickham had his own troubles. She saw how he'd watched that pretty blond girl in the "coat of many colors," gliding over the ice with a lightness and grace Kate could scarcely remember owning herself before the pregnancy ... before the drinking. Wickham loved that girl, and he must trust himself to confess his love to her and begin a life together. Kate wanted Wickham, who'd done so much for her, to do as much for himself.

As the pressure eased and the achiness diminished, Kate opened her eyes and glanced down at the tabletop. There, written in neat letters in the flour was the name ... *Gabby*.

As per the instructions in the note, Zach rode to the cottage without the company of either servant or friend. It was a simple enough demand on paper, requiring minimal wordage, but it really took quite a bit of doing to accomplish. First he'd had Malcolm drive him back to Charlotte Square, and there, without changing his clothes or giving his servants any sort of explanation, he'd instructed the stableboy to saddle a horse.

Zach had not brought his dapple gray with him to Scotland, and he suspected that the big fellow was eating to his heart's content in the stables at Pencarrow and growing quite stout. He'd have to borrow one of the Murrays' steeds. He chose a powerful roan stallion, a horse that looked as though he could easily carry two people over a considerable distance without getting winded. As soon as this was done, Zach rode off, leaving Malcolm and John scratching their heads in bewilderment.

The cottage was just outside Edinburgh, distantly attached to a little village called Dirleton. From a small snow-crested hill above it, he could see the cluster of stone houses with smoking chimneys, and the kirk with its square of graveyard and its crooked rows of tombstones. He descended the hill, keeping wide of the village, not wishing to draw any attention to himself. If the inhabitants of Dirleton knew the cottage was supposed to be empty just now, they might feel bound to investigate if someone appeared to be heading there.

Though why anyone would want to stir from their fireside on such a bleak afternoon was more than Zach could fathom. The pleasant morning had given way to an early, growing darkness. In the last hour the wind had risen, and naturally the temperature had dropped. He could feel the icy breath of the Firth of Forth through the thick of his redingote and hear its keening howl slice through the shivering trees. The storm was nearing.

Zach wondered if Gabby was warm, or if that villain McKeen had stowed her away in some freezing chamber without any consideration for her comfort. He knew that McKeen wouldn't dare build a fire in the deserted cottage for fear of attracting attention to the place, but he hoped that McKeen would have supplied Gabby with blankets.

Worse than the lack of a warming fire or blankets, Gabby could have been hurt by McKeen. If he could knock about his pregnant wife, he'd probably have no compunction about doing the same to Gabby. Particularly if he had been drinking, McKeen could easily lose patience with Gabby because it was against her nature to meekly acquiesce to being manhandled and ordered about by McKeen, or anybody. Zach had a lump on his head to attest to that!

Zach thrust aside the image of his feisty Gabby, subdued, cowering, her face and her beautiful white body covered with ugly black bruises. All because of him again! If not for his involvement in the women's shelter, Gabby wouldn't be held hostage by Kate's revengeful and desperate husband. But he refused to believe that McKeen had lost control and beaten Gabby. He refused to think the worst. He would think of something else, force himself to concentrate on his surroundings.

Even in the blighted dead of winter, Scotland was beautiful. It wasn't Cornwall. Nothing was as beautiful as Cornwall, Zach decided, without feeling a trace of prejudicial guilt. But Scotland came close. It was as free and sweeping, the land not as segmented as England's middle countries with all their charming hedgerows and privet shrubs. Here and there drystone dikes etched a pattern against the ironhard winter ground, but for the most part there were fields and fields of heather, frostbitten now, as colorless as the rest of the landscape, but with the promise of its plum-colored bloom waiting in the hibernating buds. Stands of pine, like horizontal brush strokes of black ink, were silhouetted against the white hills.

The cottage stood nestled at the bottom of one of these hills. The door was painted yellow and appeared quite new, devoid of sun blisters and other signs of age and neglect. Bright curtains the color of sunshine hung in the windows, and the garden and enclosing stone walls and outbuildings looked to be in good repair. The owners took pride in their little getaway cottage and kept it well maintained.

Zach looked about the area for movement of any kind, but saw nothing and no one. He tugged at the reins of his roan, and they cantered round to the back of the cottage toward the stable. This was the place McKeen had designated as their rendezvous point. The stable was a small stone building with a large door, which, he could see, was standing slightly ajar. He supposed this was an invitation to come inside, since it appeared that McKeen wasn't coming out.

Zach dismounted his horse and led it by the reins to the stable door. He would take it inside with him, as well, out of the wind and out of sight of any possible passersby. The rusted hinges of the door creaked in protest as he pushed it wide enough to accommodate the girth of his horse, then closed it shut behind them.

Once inside the dimly lit building, Zach tethered his horse to a post and waited for McKeen to show himself. Zach knew he was there, because a piebald horse was munching oats in one of the stalls. When he did not appear immediately, Zach cautiously cast a look about the dark stalls, the rafters, and the cobbled floor strewn with wet hay. Lingering in the air was the scent of horses and leather and fragrant alfalfa. He saw a ladder at the far end of the stable, leading to a small, enclosed loft—minuscule, really—which was probably used to house the occasional hired hand. Still no one stirred from the quiet shadows.

Zach felt a moment's doubt. Had he misunderstood the exact location or the time? Or had McKeen tricked him into coming out here for reasons Zach didn't as yet understand? He hadn't checked before he left Charlotte Square ... Was it possible that Gabby wasn't even being held hostage?

"Gabby?" he called. "Gabby, are you here?"

Near where the ladder jutted out from the stalls, the tall, lanky form of a man appeared out of the darkness. McKeen. So, this was Kate's Douglas. This was the man she loved. This was the man who beat her black and blue. Zach didn't know what to think of him, how to feel. His first instinct was to give back to McKeen some of the same treatment he'd given his wife.

Then he remembered all the things Kate had told him about the way she and Douglas were before he got to drinking so heavily. Happy. In love. Maybe McKeen was decent when he wasn't awash in whiskey. Maybe, like so many of the women who came to Zach's shelter, this man was redeemable. He'd like to believe that was true... for Kate's sake, especially.

McKeen approached till they were separated by no more than six feet. Their eyes met across this short distance, bloodshot icy blue clashing with golden sorrel swirls. "Ye bloody bastard. Ye dinna bring 'er."

Zach had known that McKeen would be furious with him for ignoring the most important of his instructions—to bring Kate. "No, I didn't bring her. It's a nasty afternoon. There's a storm brewing. She's better off where she is."

McKeen's jaw worked agitatedly. "She's better off bein' where she rightfully belongs. With 'er husband. With me."

"I had no idea what condition you'd be in, or how you intended to take care of her."

"The same as I always have. B'sides, she's no concern o' yers."

"She became my concern when I nearly ran her down with my coach on New Year's Eve. She was drunk, sick, chilled to the bone, hugely pregnant, and covered with bruises. Is that what you call 'taking care' of someone?"

McKeen had the grace—the conscience, apparently—to look shamefaced. Zach noticed how his hand shook as he lifted it to pull work-roughened fingers through his thick black hair. He was already half drunk, though not near the deplorable state he'd be in by nightfall. "She run away, the little fool! 'Tis no fault o' mine she put herself in the way o' yer bloody 'orses! I dinna know why she took the notion t' run off, neither."

Zach remained implacably calm. "You know very well why she left you, McKeen."

McKeen's eyes darted, and his already florid complexion

deepened in color. "I dinna know what ye're talkin' 'bout."

"Yes, you do." Zach did not point-blank accuse McKeen of beating Kate. McKeen knew he had. Zach knew he had. It was an unspoken fact that riddled McKeen with guilt and filled Zach with unintentional but unavoidable disgust, creating a wall of silence between them. Zach tried to separate the man, McKeen, from the sordid act of wife-battering, as Kate did. But it was hard.

It was also damned hard to hold back his pressing anxiety about Gabby's whereabouts, hard not to take McKeen by the neck and choke the information out of him. But he had to remain cool and in control. Things could get violent very easily, and Zach had learned to abhor violence, especially at his own hands.

"How were you going to get Kate back to your place in town, McKeen?" He gestured toward the piebald horse. "On that? She's pregnant, you know, and the ride would be damned uncomfortable, if not dangerous. If you hadn't thought of that, it makes me wonder even more how you can profess to care about her when you don't consider her delicate condition and think only of your own selfish wishes."

McKeen pressed his lips tightly together.

Zach continued. "I left her in the kitchen at the shelter, happily pounding a mound of bread dough to pieces. She was clean and sober. Remember, McKeen, how she used to be when you were first married, before you foisted your drinking habit on her? She's healthy now for the first time in years, and she's round as an apple, full of your children."

McKeen's eyes glinted. "Children?"

"Yes, you're going to be the father of twins."

While McKeen, stunned, digested this news, Zach went on. "She talked about you. She told me how much she wished you back the way you used to be, before the drinking."

Instantly on the defensive, McKeen said gruffly, "All men drink."

This was the sore spot. This was where Zach knew he'd run into resistance, where Douglas would balk and deny. But he had to say it. "Yes, McKeen, most men drink, and women, too. For some, however, the liquor becomes an addiction, a crutch. It works on them like a poison, bringing out the worst."

"I'm not addicted to anythin', Wickham," snarled McKeen. "I dinna need no crutch!"

"We're willing to help you, Douglas. If you come to the shelter, we can—"

"Ha!" McKeen spat on the ground to show just what he thought of Zach's offer of help. "I'm not one o' yer moonyeyed womenfolk, swept off 'er silly-arsed feet by the pretty likes o' you, and shut up and preached to by some mawkish Quaker! And ye've not fooled me, Wickham! I know ye're jest sayin' these things t' justify keepin' me wife. Ye're in love with 'er yerself, and ye dinna want t' let 'er go!"

Zach sighed. "That's a lie, as well you know. I'm not in love with Kate."

McKeen smiled, the rancorous smirk of a desperate man. With sinister sweetness, he said, "Are ye in love with the little blond princess I've got locked up in the loft yonder, then?"

Disbelief and rage gripped Zach's heart like a vise. His gaze darted to the loft where Gabby was incarcerated in its airless, cramped, dark interior. He'd thought McKeen would have put her inside the cottage. He squeezed his eyes shut, dizzy, gripped in empathetic terror. Zach couldn't imagine anything more horrible. *God, poor Gabby.* Zach opened his eyes, locking his gaze with McKeen's. Hostility pulsed between them. "Let her out."

"But ye dinna bring Kate t' exchange."

"Did you really think I would? And I didn't bring Kate not only because it would be dangerous for her and the babies, but because I didn't want her to know to what low methods you have resorted in trying to achieve your own selfish ends."

"'Tis not low to want yer wife back."

"Let Gabby out now, McKeen, or I'll fetch her myself."

McKeen pulled a pistol from his back trouser pocket and aimed it straight at Zach's heart. "Oh, will ye? Rather I think it might be a good notion t' put ye up there with 'er till ye think better o' yer meddlesome ways. Mayhap a few hours in that scurvy little rat's hole, so like me own garret back in Auld Reekie, will change yer way o' thinkin' t' be more like mine. Then the two o' us can go back t' that blasted shelter t'gether and fetch me Kate. Now move, Wickham. Straight up the ladder wi' ye, or I'll blast a hole right through yer chest."

CHAPTER SEVENTEEN

Gabrielle's hip was sore from lying on her side, but she couldn't very well turn on her back because Douglas had tied her hands behind her with a length of rope. It would be rather painful to put all her weight on her arms and hands, especially since her fingers were already going numb from lack of circulation. Besides, her feet were tied together, too, and she was a little afraid that she'd end up like some poor turtle, flat on her back on that narrow bed and unable to remedy the situation.

As for lying on her front, her face would be pushed into the bed ticking, which had a sweaty, earthy odor clinging to it, most probably accumulated over time from all the hardworking fellows who had collapsed there in exhausted sleep. In an unexpected show of consideration, Douglas had thrown a scratchy, damp-smelling woolen blanket over her which Gabrielle feared was infested with horse fleas. But with that as a buffer against the frigid air that permeated the tiny loft apartment, and her warm mantle, boots, and mittens, she seemed in no immediate danger of freezing.

Not so considerate of Douglas was the gag he'd fit between Gabrielle's teeth and tied snugly behind her head. The rough cloth bit into the sides of her mouth and made her jaw ache. As they were out in the middle of nowhere, Gabrielle couldn't understand why Douglas felt it expedient to gag her. As well, she couldn't believe that in that short space of forty-eight hours she'd managed to *twice* find herself trussed like a chicken! It was making her extremely cross.

As the afternoon dragged by, the room got darker and darker. There was only one window in the tiny chamber, and it had been boarded up from the outside. The only indication that it was still daylight came from a crack in the corner of the ceiling where a splinter of thin sunshine shone through. Gabrielle kept her eye on that bit of pale gloaming, figuratively hanging on to its friendly light for moral support. Surely Zach would come before the room had gone completely dark.

She hated the darkness. Ever since she'd been lost in that tin mine as a child, Gabrielle had disliked having to snuff her candle at night before snuggling under the covers. Most often she'd stir up the fire, leave her bed curtains open, and drift off to sleep watching the tiny flames lick at the cinders of a shrunken log, the golden embers blinking like sleepy cats' eyes.

The wind was building up, too. It pushed against the barn, wailing and lowing like a lost calf looking for its mother. The mournful sound fretted at her, making her all the more anxious and worried, not that Zach wouldn't come for her—she knew he would—but wondering what would happen between Douglas and Zach when he did come.

Knowing Zach, he'd not bring Kate with him. He'd face Douglas alone. Douglas would be angry, and they'd fight. She didn't know whether Douglas's consistent drinking from the moment he'd picked her up outside the Tuttles' till now would help or hinder Zach. Although excess drinking could slow a man's reflexes and befuddle his thinking, Gabrielle was well aware that it could also lend him foolhardy courage and make him violent and vicious.

The time for speculation was soon to be over, because she heard Zach's voice calling her. Her heart leaped with joy. As if just knowing he was nearby might give her extra strength, she strained at the ropes that tied her hands and feet. Realizing the futility of that, however, she quickly settled again and listened.

Douglas was talking. Their voices were raised, so she was able to hear the whole conversation between them, losing only an occasional word under the howl of the wind. Just as she'd expected, Zach had not brought Kate. She was proud of him for not giving in to Douglas's blackmail tactics. Zach apparently was even willing to help Douglas to sobriety. But Douglas would have nothing of it. He had produced a gun. Now they were climbing the ladder, and unless Zach did something foolish, soon he'd be joining her in the loft.

Gabrielle held her breath. She knew it would rankle Zach to be held at gun point, but she prayed fervently that he'd do as Douglas told him. She didn't want Zach to end up face down in the hay with a bullet in his back. The very image this possibility conjured up filled Gabrielle with unspeakable terror.

The bolt lifted, and the door creaked open. There was a flood of gray light, Zach's tall figure outlined against it for an instant, then a jerky step forward as if he'd been pushed. The door slammed shut, the bolt scraped into place, and she could hear McKeen climbing down the ladder. She was alone with Zach.

"Gabby?"

Zach's eyes had obviously not adjusted to the darkness. Unable to call to him, she wriggled about on the bed till he heard her movements and turned to peer at her through the gloom.

"Gawd!" he muttered vehemently beneath his breath as he sprang forward and kneeled beside the bed. "The bloody bastard! What's he done to you?" Gabrielle found herself in the ludicrous position of trying to smile around the gag, wanting to reassure him that though she had been made extremely uncomfortable, she wasn't harmed.

Zach started with her feet, untying the ropes with impatient tugs, then her hands, and finally the gag. He helped her sit up, then massaged life back into her hands while she rubbed her aching jaw.

"Why didn't you take off the gag first, Zach?" she wondered aloud.

"Because, sweeting, with the gag off, I'd not have been able to stop myself from kissing you, and I have a horror of kissing trussed-up females! Shut up, because I'm going to kiss you now!"

Still on his knees, Zach pulled Gabrielle into his arms and kissed her bruised mouth, knocking off his hat in the process. The pain of it was blissful. Then he just held her close. Gabrielle never felt so safe or so happy as when she was in Zach's arms. It didn't matter where they were, or what horrid mess she'd got them into, as long as they were together.

Presently he pushed her away slightly and squinted to look at her. His golden eyes appeared pale gray in color, transmuted to the shadowy mist of a waning eventide. The night was gathering swiftly now. In just a few moments, the loft would be pitch black. But, as she'd told Bella on Christmas Eve, Zach was Gabrielle's bit of sunshine, and with him she wasn't afraid of the dark.

Zach's fingers were firm on her shoulders. "Tell me the truth, Gabby. Did he touch you? In any way, did he... hurt you?"

"He only tied me up, which isn't a bit comfortable, but he didn't hurt me."

"I thought he might have—" He didn't finish.

"You thought he might have beaten me, like he beat Kate?".

"How do you know about Kate?"

"Mr. McKeen, while being rather confused at the moment between the right and wrong way to get back his wife, is not uncommunicative."

Zach sat back on his heels, his hands sliding down to rest on his thighs. "You know about the shelter, then?"

"Yes." She gave a rueful smile, lost no doubt in the darkness. "I've learned a lot about you from strangers in the last couple of days. How long have you been running the shelter?"

"For about three years."

"Why Edinburgh? Why not London?"

He hesitated. She could imagine his lips pursing, considering his answer. He sighed. "Well, you might as well know all." Then almost to himself, he said, "I vowed to tell all." In a louder voice, "There's another in London. And in Liverpool."

"So that's where you've been going all these years on your long absences from Pencarrow? You've been visiting your shelters, checking up on the management of them, I presume?"

"Exactly."

Gabrielle gave a little laugh. "And in St. Teath and round about Bodmin Moor, people said you'd gone off to lose yourself in dissipation and debauchery! You must have known they were saying such ghastly things about you. Why did you never set them straight?"

"You mean, why didn't I tell people about the shelters? I suppose because I didn't think it was any of their business."

"But you never even told *me*, Zach!" cried Gabrielle, unwilling to be put off with such an elusive answer. "You always used to tell me everything!"

"Not everything, Gabby. Some things are best not discussed, particularly with impressionable young girls with clean, fresh minds and hearts. Why disillusion you and sully your innocence?"

Gabrielle leaned forward and put her hands on each side of Zach's face. "But secrecy can lead to appalling misunderstandings! I thought Kate was your mistress or—worse still—your bride-to-be!" She felt his lips turn up in a smile. She slid her thumbs into the laugh lines that bracketed his mouth.

"No, Gabby. Kate is just a friend."

"McKeen doesn't think so."

Zach's smile fell away. "He's a jealous fool. I pity him, but I know how he feels." There was a pause. Gabrielle waited for him to continue. This was a promising beginning. She was about to brazenly prompt him to elucidate when he returned to the original topic. "I never told anyone—not even you—about the shelters because, I suppose, I was a little embarrassed."

"Embarrassed? You don't mean—?"

"No, I don't mean I was embarrassed about being criticized for fraternizing with so-called fallen women, though I'm sure some people would think it degrading. I was embarrassed to think that people might look on me as some sort of attention-craving philanthropist. I wanted neither criticism nor praise for what I was doing. I just wanted to do it. The shelters exist for the benefit of women who need help restarting their lives, and I draw satisfaction from their successes without having to discuss it with anybody other than my administrators and other workers at the shelter."

"Like Mr. Blake?"

"Yes. There are other anonymous people, you know, who make contributions to the shelters—some of them on a regular basis. Maybe they feel as I do, that, in a way, something would be taken away from the merit of it if I told my friends and family about the shelters. And I suppose it was selfish of me to want to protect my good feelings by keeping mum. But I'm a selfish man."

"I'm selfish, too, so you see we're destined to be together." Gabrielle had said it teasingly, but she meant it with her whole heart.

Zach turned his head and kissed the palm of her hand. "As I told you last night, sweeting, we have to talk. I have lots of things I must tell you, so you'll understand why I've been so—" He stopped abruptly, and Gabrielle could feel a slight tremor go through him.

"What's wrong, Zach?"

"Nothing … Lord, it's just so damned stuffy in here!"

"How can you say so? It's positively icy!"

He caught her wrists and pulled her hands away from his face, standing up. "It can be cold, but the air can still be stale, musty-smelling… Like an old cellar, or a crypt, or a cave… You know what I mean?"

He was pacing the floor. She could just make out his tall figure going back and forth, back and forth. "I admit it does seem a little close in here, and smelly. But there are so many gaps between the boards, plenty of cold air is getting through. Especially in this wind."

"He's boarded up the window. We can't even open a window!"

"Who would want to?" She gave a little laugh, but Zach did not reply or respond in any way. He just kept pacing. "Zach, shouldn't you stand still or come sit by me? You're going to trip in the dark—catch your boot on a nail or something—and fall down."

"I can't sit still. We have to think of a way out of here." His voice was brittle with tension.

"You know there's no way out of here. You know we're going to have to wait till Mr. McKeen is good and ready to let us out. He's hoping to change your mind about Kate."

"There's a storm brewing. We could be holed up here till spring!"

There was panic in Zach's voice. He was usually so calm and capable, unflappable even in the face of the most frightening possibilities. Why was this time different? But then she remembered another time… He'd panicked at Mother Henn's. She'd been questioning him about his past. He'd felt pressured, hemmed in. Later she'd concluded that Zach had had a reaction to that clout she'd given him over the head, coupled with the stress of fending off her persistent questions. But this time she wasn't pressuring him. He seemed ready to talk. So why was he so distraught?

She realized suddenly that he was no longer pacing. He was standing stock-still. She stood up and went to him, finding him leaning against the opposite wall. He was shaking. Every inch of him was shaking.

"Zach? What's wrong?" She ran a hand up his arm, along his shoulder. She pressed her palm against his cheek. He was sweating. Her other hand rested on his chest. Through his thick redingote she could feel his rapid breathing—silent, shallow intakes and outflows of air. His arms were limp at his sides.

He did not speak. He was trembling so violently that she didn't suppose he'd dare try to speak even if he could. But she didn't think he could. He was having some sort of a phobic episode like the one he'd had at Mother Henn's—only worse— and she instinctively knew that the best thing she could do to help him through it was to hold him. She thought she knew, too, why he had panicked. Apparently she wasn't the only one who still suffered from that nightmarish day in the Pencarrow tin mine. She wrapped her arms around his waist and pressed herself against him, holding him tighter than she'd ever held anyone. She whispered soothing words. And she waited.

It took much longer than it had taken that time at Mother Henn's, but gradually Gabrielle could feel the tension easing out of Zach. He stopped shaking. His breathing slowed and grew deeper. His arms came up and wrapped around her shoulders.

"I've got to sit down, Gabby." His tone was that of a weary

man, as if he'd just tramped over the highest of the Pentland Hills. His long, strong legs began to buckle at the knees.

"Here, Zach? Why don't we—"

"I can't make it to the bed just yet. Give me a moment, please."

So Gabrielle sank with him to the floor. He leaned his back against the wall and drew her between his updrawn legs, fitting her neatly against him. Still they clung to each other, and presently he gave a great huge sigh.

"I was hoping to leave this to the last."

"What do you mean, Zach?"

"I've hid this from everyone for so long."

"You have a phobia."

"Yes. And it makes me feel like a coward. I can't control it. I—"

"That's why you're such a glutton for fresh air, always opening windows. You panic in close quarters. You can't stand to be penned in, cut off from easy access to the outside."

He sighed again. "Exactly. And if I lose control, as I did today, afterward I feel weak as a kitten."

"These episodes of panic happen to you because of that time when I was lost in the tin mine, don't they?"

Zach did not reply.

"Don't protect me from the truth, Zach. It was because you and I and Alex were almost buried under all that earth. It's my fault you have a phobia."

"No! It's my fault because if it hadn't been for my irresponsibility, that tin mine would have been boarded up. And you'd not have been looking for knackers, either, but I insisted on letting you listen in on one of Pye Thatcher's drolleries. Beth said you were too young. She was right. I was wrong."

"Oh, Zach. I hope you aren't still blaming yourself for all that! It was so long ago."

"I've thought about it at length, Gabby, and I don't think I developed this phobia exclusively because of the guilt connected to the accident, but also because I nearly lost the two people I love most in the world—you and Alex."

"But if you understand—"

"I've learned that insight into a problem and the resolution of it don't always go hand in hand. I can't seem to stop the panic I feel in close quarters." He paused to take a breath. "And that other problem I have …"

"You mean your inability to embark on a relationship with a woman?"

He squeezed her, gave a chuckle. "You sound so clinical, Gabby! But, yes."

"That's why you haven't been able to admit that you love me."

"If I admitted to loving you, then I'd be committing myself to belong to you, and you to belong to me. I don't seem to be able to hold onto the women I love. First my mother, then Beth, then Tess… I think I've been afraid that if I openly loved you and made you the central part of my life, I'd lose you. I'd hurt you somehow. Do you understand?"

"I understand, but it isn't logical, you know."

"No, I know it isn't. But there it is."

"Tell me about Tess."

There was a long pause. "I don't know if this is such a good time to talk about Tessy."

Gabrielle snuggled against him. "I don't think we're going anywhere for a while. McKeen will get drunk and go to sleep, or in a bit he'll get impatient to see Kate and let you out to fetch her. But I feel fairly sure we've got time to talk. Tell me, Zach. Tell me about Tessy."

And he did.

Over the years Gabrielle had heard bits and pieces of gossip about this young woman called Tessy, her full name inscribed in the church records as Mary Teresa Kenpenny, and buried with her child beneath the large limbs of the horse chestnut tree by the old chapel at Pencarrow. But hearing the whole story from Zach, all the details of the short life of this tragic girl, made her seem as real as if Gabrielle had known her personally.

Zach had been engaged to Beth, Gabrielle's sister, and everyone knew that she had broken off the engagement to marry Zach's older brother, Alex. But while Zach was betrothed to Beth, he was keeping a little cottage outside of St. Teath, where he had ensconced his seventeen-year-old mistress, Tess.

She was beautiful. She had cornflower blue eyes and golden hair. She was delicate and soft-spoken. She was too sweet for her own good. Zach's mistake, apparently, had been to at first underestimate the strength of his passion for her, and secondly, to be so shaken and frightened when he finally understood how much he loved her that he determined to put an end to their arrangement before he did something foolish—like marry her. He had given her a pouch full of sovereigns and the house, wishing her well in her next relationship.

Tess had confessed that she couldn't bear the thought of another man touching her. She loved Zach and was perfectly content to remain his mistress, marry whom he will. Zach, miserable at the idea of separation from Tess, was about to give in when he discovered that Tess, whom he had seen very little of in the last few weeks, had been hiding a pregnancy.

This fact, seen by Zach as a ploy on her part to dupe him into marriage, was the final straw. He coldly informed her he would provide for her and the child, but the money would be arranged through a solicitor. She would never see Zach again.

Probably precipitated by the emotional distress, later that day Tess delivered a seven-month babe, then died from complications of the difficult birth. Too late Zach realized how much he loved Tess and how little it mattered that she was socially inferior to him.

Zach had been dealing with unresolved guilt since his father blamed him for his mother's death while giving birth to Zach. Tessy's death only added to his guilt, making him afraid to love another woman and perhaps bring tragedy into her life, as well. He felt worthless and unlovable. Didn't his own father send him away to be raised in distant Cornwall by his grandfather?

"Oh, Zach, you must understand that your father was a bitter man!" said Gabrielle at the end of this recital. "His behavior toward you—an innocent child!—was appalling. His rejection of you was wrong. You were not to blame for your mother's death!"

"Not directly, I suppose. And Alex has tried to make me see how useless it's been for me to feel responsible. If only Tessy hadn't died in the same manner... It makes me feel as though I'm a curse or something!"

"Never say so! You've brought nothing but happiness to my life, and saved my skin on several occasions, too, I might add! And look how you've helped all those women by opening the shelters."

"The shelters were like a gift to Tess. I felt I'd failed her, and I suppose I've been trying to make up for that by helping other women in similar situations. Restitution, as it were. I wanted my philanthropy to be 'the cure for what ails me.' It's helped, but I still feel like something's missing."

"The best gift you could give Tess is to go on with your life. The shelters are wonderful, but you do need something more, Zach." She kissed his cheek. "You need me! Let my love be the balm for your wicked soul, Zachary Wickham!" she teased. "And if you feel the need for punishment, let that punishment be me, as well! Let me curse you with a lifetime of pulling me out of the briars, out of all the scrapes I seem to attract like bees to honey! I'm perfect for you, Zach. Admit it! I'm the rose *and* the thorn!"

Zach laughed, the deep comforting sound filling the dark room, scattering its gloom, making it warm and secure. "You expound a convincing argument, Gabby. You do make me feel better. Just your holding me helped get me through that stupid episode just now. If you truly want to be part of my life, though, you have to realize that there may be other times you'll have to hold me while I shake and sweat like a deranged lunatic. I may need a hefty dose of your particular medicine to cure me completely, sweeting."

"I think I can force myself to endure holding you now and then." There was a smile in her voice. "Will you promise to hold me, too, whenever I should happen to need *you?*"

His arms tightened around her. "With all my heart, Gabby. With all my heart."

A comfortable silence fell over them as they huddled together. Feeling blissfully satisfied to have finally talked things out with Zach, and so safe and protected in his arms, Gabrielle forgot for a time that they were being held prisoner by a dangerous man with a gun. She was reminded of this reality when she heard his heavy footsteps coming up the ladder. She felt Zach tense. "So soon?" he whispered. "You were right, Gabby, McKeen's more impatient to see Kate than I thought."

The bolt was yanked up and the door opened. McKeen stood in the doorway with a lantern hanging from one hand and his gun in the other. The bright yellow glow of the flame blinded Gabrielle for a moment, but as her eyes adjusted, she could see that McKeen was swaying a little. She suspected that he was deep in his cups and near to passing out.

"A cozy pair, ain't ye?" he sneered, his words a slur. "But I s'pect ye dinna want t' stay in this rat-hole no longer. B'sides, there's a bloody blizzard started outside. We have t' get back t' town soon, or we'll be stranded 'ere. Not a lovely thought, eh? I s'pect ye're ready and willin' t' take me t' Kate now, Wickham."

Zach did not say a word. He gently assisted Gabrielle to her feet, then unobtrusively pushed her to the side. She realized that he was putting her out of the line of fire. He was planning to do something—surprise McKeen and take away the gun, perhaps. She darted Zach a pleading look. *It's too dangerous!* her eyes seemed to say. But he did not so much as glance at her. All his concentration was centered on McKeen.

Zach flashed a charming smile of chagrin, lifting his hands in a surrendering fashion. "Well, McKeen, it looks like you're going to get your way this time, so I may as well go in good grace."

McKeen smiled back. "Al'ays a gentleman, al'ays doin' the pretty, ain't ye, Wickham? Move along wi' ye." He stood back and waved his gun, indicating that they precede him through the door.

"Just let me get my hat—" Zach moved toward the bed where his hat lay, coming within inches of McKeen. Then, in a quick movement that took McKeen completely by surprise, Zach grabbed the wrist of McKeen's right hand—the hand that held the gun. He yanked his arm skyward, McKeen's finger tightened in panic, and the gun went off with a deafening report.

"Bloody 'ell!" shouted McKeen, letting go of the lantern handle to free his left hand for defending himself. But Zach was too quick for him. He gave McKeen a neat clip to his jaw, and down he went with a thud. While Zach removed the gun from McKeen's limp hand, Gabrielle scrambled to retrieve the overturned lantern from off the straw-strewn floor before something caught fire.

"Goodness, that was quick," said Gabrielle, standing over McKeen's supine form.

"Not particularly meritorious on my part," grumbled Zach, "hitting a drunkard who might have as easily been knocked over by a feather."

"I'm sure you didn't hit him any harder than you needed to," Gabrielle said to soothe him. "Besides, what else could you do?"

"Nothing comes racing to mind. Wait here, Gabby. Keep the light on McKeen, in case he moves." He handed her the gun. "If he stirs—which he won't—point this at him till I get back. I'm going to check on this blizzard he was prattling on about, then we'll decide what to do."

Gabrielle waited in the little room while Zach descended the ladder, holding the lantern obediently near McKeen, but avoiding looking at him. She heard the barn door creak open, then shut very shortly afterward. Zach soon returned to the room, his redingote dusted with snow.

"Don't tell me you got all that snow on you simply by opening the stable door."

"Exactly." Zach brushed at his jacket and eyed McKeen. "He was right. It's a blizzard out there. We don't dare try to ride back to town because the snow, combined with this wind, might blind us. I don't fancy bouncing down some rocky hillside on my head."

Gabrielle looked around the tiny room. "You mean we're stuck here till the storm is over, and with him? What happens when he wakes up? He'll be cross as a bear with a sore ear."

"I don't think he's going to wake up till morning. I suspect he passes out in a like manner every night, sleeping off the booze for several hours."

"Well, I still don't like the notion of being holed up here all night."

Zach rubbed his jaw in a ruminative fashion. "We don't have to stay in this loft, you know."

Gabrielle grinned. "You mean we can go downstairs and while away the hours making houses out of hay?"

Zach looked at her. In the glow of the lantern, his face was strangely planed with shadows, his eyes a rich brandy amber. She felt an anticipatory shiver run down her spine, but she wasn't sure what she was anticipating. "No, we can go to the house and build a fire. In this storm, nobody's going to come and try to oust us. Besides, whoever owns the cottage couldn't possibly begrudge us taking shelter in it during the storm."

Gabrielle imagined being with Zach, alone in that cozy little cottage with the sunshine-yellow curtains. Her conscience dispelled this pleasant picture, though, when McKeen shifted slightly and commenced snoring. Deflated, she said, "But what about him?"

"He's too heavy to carry down the stairs. If we didn't kill ourselves attempting it, we might kill him. We'll put him on the bed and cover him with the blanket, as well as both our redingotes. He'll be warm as toast, I promise you. He won't care where he's sleeping, and he won't peep open an eye till sometime tomorrow. Now, let's get busy while we can still see our way to the house."

Still hesitating, more because it seemed too good to be true than for any other reason, Gabrielle said, "But won't we be cold without our wraps?"

"Just till we get to the house, sweeting. Inside we can build a fire." Their eyes met. "And I'm sure we can think of other ways to keep warm."

CHAPTER EIGHTEEN

Blinded by the blowing, stinging curtain of snow, Gabrielle simply shut her eyes and allowed Zach to pull her along till they were safely standing under the small wooden portico that jutted out over the cottage door. Shriveled wisteria vines trailed down and swung in the wind.

"At least we found it," she said through chattering teeth, pressing as close to Zach as possible.

"Did you doubt me?" Zach retorted mildly. "But now the question is, how to get inside without doing irreversible damage to the door."

"If you hurt the door, you can always leave them money to repair it," Gabrielle suggested reasonably. "Kick it in if you must, Zach. I'm freezing!"

Zach did kick it in, breaking the lock in the process, but luckily doing no harm to the door. They stumbled in and shut the door behind them. Zach put the lantern down, incredibly still burning brightly away, and surveyed the cottage. Because of the thick snow falling past the unshuttered windows, the room seemed to have a dim preternatural glow all its own. At any rate, it was much brighter than the loft. Gabrielle shook the snow from her hair and her gown and stamped her boots against the wooden floor.

"You remind me of old Rusty when he used to come in from the moors, shaking all the bramble twigs and goose grass out of his mangy coat," Zach commented teasingly. "He used to do such a dance."

Gabrielle's hair was in a tumble, and she had to push back a lock in order to glare at Zach reproachfully. "I'm terribly flattered."

Zach grinned unrepentantly and began to unbutton his jacket. "He was a good old dog—"

"What are you doing, Zach?" Gabrielle stared as Zach slipped out of his mulberry-colored coat and stood before her in his shirtsleeves. The crisp white brilliance of his shirt showed off his golden-brown skin and played up his beautiful white teeth.

He shrugged and flashed that charming straight-toothed smile. "My jacket's damp. I'm going to dry it by the fire."

"B-but there is no fire," she pointed out.

"There will be in a moment." He draped his jacket on the back of a chair, then walked briskly to the fireplace. "How obliging! There's some kindling and logs in the basket, even some coal. The people who keep this place must have been here recently, perhaps up for some winter geeseshooting. Everything is still so clean and orderly." He bent and made up the fire, talking to her over his shoulder. The flames were soon leaping up the chimney, and the room became bright and cheerily alive.

Gabrielle looked about her. The cottage was made up of just three main rooms. Through an open door she could see the kitchen and dining area, overlooking through a spacious mullioned window what was probably a small garden. She stood in a cozy parlor with a large fireplace central to the room, all of the furniture arranged around it. Another door, to the left of the fireplace and closed, could only lead to a bedchamber.

Now that the parlor was illuminated, she took the lantern into the dining area and set it down on the table. There were pots and pans hanging in the kitchen, and pottery and china in a hutch by the back door. There were stairs in the corner of the kitchen which probably led to a loft with sleeping accommodations. Gabrielle was sure there would be plenty of sheets and blankets stored about the place, and possibly the bed in the main bedchamber was already made up. She walked back to the parlor. She had a tremendous urge to throw open the bedchamber door and check for herself, but she wasn't sure how Zach would construe her curiosity about the bed, which was, of course, perfectly innocent.

"Do you suppose that's the bedchamber?"

Gabrielle started, embarrassed to have been caught staring at the door in question. Zach had got the fire blazing, had moved the chair he'd draped his jacket on nearer to the flames, and was whisking his hands together, presumably ready to tackle the next task. "I can't imagine what else it could be," she answered as if she couldn't care less, then blushed furiously when Zach arched a disbelieving brow.

"Well, why don't we see? I hope the bed's made up." Zach went to the door and opened it, then disappeared inside. Gabrielle couldn't see anything from where she stood, so she hesitantly stepped closer, craning her neck. Suddenly Zach's head popped round the doorjamb, very nearly causing Gabrielle to jump out of her skin. "Well, don't just stand there. Come in."

So she did. What she saw delighted her. The room was small, but there was a window in it, which would make Zach happy. And monopolizing the room was a huge brass four-poster bed with a blue-sprigged counterpane covering it, which, judging by the speculative way he was eyeing it, also made Zach happy.

Then he turned his speculative gaze on Gabrielle. She waited for him to say something either quite banal and disappointing like, "You can sleep here, and I'll make a bed on the floor in the parlor," or something quite outrageous and deliciously frightening like, "Well, what do you say, Gabby? Shall we hop in?" But he said neither. He said instead, "I'm ravenous. Let's see if there's any food in the kitchen."

He slid past her, and she followed him, watching from the doorway as he rifled through cupboards. "Nothing! Drat."

"Well, you didn't really expect to find something, did you? Food would spoil between holidays, or the mice would have a tremendous party dining on it."

"Eureka! There's a tin of tea here, and coffee. And some sugar, and what's this...?" Zach had found a shelf with several canisters, apparently with a few leftover staples in them. He turned to Gabrielle, his eyes bright with excitement. He reminded her of a small boy playing house. "It isn't particularly sumptuous, but there's oatmeal. We could make porridge."

Gabrielle's stomach had been growling for the past hour. Her last meal had been at the Tuttles' for breakfast. "Porridge sounds wonderful. Do you like it thick or thin?"

Zach turned. "I'll make it. As I recall, though you always used to enjoy making gingerbread when you were little, you were never too adept at cooking. Why don't you go and tidy up? I know you want to."

"I haven't any water."

"I'll get some snow and heat it in a kettle over the fire." He winked at her. "It's rather like being gypsies, isn't it, Gabby?"

She laughed nervously. "This would seem like a castle to a gypsy. I can't believe how lucky we are."

"That reminds me... Why don't you pull down the counterpane and the blankets on the bed and check the sheets? They could be damp. We may have to lay them out by the fire."

What had she said that reminded him about the bed? But she went and did as he suggested, finding, as he suspected, that the sheets were a bit damp. After stripping them off the bed and hanging them on chairs by the fire, her water had had time to heat up, so she carried it off to the bedchamber to freshen up. Zach had given her the lantern because he'd found a thick tallow work candle in the kitchen and was using that to see by.

Gabrielle sat in front of the dressing table and looked at herself in the mirror. She was wearing one of her more practical dresses. It was made of a soft cashmere fabric, fawn-colored and long-sleeved, with a large, lace-edged white collar. Since she was up before her abigail, Gabrielle had done her own hair that morning, and now it was half up and half down. She pulled it back and washed her hands and face, drying them on a tea towel Zach had found hanging on a kitchen hook. Then she took down what little of her hair was still pinned in place, and brushed it, leaving it to fall from a side part to rest on her shoulders. Unbound, it came to the middle of her back. Maybe she shouldn't have thought so, but she was quite pleased with her appearance. Her complexion glowed, her hair shined. She left the bedchamber and shyly stepped into the parlor.

Zach was sitting in a rocking chair by the fire, in front of the draped sheets. There was a little scallop-edged table pulled up next to him, and another chair just across. There were two bowls sitting on the table with a promising-looking spiral of steam issuing up from the contents of each.

"I thought it would be warmer to eat by the fire."

"Yes." She couldn't imagine why she felt so suddenly timid, but she found she couldn't even meet Zach's eyes as she moved to sit down in the chair he'd provided for her. In the past few weeks she had actually been quite forward with Zach, but now …

"You look quite lovely, Gabby. I like your hair down. I always have."

She'd sat down and was just reaching for her bowl when this comment caused her to freeze. She lifted her eyes and found him staring at her. There was a tender tug at the corner of his mouth and a warm luster in his amber eyes. He'd apparently freshened up, as well, in the kitchen, and the firelight glanced off his freshly brushed golden hair. His hands rested casually on the chair arms, his long, tapered fingers curved over the scrolled edges. His long legs were stretched in front of him. He looked infinitely patient. Infinitely loving.

"Eat your porridge, Gabby, before it cools," he said, breaking the spell. "You're going to need your strength."

Just what did he mean, I'll need my strength? Overcome with confusion and trying not to show it, Gabrielle ate.

After two or three self-conscious, dribbly bites, she decided that she was too hungry to let nervousness stand between her and a surprisingly delicious bowl of porridge. And maybe she *would* need her strength. She managed the rest without another dribble.

"That was the best porridge I've ever eaten," she said, setting down her bowl and leaning back in her chair.

Zach set down his own bowl. "Do you want more?"

"No."

Zach smiled and gave a little shove with his boot against the floor, sending his chair to rocking. *Infinitely patient.* She licked her lips, gone suddenly dry. "What o'clock is it, Zach?"

"I don't know," he said, lazily smiling. "I'd have to check my pocket watch, which is in my jacket, which is a whole two steps away. It's probably close to six."

"Are … are you sleepy?" Then, fearing he might misinterpret her question, she hurriedly added, "I mean, are you tired? You've had a tiring day."

"Do I look tired? I don't feel it. On the contrary, I feel quite refreshed after that bowl of porridge, and I'm enjoying the fire and your company, and the entrapping snowstorm immensely. I feel as though we're cut off from the world, Gabby, and for the first time it doesn't bother me in the least that I can't stir from the house." His gaze was warm and penetrating. "You were right. You're exactly what I need, sweeting. Exactly." He rocked forward, stood up, and pulled Gabrielle to her feet.

Standing so close to him, Gabrielle was again overwhelmed by a feeling of shyness. "Zach, I feel so odd. This is what I've wanted for so long. Yet… yet while I've known you all my life, tonight you're like someone new and strange. But not in a bad way, you know, in a good way!"

While she babbled, looking straight at his undone collar and the strong column of neck exposed above it, Zach ran his hands up her arms, cupping her shoulders, kneading them with strong, sure fingers. "I *am* someone new to you tonight, Gabby." She could feel his breath in her hair, soft, warm, ticklish. He continued to knead her shoulders, and she could feel the tight muscles attenuating, expanding, relaxing. "We've been friends forever. Good friends. And now, tonight, we're going to become lovers."

Gabrielle's heart did a little jig. "We are?"

He put her slightly away from him and bent his head to look into her eyes. "Unless you'd rather wait till we're married."

Gabrielle felt a delirious urge to giggle. What sane woman would turn down the opportunity of making love in a charming cottage during a romantic snowstorm, with a golden Adonis-like Zach? No one she knew, and surely not *her*. And he'd said such a lovely word, a word that conjured up possibilities of endless romantic snowstorms and love-filled nights—*marriage*. Besides that, she loved Zach and would have made love with him no matter what he could promise her in the way of commitments.

She felt her shyness receding. As she had been telling him forever, she wasn't a child any longer, and tonight would mark her symbolic and literal passage into womanhood. "I don't want to wait another moment, Zach."

He chuckled. "I always knew you'd be a handful. But we've got plenty of time. The storm isn't likely to let up soon, and we can only hope the Murrays will depend on you being with me again and won't worry too much. But there's nothing we can do to change the weather, so we might as well make the best of it."

Warming to the idea, as she always warmed to ideas that greatly appealed to her, Gabrielle lifted her arms and locked her fingers behind Zach's neck. "Then let me start."

Zach looked surprised. "Do you know how to start, sweeting?"

She nodded her head. "I love you, Zach."

He smiled, and the lines around his eyes crinkled. "Yes, that's a logical beginning, the truest and best beginning. I love you, too, Gabby."

He bent his head and kissed her.

Zach had told her that they'd plenty of time. Time to discover each other as lovers. Time for tender caresses and exploring kisses, while he patiently prepared Gabby for their ultimate joining. But her mouth was so sweet and full of promise, her body was so eagerly pressed to his, her curves so pliant and molding against his hardness, that Zach felt his desire spark like flint to dry kindling.

His restless hands roamed over her back, down to her slim waist and the subtle flare of her boyish hips, up again to the smooth nape of her neck. He pushed her hair back and kissed her there, just above the collar of her modest gown. Then he threaded his fingers through her hair, each cool, silky strand sliding sensuously over his tender palm.

He could feel her own tentative, curious explorations, her hands moving over his shoulders, small nimble fingers burrowing into his hair, drawing him closer, holding him with a fierce possessiveness. He loved it. He loved her eagerness, her wholehearted participation. He loved her more than life itself.

Gabrielle's heart was jarred into a frantic rhythm, each beat pushing heat and urgency through her veins. He tasted so good. He smelled so masculine, like sandalwood soap and the faint tang of salty perspiration. He felt so substantial, so real, yet so new and exciting. A little dangerous, even. A little scary. Her skin felt rough with gooseflesh, thinking about what they'd do, about what she wanted to do with him more than anything. He moved a hand between them and cupped her breast, brushing her nipple through the soft material of her gown with the hard pad of his thumb.

Zach watched her face, every stroke of his thumb reflected in her expression. She didn't hold anything back. She was completely natural with him, unashamed of her own pleasure. Gabby, the consummate actress, became as genuine as sunshine during lovemaking, as free as the wind. His pent-up need for her, the need he'd denied and suppressed ever since she'd grown into a woman, was demanding full expression, complete release.

"Gabby," he whispered against her warm cheek. "It's time, love. Time to let me undress you." In response, a tremor ran through Gabby. He pulled back and looked into her face, questioning, fearful that he'd gone too far, too fast. "Are you frightened, sweeting? Do you want to wait?"

She lifted her chin slightly, her hazel eyes softened to the color of sea-foam green. "No," she said with conviction. "No, I'm not frightened, and I truly don't want to wait."

He tenderly caught her chin in his hand, kissing her very gently on the mouth. Then, without speaking, he bent his gaze to the front of her gown and dexterously began to unhook and unbutton all the fastenings.

Gabrielle watched him, her eyes following his beautiful fingers at work on the front of her gown, the concentrated furrow of his tawny brows, the lowered sweep of his dark-brown lashes. His skill at disrobing her was not unattractive, either, though it inferred that he had not, as Rory had suggested, been celibate over the years. It made her feel as though she was in capable hands. And since she already loved him, and would have endured the most clumsy fumbling, it was all the more exciting to feel confident that Zach would know exactly how to love her. Exactly.

The gown was unfastened as far as it would go, and now Zach gently tugged at the sleeves, pulling them down her shoulders. With her arms free, and not much in the way of hips to slow its progress, her dress fell to the floor in copious folds of cashmere. She stepped out of the soft puddle of fabric, and Zach gathered it up and lay it over the same chair he'd hung his coat on.

Now Gabby stood in her underthings, her bottom lip caught between her teeth. Below the hem of her petticoat, Zach saw how she stood with one foot set on top of the other. She looked adorable, like a young girl waiting to be asked for her first dance. Eager, but shy. Excited, but nervous. As if she didn't quite know what else to do with them, she'd crossed her arms over her chest.

"You aren't cold, are you, Gabby?" he asked her.

She quickly shook her head, allowing her arms to fall awkwardly to her side. She blushed in the warmth of Zach's smile. The firelight flickered over her smooth white arms, the full, creamy exposure of breasts above the lace ruching of her corset. "The fire's quite nice and toasty," she mumbled, ducking her head.

"So it is," Zach agreed, "and because the fire's so nice, we'll take off the rest of your clothes."

Gabby darted him a look alight with delighted alarm, then caught her lip between her teeth again and waited. He did not linger over the task, as he might have done if he'd been a little less in love, a little less demented with desire. Quickly and efficiently, though with infinite gentleness, he took off her petticoat, her corset, her bustle, her chemise, her stockings, her half-boots, and her silk bloomers.

Completely naked now, Gabby stood there, like a diffident statue of exquisite white marble. She seemed willing to be looked at, but unsure of exactly how to behave while being thus observed. To Zach's loving eye, she was perfectly formed. Slim and firm, with proudly erect breasts and narrow hips, and legs that were as long as summer twilight. The tangle of crisp curls at the apex of her thighs was reddish-gold in the flame-glow of the fire. He took her chin between thumb and forefinger and lifted it, making her look at him. He wanted her to see the love, the adoration, the gratitude he felt for her, for her giving of herself, for her loving him...

"It's part of the act of loving, Gabby," he explained.

"To look at me, you mean?" she asked him, wanting to make perfectly sure she understood before she expressed her own delicious thoughts on the subject.

He nodded. "Yes. You're so beautiful. Just looking at you gives me the most exquisite pleasure."

Gabrielle smiled then, and lifted her hands to place them against the front of his shirt. Through the fine lawn, she felt his heartbeat, strong and rapid. She felt the swift rise and fall of his shallow breathing. "That means, then, that I can look at you, too." She began to unbutton his shirt.

Zach made himself relax, at least as much as was humanly possible under the circumstances. Her fingers trembled, and her movements had an endearing clumsiness. Just the brush of her fingers against his bared chest made his pulse leap and the nerves below his skin writhe with awareness. He helped her, lifting his arms at appropriate moments, but without seeming to imply that she needed help.

He was enjoying this. He loved the way she looked at him, her eyes wide and curious. He loved the way she wet her lips and, now and then, gave a little gasp of pleasure. He was ready to burst with wanting her, but he was loving every second of the torturous waiting. Her being completely naked intensified the sweet agony. Her creamy breasts jiggled and hovered tantalizingly close to his own bare skin. Her nipples were taut and rose red. He wanted to touch her, but if he did he wouldn't be able to wait any longer to make love to her.

He'd helped her remove his boots and stockings, and now there was nothing left but his trousers. Gabrielle was especially clumsy with his trouser buttons. Zach's breathing was heavier now, and she got the definite impression that he was holding himself tightly in rein just to allow her the pleasure of undressing him at her own inexperienced pace. She was grateful for his patience and restraint, because she was enjoying herself. It was like unwrapping a long-awaited and much-wanted present. It was like the best Christmas morning of her life.

Finally his trousers and drawers were off, and Zach stood before her in all his glorious nakedness. She had always compared him to Adonis. And even without his smart tailoring to support the image of a fine figure, he was perfection. Perhaps more so, because she realized every beautiful lean muscle visible through his sleek-fitting and richly textured clothes had only hinted at his body's strength and beauty. Here was one man who looked even better without his tailor's help.

His nipples were wine colored and small against a smooth expanse of well-defined chest muscles. He had no hair on his chest, but a narrow golden line started just below his navel, the trail widening the further down it went, just like her eyes were widening... But how could she help herself? He was magnificent.

Zach was afraid of how Gabby might react when she saw his arousal. But there wasn't much he could do about it. The little baggage had made him as hard and swollen as he'd ever been. He was even more aroused when he realized that he hadn't frightened her at all. Her wide-eyed stare was full of fascination and absorbed interest. Gawd, the girl was going to make him lose complete control of himself in a moment!

"Have you looked enough, sweeting?" he asked her, the tension in his voice as obvious as his arousal.

She looked up, her pupils large, her eyes green and luminous in the firelight. "I could look forever, Zach," she told him with blunt honesty and an impish grin.

"But I can't," he retorted. "Not without touching. And if I touch you, there will be no turning back, Gabby, because, as you can see, I want desperately to make love to you."

Gabby sobered. "Yes, I do see. Believe me, Zach, I want you just as much."

Of one mind, they came together. The shock of fire-warmed skin against skin was a sensory explosion of incredible pleasure. He caressed her, his hands moving over her body with worshipful urgency. Her hands were just as busy and curious, just as adoring. Their kisses were deep and greedy now, their breathing sharp and labored. Zach knew that if he didn't lay down with Gabby this minute, he'd have her against the wall. And against the wall was no place to lose one's virginity, though it was an interesting position to contemplate for future enjoyment.

"Damn," he said between pants. "There are no sheets on the bed!"

"It's warm by the fire, Zach," Gabby suggested breathlessly. She gave a shaky laugh. "My legs are so weak, I don't think I'd make it to the bed anyway!"

Convinced by Gabby's ingenuous admission of passionate weakness, Zach threw one of the sheets on the rug to keep its scratchy wool from irritating Gabby's tender skin, then he lowered her gently down in front of the fire. He promised himself that next time they'd go slower. Next time he'd show Gabby all the delights of prolonged sexual foreplay ... a leisurely bonfire. He'd make her come again and again, all through the long, sweet night. But tonight he would do well simply to temper his ardor long enough to take her virginity as gently and painlessly as possible.

Zach rolled up his discarded shirt and put it under Gabby's head to serve as a pillow. "Are you quite comfortable, sweeting?" he asked her, as he lowered himself beside her, propping his chin in his hand and letting his gaze wander over the beautiful, stretched-out span of her. *Mine, all mine,* he felt like gloating aloud. He felt deliriously happy and lucky.

Gabrielle dimpled up at him. "I'm as comfortable as I can be, considering I'm waiting to be ravished." She turned sideways and stroked his chest with her hands, then his stomach, and finally wrapped her curious fingers around the velvety hard length of his manhood.

He gave a moan of pleasure that thrilled Gabrielle to her bones. She loved the power of pleasuring him. She loved his power over her, too.

Then he was on top of her, his weight supported by both arms on each side of her, his slim hips fitted between her legs, his manhood heavy and tumid against her stomach. He kissed her again, deeply and passionately. He lowered his head to her breast to suckle, to tease and tighten her nipple with his clever tongue. She felt as though she were losing her mind, crazed by the sheer joy of lovemaking with Zach.

Gabrielle's muscles were bunching, tightening like little fists of tension, like bubbles of pleasure that were growing bigger and bigger till they'd certainly burst from the internal pressure. Heat coiled in that most sensitive part of her, and she instinctively rocked her hips against Zach, his manhood pushing against her tender stomach. It felt good, it felt right, and she wanted the rest.

Zach knew she was ready, and he positioned himself to enter her. He pushed the hair away from her flushed and tortured face and kissed her mouth. "Open your eyes, Gabby, and look at me." She did, and her look was full of trust. His heart flip-flopped with love. "This is going to hurt at first. You know that, don't you?"

She nodded, smiling faintly. "Yes, I know. But the pain goes away, doesn't it?"

Zach smiled back. "Yes, love. And then there's only pleasure. Are you ready?"

She nodded again and closed her eyes. Zach slowly entered her, waiting with each slight forward thrust for the tight channel of her womanhood to stretch and adapt to him. He watched her face and saw the tiny furrow of pain between her brows and the way she bit her lip. She was being brave and quiet, and he loved her all the more for trying to pretend that it didn't hurt like bloody hell. "You can scream if you want to, Gabby," he told her, but she shook her head. She opened her eyes, and he saw tears sheening there, but she smiled, saying, "I love you, Zach."

He smiled back. "I love you too, Gabby. Does it still hurt, sweeting?"

"Just a little." She lifted her hips and pushed him deeper inside her, her eyes fluttering shut and a little gasp of pleasure breaking from her parted lips. "But it feels much more good than bad."

Zach couldn't agree more, and that last little lift of her hips had nearly sent him over the edge. He needed to love her. He couldn't wait one minute more.

Still tempering himself, he pushed into her, setting a slow, gentle tempo to their lovemaking. But she was as needful as he, as eager to consummate their love with all the pent-up passion of years of pretend and denial. Her hips rose to meet his thrusts, her own innocent desire setting a much faster, much more forceful rhythm than he had planned on. It was devastating to the last shred of control he thought he owned. He was lost in Gabby, lost in her sweet, eager body, in the sound of her tiny mewls of pleasure, and in the womanly, orchid scent of her. He was coming, and he couldn't stop it. He was lost in love for Gabby…

Gabrielle felt the bubbles bursting like fireworks—bright sparks of euphoric pleasure against the black background of her spinning consciousness. Her muscles contracted and released with mind-rending intensity. She was lost, lost in a vortex of sated sensuality. Lost in love. Lost in Zach.

CHAPTER NINETEEN

"Ralph, are you quite sure you've told us everything?"

Lying on his stomach on the striped damask sofa in the little morning room off the kitchen, with a snow-filled washcloth shaped into a pouch and pressed to the back of his head, Ralph lifted his eyes to Sir George and nodded glumly. "Aye, sir, that I have. 1 woke up 'neath the stairs with Mrs. Tuttle and her bairns hanging over me, worried-like. Whoever did this must've been waitin' fer me outside the door when I went t' fetch Miss Tavistock a hack. After 'e done 'is black deed, he drug me into the shadows so's she'd not be suspicious of any foul play goin' on." A purse-lipped Flossie, the cook and self-declared foster mother of Ralph, rearranged the bulging snow-pack and Ralph winced. "Hit me hard, sir, and knocked me clean out, or I'd never have let Miss Tavistock out o' me sight."

With an elbow cupped in one hand, Sir George pulled thoughtfully on his chin with the other. "I don't blame you, Ralph. You couldn't help being struck on the head any more than you could have said no to Miss Tavistock last night when she required you to escort her to Old Town, I suppose."

"It's not me place t' gainsay me betters, sir," Ralph agreed, only too willing to exonerate himself, since he'd had misgivings about Miss Tavistock's foray into Old

Town from the beginning. "But what are ye goin' t' do, sir, if I might ask? In a bit I'll be feelin' as good as new and I'd be pleased t' help ye look for the lass. I'm afeared she'll come t' no good in Auld Reekie."

Sir George did not reply, nor did any other of the occupants of the small room feel inclined to voice aloud their similar opinions on the subject. It was quite obvious from all their faces that Rory, Regina, Lady Grace, Aunt Clarissa, and even Flossie the cook, believed as forcefully as Ralph did that Gabrielle had once again flung herself headlong into the briars. Only this time there was some doubt about her getting out.

"It's nearly seven o'clock," said Rory, who was standing with his back against the mantelpiece. "Zach hasn't returned yet, either. He's never missed dinner unless he's sent word. I think it possible that Gabrielle's with him."

Aunt Clarissa fluttered her hands in front of her and sprang up from the wing chair in a spasm of nervous movement. "You don't know how very much I would like to believe that Gabrielle is with Zachary, as he's certainly saved her from dire consequences more than once over the years. If only we knew for sure!"

"Has anyone thought to ask Zach's servants if they know anything?" Regina interposed, sitting on a footstool near Rory and holding his hand.

Flossie spoke up. "Mr. Wickham's carriage 'as been in the stable since early afternoon. I heard from one of the lads that he borrowed Sir George's roan and went off again right after he come home without so much as a by-your-leave."

"He didn't mention to his servants where he was going or when he'd be back?" Lady Grace inquired, perched anxiously on the edge of the settee.

Sir George pulled the bell rope which hung near the fireplace. "I'll summon his manservant, who, of all his men, might know the whereabouts of his master, though it is entirely possible and reasonable that Zachary didn't tell anyone where he was going. After all, why should he? He's a gentleman and completely free to do as he pleases without announcing his intentions. Like as not, he's simply unable to get home through this blasted blizzard." A footman appeared, and Sir George issued his order to fetch Mr. Wickham's manservant. The footman immediately bowed himself out the door to do as he'd been told.

"The weather makes it well nigh impossible to undertake a search for her, as well," Sir George muttered gloomily. "Frankly I don't know what to do. Anything could have happened to her, though abduction seems a likely possibility."

Rory and Regina exchanged glances. He could tell by Regina's expression that she was wondering whether or not they ought to tell the Murrays about Gabrielle's run-in with Mother Henn. He greatly feared that the madam from the brothel may have had a revengeful hand in Gabrielle's sudden disappearance and Ralph's goose-egg. But, since he wasn't sure that that was the case, and it probably wouldn't help a bit in finding her even if Mother Henn were indeed involved, Rory was unwilling to further upset the Murrays and Aunt Clarissa by detailing to them Gabrielle's scandalous adventure of just two days before.

Regina read his thoughts. He could tell she'd read them just as plainly as if they'd been inked on his forehead. Her keen brown eyes telegraphed quite ably her understanding of his logic and her perfect agreement with it. He'd been communicating with his childhood friend in this manner since they were both on leading strings. Why, he wondered now as he smiled tenderly down at her, why had he never realized she was in love with him and he with her? He'd been too puffed up with conceit, he suspected, and bent on engaging every lass's heart from Edinburgh to Glasgow.

Thank God Zach had spoken up last night at the Garrisons' party and awakened Rory to the realization of Regina's great worth and her unwavering devotion to him! He'd gotten so used to her always being there that he'd become rather cavalier, enjoying her company as freely as he drank water, and taking it as much for granted. But when forced to think about the possibility of being without Regina—say, for example, if she married and moved away—he appreciated how dear she was to him, how necessary to his happiness. She was as essential to his well-being as his daily consumption of that cool water he'd thought of as a metaphor for Regina's own particular brand of refreshment.

He squeezed Regina's hand, rejoicing in the gesture because he knew it would not be disapproved of by her parents. He'd confessed their guilt in the betrothal charade at the exact time he and Gabrielle had agreed to make the confession together— precisely at one, after nuncheon—even though she'd not been present. At the time, Rory simply thought she'd been delayed, or had even possibly been too frightened to face up to the Murrays and left the task to him.

Manfully, he'd faced the Murrays alone. Then, while they frowned in disapproval and disappointment, he risked his future on their merciful goodness and lifelong affections by confessing something more. He was in love with Regina, and would they mind terribly much if he requested her hand in marriage?

The Murrays were left speechless, too surprised and delighted by Rory's second confession to be inclined to scold him for the wrongfulness of his behavior as revealed by his first confession. Despite his frivolous ways over the years, the Murrays had always been fond of Rory and knew there were merits beneath his rakish facade. Furthermore, they had always suspected Regina's love for Rory and they had been amazed by her seeming unconcern when the engagement between Gabrielle and Rory was announced.

Now all made sense. Even though they had wrung out of Regina an admission that she, too, had been part of the betrothal charade, they were now very glad to make their daughter happy by bestowing her hand on the Marquess of Lome. They were also ready to forgive Rory and Gabrielle their sins against themselves, and indeed against all of Edinburgh and half of Cornwall. Later, basking in the glow of Regina's happiness, they felt most indulgent and almost eager for Gabrielle's return from whatever mischief was keeping her away.

Later they discovered that the lass had probably coerced Ralph, one of their footmen, into an errand they'd strictly disapproved of. According to the scullery maids' descriptions of the bundles of food and blankets and other creature comforts Ralph had been toting, Gabrielle had apparently disobeyed Lady Grace and gone off to personally administer to the poor. When Ralph showed up in a hack with his goose-egg this afternoon, they realized that that was exactly what Gabrielle had done. But her secret philanthropy had proved to be an even more dangerous undertaking than they thought it might be. She was missing in the sometimes sinister streets of Old Town.

"You summoned me, sir?" Bleader's arrival prodded everyone from their grim thoughts. His hair was slicked down as if by a hasty spit-bath, his large ears seeming to stick out all the more by the relative flatness of his scalp. Rory thought he looked worried. There were puckers of concern between the manservant's brows.

"You're Mr. Wickham's valet?" queried Sir George, making quite sure he'd got the right man.

"Yes, sir." Bleader bowed respectfully.

"Do you know where he is?"

"No, sir, I don't," Bleader replied, the puckers deepening. Then came the validation of Rory's suspicions. "And I'm right worried about 'im, sir. 'Tisn't like the master t' not tell 'is servants what he's about. At least not fer such a long spell."

"I suppose you're aware that Miss Tavistock is missing, too?"

"Yes, sir. Hard not t' know what's goin' on when everybody's in such a pucker."

"Er… yes. Do you think they're together?"

Bleader paused, pursing his lips consideringly. "Could be, sir. Indeed, sir, 'tis more'n likely that if Miss Tavistock is in the briars, so t' speak, Mr. Wickham is tryin't' pluck 'er out. Happened all the time back home. She's prone t' findin' trouble, that one, and Mr. Wickham has what ye could call a knack fer knowin' when she's found some."

"Goodness!" exclaimed Lady Grace. "You make it sound as though he's fey! It seems extremely fantastic to me that Zachary would know when Gabrielle is in trouble and somehow make himself available to save her."

"Fantastic, indeed, Lady Grace," agreed Aunt Clarissa with a self-important nod of her head, "but I can tell you from personal experience that what Bleader is saying is true. While I cannot believe that Zachary was involved in Ralph's injury, I can readily believe that he is somehow involved in Gabrielle's disappearance. I would be much more concerned about her safety if Zach were standing in this room with us right now. Since he isn't, I can only hope they're together somewhere." She nodded decisively. "In fact, I firmly believe they are!"

Unlike Aunt Clarissa, Rory couldn't be made comfortable by what he considered mere wishful thinking. It was late and dark, and the streets were piled with snow, the air full of the blinding snowflakes that could look so beautiful and harmless as they drifted lightly down in the still air, yet turn so hazardous when caught up and tossed around by the stiff wind from the firth. It was not a night for a female to be missing, but only a fool—or a hero—would venture forth in this weather to find her. As Rory reached for the bell rope to summon the servant to fetch his redingote and hat, his stoutest boots, and thickest woolen scarf, he thought he knew which of the two he was!

"I can't just stand here, warm and dry and safe, and wait while something dreadful could be happening to Gabrielle," he announced. "I have to do something, go somewhere."

Regina stood up and squeezed Rory's arm. "You'll be careful, won't you, and—"

"If'n ye're wantin't' go somewhere, sir," Bleader interrupted in a different voice, but with a determined look, "I know a good place fer ye t' start."

Rory, desperate to have somewhere to start, some hope to grasp onto, was all attention. "Where's that?"

Bleader shifted from foot to foot. "Mr. Wickham doesn't like people to know about it, but he's got a charitable institution in Old Town he runs fer unfortunate woman, so t' speak. He could be there ... that is, if'n he ain't with Miss Gabrielle. Maybe she's there, too. Or if nothin' else, maybe the folks there know where Zach was headed this afternoon."

Ignoring the astonished gasps from the others at Bleader's revelation concerning the women's shelter, Rory asked, "Will you go with me, Bleader, show me the way?"

Bleader nodded, the puckers between his brows smoothing somewhat. "'Twould be a pleasure, sir. It's makin' me twitchy-like just waitin' 'round t' see what happens."

"Good," said Rory, nodding his thanks. Then he turned to Sir George. "Do you approve, sir?"

Sir George looked sober. "I don't know if I approve, so much as I understand your need to do something. I ought to go myself."

Lady Grace put her hand to her heart, saying, "My dear, you couldn't possibly go! I'd be sick with worry if you went out on such a night. You're much too old for such heroics!"

"Thank you, my dear," Sir George murmured wryly. "I suspect you're right, but 'tis rather unflattering to be thought too old for anything."

When the footman came, Rory ordered his winter outerwear and once more firmly but kindly refused Ralph's offer to come along. He also ordered that his horse be saddled, and another for Bleader, since it would be impossible for a carriage to get through the snow-clogged streets.

"We're off," Rory announced, kissing Regina soundly on the mouth under the benevolent watchfulness of her parents. Regina blushed, then grew teary-eyed as she watched Rory and Bleader step out into the blasting, blinding snowstorm. Love was cruel, she decided, looking out the window after Rory even though it was impossible to see anything but a blur of white. Love was cruel because it made one so happy, and then sometimes so very sad and anxious…

Douglas woke from his stuporous slumber with a start. He had no idea where he was. Everything was black. He wasn't cold, which was an unusual happenstance. He was always cold in that dreadful garret he lived in with the rats. Then he realized he wasn't home at all, and he was warm because he had a blanket over him and two heavy wool wraps, one smelling of orchids. Then he remembered.

He was in McSwain's stable, in the loft. Wickham had tricked him and then neatly clipped him in the jaw. Like a babe he'd gone right to sleep. Douglas rubbed his jaw. It ached a bit, but not nearly as much as his head did. Then he realized something else. He ought to still be asleep. He'd finished a goodly amount of whiskey that day, and it usually took him all night to sleep it off.

Douglas felt for his pocket watch, then remembered for the

umpteenth time that he'd sold it, and even if he hadn't sold it, it was too dark to read the time. It was night, that was all he knew, but he suspected that he hadn't been asleep very long.

Why was he awake? Douglas sat there, thinking. The wind was howling like a banshee, so maybe that's what woke him. But he'd been known to sleep while inebriated through gunshots and screams and every other sort of sound that might be expected to wake the dead. No, the wind wasn't the reason he was awake.

Douglas sat very still, listening. Then he knew. In his heart, something was aching. Distantly, someone was … calling. Yes, Kate was calling. Kate needed him, wanted him. He stood up, flinging off the blanket and the good-smelling wraps. He reeled for a minute, then steadied himself and groped for the door.

He didn't understand why, but Wickham hadn't locked him in, and he was in too great a hurry to puzzle it out. He didn't know why he'd bothered to cover him up with the blanket and redingotes off their own backs, either, or how the two of them had ridden back to New Town without freezing. He thought of the cottage then, and the storm, and realized that they were probably holed up there for the night, or at least till the storm blew over.

Douglas felt a sudden shiver, then stooped and picked up Wickham's redingote and put it on over his own ragged, inadequate clothing. It was heavy and warm and felt damned good. Douglas carefully descended the ladder, each step accentuated by a corresponding throb of knife-sharp pain in his temples. When he saw Wickham's horse in the stable, his theory about where the two of them were was confirmed. He had no desire to burst in upon them at the cottage, though, snatching back his gun and demanding Kate's release again. He didn't have the heart or the time. Kate needed him, and somehow he was going to make it back to Old Town and the shelter.

Douglas rubbed the piebald mare's nose in apology for making it face the horrors of what lay beyond the stable door, then led it into the blast of snow and bone-chilling wind. He mounted it, and, head down, urged the poor beast forward into the darkness.

Douglas prayed to God he wouldn't end up in the bottom of some icy ravine. Yes, for the first time in a long time, he felt like bargaining with God. He'd do anything... *Anything*. Yes, even that. Just to be there for Kate, he'd give up the bottle. God, please, just let him be there for Kate.

Bleader couldn't believe they'd finally arrived. It had taken much longer than normal, pushing nearly-blind through the gale-force winds and sheets of snow, but they'd made it, and he was never more happy to see the interior of a place in all his born days. He'd never been inside the shelter with Zach, but he knew it was on the third floor. Since there was no place to stable the horses, they took them right into the hall and tethered them to the posts of the stairwell. No one would blame them for saving the horses from a possible death by freezing if they were left outside.

They trudged up the stairs, Bleader rubbing life back into his fingers, which he knew were red and swollen inside his wet gloves. He felt dazed and numb, not as yet used to the cessation of weather-induced misery he'd endured for the past hour. Lord Lome was just as quiet, feeling, no doubt, just as stiff and wretched as Bleader did. Below the brim of his hat and above the folds of his thick woolen scarf, his lordship's face was chafed raw by the wind, his eyes bloodshot and irritated, his brows and lashes frosted with tiny ice flecks.

The building was obviously full of humanity, there being some traffic on the stairs and in the halls and much noise coming from behind the doors. Bleader was grateful he was a well-paid, well-appreciated servant of a good man like Zachary Wickham, living most of the year in the blessed peace and openness of Cornwall. For Zach's sake, as well as his own, he hoped Miss Gabrielle's antics hadn't brought Zach, like a cat, to his ninth and last life. Heaven knew he'd had several close calls with mortality already.

They were at the door, made conspicuous by the sturdiness and newness of it compared to the others they'd seen as they traversed the hall. Bleader knocked and waited. Several locks were heard to unlatch from the other side, and the door was opened a slit, though there were still chains hanging across the opening at the top and the bottom. Charlie, the shelter's guard and general servant, peered into the hall at Bleader.

"It's me, Charlie," said Bleader, surprised at how difficult it was to move his frozen lips, but so far he'd had no compelling reason to talk. "You know me, Mr. Wickham's manservant, Bleader. I'm sure ye've seen me from the window afore."

Recognition finally lit in Charlie's sharp blue eyes. He nodded slightly, then cast a questioning gaze in Lord Lome's direction. "It's all right, Charlie," said Bleader. "He's Lord Lome, a gent who's well acquainted with Mr. Wickham. We've come in this dreadful weather on account o' Mr. Wickham. Let us in, won't you, so's we can thaw by the fire?"

Charlie hesitated a moment, then closed the door, undid the remaining chains, and opened the door. He stood back and allowed them to enter, but Charlie kept a suspicious eye pinned on Lord Lome. Automatically they made a bee-line for the fire, extending their hands to the flames. "Is Mr. Wickham here, Charlie?" asked Bleader.

Charlie shook his head, but Bleader hadn't expected any other answer after seeing no horse tied up downstairs. He knew his master would never leave an animal out in this weather. "Will ye fetch Mr. Blake, then?" said Bleader over his shoulder. Charlie nodded, frowning, and left the room.

"Why can't we ask this Charlie what he knows about Zach's possible whereabouts?" Lord Lome inquired, in the same indistinct articulation Bleader had been forced to push through stiff lips. "Seems a taciturn fellow, but surely he'd help us if he could."

Bleader worked his jaw, warming up the hinges. "He can't talk, that one."

"He can't talk?"

"No, ain't spoke a word since he come here t' work five years ago. We'll save time, m'lord, askin' our questions of the Quaker gent what runs the place."

"I thought you said Zach was the owner?"

"He is, m'lord. But he don't run the place, 'cause he don't live in Edinburgh year round." Bleader should have thought that that was self-evident. He excused his lordship from his inability to deduce, however, in supposing his brain cells were frozen along with other parts of his noble body. For good measure, he further explained, "He's got two other shelters in England proper, and he pays them all visits, but hires managers to run 'em."

Lord Lome nodded in understanding as he turned round to thaw his backside in the warmth of the fire. As they stood there in the small neat parlor, gratefully toasting themselves like bread for tea, their peace was disturbed by a bloodcurdling female scream.

"Good God, what was that?" exclaimed Lord Lome, giving a little start and darting an anxious look toward the door leading into the hall. "This isn't a home for the mad, is it?"

"I don't think so," Bleader answered, unable to completely reassure his lordship because he wasn't sure himself exactly what sort of females Zach gave shelter to. "I think they're mostly women what's been beat, or out on the streets 'cause they're breedin' or drunk or have the opium sickness." Bleader shrugged. "Mayhap a mad one shows up now and again."

There was another scream. "Where's this Blake fellow?" complained Lord Lome, shedding his damp jacket and draping it on a chair to dry.

"It sounds like he's busy," Bleader ventured.

"But surely not with anything more important than what we've come to talk to him about!"

Bleader did not reply, but wisely kept mum while Lord Lome paced the hearth rug impatiently. As with his own master, he knew when there was no use saying anything. Finally the door opened, and Mr. Blake entered the room. His heavy face sheened with perspiration, and he looked rather harassed, Bleader thought. But he was unfailingly polite. He walked hurriedly over and shook Bleader's hand, paying no attention to the rules of worldly society which would surely dictate that Bleader, a mere servant, be ignored while Mr. Blake made his acquaintance with the obvious gentleman. But Mr. Blake was not your usual sort. He was an odd'un. He was a Quaker.

"Friend Bleader, how nice to see thee again. I don't believe thou hast ever actually been inside the shelter. I hope the fire is making thee a mite more comfortable. What can have brought thee out on such a godforsaken night, pray? And who is this gentleman with thee?"

"This is his lordship, the Marquess of Lome," he said, stressing the lordship part, hoping Mr. Blake would call him by his proper, respectful title and not "Friend."

Mr. Blake smiled and extended his pudgy hand to Lord Lome. "Friend, I'm pleased to make thy acquaintance. Thou must forgive me, as we're at sixes and sevens here. One of our residents is in the midst of birthing twins, and having a hard time of it, I'm afraid."

After a slight hesitation, Lord Lome shook hands with Mr. Blake, automatically exchanging the usual pleasantries, after which Mr. Blake took out a large neatly folded handkerchief from his jacket pocket and mopped his brow. "Wilt thou sit?" He motioned to the two chairs by the fire.

"We haven't time to sit. We've a crisis on our hands," Rory said, finding his voice at last despite all the surprises he was running into at Zach's shelter. Sympathetic to his lordship's plight, Bleader admitted that a mute, a screaming female birthing twins, and a Quaker, and all three of them sprung upon one in the space of ten minutes, was a bit much to absorb, especially when one's brain cells were only just thawing.

"Tell me," urged Mr. Blake, all solicitous attention.

"Miss Gabrielle Tavistock, a friend of Mr. Wickham's, who is a houseguest of the Murrays at Charlotte Square, is missing."

"I am aware of who Miss Tavistock is," Blake murmured gravely. "And she's missing? That's dreadful! Dost thou know particulars?"

"What we know is that she left Charlotte Square this morning just after dawn with one of the Murrays' servants, a large fellow named Ralph, whom I'm sure she chose because she thought he would keep her safe."

"Did she say what she was afraid of?"

"She was planning to visit an impoverished family here in Old Town. She became acquainted with the children on Christmas Eve. The Tuttles."

"Ah, yes. The Tuttles. A worthy family."

"But she had had a rather… er … troublesome experience in Old Town just two days earlier, and she was naturally concerned that she might… er… be *troubled* again."

"Yes, I had heard something of it," admitted Blake, still in a very grave tone.

Bleader listened with interest. Apparently both the marquess and Blake knew about Miss Gabrielle's close encounter with Mother Henn. He had been told by John and Malcolm, who knew that the information would go no further. All of Zach's servants held Miss Gabrielle in considerable affection, though she sometimes tried their patience with her propensity for the briars and Zach's sometimes difficult task in getting her out of them.

"Well, coming out of the Tuttles' apartment to fetch Miss Tavistock a hack, Ralph was hit over the head by someone and dragged into a dark corner beneath the stairwell. There he stayed till Mrs. Tuttle and the children found him some several hours later when she returned home from work to take tea."

"And Miss Tavistock left the apartment after Ralph and has not been seen since, I gather?"

Rory was about to speak when the woman who was giving birth to twins screamed again. Mr. Blake tugged on his bottom lip with his teeth and glanced worriedly toward the door.

"Do you need to go?" asked Lord Lome, his sympathy for the girl apparently inspired once he understood she was not mad, but only birthing.

"There is a doctor with her and my capable helper, Mrs. Stark. What she needs is her husband. Or at least that is what she thinks she needs. Near out of her mind with the pain, she's been asking for him rather pitifully, looking at us as though we're keeping him away."

"Well, ain't ye, sir?" As soon as he'd said it, Bleader wished he'd held his tongue. 'Twas a delicate business, what went on at the shelter. But he knew full well that most of the husbands of these women were unworthy individuals who did more harm than good.

"If he were sober, I'd welcome him," Blake answered, unoffended by Bleader's bluntness. "Mayhap seeing his own children coming into the world, and knowing how he might make it a better or a worse place to live in, might do him good. But I interrupted thee, friend. I asked thee if Miss Tavistock was supposed to have disappeared when she left the Tuttles, once the villain had rendered Ralph unconscious."

"Yes. That's what we assume. But we don't have any idea, beyond Mother Henn, of course, who might have been motivated to abduct her."

Blake's chest puffed out in an uncharacteristic swell of pride. "I think we can rule out Mother Henn, because she's abandoned her tawdry business for now."

"I'm relieved to hear it," said Rory. "Since Zach is also missing, perhaps he's with her, or involved in some way. His servants said he was here this morning, but returned to Charlotte Square hastily and then left on horseback without telling them where he was going or when he'd be back. If you could shed a light, I'd be very grateful."

Blake pursed his lips consideringly. "Well, there was a note delivered this morning for Friend Zachary, but no one knows what was written in it. Kate—she's the girl birthing twins—seemed to think that it was bad news. She even mentioned that she was hoping her husband wasn't involved in some way."

"Her husband? Why would he—?"

A heavy knock on the door interrupted them once more. Blake frowned, saying, "Who could that be, now? We get less visitors on a bright day in June! What a blustery night for people to be out and about!" Charlie, apparently making himself useful in the back apartments, did not appear to open the door, so Blake did it. He left two chains in place and peered into the dimly lit hall.

"Good gracious! Is it Douglas McKeen? Friend, thou art

injured!" After these exclamations, Blake quickly undid the two remaining chains and flung the door wide, revealing to the two other occupants of the parlor a half-frozen, hatless man, with a gash in his forehead and blood trickling down his neck and onto the lapel of a handsome, black wool redingote which Bleader instantly recognized as … Zach's!

With glazed eyes and uncertain gait, the man took two steps into the room and collapsed.

Chapter Twenty

"I'm beginning to feel guilty."

Zach propped himself on an elbow and looked down into Gabby's radiant face. With her long hair in a tumble about her shoulders and the white sheet tucked round her delightful curves, she reminded him of a naughty angel—her purity, like a halo, just slightly askew. "Gabby, how could you feel guilty? What we just did was absolutely beautiful and pure—"

"What we did for the second time, I might mention—"

"Gabby, we're going to be married!"

Smiling, Gabby reached up and placed two fingers against Zach's lips, effectively silencing him. "You goose. I'm not talking about our lovemaking. I could never feel guilty about that. I'm talking about Douglas McKeen. I'm worried. Perhaps he's cold. We ought to check on him."

Zach sighed and glanced at the window. For the past hour he'd noticed that the wind had died down considerably, and the snow was lessening. He'd tried to ignore these facts, though, because he knew that if it were at all possible, they should return to Charlotte Square and relieve the worry the Murrays and the others were feeling on their behalf. As for McKeen, Zach had been thinking of him, too. Mainly he was wondering what they'd do with him if they did return to Charlotte Square that night. Should they drag his inert body down the ladder and sling him over the horse? No, not even McKeen could sleep through that. And what would he do once he was so rudely awakened? Zach sighed again.

"What is it, Zach? Are you thinking we ought to go back to town tonight? I hope so, because I'm thinking the same thing. Don't misunderstand me, however. I'd much rather stay here with you all night, in fact all week!"

Zach chuckled, pulling Gabby against his bare chest, reveling in the wonderful feelings she engendered. "Thank God, now that I've come to my senses, we'll have the rest of our lives to be together. I suppose we ought to be unselfish enough to think of our friends this once, and even those who aren't our friends, and forgo the pleasure of spending this entire night in each other's arms. But it's a sacrifice!"

He bent his head and kissed Gabby's smiling lips, their warm, soft fullness and the press of her eager body against him threatening to make his words nothing but meaningless rhetoric. Her arms slipped round his neck, holding him close, and he felt himself becoming aroused once more. With monumental willpower, he pushed her gently away. "Don't kiss me like that, Gabby, unless you really don't care a fig whether or not McKeen is cold, or if Aunt Clarissa has pulled out her hair by the roots in a frenzy of worry."

"You're right," Gabby conceded, scooting away and putting space between them. "I vividly see Aunt Clarissa just as you describe her, and it's a picture that's bound to spoil our evening if we stay here all night making love." Her voice wavered a little on those last words, her desire made apparent by this, and by the way her ruby-red nipples made distinct, erect protrusions beneath the sheet she'd pulled tight against her. Zach couldn't look an instant longer; he had to get up and put his pants on or they'd never get out of there in a month of Sundays.

Zach stood up, welcoming the cool draft of air as it hit his naked skin when the sheet fell away. He hurriedly dressed, glancing only once at Gabby as she lay there watching him. Drat the little baggage; those big greedy eyes of hers were enough to cause a man more than a bit of difficulty in buttoning up his trousers! But he managed it at last, and, now that everything was tucked in and hid under layers of clothing, he tried to make himself believe he was no longer aroused.

"I'll go check on McKeen while you dress," he announced.

This comment seemed to stir Gabby from her sensual daydreaming. "I'd better go with you! Who knows what he may try to do if suddenly awakened."

"All the more reason why you should stay here."

"Well, I won't," she declared, flinging off her sheet and exposing those delectable breasts of hers. Zach quickly looked away, walking into the kitchen to pick up the lantern and relight it with a taper he'd carried from the parlor. "I'll be dressed in a trice," she called after him.

"Not soon enough, I'm afraid," he said with good-humored contrariness, leaving the cottage by the back door and plowing in his boots through the snow to the stable. He relished the cold air and the icy snowflakes on his shirt that seeped through and made his skin tingle. It cleared his mind and most effectively subdued his ardor. But he didn't imagine he'd relish the cold for very long. He knew he'd be wanting his redingote for the long ride home.

Once inside the stable, his ardor was squelched completely by shock. McKeen's piebald mare was nowhere to be seen! He couldn't imagine the animal getting out of the stable on her own, nor even wishing to if she could. McKeen must have gone! Just to confirm this fact, however, Zach quickly ascended the ladder to the loft and went inside. He felt a shiver of remembered apprehension just entering that little room, and turned around quickly as he suddenly imagined that McKeen might have tricked him into coming up there with plans to close and lock the door behind him.

Of course there was no one there. McKeen wasn't closing the door and locking him inside that minuscule chamber, but Zach's heart still beat heavy and hard, making a sloshing, deafening echo in his ears. He wanted to run out of that room as fast as he could, but he made himself stay till he'd calmed down. He wanted to leave of his own accord, not be driven out by demons of irrational fear.

Zach breathed deeply and thought calming thoughts, finding the most soothing images were of Gabby holding him, loving him. Presently he felt quite composed—tranquil enough to sit in that room till dawn broke. But he couldn't, nor did he want to. He had other more pressing things to do. He had a feeling that when McKeen left the loft, enduring a horrendous hangover to boot, he'd headed straight for the shelter. McKeen was a desperate, unhappy man, and he had a headache that would make the devil himself water at the eyes. Those were not sensations one would wish to feel all at once, nor even separately. And they were not conducive to rational behavior.

There was no choice in the matter. Instead of going straight to Charlotte Square, Zach must take Gabby with him and go first to the shelter. He had to make sure that all was well there, that Kate was safe. She was due to deliver those twins any day now, any minute. She did not need aggravation, and who knew what mischief McKeen was up to?

Gabrielle had never seen a door with so many locks. And once inside, she'd never seen so many happy male faces. She found this rather a diverting idea when she thought about it—the parlor of a women's shelter full-to-bursting with men. She would have laughed, except that her mouth was still frozen from the long ride. She could only imagine how chilled Zach was. He'd not even had his redingote to fend off the nippy wind, but only the smelly blanket from the loft and her arms wrapped tightly round him.

She'd been shuttled close to the fire the instant she'd entered the room, surrounded by the happy men, some of whom she recognized and some she didn't. In truth, the returning warmth to her body was bringing with it a kind of pleasant stupor, and she smiled equally on them all whether or not she knew them. They were each obviously pleased to see her, and that sort of agreeableness deserved a smile, didn't it?

Zach immediately asked about Kate and McKeen and was preceded out of the room and down the hall by a stout, pleasant-looking man in plain clothing, his soft-voiced conversation punctuated by "thees" and "thous." A Quaker, she surmised, smiling. How nice. She supposed he always spoke softly, but she was encouraged by the attitude of Mr. Blake—who else could the gentleman be?—and decided that Kate must be all right and

Douglas McKeen must not have come there, after all. But where was he, then? She couldn't help but worry.

Rory was there, relief and affection written all over him. He leaned down once to where she was snuggled into a chair beneath several blankets and pushed as close to the fire as she could tolerate, whispering, "I've told the Murrays everything. You don't need to worry about that, so don't. And there's something else." He leaned closer, his blue eyes dancing with happiness. "Regina and I are engaged."

Gabrielle smiled, whispering back, "I'm very happy for you! Zach and I have come to an understanding, as well. Mama will be thrilled"—her smile broadened—"even though Zach is not a marquess like you, Rory. But I can say without equivocation that he does share one of your talents. He's a first-rate kisser!" Rory whooped with laughter and moved away to fill a cup with hot tea for Gabrielle to drink, now that her teeth had quit chattering.

A very large man with sandy-blond hair, whom Gabrielle believed was the person who had opened the door and let them in, leaned against the far wall. He was smiling, too, but he didn't join in the conversation with the other men. In fact, she didn't remember hearing him say anything since they'd arrived. But he had an aura about him of serenity and strength and security, like a mountain—like the rugged, benign mountains of Scotland. She smiled at him, and he blushed, looking hastily away.

Bleader was there, too, standing at a discreet, respectful distance, but grinning from ear to ear, looking for all the world like a tomcat who had just snared himself a fat mouse. Returning his smile, she remembered Ralph, and her smile fell away. "How's Ralph, Bleader? Is he all right?"

"Right as rain, miss, though he's sportin' a knot on 'is noggin 'e didn't have this mornin'."

"That was too dreadfully shabby of McKeen, and I told him so!"

"I told him as well, Gabrielle," said Rory, shoveling spoons full of sugar into Gabrielle's tea.

"You told him as well? McKeen's *here*, then?"

"Yes, sitting with his wife in one of the back bedchambers.

He fell off his horse trying to get here from the cottage, hitting his head against a rock, which was, perhaps, Providence's way of getting back at him for Ralph's goose-egg."

"So, you know all about where Zach and I've been? You know that McKeen abducted me?"

"We know everything," Rory informed her calmly. "We got it all from McKeen. He was in dreadful shape when he got here, but he was revived with heat and bandages, food and plenty of steaming coffee. As he was wearing Zach's coat when he arrived, we feared the worst and were ready to draw straws for the privilege of beating him senseless again once he regained consciousness. Though I daresay Blake wouldn't have allowed it," Rory added regretfully. "When he assured us that you and Zach were both perfectly safe, we were persuaded to let him live, unless, of course, he was proven later to be lying."

Rory put a generous dollop of cream in Gabrielle's tea and commenced stirring. "It's just as well we didn't beat him, as it happens, because his wife was having twins and calling for him."

"She's had them, then? Is everyone all right?"

"Yes. It was rough going for a while, but she came through. A plucky lass, Blake tells me. Both are boys. She'll have her hands full taking care of them, I have no doubt." Rory offered her the tea at last, and Gabrielle pulled her hands free of the blankets to take it from him.

She took a swallow, relishing how the hot liquid eased down her scratchy throat.

"I am delighted for Kate," said Gabrielle, staring into the fire as sober thoughts took the edge off her happiness. "But she's got more on her hands than those boys to raise. What about her husband? What about his drinking and his ..." Her voice trailed off.

"It seems Zach had extended an offer to Kate to take Douglas into the shelter and help cure him of drinking," Rory told her.

"Zach extended the same offer to McKeen at the cottage. But McKeen didn't seem inclined toward taking him up on it."

"Well, he has now. And if he's cured of the drinking,

perhaps the other will remedy itself. But if it remains a problem, Kate has told her husband that she will by no means tolerate any sort of bullying again. She has friends and resources she can turn to now, and McKeen knows it. He's been warned, and I think he's a sober man tonight in more ways than one."

Gabrielle nodded, encouraged. "Does he like the babies?"

"He's smitten," Rory admitted with a grin. "I think we all are, aren't we, Bleader? Aren't we, Charlie?"

Bleader grunted and Charlie shrugged, unwilling to admit they were smitten with anything.

"How do they look? Are they awfully small? Are they handsome?"

"Why don't you come see for yourself, Gabby?"

Gabrielle turned at the sound of Zach's voice coming from the door that led into the hall. Zach had shed his jacket and hat, and the snow on his hair had melted, making his straight bright hair glisten with dampness. "But aren't you cold, Zach? Shouldn't you warm yourself by the fire?" She didn't want him dying of a lung inflammation just when she had finally got him exactly where she wanted him!

"I'm quite warm. Come, do you want to see the babies before Kate goes to sleep?"

Gabrielle certainly wanted to see the babies, and Zach knew it. Even as a small child she'd been fascinated by anything infantile. Puppies, kittens, piglets, bunnies, even a nest of barn mice. They all held a measure of charm and attraction for Gabrielle. She pushed off her blankets and stood up, a little wobbly on her recently thawed legs. Zach obligingly stepped forward and gave her his arm to lean on. Oh, how nice it was to know that his arm would always be there for her, the two of them—God willing—growing quite old and rickety together.

As they walked to Kate's bedchamber, several women found something to do that necessitated leaving their rooms and hovering in the hall or the doorways so they could look at Gabrielle and Zach, some gaping openly, some smiling shyly from behind a curtain of hair. Some were pregnant. Some had obvious bruises. Some were so thin they looked as though they might snap in two. Gabrielle smiled at all of them, her heart full of empathy. But she was glad for them, too, because they were in the shelter, exactly where they needed to be to help them work through their problems and start life anew. She squeezed Zach's arm. She was so proud of him.

As they entered Kate's bedchamber, a room she shared with two other women, Gabrielle's gaze first fell on Douglas. Kate had the center bed, and Douglas was sitting next to it in a chair, holding one of the twins. Mr. Blake stood at the foot of the bed, benignly looking on and, just possibly, keeping an eye on Douglas. Douglas didn't notice when they came in; his head was bent, looking at the baby. He had a bandage over one brow. His hair was combed neatly back from his brow, and his face and hands had been scrubbed clean.

Gabrielle wasn't sure how to feel toward the man. Everyone seemed to have forgiven him everything and was supporting him in his endeavor to change. She wanted to feel the same way, she wanted the magic of the moment to fill her with confidence for the future, but she instinctively knew that the glow of fatherhood wouldn't be enough to get Douglas through the horrors of liquor withdrawal. He would need to make up his own mind to do it, not just for the babies and Kate, but for himself as well.

Gabrielle turned to Kate, who was holding the other child. Kate looked back at her, a tentative smile tilting her lips that conveyed a friendly curiosity. She was a pretty, petite girl, though rather pale and tired at the moment from having given birth to a couple of strapping boys. She hardly seemed old enough to have children of her own, but they were hers, all right. She glowed with maternal pride. Gabrielle could see why everyone was so willing to forgive Douglas and hope for the best. It was for Kate's sake. She was charming—instantly likable.

"Ye're Gabby, then?" She blushed, correcting herself. "I mean, Miss Tavistock."

Gabrielle smiled reassuringly. "Do call me Gabby, if that's how you know me."

"I do feel I know ye a little, miss. Wickham has talked of

ye considerable."

Gabrielle smiled up at Zach, who shrugged his shoulders and looked slightly sheepish. "Good things, I hope," she teased, then turned back to Kate. "I've come to see the babies before you go to sleep, which I'm sure you're dying to do."

"Aye, miss, 'tis a pleasure t' show 'em to ye, but first me and Douglas have somethin't' say. We're more'n sorry fer the trouble and—"

"No, Kate," Douglas broke in, lifting his head and looking Gabrielle straight in the eye. "You dinna do nothin' wrong, Kate. It was me, and it's my place t' beg the lass here t' pardon me wrongdoin'." The baby made a wee squeaking sound, and Douglas bounced it gently, as natural as can be in his new role as "Da." "I've been a villain, Miss Tavistock. I've been sick with the bottle fer a long time and doin' things I should'na do. When Kate run away, 'stead of realizin' it were my own fault, I blamed my misery on Wickham. All I wanted was me Kate back, but I dinna think beyond that. I hurt ye and scared ye and I'm sorry fer it. I hope someday ye'll find it in yer heart t' forgive me."

"You have my forgiveness already, Mr. McKeen, if you keep your promise to Kate and take up Zach's offer of help. I want you to succeed. I can see you're going to make a first-rate father and enjoy a wonderful family life, if you learn to control your drinking."

Douglas looked grateful and humble. "I will, miss. I promise I will."

The apologies given and accepted, Gabrielle's favorite part was at hand—the inspection of the babies. Zach lifted the one Kate was holding and placed him in Gabrielle's eager arms. He was tightly swathed in a flannel blanket. Gabrielle gazed down into the tiny red face, the eyes slightly swollen from the trauma of birth. She nuzzled her nose against the wispy dark hair on his head and breathed in the "new" scent of him. Then suddenly Douglas was there, handing her the other twin. They were so light, it was easy to hold both of them. She kissed the newcomer. They were exactly alike. Exactly.

Zach's heart was bursting with love for Gabby. Standing

there, holding the twins, her fair head bent over them in delighted examination, she radiated womanhood. She was right. She'd been right all along. She wasn't a child. She was a woman ready to have her own children, *their* own children.

Zach felt a tug of prideful hope. Maybe she was already breeding. Maybe they'd already started a baby together today, in the cottage, by the fire. Just in case that were true—his chest puffed out a little at the possibility—they had better get married right away. In Scotland it only took two witnesses and a willing lass. He knew his lass was willing, and he'd witnesses to spare. It was as good an excuse as any to hasten the nuptials. And frankly, any excuse would do.

He leaned over and kissed her, above the babies, in front of everybody, and didn't feel the least bit embarrassed.

The wedding was a small affair, held in the Murrays' drawing room two weeks after Kate's babies were born. The guest list was limited to a select few. The Murrays were there, of course, and Regina, Rory, Aunt Clarissa, and the servants. The Tuttles, all five of them, were in attendance, sitting with Ralph, with Bella holding on to his hand as if he might lift off like a hot-air balloon should she dare to let go. Will had been seen by the doctor, and his ears were already on the mend. They all looked spruce and clean and happy. In fact, they looked so respectable that Lady Grace was forced to modify her general opinions about the poor and decided to sponsor them.

Gabrielle had already made up her mind that Ralph would marry Mrs. Tuttle—Caroline was her given name—and move to a little farm in the country. Mr. Tuttle could be located and a divorce demanded. Gabrielle wasn't sure yet if the parties involved would fall into her plans as readily as she thought them up, but she had great hopes. The children already loved Ralph, and judging by the way Caroline slid shy and admiring looks in Ralph's direction, it was apparent that that lady's affections were speedily blossoming. That left only Ralph to deal with, and Gabrielle had great confidence in female persuasiveness and charm, which she'd no doubt Caroline possessed in the usual quantities and was eminently capable of exercising.

Mr. Blake came from the shelter, but it was understood that Kate and Douglas would not be able to attend. Kate sent word that she was thinking of them and imagining how beautiful Gabby would look in her wedding finery and how braw Zach would look in a kilt.

Everyone knew that Douglas wouldn't be thinking much about the wedding at all. He'd be concentrating on getting through the day without a drink. The first week was always hellish, and he was in hell, sure enough. His nerves were on fire. His head ached, and his stomach rejected food, only wanting whiskey. They were patient with him at the shelter, but unwaveringly firm. When he ranted and raved, they restrained him. When he begged and entreated, they listened sympathetically but didn't budge an inch.

In his saner moments, he thought of Kate and the babies and looked forward to the time when he could face them a sober man. He wanted to get on with his life, resume gainful employment, and come home at night to his smiling Kate and his strapping boys. He was going to do it for them, and for himself. After all, he'd promised.

As for Charlie, he couldn't be spared from the shelter, especially with Douglas needing to be tended. Gabrielle would send him some cake.

Dressing for her wedding, Gabrielle had thought of her mother, Beth, Alex, and the children. She wished they could be there, but she knew it was impossible at such short notice and in such inclement weather and traveling conditions. They had sent their love in long letters, and it was apparent that each of them had been hoping that Zach and Gabrielle would make a pair. In fact, Beth and Alex's letter implied that they had expected Zach's trip to Scotland to settle the matter one way or the other. Their approval and deep satisfaction over the way the matter was settled at last resonated from each affectionate sentence. Gabrielle had never imagined she could be so happy.

Her dress was made in a great hurry by Lady Grace's usual

modiste, and done discreetly so as not to alert the whole of Edinburgh to the news of the wedding. The Murrays decided to keep the developments of the past few days a secret for a while, giving Zach and Gabrielle time to leave town on their honeymoon without having to dodge a lot of questions and impudent stares. Shortly after, they would announce Rory and Regina's engagement and give a short explanation about "the young people finally realizing who they were actually in love with," and leave it at that. The persistently curious would be snubbed.

Gabrielle's dress was a dream, made of white silk brocade and embossed with white roses. An off-the-shoulder deep ruffle exposed her shoulders and the line of her neck. Her hair was swept up in a coiffure dubbed by the fashion plates as *"Cimodocee,"* named after the Greek sea nymph Cymodoce. Naturally Gabrielle's fanciful imagination had been intrigued by the name, but she liked the style, as well. It was rather simple, her hair pulled back and braided and looped in a sort of whimsical topknot. A wreath of myrtle crowned her head, with a diaphanous flowing veil attached at the back, hanging nearly to the floor.

The ceremony was a blur, the words of commitment a vague, poetic recital. Gabrielle didn't need anyone to tell her that she belonged to Zach and he to her. She'd always known they belonged to each other. Always. Her thoughts were consumed and her senses were inundated by the man who stood next to her.

Zach was splendid in a black velvet jacket, pristine white shirt and jabot, and a tartan kilt of variegated colors of green and russet. Sir George had traced Zach's genealogy and found Scottish blood in his family tree, as he knew he would if he tried hard enough. Zach, it seemed, was entitled to wear the clan colors of the MacKays. Zach was willing to do in Rome as the Romans do, so to speak, and was happy to show off his legs in the same manner as Rory had been showing off his since Zach's arrival on New Year's Eve. Truth to tell, he'd been rather jealous of Rory's kilt-wearing and felt as if he were finally getting some friendly revenge. Besides, Gabby had confessed a fondness for that particular part of his anatomy, and he was determined to please Gabby at all costs.

They spent their wedding night at a little inn outside of Edinburgh, en route to Cornwall and home. They would go at a leisurely pace, not minding the gray and unpredictable skies in the least. So what if they were stranded at some charming inn by rain or snow? That had happened before, and they'd not wasted a bit of time repining over the weather.

They were making love now, slow and luxuriously, just as Zach had wanted to do that first night together. He was building a leisurely bonfire, a bright, huge conflagration that began with a single spark. But all these thoughts of fire were perhaps making Zach imagine he smelled smoke. He pulled back, gazing into Gabby's flushed face, her luminous eyes and parted lips. She squirmed beneath him. "Oh, Zach, don't stop now!"

"I don't intend to, Gabby," he said, his voice raspy and breathless. "But, sweeting, do you smell something burning?"

Gabby giggled. "Just me!"

"No, 1 think perhaps they've scorched something in the kit—" Zach looked over his shoulder and observed that the counterpane, shucked off by Gabby in the excitement of the moment, had connected with the candle on the bedside table and was just about to burst into flame. Zach jumped up from the bed, threw the counterpane to the floor and stamped out the smoldering fibers. "Gawd!" he muttered. "We might have been burnt alive in our beds!"

Gabby, propped on her elbows, looked on with amusement. "But we weren't. Come back to bed, Zach. I like the view from here, of course, but we aren't likely to get much done at such a distance from each other."

Zach shook his head, grinning. Leave it to Gabby to minimize the crisis and put the emphasis back where it belonged—on their love. What a coquette she was, lying there all milky-white and come-hither, smiling like an imp. She was right. Who cares what might have happened? The important thing was their lovemaking.

Besides, he thought philosophically as he climbed atop his bride, as long as he was married to Gabby he'd have to get used to living in the briars, constantly facing crises and challenges. It would never be dull. He lowered his head and claimed her lips in a passionate kiss. No, never that.

EPILOGUE

Pencarrow
Cornwall, England
May 1841

Spring had come to Cornwall. The air was sweet with the scent
of budding trees and wildflowers. The moors were green with
new bracken and feathery tamarisk. Gulls swooped and cawed
over the mellow terra-cotta stone walls of the Tudor mansion
called Pencarrow.

It was twilight, and the rays of the sinking sun filtered
through the air, turning it blush-gold. Long shadows stretched
across the closely scythed lawn. A soft breeze stirred the leaves
of the tall horse chestnut by the ancient family chapel, whispering
over Tessy's well-kept grave like a benediction. The honeysuckle
vines that decorated the trellised lych-gate leading into the family
cemetery trembled in the warm, moist atmosphere.

A door opened, the slight creak of the hinges punctuating
the silence. From behind the walls of the kitchen garden,
footfalls sounded on the cobbled walkway. The gate opened
and Gabrielle and Zach emerged, arm in arm. Despite her
obvious pregnancy, Gabrielle walked with a spring in her step,
the flounce of her yellow dress flipping up to show her ruffled
petticoat. She would give birth in July. She hoped this one would
be a girl, a little sister for Matthew and Adam to spoil and tease
and protect. A daughter Zach could claim as his own.

They took a well-worn path to the creek, the water rushing
high against the banks, its sound the watery chuckle of Mother
Nature. They sat down in the tall grass beneath the great span of

a gnarled oak. Rooks quarreled amongst themselves and hopped about in the leafy branches.

Bareheaded, Zach's golden hair stirred gently in the breeze. Gabrielle rested her cheek against his shoulder. His shirt-sleeves were casually rolled an inch above his wrists, showing off the lean brown beauty of his hands. He smelled like the moor, of earth and sunshine. He bent his head, saying softly, "Did Matthew and Adam go to sleep right away?"

"Yes. They were quite done up, the poor dears. Matthew's been so happy to be home on holiday, he has not sat still a moment, and Adam follows him around like a puppy."

"I was the same way at Matthew's age. Nine-year-old boys are constitutionally unable to sit still, especially on holiday."

"Matthew has adjusted very well to Eton, I think. I was worried."

Zach squeezed her arm. "I know."

"I'm glad he'll be going to London with us for Torie's wedding. Now everyone will be there. Even your entertaining Aunt Saphrona."

"I hope she hasn't brought her pet raccoon to London with her."

Gabrielle laughed. "All the way from New Orleans? I should hope not! Torie will be so pleased to have everyone there. I can't wait to see her in her wedding gown. She'll be lovely. She's lovely already, of course. She looks like you."

Zach did not reply.

"Do you wish you were giving her away instead of Alex?" Gabrielle waited patiently. She knew Zach wasn't angry with her for bringing up the subject; they talked about everything. He was simply thinking about his reply.

She remembered when Zach first told her that Victoria Wickham, supposedly Alex and Beth's eldest daughter, was really *his* daughter. His and Tess's. When Tessy died during childbirth twenty years ago, everyone believed that the child had died and been buried with her in the coffin that had been nailed shut before the funeral. But it had been a colossal ruse, effectively pulled off to fool everyone except those particularly included in the secret.

It had been Beth's idea. She wanted to spare Tessy's daughter the same social prejudices—and possibly the same fate—her mother had endured because she was born illegitimate. Thus a complicated, well-executed scheme was concocted to send the child off to Italy with Beth and Alex, where they stayed two years at a secluded villa. A premature child, and petite by nature, Torie was believed by everyone to be nine months younger than she actually was, conceived and born while Alex and Beth were honeymooning.

With Zach's wholehearted cooperation, Alex and Beth raised Torie as their own. Zach wanted the best for her, and if the best did not include acknowledging her as his own child, so be it. He loved her and doted on her, not as "Papa," but as "Uncle Zach."

"No, I don't wish it. I don't regret any of it, Gabby. Look how well she's done for herself. That would never have been possible if I had raised her as my own."

"Lee seems a very nice young man, well positioned in society, and well able to give her a good life. But, most importantly, I believe they are suited to each other. He seems to adore her."

"Who couldn't?" said the indulgent father cum uncle.

"She's incredibly lovely, as I've already said. But best of all, she's full of life and enthusiasm. Very kind. Needle-witted, too. Your buttons must be bursting, Zachary Wickham."

"Well, maybe a little. But I give all credit for Torie's outstanding qualities to her upbringing. Alex and Beth have made her the sweet, lovely, intelligent girl she is today."

"Having a bit of you in her doesn't hurt, either," persisted Gabrielle, too fond of her husband to allow him to be so completely modest.

"I got a letter from Blake today," said Zach, changing the subject.

"And how are things at the shelter?"

"Going well. You'll have to go with me next spring when the baby's old enough to travel. Rory and Regina would love to have you stay in Perthshire with them while I attend to business in Old Town. Blake mentioned Kate and Douglas. They've saved up enough money to lease a farm and get the first crops in this spring. They'll miss Douglas at the shelter. He's done a wonderful job working with Charlie. Extra help was needed even before we extended the shelter into the adjacent apartment and took in more women, but now it's imperative that Douglas be replaced when he leaves. I hope Blake is successful in finding just such another excellent fellow to help out."

"But a farm! How splendid for Douglas and Kate! And at the rate they're going, with six children to do chores about the place, they'll have plenty of help. Who would have thought Kate would be such a fertile little thing? I hope their land is just as fruitful!"

Gabrielle hoped Zach didn't hear that note of wistfulness that had crept, quite unintentionally, into her voice. Though she was terribly happy for the McKeens, and very proud of Douglas for sticking to sobriety all these years—never once lifting a finger to hurt Kate—Gabrielle was envious of Kate's ability to conceive. Gabrielle had conceived Matthew on her honeymoon with Zach, and Adam came just two years later. But after Adam's difficult birth, she had developed a few related medical problems and had been unable to get pregnant again till last fall. Because she was afraid that this might be her last chance to give Zach a child, and because he'd had to give up Torie, Gabrielle was praying that this baby would be a girl.

"Sweeting, I hope you aren't thinking I'll be disappointed if this child is another boy."

Gabrielle felt a lump form in her throat. Zach always knew exactly what she was thinking. Exactly. "It would be nice if it is," she said, ducking her head, averting her watery eyes from his loving gaze. When he looked at her like that, it made her want to either laugh or weep. But since she was pregnant, she tended more toward weeping. What a bother!

"I don't care what sex the child is. I'm frankly more concerned that you weather this pregnancy in fine fettle. You're the most important thing in my life, Gabby. You know that, don't you?" He tilted her chin with the tip of his forefinger, gently forcing her to look at him.

Looking into those golden eyes, Gabrielle could be convinced of anything. "Yes, I believe you." Blinking back the bothersome tears, she smiled teasingly. "I'm so glad, too, because you're a first-rate kisser, you know."

Gabrielle parted her lips and waited. She saw how Zach's gaze drifted to her mouth. She saw how he was debating inside that wonderful head of his.

"You need your rest, sweeting," he said hoarsely. "It's going to be a long day tomorrow, knocking about in that carriage. Two days of travel are ahead of us, you know."

"I shall be sitting still, doing nothing. I'm sure I'll be just fine." Her eyes drifted shut. She waited. When he still debated, she opened her eyes and arched a brow. "Zachary Wickham, please believe me, I shall be in much better fettle for the journey tomorrow if we make love tonight! Can't you see, dearest, that I'm *dying* to be ravished?"

Zach smiled. He was convinced. He bent his head and kissed her laughing mouth, the both of them sinking into the soft, sweet-smelling grass of Cornwall.

ARMS OF A STRANGER

The lure of intrigue leads a young woman down a path of danger and into the passionate embrace of a daring stranger.

Bored with the dull suitors and shallow admirers of London, Anne Westin sets out for New Orleans in search of a new kind of man. She finds what she's looking for in the form of a brave stranger who helps a family of slaves escape—before pulling Anne into the shadows to steal a kiss.

Lucien Delocroix, the careless, lazy son of a wealthy plantation owner, is more concerned with the cut of his coats than the running of his estate. And yet, Anne knows there is more to the charming dilettante than meets the eye, and that he's willing to risk everything for what he knows to be right.

Swept into the secret life of a daring rogue, Anne finds herself drawn to the excitement of danger—and the fervor of passion.

BELOVED RIVALS

Estranged as boys, Alex and Zachary Wickham are reunited by tragedy. With the help of Beth, Zachary's beguiling fiancé, the brothers find peace in one another, finally confronting a past that tore their family apart and, at last, putting it behind them.

But as Beth becomes helplessly drawn to Alex, the men will discover that the same woman who aided in mending their wounded relationship may be the very woman to tear it apart for good.

REMEMBER ME

Secrets from a dark past threaten to destroy the promise of one man's future.

Out on a daring rescue mission, Amanda Darlington feels duty-bound to care for an unconscious gentleman after he stumbles drunkenly into the path of her carriage. Aware of the dangers in nursing a potential scoundrel back to health, she nevertheless takes a chance on the handsome stranger—especially when he awakens with no memory.

When Jackson Montgomery comes to, he is greeted by a vision of beauty that instantly sparks the fire of passion within him. But as his memory returns, the shattering secrets hidden in his past threaten to destroy any chance he has of winning Amanda's love. Only through feigned amnesia can Jackson capture Amanda's heart, but can he do so before she learns the truth of his brazen charade and his dark past?

THE PERFECT GENTLEMAN

He is supposed to be teaching her the ways of the world, but she may teach him the ways of love instead.

Samantha Darlington is the illegitimate daughter of a respected man. Her father's deepest shame and darkest secret, she has spent all of her seventeen years hidden away on a remote island. But when her half-sister, Amanda, discovers the truth of her existence, Samantha is rescued from her life of exile and thrust into a new world to be polished and educated. With the help of Amanda and the dashing and mysterious Julian Montgomery, Samantha will claim her rightful place in society.

When Julian agreed to tame the rebellious Samantha in order to find her a suitable husband, he hadn't anticipated that Samantha already had eyes for only one man—Julian himself. Now Samantha, determined to make Julian her own, is stirring up a frenzy in his elitist world—and his impenetrable heart.

THE SPRING BEGINS

Still grieving the death of his wife, Adam McAllister has isolated himself from the world—even from his children—shrouded in a gloom of perpetual winter. But the first blush of spring seems to appear again in the form of his children's feisty new governess, Letitia Webster.

As a flame of passion begins to warm their cold home, both Adam and Letitia must leave behind their painful pasts before they can embrace their future.